CRITICS PRAISE THE FRIGHTENING WORK OF BRYAN SMITH!

QUEEN OF BLOOD

"I can't see any fan of 80s-style pulp horror novels not leaving this one with a huge, gory grin on their face."

—*The Horror Fiction Review*

"*Queen of Blood* is a great follow-up...taking all the elements that worked so well in the first book and ramping them up. Not just the gore or the violence, though there's plenty of both, but the characterizations Smith is so adept at as well. He has weaved a very intricate tale with multiple levels of deception and sadism and managed to have it all make sense and be a helluva lot of fun at the same time."

—Dread Central

"A non-stop thrill ride...*Queen of Blood* is flying off the shelves. Bryan Smith seems poised for a major career explosion, and if you want to be trendy, read him now, before he becomes a household name. Incidentally, although *Queen of Blood* has a definite conclusion, there is plenty of room for a third volume in the same series. You can count me as someone who is eager to read it."

—Skullring

"Dark fantasy and psychological suspense might be the new norm, but the old slice and dice set hasn't kicked the bucket yet. Smith's lean and mean prose never lets up, allowing for a smooth, leisurely reading experience...a refreshing change of pace."

—Fear Zone

Her True Face

Myra sprang out of the chair and clamped a hand around Penelope's throat. Penelope struggled for air. The strength of the girl was astonishing. She tried to pry Myra's hand loose, but to no avail. Myra only squeezed harder.

"Are you going to obey me now? Are you going to shut up?"

Penelope was beginning to feel light-headed, but she managed a nod. Myra loosened her grip, allowing her to suck in a lungful of air. Penelope felt better, but the girl was still holding her by the throat.

"I have something to show you," Myra said. "Something simply amazing, Ms. Simmons."

Myra's flesh began to ripple and stretch, its smoothness shifting to a rough, scaly texture. Then she grinned. Only it was a hideous, hellish parody of a grin. Her mouth doubled in size. Tripled. Quadrupled. Her teeth grew and multiplied, become sharp like razors, glistened with saliva. There was something at the back of the mouth, something yellow and pulsating, something obscene....

BRYAN SMITH

SOULTAKER

LEISURE BOOKS NEW YORK CITY

This one's for my mom, Cherie M. Smith.
For everything you and Dad did for me through the years.
It has not been forgotten.

A LEISURE BOOK®

February 2009

Published by

Dorchester Publishing Co., Inc.
200 Madison Avenue
New York, NY 10016

ISBN 10: 0-8439-6193-7
ISBN 13: 978-0-8439-6193-5
E-ISBN: 1-4285-0601-2

Visit us on the web at www.dorchesterpub.com.

ACKNOWLEDGMENTS

Some readers of this book may imagine they detect a whiff of autobiography within these pages. This is not the case. While I do share one or two superficial things in common with the protagonist, Jake McAllister, he is not meant to represent me in any way. I come from a much, much less deprived background, and I was raised by wonderful parents who always did their best by me, even when I was struggling. Without the love and support of my mother, Cherie Smith, and Lonnie Smith, my still deeply missed late father, I could never have come as far as I have. I was also blessed enough to have two of the greatest brothers anyone could ever ask for in Jeff and Eric Smith. My brothers, thanks for making a big chunk of my younger days so memorable and fun. And as always, my love and gratitude to my wife. Rachael, without you sharing my life, the world would be a much darker place indeed.

Thanks also go out to the usual cast of colorful characters and friends: Shannon Turbeville and Keith Ashley, without whom the good old days would just have been the old days. Kent Gowran, Tod Clark, Mark Hickerson, David T. Wilbanks, Derek Tatum, the denizens of Brian Keene's message board, Brian Keene, Don D'Auria (for making it all happen), and the core MySpace gang (keep those comments and messages coming).

Last, but not least, thanks to the readers for buying enough of these things to keep them coming.

SOULTAKER

CHAPTER ONE

The boy and the girl eyed each other nervously as they stood in the clearing in the woods. The distant buzz of speedboats on the lake and the chirruping of crickets were like dim signals from another world, alien transmissions neither boy nor girl perceived. The whole of existence was comprised of their bodies and the aching space between them. Adolescent urges raged inside the boy, needs he could never quite articulate and only half understood.

All he knew was nothing in all of creation mattered more than this girl. He was horny, yes. Filled with lust, as any boy his age would be in his place. But it was more than that. He felt such great love for her, the kind of grand, pure love that was the stuff of fairy tales. She was a damsel, a radiant princess, and he was her shining knight. Thinking this made him feel silly, but he could at least be honest with himself—it was how he really felt.

Yet, he felt fear, too.

One thing he'd learned in his short time on the planet was that within love lay the potential for great hurt. He'd lost loved ones to death, drugs, and divorce, and he feared the hurt this girl could bring him if things went wrong, if he somehow failed to be everything she needed him to be.

Trey McAllister glanced heavenward and said, "Full moon tonight."

Myra Lewis shrugged. "So?" She took a drag from her clove

cigarette and blew fragrant smoke Trey's way. "You're not su-
perstitious, are you?"

Trey made a face and waved the smoke away. "Jesus Christ.
Those cloves fucking stink."

Myra smirked. "You don't like it, you can find someone else
to hang out with." She blew another cloud of smoke his way.
"Maybe one of those preppy chicks your buddies fuck. Or one
of those Paris Hilton or Lindsay Lohan wannabes. Rockville
High's full of both."

Trey frowned. "I don't want one of those girls. You can't
talk to a girl like that. Not really talk, I mean. The way, uh, you
and I talk."

Myra rolled her eyes, but she ran a hand adorned with multiple silver pagan rings and black nail polish through her
choppy jet-black hair, a self-conscious gesture. "Yeah. I'm special."

Trey wrapped his arms around her and drew the girl's small
body close. "You are, you know. I've had other girlfriends,
but they never meant much to me." He smiled. "That was
kid's stuff. You're the first girl I've ever wanted to have a
real . . . relationship . . . with."

Myra laughed. "You're just saying shit you heard on *Dr.
Phil* or something. You're seventeen, Trey. You don't have real
relationships when you're seventeen."

"I'll be eighteen next month." He slipped a hand under the
silky fabric of her blouse and shuddered at the feel of her bare
flesh. "And my parents got married right after high school.
We're almost adults in the eyes of the law."

They'd only been going together two weeks. She'd told him
it was too soon to be fucking. But sometimes girls said things
like that and didn't really mean it, or only half meant it. Sometimes they were so hard to read, as complicated and hard to follow as one of the old novels you had to read for English class.
But maybe she was beginning to relent. She seemed to melt
against him. His arm moved higher, lifting her blouse as his fingers slipped under her bra. He leaned into her for a kiss. She

cupped both sides of his peach-fuzzed face and matched his carnal hunger.

Trey pulled back and said, "I want you."

Myra was breathing hard. She stepped out of his embrace and tugged her blouse down. The gesture was instinct, Trey thought, maybe some remainder of her mother's attempts to make her believe in the virtues of teenage chastity. He gripped her wrist and drew her back into his arms. She did not resist. His tongue probed her open mouth, making her moan. She cupped the bulge at the crotch of his jeans and gave him a squeeze. The way he reacted—with a squirm and a husky grunt—obviously pleased her. It made her feel powerful, like she could make him do whatever she wanted with just the right touch.

Trey managed to say, "Are we . . . are we . . ."

Myra gripped a handful of hair at the back of his head. "Yes."

This brought a trembling smile to his lips. "I don't have a condom."

Myra unsnapped his jeans. "And I don't care."

"But—"

Myra reached inside his jeans and said, "Shut the fuck up. You can pull out."

"But—"

Myra gave him a squeeze. "I told you to shut up." Then she released him and tugged her blouse off over her head. The blouse fell to the ground. "Your turn."

"Wha-what?"

She laughed. "Take something off."

Trey Marshall was eager to do as she commanded. He'd dreamed of this very thing for months, from the moment he'd laid eyes on the strangely alluring new girl at the beginning of the school year. He'd still been dating Hannah Crawford, his girlfriend since Christmas break of the previous year, but the blonde and busty preppy girl soon seemed so ordinary to him, a bland and uninteresting bubblehead compared to this exotic creature. For months he'd worked up his courage, then, finally, he dumped Hannah and asked Myra out.

He'd expected to get shot down. He was a good-looking guy. One of the popular kids at school. The opposite, he'd been certain, of anything that would interest Myra Lewis. So he'd been surprised when she'd accepted his offer of a date. That first date was a real eye-opener, too. She took him to an all-ages punk show at a downtown club, where they saw a band called The Cramps. This was a seriously weird, loud band with a freaky-looking lead singer and a hot chick guitarist in high heels and a tiny dress. He'd felt so self-conscious in his Joe Straight clothes. Everyone else at the club was decked out in punk or goth gear. But Myra, who of course did look as if she belonged, clung to him throughout the evening, making him feel like he belonged, too. Just two weeks had passed, but his whole life seemed different now. He didn't just love her, he idolized her. He burned copies of her favorite albums and listened to them incessantly. He memorized titles of books from her library and ordered his own copies from Amazon.com. They went to more shows. Always the same kind of thing. The Voluptuous Horror of Karen Black. The Genitorturers. His friends joked about his obsession with the "weirdo" and called him "whipped," but he just didn't give a shit what they thought anymore.

Myra.

Fuck. She was everything to him.

His hands shook as he began to remove his shirt. God, how he loved the way the brilliant moonlight sparkled in Myra's eyes. She was so beautiful, like some kind of gothic angel. He was so enraptured the approaching noise took longer to register. He paused with the shirt bunched up around his shoulders, squinting at the dark line of trees beyond Myra.

She frowned. "What's wrong?"

Trey tugged his shirt back down and stepped past her. "Someone's coming." He stared at the black line of trees, straining to see what was out there. Then he saw a flicker of light, a burning flame moving at shoulder level. Then more flickers, like a line of approaching torchbearers. The flickering lights grew brighter and he began to hear the crunch of twigs beneath multiple pairs of feet. And he began to perceive another sound; a soft, rising murmur, a chantlike cadence drifting closer on the gentle evening breeze. He took an unconscious step back and gripped Myra by the wrist again. "Come on."

Myra knelt to grab her fallen blouse. "Jesus, Trey, what's the big deal?"

Trey didn't have an immediate answer for that. His panic was fueled by instinct. Something about this new presence in the woods bothered him on a primal level. He was pulling Myra toward the opposite side of the clearing even as she struggled to get her blouse back on. As they stumbled over the uneven ground, the chant grew louder and more distinct. The words were Latin, so Trey had no idea what was being said. Not that the actual substance of the words was all that important. A bunch of people carrying torches and chanting Latin phrases at night in the woods couldn't be up to anything good.

The teenagers slipped into the woods mere moments before the leading end of the strange procession entered the clearing. Trey pulled Myra behind a thicket and hunkered down with her on the ground. Through a small opening in the thicket, they watched the interlopers form a circle around the site of an extinguished campfire. Only a few members of the group were carrying torches, but there was enough light to distinguish a few new things. The torchbearers were all nude males with black hoods over their heads. The others wore monklike dark robes with hoods.

Myra wriggled closer to Trey and put her mouth to his ear to whisper, "Look at those dudes with their dicks out in the air. Fucking hilarious."

Trey cringed. He didn't want to risk drawing the attention of the—what the hell was it? A coven? Some sort of satanic cabal?—and even a whisper was too much noise. He turned his head to meet Myra's gaze and put a finger to his lips.

Myra scowled. "What, you're afraid?"

Trey winced.

She snorted. "You are, aren't you? You're a fucking pussy."

The words stung. Trey figured he was as brave as the next guy under normal circumstances. He wasn't the type to back away from a fight. He would never start anything without just cause—he just wasn't that type—but he wasn't shy about standing up to assholes. But these weren't normal circumstances. This constituted what you could maybe call supremely-fucked-up-to-the-nth-degree circumstances. This was twilight zone type of shit. He had no frame of reference for dealing with . . . well, for dealing with whatever the hell was going on here. And Myra should know that. He couldn't fathom why she wasn't as freaked the fuck out over the tableau in the clearing as he was. Sometimes, hell, a lot of times, she had a sharp tongue, snapping off a string of caustic words that sliced through the vulnerable parts of his psyche like a razor. It didn't bother him most of the time, because she always seemed to sense when she'd gone too far. This time, however, there was no evidence of regret on her part.

She put her mouth to his ear again. "Coward."

Now Trey was mad enough to speak. "That's not fair, Myra," he said, his voice a low hiss. "I'm no coward, but I'm not fucking stupid, either."

Her eyes narrowed to slits. "Oh yeah? Bullshit."

Trey flinched. She was getting upset, and the volume of her voice was near normal speaking level. He hoped like hell the people in the clearing were too immersed in their ritualistic weirdness to perceive anything occurring outside their little circle.

Trey said a silent prayer before saying, "Nothing. I'm sorry."

But Myra wasn't backing down. "No. Fuck that. You're fucking chickenshit."

Trey's fingers clawed at the damp ground. Part of him wanted to dig a hole deep into the earth, just wriggle into the ground like a worm, where he'd be safe from the chanting weirdos and the piercing glare of the girl he loved—who, he was just realizing, was a little bit mean. And who, if her voice went up another notch or two, would be yelling.

"Please, Myra." A pitiful, helpless whimper escaped his throat. "I'm begging you. Let this go for now. You can rip me a new one later, okay?"

She grunted. "Count on it."

But Trey was content—her voice had dropped back to a whisper.

The group in the clearing had taken up a new chant. This also wasn't in English, but it wasn't immediately recognizable as Latin, either. It sounded like some alien language. He half expected to see a shimmering mother ship descend from the heavens. The words seemed more rhythmic than before, more musical and sensual. The robed figures began to move as their voices rose from a whisper to something approaching an ecstatic roar. Trey began to recognize repeating patterns in the chant, like the choruses of a song, and the end of one such passage seemed to act as a signal to discard clothing. Robes fell to the ground and Trey gaped at the sight of a dozen nude women dancing and whirling around the freshly lit campfire. Their faces were obscured by white masks that resembled the comedy and tragedy masks of theater. But they were all beautiful, the flickering torchlight licking at their tall, full-figured bodies like eager tongues. The breasts of each woman were high and large. They all had long legs, trim waists, and flat stomachs. Trey imagined some bizarre underground society of ex-models, Playmates for Satan, something like that. Absurd, yes, but everything about this was surreal. So maybe he was dreaming. Or maybe Myra had slipped some weird drug into his last beer.

What kind of drug could conjure visions like this, though? He noticed that the dongs of all but one of the male torchbearers stood erect. Maybe the lone limp-dick was gay. Or maybe not. He was standing well-removed from the rest of the group, and Trey could just make out his hooded head moving in a slow arc, his gaze taking in the periphery of the clearing.

Trey shuddered. *He's standing watch. Oh God, what if he sees us?*

He nearly jumped out of his skin as he felt something cold

on his back. But it was just Myra, sliding her hand up under his shirt. She wriggled close to him again and curled a leg around him. "Let's do it." Her voice was husky in his ear. "Right now."

Trey's eyes widened. "What?"

She sat up and, again, pulled her blouse off over her head. She flung it away into the darkness. Then she unsnapped her bra and her breasts popped loose. Trey opened his mouth to speak again, but no words came forth. Her breasts weren't as large as those of the women in the clearing—who looked like fucking Amazons—but they were a nice size anyway, with stiff pink nipples that she pinched to erectness.

Trey experienced an epiphany in that moment. He loved Myra, yes. Enough to do practically anything she wanted. But she was, without question, stone-cold crazy. The spectacle in the clearing was making her horny! She ought to be shaking with fear, but instead was consumed with lust. Trey mulled over any number of ways to defuse that lust without making her angry, but none of them seemed workable. Then there was the matter of his own libido. His erect cock was straining painfully inside his jeans. So he was crazy, too. He breathed a loud sigh of relief as Myra unzipped him, releasing him into the cool night air. He moaned and fell onto his back as she knelt to take his hard length into her mouth. He closed his eyes and clawed at the ground as she expertly manipulated him with her tongue. Good Lord, how could any girl her age be so skilled at this?

He was so consumed with the incredible pleasure provided by Myra's mouth that all thought of the cavorting cult vanished. There was no room for anything in his consciousness but this pure ecstasy.

Which was why he failed to perceive the approach of the hooded guard he'd noticed earlier. A pair of strong hands seized him about the wrists and yanked him to his feet. The initial sense of dismay he felt when his cock popped out of Myra's mouth gave way to terror when he looked into the eyes of the hooded man, which were visible through ragged slits cut in the coarse fabric. The terror paralyzed him for a few moments; then he tried to tear out of the man's grip but was hampered by the man's incredible strength. That, and the fact that his jeans were tangled up around his ankles. The man had little difficulty pulling him out of the thicket and out into the clearing.

Trey looked at the masked dancers, who were no longer dancing. Twelve masked faces and three more hooded ones turned to face him. The bodies of the women were even more astonishing in their utter perfection up close. Though he knew he was in mortal danger, his hormones compelled a quick inspection. He saw stiff nipples and pubic thatches glistening with moisture. Maybe the chant they'd been doing was some sort of sexual spell. That would account for Myra's otherwise inexplicable behavior. And his own.

Myra.

"Myra!" he screamed. "Run! Get the fuck out of here!"

The man tugged him into the center of the campfire circle and tossed him to the ground. The heat of the nearby flames baked his skin. Trey reached for his jeans, meaning to pull them up, but the guard kicked him in the stomach, making him curl into a tight ball on the ground. He squeezed his eyes shut against the pain. When he opened them, he saw the night's most shocking scene yet.

Myra, nude, strode into the clearing.

The masked women bowed as she stepped through their circle.

Trey rolled onto his back and stared up at her. She stood over him, a strange, small smile touching the corners of her pretty mouth. "Trey, darling?"

A tickle of nausea touched the back of his throat. The only response he could manage was a moan.

Myra's eyes glittered in the firelight.

"Remember when you told me how you wanted me from the moment you laid eyes on me?" Her voice mocked him, a tone of sadistic amusement that tore at his heart, pulverizing the love he felt for her. "Be careful what you wish for, idiot."

CHAPTER TWO

Raymond Slater, principal of Rockville High School for this past decade, was in his office at the school. It was midnight, an hour at which the school was thought to be deserted. But Principal Slater was often here at odd hours. He and the night watchman had an understanding—an understanding reinforced with a generous weekly outlay of cash.

It was important that his nocturnal activities at the school remain a secret for one very simple reason—the activities in question would be considered perverse by just about any objective set of community standards.

Principal Slater was not alone in his office. Penelope Simmons, a ravishing young Senior English teacher, was slumped in a recliner opposite his big oak desk. The way she was dressed would shock her students, who were used to seeing her wear far more conservative clothes. She wore black, knee-high boots with stiletto heels and laces up the sides, black crotchless panties, a black bikini top with conical, bulletlike cups, and a black cap with a shiny brim that resembled the kind worn by Hitler's SS. The hat was tilted low over her pale face. Her full lips, painted a whorish bright red, looked blowjob ready. The middle finger of her right hand pushed through the open slot of her panties and slipped into her sex.

Her hand flexed.

And she writhed minutely on the leather recliner, her red lips forming a wide O of ecstasy.

Principal Slater sported an enormous erection, which strained the fabric of his trousers. He would use it on Penelope when the time was right, but that time had not yet arrived. He turned away from her and faced the little mirror above the display case of his various plaques and awards for community service. The image in the mirror showed a man with short black hair shellacked in place. His dark eyes were hard and pitiless. He smeared a dab of spirit gum above his upper lip and affixed a fake mustache. Once he was satisfied with the way it looked, he stepped back and snapped off a stiff-armed salute.

"Heil!"

He spun away from the mirror on the heels of his vintage jackboots, glared at Penelope, and barked, *"Achtung!* Activate the boombox, wench!"

Penelope leapt off the recliner and stood ramrod straight. She looked sleek and delectable, a dazzling Aryan goddess. *"Ja, mein* principal!"

She pushed the play button on the boombox, which was on Slater's desk. The recorded voice of a dead German dictator filled the room. Penelope leaned against the edge of the desk and watched Principal Slater goose-step back and forth.

She imagined ranks of Third Reich troops marching around a town square. The image sent a shiver of delight down the length of her trim body. She closed her eyes, lifted one long, sleek leg, and placed the sole of a boot on the edge of the desk.

Then she reached between her legs again.

And her mouth formed another O.

Outside, perched on a low-hanging tree branch, a crow as black as the night itself observed the decadent scene through the principal's office window. Principal Slater often neglected to close the blind when indulging his secret lusts. His office window was not visible from a street, and there was no one around at this time of night to bear witness to his Third Reich fetish.

It would not trouble him to know the crow was watching.

The crow flapped its wings and took to the air. Had Principal Slater been able to track its flight path, he would've cursed his carelessness. The crow flew high over the small town, leaving the school and the nearby main drag far behind. It flew past a residential area and over a wooded area, homing in on a flickering campfire in a clearing.

It began to descend.

Sensing its approach, its mistress turned her face skyward and smiled.

The crow landed on her shoulder and whispered in her ear.

CHAPTER THREE

No one noticed the blue Camry parked outside the Good Times Bar & Grill, which was fine with the man slouched behind the car's steering wheel. He rolled what appeared to be a coin between the thumb and forefinger of his right hand, a shiny gold-plated disc roughly the size of a quarter. Engraved in the middle of the coin on each side were the words "One Year." The AA chip was the ultimate symbol of the new life the man had built for himself in St. Paul. A new life that had effectively ended a day ago, when he got the call that had brought him back here to Rockville. The last thing in the world he'd ever wanted was to come home, but there was just no way around this. This was duty.

But Jake McAllister couldn't face what he had to face sober. He flipped the chip through the Camry's open window and heard it strike the pavement. It rolled under a pickup truck parked at the bar's entrance, then disappeared down a storm drain. Jake reached into the plastic Kroger bag on the passenger seat, pried a Bud tall-boy can from its plastic ring, and popped the tab. The beer felt good in his mouth, refreshing, like a reminder of something sweet from his youth, a salve for the psyche, and he felt a sense of immense relief. Getting that first swallow out of the way had been hard, but now it was done. Now he could walk into this bar without feeling like a condemned man walking into the gas chamber. He finished the contents of the tall boy, crushed it, and tossed it into the back-seat, a reflex left over from the bad old days.

He got out of the car and walked into the bar.

Stepping through the door, he smelled beer, meat on a grill, and cigarette smoke. Jake slid onto a stool at the bar and ordered a shot of tequila and a Grolsch chaser. He threw back the tequila, winced at the familiar burn, and savored the Grolsch.

The burly bartender had shaggy blond hair and a thick mustache. The sleeves of his white button-up shirt were rolled halfway up bulging forearms. Jake felt a spark of recognition, but he couldn't quite place the guy. "I haven't set foot in this town in ten years, but I'm sure I know you."

The bartender's eyes crinkled a little as he smiled. "Yeah, you do. You're Jake McAllister. I'm Stu Walker." He shook Jake's hand across the bar. "You were about five years ahead of me in school, but I used to hang with your little brother." Stu's smile faltered a bit. "Shame what happened. Mike was a cool dude. We used to party a lot. I still miss the guy."

Jake felt a brief flash of the old grief at the mention of his dead brother's name. A familiar blackness loomed somewhere within him. He swallowed some more Grolsch and willed thoughts of the fucked-up past away.

"Yeah. Honestly, I don't think about it much anymore. What happened, I mean."

Stu cleaned some pint glasses with a cloth. "Yeah. It was a long time ago."

Later, as Jake finished his second Grolsch, he did a quick booze-intake inventory. In less than a half hour, he'd consumed three beers and a large shot of tequila. It was tempting to go ahead and get hammered, but he knew it wasn't wise. He had some serious matters to attend to, including some face-to-face encounters with people he'd hoped to never see again. People he hated. His mother, for one. And his beer-bellied, quick-with-a-backhand evil bastard of a stepfather, for another.

Stu set a fresh Grolsch on the bar in front of Jake. "So . . . what brings you back, man?"

Jake picked up the bottle, but didn't immediately drink from it. He rolled the cool glass between his hands and stared into the open mouth of the bottle. "You know my mother had another kid by that asshole Hal, right?"

Stu grunted. "Yep. Trey. He reminds me of you."

"Yeah? That poor bastard."

Jake took a big swallow of beer. He'd allow himself one more beer while he talked with Stu; then he'd get out of this place. He had enough discipline left to do that, he hoped. Because he was pretty sure he'd be here for the night if he stayed for even one more drink beyond that.

A blonde girl with nice legs displayed pleasingly in a short skirt and ass-lifting platform heels leaned over the bar next to Jake and ordered a Long Island iced tea. While Stu mixed the drink, the girl glanced Jake's way. She looked maybe twenty years old, with straight white teeth, pretty blue eyes, and marvelous cheekbones. When she smiled at him, Jake forgot about everything else for a moment.

"Hello."

"Hey. Haven't seen you here before." Her voice was sweet and lilting, but she sounded a little tipsy. "You're kinda cute for an old guy."

Jake chuckled. He was thirty-nine and not quite ready to shuffle off to the old folks home. But it was all about perspective. From this chick's point of view, he was old. And maybe she was right. He didn't like to think about that looming milestone birthday, but it was right around the corner and coming up fast.

He tipped his glass at her. "Thanks. I guess." He drank some more Grolsch. "I'm new here. Sort of."

"Sort of?"

Jake shrugged. "I grew up in Rockville, but I've been gone a long time."

Her brow furrowed some. "You back to stay or just visiting?"

"Definitely just visiting. But I'll be around a while, taking care of some family business."

The girl's smile returned. "Wonderful. I'm Bridget Flanagan. I'm a student at RCC."

Jake tipped his glass at her. "Jake McAllister."

She accepted the finished drink from Stu and sipped tentatively from a thin straw. "Lovely. Well, Jake McAllister, hang out at the Grill enough and we'll see each other again. But now I must be off."

"Good-bye."

"Ciao."

Jake watched her return to a table occupied by several other college-age girls. She moved like she knew he would be watching her, swaying her hips a little more than she normally would.

Stu laughed. "Work that ass."

Jake watched her smooth her skirt and fold herself into a small chair. "I'm way too old to be flirting with a girl that young."

Stu indicated the nearly empty Grolsch bottle in Jake's hand with a nod. "You 'bout ready for another?"

Jake tilted the bottle and studied its remaining contents. It still held another good swallow or two. He sighed, remembering his pledge of only minutes ago. "No. This is it for tonight, I think."

"So, why are you back, Jake?"

Jake sipped some Grolsch. "My mother called me yesterday, begging me to come back to Rockville. Her 'baby,' this is Trey we're talking about, this is the term she uses for a kid almost out of high school . . . anyway, her 'baby' has apparently suffered some sort of massive psychological trauma, something he won't tell her about no matter how much she pries. My opinion, just living with her is plenty trauma."

Stu's expression was grim. "I hate to say it, but I agree. Her and her old man aren't gonna win any popularity contests, put it that way. Trey, though, is a good kid, from what I know of him. Smart, like you. So you're here to put the boy straight, huh?"

Jake laughed. "I guess. My mother, God knows why, has

this idea I'm some kind of paragon of maturity and success. She thinks Trey looks up to me. Which is funny, I haven't accomplished shit, other than escaping this place. But go figure, she reckons my mere presence will be enough to steer Trey back to the straight and narrow path. Pure bullshit. If I'm the kid's role model, he's already in trouble. Luckily, I've got an alternate plan."

Stu poured a Bud draft for a factory worker and passed it across the bar. "What, hire a hitman to whack his parents?"

Jake smirked. "Now, that ain't a bad idea. But no, what I have in mind is nonlethal but hopefully just as final. Trey graduates from Rockville High in a little over a month. I'm gonna hang around until then, play the role model to pacify Mom, then, when Trey has his diploma in hand, I'm gonna put him in my car and get him the hell out of Rockville."

Stu's eyes widened. "Really? You sure he'll go along with that?"

"Don't know. Gonna give it a shot, though."

A smile tugged at the corners of Stu's whiskered mouth. "That's a pretty bold plan. Maybe even a little crazy." The smile broadened. "Shit, it might even work."

Jake sucked down the last of the Grolsch and pushed the empty bottle across the bar. "I won't force him to come with me. I'm just gonna roll the dice and see what happens."

"Where will you be staying while you're in town?"

Jake sat back on his stool and rubbed fatigue from his eyes. "Man, I'm bushed. I figured I'd look for some kinda weekly rental type place."

Stu snapped his fingers so abruptly Jake almost slid off his stool. "Nah, fuck that, man. You can stay with me."

Jake blinked. "But—"

"I'm serious. And you don't have to worry about imposing. I rent a house in Washington Heights. Plenty of room." Stu grinned. "And the price is right."

Jake frowned. "Ah . . . my, um, funds aren't . . ."

"You asshole, I ain't chargin' you."

Jake thought about it a moment longer, then nodded. It wasn't like he had a lot of options. "I appreciate it, man."

Stu nodded. "Not a problem, bro. Hang out a bit longer. I'll fetch my extra house key from the Jeep when I get a chance."

Stu poured some more drafts and set another Grolsch in front of Jake. Jake was drinking it before he realized he'd broken his pledge. He decided not to worry about it. He'd been looking for an excuse to postpone the meeting with his mother anyway. It could wait one more day. A little more time to mentally prepare himself couldn't hurt. Rationalization firmly in place, he cast his gaze about the Grill and saw Bridget Flanagan giggling with her friends. Something about the way she cocked her head when listening to one of her friends reminded him of someone else. He frowned, unable to place the dim memory, then it came to him.

Moira Flanagan.

The love of his life—once upon a time.

Bridget was her kid sister.

If anything, Bridget was even prettier than Jake's former love. Looking at her had the uncomfortable effect of stirring some of the old lust he felt for Moira. An image flashed in his head, disturbing and vivid—Bridget kissing him, fondling his crotch as Moira always so boldly did when they'd made out in her bedroom at her parents' house. Jake wrenched his gaze away, not wanting the girl to see the desire in his eyes.

Jake looked at the bar.

His heart raced in his chest.

And he thought, *Oh God . . . Moira.*

CHAPTER FOUR

Bridget was having a good time. She liked to mess with people. Get their motors running, build up their expectations, then crush them. The old guy at the bar, for instance. Her new work in progress. She looked forward to seeing him again. Being a guy, he was gullible. It would be easy to lead him on, make him believe she wanted his old ass. The look on his face when he learned the truth would be well worth the effort. Something within her found deception of any type enjoyable. The girl across the table, a petite brunette with a pixie-style haircut, was another good example. Thinking of Bridget as a confidante, she'd tearfully confessed her sexual confusion to her the night before. Bridget fended off the girl's tentative advances while professing profound respect for her courageous decision to out herself. Which, it turned out, wasn't what the girl wanted at all. She just wanted to "experiment," she claimed, and she begged Bridget not to ever tell anyone else about the episode. So Bridget made a solemn vow to take the secret to her grave if need be.

The memory made Bridget feel delightfully wicked.

"You guys want to hear something shocking?"

The women seated around the table looked at her with expressions of expectation. The girl across the table looked troubled. Not quite alarmed. Not yet. Just troubled. Her name was Jordan Harper. She believed Bridget was just about the sweetest girl in the world. Or so she'd told Bridget.

Jordan stared at her. "Bridget—"

Bridget smiled. "Jordan's a dyke. She came on to me last night."

The revelation was like a grenade rolled into the conversation. All giggling ceased. There was a long moment of uncomfortable silence. The silence was broken by the ragged sob that tore out of Jordan's throat. "I can't believe you. You said you wouldn't tell."

Tears streaming down her face, the girl bolted from the table and ran out of the bar.

Bridget laughed.

Angela Brooks gaped at her. "That was so mean." Then she grinned. "It was fucking beautiful."

The others laughed.

Jordan Harper had never been fully accepted into Bridget's circle of friends. She had no way of knowing it in the midst of her current misery, but she was fortunate to have escaped with just this fresh psychological scar. Had Jordan been deemed worthy, she would have been ritually inducted into the Sacred Circle.

A transformation that would strip her of her humanity.

As had already happened to Bridget and the other girls at the table.

Bridget enjoyed a few more drinks with her friends as the evening wore on, strong, high-alcohol drinks. Her girlfriends deferred to her at every point in the conversation. Although they were Sacred Circle members, they had not yet attained the privileges Bridget had been granted.

They were Novices.

And she was Adept.

She had learned some things, special secrets, the simpler aspects of what Lamia, the Dark Mother, called the Mysteries. She craved so much more. One day she would wield the power of a Priestess, become one of Lamia's chosen ones, and how glorious that would be!

She eyed the Grolsch-drinking man at the bar, so familiar, and she slid a hand up a bare thigh as she imagined possessing the ability to reach into his mind and make him do as she pleased. She pretended not to notice his occasional, surreptitious glances her way, but she knew the man was entranced by her. He clearly desired her body. She could, of course, manipulate him sexually, but that would be too easy. And not nearly so fun as the other thing she could do.

She smiled.

And hoped his "family business," whatever it was, would keep him around until she was able to fully harness the power Lamia had promised would be hers.

Then she would pull his strings.

Make him dance for her.

Fall down for her.

Like a helpless little puppet.

CHAPTER FIVE

"Crawl."

Trey fought a brief mental battle against the command, but it was no use. He was helpless. Always helpless. He might have felt despair had he not already endured so much humiliation, but all he felt now was a deep numbness. His momentary resistance was just the flinch of instinct. He knew he was powerless.

He fell to the concrete floor and crawled toward where Myra, nude, straddled the body of a dead security guard. The guard's head was a bloody pulp. Staved in with a brick. Trey tried to blot out the image of the man's head collapsing beneath a flurry of blows, but the mental replay unspooled anyway and Trey saw himself slamming the brick down again and again, the motion of his arm controlled by something else.

By the evil thing, the Dark Mother, that lived inside Myra's body.

Lamia.

Myra grinned at Trey as he drew near. Her teeth were bloodstained and bits of gleaming viscera were visible on her body. She reached into the dead guard's body and drew out another loop of intestine.

Trey felt only a slight tickle of nausea.

He'd seen her do too many other awful things, many of them far more depraved, far sicker, than even this. But then her grin became a leer, a horribly knowing expression, as if she could read his mind.

She laughed. "Come to me like a dog, Trey. On all fours."

Tears welling in his eyes, Trey rose to his hands and knees and did as she said.

"Sit."

Trey sat, mimicking a dog's posture.

Myra proffered the length of viscera.

"Feed."

Trey whimpered.

He drew the dead guard's guts into his mouth and began to chew, and as he did he retreated to a remote area of his mind, a corner of his consciousness where his essence, the real Trey, went to hide when the *really* bad things happened. Myra's laughter sounded dim and far away, like an echo from deep within a dark cavern.

"Do you still love me, Trey?"

Her voice sounded sweeter, a dulcet, almost angelic tone— it brought him back to the here and now. Myra knew when he was shutting things out. Sometimes she allowed it. Not this time. Trey mumbled an affirmative reply around a mouthful of intestine.

Myra stroked his hair. "That's a good boy, Trey. That's a good little doggie."

He really did still love her.

Trey was convinced that the real Myra was the girl he'd always believed her to be, and that her body was being used as a vessel by this thing that called itself Lamia. It was the only way he managed to maintain even a loose grasp on sanity. He refused to believe Myra was some kind of evil incarnate. And he held on to the hope that one day, somehow, he'd be able to cast the thing out of her body.

But it just seemed so fucking hopeless.

He couldn't even control his own body.

Myra scooped up another handful of dead security guard and pushed it into Trey's open mouth. "Try some brain soup, baby. It's good for you."

Trey gobbled it down.

There was a sound of approaching footsteps behind him.

A male voice said, "That's all of it. We should get out of here."

Myra sighed. "Aw . . . just when I was starting to have fun."

She stood and stretched, her lean body magnificent in the dim light. She looked to Trey like a warrior goddess of myth, her body bathed in the blood of battle, but he knew the truth was nothing as fanciful as that. A warrior goddess, or just about any other significant source of power, would quake with terror in Myra's presence.

She donned a cloak, beckoned to Trey with a slap of hand on thigh, and they followed the other members of the Sacred Circle out of the building.

Outside, the wind that came up was like a cold hand closing around Trey's bare flesh.

CHAPTER SIX

Jake dreamed of the hot blonde girl he'd flirted with at the bar, the delectable little thing he'd belatedly realized was Moira's baby sister. In the dream, they were on their first date. They were at a drive-in movie theater showing an all-night marathon of B horror movies. There hadn't been a drive-in theater in Rockville since the early '80s, but that's where they were, and they were engaged in the traditional activities of a couple on a drive-in date—kissing and groping. Then the dream shifted, the way dreams do, and they were walking through a fog-shrouded cemetery. Jake felt a sense of dread, and he tried to coax Bridget back to the car. He didn't know why they were here—Bridget wouldn't tell him—but he knew she was up to no good.

Bridget came to a stop at a grave with a large headstone flanked by identical granite goblin statues. Jake read the gravestone's inscription and felt a chill crawl up his back: "Here lies Moira Ann Flanagan. May she rot in hell."

Then Bridget began to disrobe, shedding her blouse and exposing large, milk white breasts to cold air. It was a dream, yes, but Jake knew it was cold by the way Bridget's large pink nipples jutted. She stepped out of her skirt, seized Jake by the wrist, and pulled him down to the ground. He was already nude and erect. He didn't remember undressing, but his clothes were gone. Bridget pulled his erection into her, and Jake was buffeted by conflicting feelings of erotic exhilaration and disgust at the obscenity of fucking young Bridget on her long-dead sister's grave.

But that wasn't the worst thing.

The worst thing was what happened to Bridget's face just as he was about to come.

It began to change.

Jake awoke with a gasp, and sat up panting in the bed in Stu's guest bedroom. He couldn't remember precisely what had happened to Bridget at the end of the dream, but whatever it was had been awful enough to propel him instantly out of sleep. Jake drew in a few more big breaths and waited for his heart to slow to a normal rate. He almost never had nightmares, and the few he could recall tended to be mundane, such as falling from a great height or inexplicable classroom or mass transit nudity.

He recalled some of the more disturbing details and felt fresh disgust. Not wanting to think about it further, he threw back the covers and bounded out of bed. His head throbbed at the sudden motion, and he gritted his teeth against his first hangover in more than a year. It was mild, but its presence was unsettling. He popped some Tylenol, showered, dressed, and left Stu's house, locking up with the spare key his new roommate had given him the night before.

Stu lived in a middle-class neighborhood at the southeastern edge of Rockville called Washington Heights. Most of the houses were single-story redbrick cookie-cutter prefabs, and Stu's rental was no exception. But Jake had lived in apartments most of his adult life, so the little house was like a sprawling manse by comparison.

Jake climbed into his Camry and drove out of Washington Heights. His destination was a far less reputable address, the Zone. Short for Combat Zone. The Zone was a sprawling maze of cheap living units that had once housed thousands of soldiers during the Second World War. The Rockville army base was decommissioned after the war and the area became home to hundreds of low-income families. One of those families had been the McAllisters. Generations of McAllisters grew up, lived, and died there, some of them spending the bulk of their lives within its confines, subsisting on welfare and food stamps, rarely venturing farther than the corner store for a case of Old Milwaukee and a carton of smokes.

As Jake drove into the Zone, he was surprised to see that there had been some drastic improvements in his long absence. Many of the houses had been renovated, and the kids wandering its narrow streets looked clean and healthy. He didn't see any cars on blocks, or any aluminum litter glittering in the sun. The Zone had once been a great repository for empty beer cans. Not so anymore. It was amazing. Somewhere along the line the residents of this formerly blighted place had discovered some fresh sense of community pride and spirit. It was still a poor neighborhood—this was evident in a number of little ways—but it no longer reeked of decay. It was alive and vital.

Well, holy shit, Jake thought.

The change struck him as nothing less than miraculous.

And so he experienced a profound disappointment when he arrived at his childhood home. Aside from some obvious renovations to the small house's exterior, little had changed. The yard was overgrown. A Camaro was up on blocks in the middle of the yard. The telltale glint of crumpled beer cans was evident even through the tall grass.

Jake parked the Camry and got out. As he walked up the short drive to the front door, he had an impulse to turn around, get back in his car, and get the hell out. He didn't want to be here. Didn't want to see these people. Not now. Not ever. His body rebelled against it. His forefinger trembled as he stabbed the doorbell button. He waited a while before realizing the button didn't work. Then he steeled himself and rapped a fist on the glass outer door and yelled, "Mom! It's Jake!"

He heard a crash from somewhere within the house—glass shattering on a floor, from the sound of it—followed by a screeched curse. Then there was a clomp of bare feet on linoleum and his mother was scowling at him through the pane of grime-stained glass. She pulled the door open, seized him by the wrist, and pulled him inside.

Jolene McAllister slapped him hard across the face. "That's for being gone ten goddamn years. Don't your family mean nothin' to you?"

Jake gaped at her. He hadn't expected any tearful reunion, but this was ridiculous. Then again, it was just like the McAllisters he remembered. Hit first, ask questions later. Jolene's aggression was a direct link to that awful past, and being hit made him feel like he was seventeen again, the age he'd been when he'd finally left this fucking hovel to move into a friend's apartment on the other side of town.

Jake put a palm to his stinging cheek and rubbed it slowly. "You still pack a wallop, Mom. But get this straight. I came here to help Trey. I still care about him. You, I don't give a shit about." His mouth curved a humorless smile. "That answer your question?"

Jolene's bloodshot eyes narrowed to slits, and he could see the muscles in her neck working as she ground her teeth. Jake braced for another slap. If it came, he was out of here. He'd find another way to help Trey.

Then Jolene started crying. Tears welled in her eyes suddenly, then streamed down her face, etching messy trails through her heavily applied mascara. She put her face in her hands and sobbed. Jake rolled his eyes and waited for the storm to subside. Other than being older, his mother hadn't changed a bit. She was still mean. Still abusive. Still a drama queen. And she still dressed the same, wearing a skimpy pink tank top and cutoff denim shorts that hugged her narrow hips and rode up high on her blotchy thighs. Also present was the same old profusion of cheap jewelry—clacking silver bracelets, large, dangling earrings, and several necklaces. Her long fingernails were painted a tacky shade of glittery purple, and her huge helmet of permed blonde hair would have made even the most shamelessly garish '80s hair-metal singer cringe.

She looked exactly like what she was—an aging white-trash slut.

"Mom?"

Another round of sobbing followed the sound of his voice.

"Is Trey here?"

"My bay-beeee!"

Jake scowled. "Jesus. I'm wasting my time here. I came back to Rockville because I wanted to help Trey, not to watch you put on a fucking show."

Jolene stopped crying. She glared at him again. "You and I ain't ever gonna get along. I get that, son. Hell, I know what you think of me. You think I'm a total idiot?" She sneered. "So let's forget about the shit between us for now. Trey's all that matters. All I ask is you listen to what I have to say."

Jake didn't say anything for a few moments. His mind showed him a series of images burned indelibly into his memory, moments of childhood terror he wished he could forget, though now it was important to recall them, to strengthen his resolve and keep his mental defenses in place. These were memories of pain inflicted by the adults in his life. First by his biological father, a bitter man who was almost a prototype of a typical Zone man. He still bore the scars left by cigarettes extinguished on his flesh by Lou McAllister. Lou was shot to death when Jake was just eight. He hadn't wasted a second mourning the son of a bitch. But the abuse did not end then. Jolene McAllister never put cigarettes out on her boys, but she was no less vicious than her deceased husband. Her favorite disciplinary tool had been a belt with a huge Confederate flag buckle. Then the worst possible thing happened. Jolene remarried. And Lou's successor was even more of a sadistic bastard. The beatings Jake and Mike endured at the hands of that man had been beyond brutal.

Jolene's thinly veiled attempt to characterize their troubled past as little more than the normal tensions existing between parents and rebellious children was ludicrous. She could never admit her faults, never recognize her past behavior as abusive. So he couldn't confront her, couldn't make her acknowledge the damage she'd wrought. There was no closure to be had here. Not now. Not ever.

"All right, Mom. Let's forget about the . . . shit . . . between us. Tell me about Trey."

"Okay, but let's move this heartwarming reunion to the kitchen." She turned away from him and padded down the short hallway, then stepped through an archway into the kitchen. "I don't know about you, but I could sure use a drink."

Jake followed her into the kitchen. The sink was piled high with dirty dishes. An odor of shit emanated from an overflowing litter box. The ancient linoleum was stained and curling up in places. Another odor permeated the air in here, a ghost smell just detectable beneath the stench of cat shit. A puke smell. On the floor near the refrigerator was a pile of jagged glass shards, the remains of a shattered jar.

Jake took a seat at the wobbly kitchen table. Jolene pulled open the refrigerator door, popped two cans of Old Milwaukee off a plastic binder, and set one down in front of her son. She plopped down in the seat opposite him, popped the can's tab, and knocked back a long slug of cheap beer. Jake hated Old Milwaukee, but he needed a beer. More than ever, he needed a goddamn beer. He opened the can and took a sip.

He shuddered and put the can down. "So what's going on?"

Jolene pushed her chair back and set her feet up on the edge of the table. She had some kind of vine tattoo around her left ankle. And a gold-plated anklet. And a toe ring. Jake tried to conceal his distaste. But Jesus fucking Christ. This woman was in her fifties. Did she know how ridiculous she looked?

"Trey's gotten mixed up with some punk-ass bitch."

Jake thought, What are you, Snoop Doggy Mom now?

He kept his voice noncommittal. "Oh yeah?"

Jolene lit a Doral and blew smoke at the ceiling. "This weird slut named Myra. When I say punk, I mean punk rock. You know, alternative? Hair and clothes all funny-lookin'. Piercings all over."

Jake laughed. "So what's the problem? Because I just don't see what the big deal is. So Trey's hanging with a punk chick. Real shocking, Mom. For 1978, maybe."

Jolene's feet came off the table and she leaned toward Jake, some of the previous heat returning to her voice. "Fuck you, Jake. I ain't so simpleminded as that. There's more to it than that."

"Okay. So make me understand why this girl's trouble."

"Trey's not like you or Mikey, Jake. He's a good boy."

Jake sighed.

Jolene pressed on. "He's a good student. Honors and shit. He plays sports. He's popular. He's everything you wouldn't expect a kid from the Zone to be. At least he was until that cunt came along. Now it's all gone down the tubes. He dumped his beautiful girlfriend and his grades are in the toilet. I'm not even sure he's gonna graduate." Tears welled in her eyes again. "My baby's in trouble, Jake. He could still have a bright future if he'd just be made to see how this bitch is ruining everything." She reached across the table and clasped hands with her oldest son. "Can't you help me?"

Jake doubted this Myra chick was as horrible as Jolene made her out to be. Still, if her account of Trey's abrupt and dramatic change of behavior was even partially accurate, then there was some legitimate cause for concern. A selfish, private corner of his psyche boiled with anger, though. When he and Mikey were skipping school and getting in scrapes with the law, she'd never been anywhere near this concerned. Hell, she hadn't given a shit.

"I'll try to help," he said at last. "When's the best time to see him?"

Jolene smiled. "I told him you'd be by to see him when he gets home from school today." She sniffled. "I just knew you'd help. He should be here about three thirty."

Jake stood up. "I'll be here."

"He'll want you to tell him all about being a famous writer. He just loved your books."

Jake's expression remained impassive. "Yeah. Right."

Jake had two published novels to his credit, but their sales figures were far south of "famous writer" territory.

Jolene's expression softened. She almost seemed to project

real warmth at him. "You're a good role model, son. I always knew you'd turn your life around someday."

Jake felt a headache coming on.

"Three thirty," he said.

He turned and walked out of his nightmare house.

CHAPTER SEVEN

The girl looked good enough to eat. The way she sat there all curled up in the chair on the other side of his desk was just about too sexy to take, her legs tucked beneath her, her body turned sideways, one arm draped languorously over the back of the chair. He wanted to chew on her pooched-out lower lip. Wanted to kiss her eyelids. Smudges of dark eye shadow created a false impression of fresh bruises. The eye shadow and a delicate bone structure made her eyes look big and white like fat flakes of falling snow.

Principal Raymond Slater had lusted after hundreds of the young girls who'd passed through Rockville High's not-so-hallowed halls over the years, but he'd never attempted to seduce any of them. He enjoyed his job and his position in the community, and he was smart enough to shy away from forbidden fruit. Still, some temptations were more . . . tempting . . . than others.

He made himself frown. "Surely . . ." He cleared his throat. "Surely you do not mean to propose an exchange of sexual favors for leniency . . . do you?"

Myra chuckled. "Do I?" Her gaze lingered on Slater a moment. Her tongue darted out and she licked her lower lip. Mischief twinkled in her eyes. She stroked an arm of the chair, gripping it the way Penelope often gripped his cock, with a delicious mixture of delicacy and firmness. "That's not really what I said, Principal Slater."

Slater swallowed hard. "You said . . ." He cleared his throat again and squirmed in his chair. "When you came into my office, I directed you to the chair you're in now. You leaned over my desk and said you'd prefer to sit in my lap."

Myra batted her eyes, licked her lips again, shifted her hips again. "Mmm . . . yes . . ."

Slater's penis leaped against the fabric of his trousers. He cursed the thing. He could feel his self-control faltering. He didn't know how much longer he could stand to watch her *undulate* on that chair. He was tempted to give her a free pass just to get her luscious little body the hell out of his office.

He glanced again at the open file on his desk and sighed, realizing that just wasn't an option. Myra had been causing trouble in lots of little ways almost from the day she'd arrived on campus at the beginning of the year. Her attendance had been spotty from the start, but today was the first time she'd deigned to show up in nearly a full week. Even so, her poor attendance alone would not have been sufficient to bring him to the brink of the decision he was about to make—to recommend her expulsion from Rockville High to the school board.

He shook his head and sighed. "I hate to have to do this, but I have no choice. I could overlook everything else. This close to graduation, nobody cares about attendance if your grades have held up, as yours have. But you crossed a point of no return when you punched Cindy Wells in the face."

Myra laughed.

Slater's expression sharpened. "It's not funny, Ms. Lewis."

Reverting to a student's surname after conversing with them more familiarly was a patented Slaterism, his way of signaling a serious shift in temper. Most students heeded the warning, recognizing at last the serious trouble they were in.

Myra just laughed some more. "I thought it was hilarious. Cheerleader fall down, go boom."

And now she *giggled*.

Slater gaped. His iron glare had never failed to instill fear in the hearts of students. "You broke her nose. You disfigured one of Rockville High's most popular students. She lost teeth, for Christ's sake! You knocked her unconscious!"

Myra shrugged.

She seemed uninterested, almost disinterested, as if the matter under discussion was of no concern to her at all and could have no impact on her life. "You may not graduate, Ms. Lewis! Don't you care about that? Why did you do it?"

There was something disturbing in Myra's oddly knowing smile. "There are times when I want to hurt people for no particular reason. This time there was a little bit of a reason. Cindy's life was a little too perfect, you have to admit. Perfect body, perfect football-player boyfriend, scholarships spilling out of her tight little ass. I thought I should introduce her to some possibilities she may not have previously considered."

Slater's brow furrowed, a topography of valleys and canyons forming across his forehead. "What!?" It was like the girl was speaking in a foreign language. "Are you insane? What the hell do you mean?"

A detached part of himself was appalled. He never lost his cool with students. Never. Oh, they knew when he was pissed, you bet your ass, but he never flew off the handle. He was always calm, cool, and when necessary, menacing. But now this infuriating girl, this strange, exotic creature so unlike any other girl at Rockville High, had him on the verge of a meltdown. She made him furious. Christ, she made him so horny! And the hell of it was there were dozens of female students more classically beautiful. Tall, busty, blonde girls with tawny skin and sleek bodies. Myra was small, barely taller than five feet, and she was so pale, her flesh just a few subtle shades removed from albino white.

Her smile broadened. "I decided I wanted Cindy to know bad things can happen to her, too. That being loved and adored won't protect her. That there's ugliness in the world and she's just as vulnerable as anybody."

Slater shuddered. "My God. You're absolutely psychotic."

Myra laughed again.

Slater shook his head. "Why was this important to you?

Did her friends pick on you? Did she slight you in some way? Please help me to understand this."

"Cindy treated me as well as anyone else in this school, maybe even a little better."

"And this is how you repay her kindness?"

"Oh, I'll make it up to her."

Slater frowned. "How do you mean?"

"I'm going to visit her soon." Myra unfolded her legs and leaned forward in the chair. "We'll kiss and make up. Then I'll make her boyfriend watch while she eats my pussy."

Slater could not conceal his shock. "Wh-wh-wha . . ."

Temporarily unable to utter complete words—much less coherent sentences—he gave up.

Myra leered at him. "Her missing teeth should make things interesting."

Slater's next words emerged in a strangled squeak: "Get out of my office . . . you . . . you . . ."

Myra stood up and circled the desk. She was straddling Slater's lap before he could even think to fend her off.

Myra's eyes widened in mock shock. "Why, Principal Slater, what's this creature in your pants?"

Slater gulped and managed to recover a measure of dignity. He imagined someone bursting into the office unannounced and felt horror. He seized Myra about the shoulders and tried to push her away, but she clamped a surprisingly strong hand around his throat.

She leaned closer and whispered in his ear. "You'll do whatever I want you to do from now on, little man. You won't suspend me. You'll trump up a reason to suspend Cindy instead. Just because. Oh, I know it seems mean, but that's the fun of it. Being mean is a good time."

Her warm breath felt good on his ear. He had to force himself to concentrate. "But—"

Her hand closed tighter around his throat. "And the reason you'll do this, other than my ability to make you do whatever I want anyway, is your reputation. I can destroy you, Raymond Slater."

Slater blinked. Swallowed. "What . . . do you mean?"

Myra drew his earlobe into her mouth, bit down.

Slater shuddered—with both pleasure and fear.

Then she told him all about what the crow had seen through his window one night.

Slater's heart paused a moment.

Myra clamped a hand over his mouth to stifle his scream.

And she laughed. "Don't be too afraid, Raymond, baby. I have such wonderful plans for you and your wench. Your future is glorious."

Then she revealed her true self to him.

This time Slater was too terrified to muster a scream.

CHAPTER EIGHT

After her son left, Jolene McAllister swept the remains of the broken pickle jar into a dustpan, dropped the glass fragments into a garbage can that was already stuffed to capacity, and went to her room. She shed her clothes and went into the bathroom to take a shower. Steam filled the room and she began to feel very mellow, some of the nervous tension generated by her oldest boy's return dissipating as she closed her eyes and leaned her forehead against the tile-covered wall. She fell asleep standing up, waking up when her knees began to buckle.

She squelched the flow of water, stepped out of the tub, and toweled off. Then she dressed herself, went back to the kitchen, and yanked open the sliding glass door that overlooked a backyard overgrown and strewn with debris. One day soon she'd have to break down and blow one or more of the Crawford boys down the street, get them to come out here with their riding mower and weed trimmer. The Crawford boys liked to talk about her behind her back, run her down like all the other Zone assholes, but they sure didn't talk shit when the prospect of putting their rock-hard dicks in her oh-so-experienced mouth was raised.

Jolene slipped on sandals and ventured into the backyard. The yard was bordered by rust-encrusted chain-link fencing, which was so old it sagged in places. A stand of trees loomed beyond the far end of the yard, the edge of a stretch of forest that extended to the man-made lake a mile north. Trey was always disappearing out there for hours at a time, and it bothered her, but she had other concerns at the moment.

She crossed the yard, the sandals protecting her against an array of sharp objects obscured by the tall grass as she made her way to the dilapidated old shed in a corner of the yard. She fished a key from a pocket of her denim shorts, opened the new lock she'd purchased last week, and stepped inside. A powerful lantern sat on a dusty worktable. She turned it on and studied the sleeping figure in a rear corner of the room.

"Wake up."

Her voice was loud in the room's stale, dusty air. The man in the corner awoke with a jerk. He looked at Jolene and muttered something unintelligible. The gag in his mouth rendered decipherable speech impossible. Not that Jolene wanted to hear anything her husband might have to say. Hal McAllister's nude, fat body looked gray in the glare of the lantern light. The bloat of his hairy beer belly turned Jolene's stomach. It sickened her to think of how many years she'd wasted allowing this shitty whale of a man to flop around on top of her.

She sneered. "You're disgusting. You're a blob. You look like a big ol' hairy pile of mashed potatoes."

More indecipherable muttering ensued.

Jolene stepped over to a wall and examined a row of rusty tools hanging on pegs. Some of them were dark with recent stains. There was a big saw that had last been used decades ago. She was saving it for some of the bigger operations to come. She looked forward to cutting off his legs with it. She reached up and removed a wire cutter from one of the pegs. Hal's eyes tracked her movements, widening when she flexed the wire cutter's blades.

She turned away from the wall and fixed him with a grin that looked both hungry and salacious. He knew by now the pleasure she derived from his pain. She walked toward him slowly, enjoying his terror, growing wet as she watched him shiver, anticipating the agony he was about to endure.

"Jake was just here, Hal. We talked about Trey and his troubles." She stood before her bound husband, her legs spread, staring down at him, using her rigid posture and position to emphasize his vulnerability. "You know what's funny? He never once asked about you. Not once."

She snipped the wire cutter at him, the blades snapping on air millimeters from his face. He whimpered. Began to cry. Soon he would begin to blubber, perhaps even go into convulsions. It had happened before.

"Nobody ever asks about you, Hal. Nobody."

Hal's chest hitched.

"Trey never asks about you. Your own son. You've disappeared off the face of the earth and he hasn't noticed. It's like you never existed." She grinned. "By the time anyone thinks to ask of you—months from now, years maybe—every trace of you will have vanished from this earth. What do you think about that, Hal, baby?" She leaned down, her mouth poised inches from the place on his head once occupied by his left ear. "Doesn't it make you feel worthless? Like scum? Like something a rabid dog might crap out its ass?"

Hal threw his head back and wailed, straining against his bonds.

Jolene groped for his right hand, pulled its forefinger rigid, and fit the wire-cutter blades around it. She paused a moment and leaned closer, getting her eyes good and close to Hal's, enjoying the sensation of power that coursed through her as she watched his milky orbs jitter. Then she gritted her teeth and squeezed the handles with all her strength. Hal's forefinger, the only finger remaining on his right hand, until now, tumbled to the dirty floor.

Hal squealed and writhed.

Jolene went to her knees and opened her mouth to taste some of the jetting blood. It filled her mouth and sprayed her face and chest. She would need another shower. She let him bleed a little longer; then she got to her feet and retrieved the blowtorch from the worktable.

She approached Hal, smiling. "This is going to hurt you more than it's going to hurt me."

She cauterized his wound and shut the blowtorch off. She

retrieved a syringe filled with morphine from a bag she kept under the worktable, stabbed the needle into a much-abused vein on Hal's left arm, and filled him with the medicine that would keep him from dying of shock.

"There, there, baby. You're going to be around a long time. Mama ain't near done with you."

She laughed.

Then she picked up the severed finger, shoved it into her pocket, and left the shack, leaving her miserable husband alone with the shadows and his nightmares.

And a few other things.

Crawling things.

Horrible, leering things that grew and changed shape.

Things that knew infinitely more about sadism than Jolene McAllister.

CHAPTER NINE

Jordan Harper staggered into her apartment and threw the door shut behind her. She shuffled into the kitchen on legs that felt like those of an old lady. Heavy and weary. Stung by Bridget's betrayal, she'd been unable to sleep all night. She'd nonetheless managed to show up for her morning shift at Mondo Video.

In retrospect, she should have stayed home.

Robbed of her patience by exhaustion, she'd snapped at several customers and a few of her more annoying coworkers. This culminated in a bitter exchange with a snide old bitch. A dispute over late fees ended with Jordan screaming at the woman, calling her a "miserable, skeleton-faced cunt hag from hell."

Thus had Jordan's less-than-illustrious career at Mondo Video come to an end. Not that she cared. She didn't give a shit about her job or anything else connected to this rotten town. Showing up for work today was just the kind of thing Jordan did, fulfilling her obligations. She felt nothing but contempt for slackers. But how could she reconcile that with her behavior today?

She poured herself a glass of juice and shut the refrigerator. "Christ, give yourself a break, girl."

Okay, this talking to herself shit was a bad sign. But the sentiment was dead-on. This was just a setback, and a minor one at that. The loss of the Mondo Video job was your basic blessing in disguise. It meant there was one less thing tying her to Rockville. Even last night's public embarrassment was a blessing. She didn't need duplicitous people in her life. She was better off without those backstabbing bitches.

She sipped her juice and contemplated her immediate future. As recently as yesterday evening, she'd planned to be in Rockville for another year, long enough to get her associate's degree from RCC. But fuck that. She was spinning her wheels here. Her first-year grades at RCC were impeccable. It was time to start sending out applications to real universities, maybe get enrolled at a good school by the fall semester, somewhere far away from Rockville.

"Sounds like a plan," she muttered.

And thought, Stop that!

Bailing out of Rockville was clearly the way to go, but there was some shame in it, too. She felt a bit like a whipped dog running away with its tail tucked between its legs. It was the sort of thing she would normally rebel against. But not this time. Enough was enough. This time running away was absolutely the right thing to do.

It was too much to think about right now. She was tired. She yawned and stretched. What she needed right now was rest. The future could wait a few more hours. She dumped out the rest of her juice, dropped the empty glass in the sink, and shuffled out of the kitchen.

She heard the dim noise of a television as she moved down the short hallway toward her bedroom. Alarm surged through her until she realized she'd probably forgotten to turn it off before leaving this morning. She'd been in a mental fog, so it was a reasonable explanation—but when she entered the bedroom, she saw that she was wrong.

Bridget Flanagan was on her side in Jordan's bed, her head propped in the upturned palm of her right hand. Her other hand aimed the remote control at Jordan's television. A white comforter was pulled up over her breasts. Her bare shoulders made it clear she was nude beneath the comforter. Jordan gaped at her a moment before her gaze went to the small pile of clothing at the foot of the bed—Bridget's skirt, blouse, and panties.

Jordan cursed herself for being so stupid. The door to her apartment had been unlocked when she came home. She'd been too tired to notice. Probably she'd left it unlocked this morning, too.

Bridget dropped the remote and sat up in the bed, holding the comforter up over her breasts. "There you are! I was hoping you weren't at work today."

Jordan felt numb as she said, "I was. I got fired. What are you doing in my bed, Bridget? What are you doing in my apartment at all?"

Bridget pouted. "I'm here to see you, silly." Her eyes crinkled at the corners as she tried to fake emotion. "I feel real bad about last night. I don't know what got into me."

"Bullshit. Put your clothes on and get out of here."

Bridget pouted some more. "I was just afraid. Please don't be mad at me, Jordan. You made me think about a part of myself, my sexuality, that I just wasn't ready to deal with."

Jordan smirked. "And now you are?"

Bridget nodded. "Yes. I . . . I want you, Jordan."

Jordan couldn't believe it. There was just no end to this chick's head games. She hated that she'd been so blind to Bridget's true nature for so long. She was a user. A manipulator. An emotional sadist. "You make me sick, Bridget. Get out of here before I throw you out."

Bridget smiled. "You don't want to do that . . ." She let the comforter fall away, exposing her breasts. "Do you?"

Jordan knew she should say something. Keep focused. But she stared at Bridget's full, firm breasts and imagined touching them. Her mouth hung open. Her eyes fluttered. Christ, she was too tired to think straight. She imagined how she must look to Bridget and felt a fresh surge of anger, directed both at herself and the evil bitch in her bed. "Get out!"

Bridget laughed. She threw the comforter back and stretched out on Jordan's bed, her long, lean body aglow in the morning sunlight slanting in through the window blinds. She lifted her legs off the bed, stretched her feet to their fullest extent, and wiggled her toes. She lightly trailed the fingertips of one hand over her smooth, concave belly, the glint of pink nail polish a sensual contrast to tanned flesh. She met Jordan's gaze and winked.

"I don't feel like leaving just now, Jordan." She pinched one of her nipples. "Why don't you come over here and put your mouth on this?"

Jordan wavered for just a moment. She saw herself caving in, submitting to this degradation. Although it would be the fulfillment of a fantasy, it would absolutely be a degradation. And knowing this strengthened her resolve.

She went to the bed and Bridget sat up, puckering her lips, anticipating a kiss. She yelped when Jordan grabbed her by the wrist and yanked her out of the bed. Bridget shrieked and struggled until Jordan drove a fist hard into her stomach, and then she was gasping for air. Still holding her by the wrist, Jordan scooped up Bridget's clothes and pulled her former friend out of the bedroom.

"What are you doing, you bitch!?"

Jordan dragged the struggling girl down the hallway. "Throwing out the trash."

Bridget tried to twist out of Jordan's grip, but to no avail. They arrived at the front door moments later. Jordan pulled it open and shoved Bridget through it. Then she threw the skimpy, silky clothes—which felt so nice to the touch—out after her. She threw the door shut, turned the lock, and leaned against it. Bridget screamed and pounded her fists against the door.

"You'll pay for this, you fucking whore!" came the muffled voice from outside. "I'll kill you! You're gonna die, Jordan! Die!"

Jordan closed her eyes and tuned out the rest of it.

So she didn't realize that Bridget's screams had turned to cruel laughter.

CHAPTER TEN

Jake stopped at a convenience store on the way back to Washington Heights. He picked up a copy of the *Rockville Times* and got in line behind a woman who reminded him a little too much of his mother. Bottle-blonde hair. A skimpy white tank top. Tattoo depicting a coiled snake visible on her left shoulder blade. Denim cutoffs that clung like a second skin to her shapely ass. She caught him looking at her and winked.

Jake's stomach clenched.

It was as if his mom had caught him leering at her. He was mortified. The woman's face had that haggard quality common to middle-aged women from the Zone. Too many years of hard drinking and hard living. She could've been anywhere from thirty-five to fifty.

She smiled at him. "I know you, sweetie?"

His face flushed. "Ah . . . no. You look like somebody I know."

Her red-rimmed eyes almost twinkled. "Well, want to get to know *me* better?"

Jake forced a laugh. "Yeah, I'm flattered, but I'm . . . married."

He tried to conceal his lack of a ring by shifting his grip on the newspaper, but the lady had an eagle eye and didn't miss the lame attempt at subterfuge.

Her smile vanished. "Oh, fuck off."

She turned away from him and set her twelve-pack of Old

Milwaukee on the counter. Embarrassed, Jake wandered to the rear of the store, where he grabbed a six-pack of Heineken from the beer cooler. The flirtatious woman hurled a final curse his way as she banged the door open on her way out. Jake paid the clerk and left the store. Back in the car, he pried the top off a Heineken, wedged the bottle between his legs, and wheeled out of the parking lot.

The Heineken was empty by the time he pulled into Stu's driveway. His hand moved to toss the empty into the Camry's backseat, but he stopped and frowned at the bottle.

He sighed. "You're on a slippery slope here, man."

But fuck it, it was done.

He chucked the empty into the back and got out of the car. He went around the side of the house and let himself in through the back door, then stepped into the kitchen and hit the light switch. The overhead fluorescent lights flickered for a bit before coming all the way on. He put the rest of the Heineken in the fridge and poured Coca-Cola into an ice-filled glass from a two-liter bottle. Then he grabbed his paper and headed to the living room.

He was in an old leather recliner and looking at the newspaper before he noticed the girl. She was curled up asleep on the blue sofa on the other side of the coffee table. She was small, with a pale face and straight, lustrous black hair tucked behind her ears. She wore a dark gray hoodie, ratty blue jeans, and striped orange-and-black socks with holes in the toes.

Jake had no idea who she was.

Stu hadn't mentioned anything about a girlfriend or a roommate. It bothered him. She didn't look like a criminal. But that didn't mean much. She could be an intruder, what did he know? He thought about calling Stu. Maybe even the cops. But he just couldn't bring himself to do it. What kind of criminal breaks into a place just to sack out on the sofa?

But hell, he knew the answer to that.

The mentally unbalanced kind.

Then Jake saw the small handbag and the key ring on the coffee table. An idea occurred to him. It was an invasion of privacy, but the idea's allure was strong. Oh, the hell with it. He folded the paper and set it aside, then got up and moved cautiously to the other side of the coffee table. The hardwood floor creaked beneath his hiking boots. He searched the girl's face for any indication of imminent wakefulness. She kept on snoring. Jake reached into the handbag, rooted through a jumble of lipsticks, pill bottles, and other ephemera, and finally extracted a lime green wallet. He undid the snap and looked at the girl's plastic-encased driver's license.

His eyes widened. "I'll be damned."

Kristen Walker woke with a yawn, startling Jake. The wallet jumped out of his hand and landed with a thump on the coffee table. She smiled and said, "Hello, Jake." She glanced at her wallet and smirked. "You know, if you're hard up for cash, you're robbing the wrong girl."

Jake covered his embarrassment with a laugh. "Sorry, I'm not robbing you. I just had no idea who you were, and my curiosity overwhelmed my good sense."

She regarded him with a cool gaze, an expression conveying both reproach and amusement. "I assume you've figured out who I am, then?"

"I have the vaguest memory of Stu having an older sister, a fact that I forgot until now. Do you live here with Stu? I thought he was alone here."

Kristen sat up and perched herself on the edge of the sofa. "He is. But he lets me stay here when I need to. Like now."

Something in her tone put Jake on edge. Her words revealed little about her real situation, but there was an undertone of distress. Maybe she was in an abusive relationship and stayed at Stu's place after especially bad domestic episodes. A surreptitious glance at her left hand failed to reveal a wedding band. But that didn't mean she wasn't involved with some creep who liked to settle domestic disputes with his fists.

He kept his tone neutral as he said, "So what brings you here this time?"

Her expression turned sour. "My boyfriend kicked me out."

Jake frowned. "Oh. Well. Um . . ."

He had no idea what to say.

Kristen seemed to sense this and the corners of her eyes crinkled. "He was justified in kicking me out, Jake. I made some promises I couldn't keep. He found out I was a lying bitch, so he gave me my walking papers."

"I'm sorry, I didn't mean to pry."

She laughed. "You're not. I volunteered my sad tale. But I'm done talking about it for now."

Jake shrugged. He felt awkward standing there, so he sat down at the far side of the sofa. He felt a little tremor of excitement as Kristen turned to face him. "Hey, wait. How did you know who I am? Stu's been gone all day."

Kristen stared at him a moment. "There's this new gizmo that's been catching on lately. Cell phones. Maybe you've heard of them. Anyway, I called my brother's cell this morning to tell him I'd need to stay here a while. He told me you might be here. But I would've recognized you anyway."

Jake cocked an eyebrow at her. "Um . . . how?"

"There was a story in the *Rockville Times* when *Blood Circus* came out. Then another when *House of the Damned* was released."

Jake frowned. "Huh."

"Something wrong?"

"No." He shook his head slowly. "I guess not. It's just the last time I knew of my name being in that rag was in the weekly crime report years ago."

"You mean nobody sent you clippings?"

Jake shook his head. "Who the fuck would do that? Me and Rockville, we've kept our distance."

"So why are you back?"

He told her about Trey's situation. She listened to him attentively through the whole tale, never breaking eye contact. She was so earnest it was unsettling. Her rapt gaze gave the impression that nothing else existed for her while he was talking.

When he was done telling her about Trey, she bit her lower

lip and cast her gaze downward. He figured she was thinking the situation over and would soon volunteer some insights.

But what she actually said was, "Whenever I meet someone new, I have a test. It's not an especially complicated test, as far as tests go. It's more subjective than most, and there's just one question. I ask you to tell me one true thing about life and existence, one thing close to your heart, one thing you believe says everything there is to say about you as a person."

Jake blinked. "Um . . ."

Her speech unsettled him. It came from out of nowhere, for one thing. And it was already evident that Kristen was a little strange. But he tried to squelch his unease. He liked her. He couldn't pinpoint precisely why, but he did. It wasn't just that she was pretty. It was a combination of the way she talked, the way she looked at him, and her relaxed physicality, the way she was so at ease being this intimate with a virtual stranger. It was all that and probably a host of more obscure things, too.

He liked being close to her.

What that might mean beyond this moment, he didn't know, but there you go.

He coughed. "Okay. Sure. But you go first . . ."

She drew in a lungful of air, then let it out slowly. "People like to say they're not afraid to die." She peered at him with an intensity that made Jake squirm a little—it was as if she were trying to see through his eyes and into his brain, probing for his secrets. "Of old age, I mean. Hell, everybody's afraid of sudden death. A killer sneaking into your room in the middle of the night. A crack addict with a gun mugging you on a city street. A heart attack that strikes you down in the prime of life. But most people, if you ask them, will say they won't fear death as the natural end to a long, well-lived life. If you get to be ninety years old, or a hundred, or whatever, the supposition is that you'll be so tired of dealing with your infirmities that you'll gladly surrender to the darkness."

Jake laughed. "Surrender to the darkness?"

Her smile was a shy one. "I'm trying to be a horror writer, too."

"No way. Are you shitting me?"

"Seriously."

Jake sat up straighter. "Huh. Well, that's cool."

A subtle hint of redness touched her cheeks. "Yes. But back to the subject at hand. Here's the thing, Jake. I'm afraid to die. Whether it happens today, tomorrow, or fifty years from now, it doesn't matter—I'm afraid. I think about it every day. I can be just sitting at my desk at work and suddenly I'll think about it. I'll fast-forward to my last moments so clearly it makes me want to scream. I see myself in a hospital bed. Impossibly old and feeble. Hooked up to machines. Laboring for breath. Clinging to life. Most people, if they imagine something so morbid for themselves, they'd say death would be a welcome relief. But not me, Jake." She leaned forward and touched his hand, making him shudder. "Even then, I'd be consumed with terror. Dreading what comes next, because I know what comes next. Nothing. A void. Nonexistence." Her voice drifted to a lower register, became almost a whisper. "I don't believe there's anything after this life. And I don't want to ever die, Jake. I don't want to stop *being*. Which just isn't possible." The shy smile returned. "It's quite the conundrum."

Jake drew her hand into both of his. "I think I'm going to drink myself to death." He swallowed hard. It astounded him that he was saying this. It frightened him, too. "I'm an alcoholic. I ended a year of sobriety yesterday. The stress of being back in Rockville had a little to do with it, but mostly it's because, deep down, I never really wanted to stop drinking. And I don't think I'll ever stop again. I mean that. That's not a poor-pitiful-me statement. That's the way it's going to be because that's the way I want it to be. I don't like the way the world really is. I don't like the way I feel sober. I need the edge off. I need reality blunted. It's going to kill me. But I consider it an equal exchange. Am I crazy?"

"You're not crazy." She laid her other hand on top of his. "And congratulations. You passed the test."

Jake felt a sudden tightness in his chest. He replayed his

words in his head, marveling at them. The sentiments expressed ran counter to every sensible thing he'd learned over the past year, but he realized that he truly did not care. His speech to Kristen marked the first time he'd ever laid bare this unvarnished truth.

Her gaze turned solemn. "Jake . . . are you feeling this like I am? Please tell me you are."

Jake hesitated. Then he sighed. "Yeah. Yeah. Holy shit, I think so."

She smiled. "Cool."

Jake shook his head. "But it's crazy. Isn't it? I've known you, what . . . twenty minutes?"

She laughed. "I know. And it is crazy. It really is. But I don't think I care."

They inched closer to each other.

And Kristen said, "Kiss me."

So he kissed her.

CHAPTER ELEVEN

The cafeteria at Rockville High came alive shortly after the noon lunch bell. Students poured in through the wide-open double doors at either end of the spacious room, filling the previously silent void with chatter and laughter. Jocks told dirty jokes, their buddies barked sycophantic laughter, and their pretty blonde girlfriends giggled and rolled their eyes. Students snagged prime table spots while their friends got in line to get food. Plates and cutlery clanked, students jockeyed for position as the tables filled, and a hip-hop beat began to emanate from the wall-mounted speakers. The small crowd around the jukebox dispersed after a few minutes, because by then it was already programmed through the lunch hour. By the time the last student cleared the lunch counter, there were precious few empty seats remaining at the overflowing tables.

There was, however, one notable exception.

A lone table with just two occupants, a big white island in the middle of a human sea.

Kelsey Hargrove and Will Mackeson sat opposite each other at one end of a jam-packed table. The tables were arranged in four long rows on each side of the cafeteria with a wide-open space in the middle. The boys normally liked to position themselves at the edge of the open space. It was a good spot for scoping out hot chicks. But today they weren't at their normal table. Today they were sitting one table over from that lone white island, conducting long-overdue reconnaissance work.

Kelsey shot a quick glance at the island, then snapped his eyes in another direction. "Fuck, man. She saw me looking at her."

Will grimaced. "Christ, don't look at them."

Kelsey stared with distaste at the untouched lasagna on his plate. He was too sick with worry to muster an appetite. He prodded it with his fork for a moment before setting it down. "There is something seriously fucking wrong with that chick. And I don't mean wrong like she's psycho or something. She's *evil*, dude, like a spawn of Satan or something."

Will nodded. "Right. Yeah. She's the fuckin' princess of darkness."

The boys weren't joking. This Myra Lewis chick their buddy Trey was spending all his time with these days was bad news. The school was still abuzz with gossip about her run-in with Cindy Wells. Cindy Wells was one of a handful of girls who could contend for the title of Ms. Rockville High. She was almost universally adored. An untouchable. Royalty among students. Myra Lewis had gone medieval on a fucking *goddess*. She should be in a jail cell. But here she was, eating lunch with her whipped boyfriend, a serene smile on her pretty face, acting as if nothing had happened.

Kelsey picked at his lasagna some more, managed to eat a forkful or two before giving up again. He eyed Will solemnly. "We've got to do something, man."

Will shrugged. "Yeah, but what? It's hopeless. Trey barely even talks to us anymore. It's like Myra won't let him."

Kelsey nodded. "It's like he's a trained puppy dog."

"More like a broken-down, beat-to-hell old hound dog." Another darting glance at their troubled friend's table rattled Will—Myra was staring right at him. Her cold gaze raised goose bumps on his arms. She had an arm draped around Trey's shoulders. While he watched, she twined a lock of Trey's hair between her fingers and twisted it, pulling it taut. It looked painful, but Trey didn't react. Feeling sick, Will looked away. "Shit."

The same sick feeling was reflected in Kelsey's eyes—he'd seen Myra's blatant display of sadism, too. "The bitch scares me, man. I mean, she really fucking scares the shit out of me."

Will shuddered. "Yeah. Me, too."

"I wasn't kidding about her being evil. I think she's some kinda demon or devil lady." Kelsey's tone was utterly devoid of humor. "I think we should look up some exorcism shit on the Internet."

Will shook his head. "I guess we could try, but what good would it do? With that kind of thing, how would we ever tell what's bullshit from what's genuine? Ain't anything in the world more full of shit than the Internet, man."

"So, what, we do nothing? Fuck that. Trey's our bro. We can't just let this demon chick destroy him."

Will looked at his food. He hadn't eaten all day, but the lasagna looked like something regurgitated by a rabid animal. He pushed the plate away and said, "Maybe we could go to Principal Slater."

"Oh, sure, right, the same Principal Slater who let her get away with knocking Cindy Wells on her ass. Wow, why didn't I think of that?"

Will flipped him off. "Okay, smart guy, what about the police?"

Kelsey shook his head. "The police will not take this seriously. Not in a gazillion fucking years. Face it, there's no help coming from the adult world."

"So we're just screwed, right? Trey is doomed to be Myra's slave forever?"

Kelsey leaned over the table and jabbed a forefinger at Will. "Wrong. We're going to do something. I don't know what yet, but something. We'll do the Internet thing. If that doesn't work out, we'll hire a mafia goon to whack the bitch."

"There ain't any mafia in Rockville."

Kelsey smiled. "Right. Otherwise that'd be plan A."

Will slumped in his chair, frustration evident in his posture. "Shit, it's not funny. We don't have Soprano motherfuckers around, but there's a shitload of Zone rednecks who'd do the job for beer money."

Kelsey grunted. "Forget that. None of those fuckers are ever sober enough to shoot straight. It'd turn out like Larry the Cable Guy meets *Pulp* fucking *Fiction*."

"So there goes that idea."

"Yeah."

Kelsey risked another glance at Trey's table and was startled to see his friend sitting there alone. It was the first time he'd seen Trey without Myra in ages. He looked at Will, who'd noticed the same thing. An unspoken communication transpired in a heartbeat. They rose from the table and hurried over to Trey.

Will took a seat next to Trey, while Kelsey sat opposite him.

Trey just sat there, barely blinking, their presence not appearing to register at all.

Kelsey glanced again at Will before addressing Trey. "Trey, man, listen up. We know something's wrong, okay? Myra is, like, evil incarnate, right? We don't know what she's doing to you, but we're gonna do something about it, I fucking promise."

Trey's voice was barely audible: "No."

Kelsey frowned. "What? You *need* our help, man. Don't even pretend like you don't know what we're talking about."

Trey pushed his chair away from the table and got to his feet with a sigh. He lifted his tray off the table and began to shuffle away from them, his head down as he moved toward the counter. He appeared listless, sapped of energy and life. Like a damn zombie. Kelsey and Will hurried after him. Kelsey cupped a hand on Trey's shoulder. "Hey, hold up—"

But Trey whirled on them. His tray went flying as he slapped Kelsey's hand away. The plate bounced off the tray and shattered on the floor. The babble of chatter and laughter around them stopped immediately.

Trey leaned in close to Kelsey, his face twisted with anger

and an inner agony. "Mind your own fucking business." His voice was a low growl. "Stay away from me, Kelsey, if you know what's good for you."

Then he bolted from the cafeteria.

Will muttered, "Oh, man . . ."

Kelsey remembered to breathe again, his breath emerging in a gasp. "Jesus . . ."

He saw Trey meet Myra at the open double doors. She drew him into her arms and kissed him passionately. Then she pushed Trey through into the hallway and directed one last smirk in their direction.

She winked.

And was gone.

Kelsey turned to Will. "My house. Tonight."

Will nodded. "Yeah. Okay."

Kelsey stared at the empty space occupied by his friend moments earlier.

And he thought, I guess I don't know what's good for me.

CHAPTER TWELVE

Hal screwed his eyes shut and tried to pretend the monsters weren't there. He didn't know what they really were, but "monster" seemed the most apt word. They were like nothing he'd seen before, not even in his worst nightmares. They couldn't be real. Nothing so horrible could be real. He was hallucinating. So he figured they'd just go away if he could keep his eyes shut long enough.

Then something snaked slowly around his leg, coiling like a cold, slippery vine. The way it felt on his flesh—so alien, so *wrong*—made him want to scream, but Jolene had gagged him with a pair of her soiled panties, sealing them in with a length of duct tape (and she took such evil pleasure in ripping the tape from his face when she wanted to talk with him). He whimpered instead, fresh tears leaking from the corners of his eyes. The slithering thing wrapped itself around a flabby thigh before probing at his crotch. It pushed at his balls, but they didn't budge—Jolene had cemented them to the slick vinyl seat of the wheelchair with superglue. The thing gave up and shifted its attention to his beach ball–sized beer belly.

Hal was having a hard time breathing through his nose. He longed to open his mouth wide and draw in great lungfuls of air. Thinking about it brought on another attack of claustrophobia. His soul screamed for release, for deliverance from this dark, scary place. He yearned to be out in the open world again, with nothing around him but nature and the sky above.

If he survived this nightmare, he would become an outdoors-man. It was one of the things he fantasized about during the long, empty hours when Jolene was away. He imagined camping out for weeks at a time up in the mountains, enjoying the solitude and achieving a real peace for the first time in his miserable existence.

The tendril curled around his throat, triggering a gag reflex that rendered the already difficult act of breathing almost impossible for several agonizing moments. But the monster's touch was actually very light. It wasn't squeezing him. At least not yet. His mind reeled with horror at the prospect of slow asphyxiation by this . . . this thing.

Hal had other fantasies, too. Extremely vivid revenge scenarios. These usually came on the strongest right after one of Jolene's torture sessions, and mostly he imagined doing some of the same things to Jolene that she'd done to him. The bitch. He'd cut off *her* fucking toes and fingers. See how she liked that shit!

But he knew the fantasies were doomed to forever remain fantasies, and so they were often followed by long stretches of utter despair. And in those moments he often thought back to the day before Jolene snapped and marched him out to the shed at gunpoint. He'd come home early from work that day to find her sitting on the mailman's face in the living room. Hal knew his wife was a slut, and most of the time he didn't give a shit, but coming home to that kind of thing wasn't acceptable. So he kicked the mailman out and went to work on Jolene, determined to whip her into place with his fists. Hal firmly believed any man who caught his wife in the act had the right to do this. But he'd gone overboard, battering her harder than a prizefighter taking out his aggressions on a punching bag, keeping at it until his clothes were drenched with sweat and his muscles ached from the strain.

In Hal's bleakest, blackest moments, he'd revisit those moments again and again.

And he'd think, *I deserve this.*

He felt something on his face, something so essentially different in texture he knew it was a different creature. It felt almost like a human hand. But not quite. Its flesh felt too rough, almost scaly. Fingers tugged at the length of duct tape, pulling it with surprising gentleness from his flesh. Hal spit out Jolene's panties and sucked in air, and he mumbled a thank-you to his unknown benefactor.

His gratitude was short-lived, however.

The tendril pushed through Hal's lips and entered his mouth. Its strange flesh was the most vile thing he'd ever tasted, like something awful from the darkest depths of the ocean. It moved to the back of his mouth and began to slide down his throat. Hal's eyes came open at last as panic engulfed him. There was something standing in front of him. One of the monsters. It stood on two legs and had shimmery, sluglike skin. It had a curved spine that lent it a hunchbacked appearance, a long, ridged tail as thick as a python's, lampreylike mouth, bulging black eyes, and a single tendril between its legs. When Hal's mind made the obvious association, he tried to bite down on the appendage invading his mouth. It went rigid inside him and he felt a sudden warmth in his chest, as if something had been expelled from the tip of the tendril. It retracted rapidly, uncoiling itself from his body and shrinking to a length a fraction of its fully extended reach.

Hal's mind reeled at the awful thing that had just happened. That goddamn thing had *raped* him! The sense of violation eclipsed anything he'd experienced in terms of sheer obscenity, and that was saying something. Jesus, this must be how that lady hitchhiker he'd picked up so many years must have felt when he—

His train of thought was derailed when the first monster, the one that had removed his gag, stepped into view. Hal's eyes widened and he opened his mouth to scream, but the lizard-woman clapped a scaly hand over his mouth and made a shushing sound.

Hal couldn't take any more of this. He'd been through a

lot, but enough was just fucking enough. He prayed for a heart attack. Or a stroke. Some sort of natural end to this horror and suffering.

But that didn't happen.

What did happen was more surprising, and perhaps more frightening, than anything he could've imagined.

The lizard-woman began to work at his bonds.

CHAPTER THIRTEEN

Rage consumed Bridget, her blood boiling as she vented her frustration by screaming threats at Jordan and banging on her door. This rejection was unacceptable. Bridget had never been spurned by anyone. It made no sense at all. She took great pride in being able to wrap sensitive little things like Jordan around her finger. Nothing gave her greater pleasure than playing with another person's emotions until she'd broken them, and this turn of events left her feeling cheated.

Her fury didn't begin to level off until a calm voice spoke inside her head: *You will have your fun with her yet. Be patient.*

Bridget gasped. The voice of the Dark Mother was clear and lovely, like a soothing spiritual caress. This communication was a privilege, a blessing bestowed. The promise in the Dark Mother's words erased Bridget's fury. Anger gave way to delight. She stopped banging on the door and threw her head back and laughed.

She laid a hand against Jordan's door.

"Soon." Her voice was a whisper, a subtle insinuation of future pain she hoped Jordan's subconscious would perceive. She pressed a cheek to the door. "Soon. I can't wait to hear you cry again."

Then she giggled.

A door opened to her right and one of Jordan's neighbors, a scrawny young man with shaggy brown hair, poked his head out to see what was going on. He gasped at the sight of Bridget's trim, tawny, naked body. Bridget saw him and smiled. "Hi there."

The man blushed. "Uh . . . is there a . . . problem?"

Bridget stepped away from the door and leaned against the wrought-iron railing that wrapped around the outer edge of the landing, displaying her body in its full glory. "Oh, just a little lover's spat."

She laughed when the man's mouth dropped open. Men were so easy to manipulate. Put an image of two women going at it in a guy's head and, presto, instant lust zombie.

Now for some more manipulation. This might turn out to be a fun day, after all.

"You're cute. What's your name?"

The man stepped out onto the landing. He wore rumpled khaki shorts and a dirty My Chemical Romance T-shirt with an indelible pizza-sauce stain just below its collar. He was nervous as hell, his hands jittering until he shoved them into his pockets. Pathetic. But then, this wasn't the sort of thing a geek got to see every day—a beautiful naked woman in the flesh. Not without paying good money anyway.

"I'm, uh, T-Todd."

Bridget smiled. "Pleased to meet you, Toddy."

"L-likewise."

Bridget knelt to pick up her clothes, deliberately extending the act to prolong the man's erotic torture. She bent over at the waist, keeping her legs straight as she stood on her tiptoes and thrust her round ass into the air. Then she stood straight again and held her skimpy clothes in front of her chest.

"Say, Todd, could I come into your apartment to get dressed and use your phone?"

Todd grinned, displaying rows of crooked teeth with bits of food wedged between them. "Sure! I'm, uh, always happy to help out a lady in distress."

Bridget sashayed past him, saying, "*Such* a gentleman."

Todd followed her into the apartment and closed the door. Bridget pushed up against him, snaking an arm around his waist. She turned the dead bolt, heard the satisfying click of the bolt sliding home, then slid her hand under his T-shirt. Todd was too captivated by Bridget's compelling cleavage to note the click of the lock. His mouth hanging open again, he stared down at the large breasts pressed against the front of his T-shirt.

Bridget smirked. "See something you like, little boy?"

Todd's jaw moved up and down, flapping like a broken gear. He seemed to have forgotten how to breathe. "Um . . . I . . . uh . . ."

"Relax, baby."

Bridget wiggled against him, pressing her thigh hard against the erection that strained the front of his shorts. The sound that emerged from his throat then was almost like a cry of anguish. Poor little fucker. He'd probably never even kissed a girl before, and now suddenly he found himself in a scenario like something out of a porn flick. Probably didn't have the first clue what do do.

Bridget reveled in his discomfort. The ease with which she manipulated him was an ego tonic following the Jordan debacle. And the sadist within her gorged on the man's exquisite agony, lapping up his misery the way a drunk guzzles cheap hooch.

"Would you like to fuck me, Todd?"

Todd shuddered. "Yes. God, yes."

"It's funny you should say that, Todd." She smiled and wiggled against him one more time. "Because I think I'd rather be shot point-blank in the face than let you so much as lay a finger on me. You're one ugly little fucker, you know that?"

Todd flinched. "What?"

She seized a handful of his hair and gave it a vicious twist. Todd shrieked.

Bridget giggled again and said, "Aw . . . did that hurt?"

Todd's initial shock gave way to anger. His voice boomed with rage as he said, "Get out of my house, bitch!"

Well, this was just astonishing. What had happened to the flustered loser?

He pointed at the door and yelled at her again. "Go on, you cock-teasing whore, get out of here!"

Bridget fumed.

Her breath emerged in great gasps.

She waited to hear again the soothing voice of Lamia, the Dark Mother, but this time there was only silence.

Todd scowled. "The fuck is wrong with you? Get your psycho ass—"

Bridget screamed.

Then she raked her long, sharp fingernails down the side of Todd's face, drawing blood. Todd clapped a hand to his face and staggered away from her. Bridget screamed again and surged toward him, her hands going to his face again. Todd tried to fend her off, spewing curses as he tried to grip her wrists. But Todd's survival instinct proved to be no match for Bridget's replenished rage. Her fingers found his eyes, and she drove her nails into the soft orbs, thumb and middle finger hooking into the sockets like the holes of a bowling ball, piercing the tissue and eliciting loud, girlish screams from Todd. She rode his thrashing body to the floor, landed on top of him, pinning his arms beneath her as she continued to drive her fingers through tissue and into his cranial cavity, where she dug around in brain matter and made his body twitch like a live electrical wire for several moments before it went still. Bridget orgasmed more than once while he died.

Then she climbed off him and stared at the utterly still body.

"Was it as good for you as it was for me, Toddy?"

Bridget laughed.

She laughed for a long time.

Then she went into Todd's kitchen and found several sharp implements. And she went to work on the dead geek's body. She felt so powerful. It was wonderful to kill! The elation she felt obliterated the previous blows to her self-confidence. She knew now there was nothing she couldn't do. This was a gift, this power, this strength. A sacred reward for her loyalty and service to the Dark Mother.

She slapped Todd's lifeless face with his dismembered hand.

He didn't react, of course, but it was fun.

Bridget again longed to ascend to the rank of Priestess. How endlessly amusing a spell of resurrection would be right now! He would be a zombie. Her slave. Like all the other men who served the Sacred Circle.

She giggled.

And slapped the dead man with his own hand some more.

CHAPTER FOURTEEN

The sensation she felt as the hard, flat plane of the wooden paddle struck her ass rendered Penelope Simmons cross-eyed with pleasure. She stood bent over at the waist, her hands braced against the edge of Slater's desk, her long skirt hiked up over her waist. Slater caressed her taut ass with one rough palm. His breathing was shallow. She knew the way she looked in this position was devastating to him—her long, sleek legs encased in sheer black stockings, toned calf and thigh muscles lent extra, exquisite definition by the high heels that lifted her perfect ass. Penelope gasped when he slipped the tip of a finger inside her. Any minute now, he'd unzip his pants and enter her from behind. Penelope tensed, awaiting the explosion of ecstasy she knew was coming.

A moment passed.

And another.

He was really drawing it out, prolonging her torture to the goddamn nth degree. It made her furious. And frustrated. But she loved it, too. This forced denial of pleasure was a pleasure itself, a divine level of sweet discipline. And every passing moment only increased the sweetness of the eventual reward. Every nerve ending tingled with sensual hunger. She was certain this would be her most intense sexual experience in a long, long time, perhaps even eclipsing the frenzy of ecstasy she'd known with her sister's husband-to-be in the back of a limo on the wedding day.

But then Slater sighed.

And set the paddle on the edge of his desk. He collapsed into his chair, triggering squeals of protest from ancient casters in desperate need of oiling. He folded his hands over his stomach and leaned back with his eyes closed.

Penelope remained braced against the desk a few moments longer. She wasn't able to process what had happened right away. All day long, she'd been unable to concentrate on her classes, her head filled with fantasy images. Mad with desire by the time the final bell tolled, she'd proceeded directly to Slater's office, knowing he'd be up to the task of giving her the rough treatment she craved. In her mind, she envisioned it being wilder than ever. There was an extra element of risk at the outset, as there always was during their rare daytime trysts. She imagined rabid, desperate couplings in every position, the two of them clawing at each other and drawing blood, throwing their sweaty bodies around the room and knocking over furniture.

This, though.

Jesus, this was more than she could have anticipated. By the time she was able to speak again, she knew she couldn't take much more. "Oh my God. Master, you are an artist. But I can't wait any longer. Please . . ."

Slater groaned. "I'm sorry, Penny. I'm not playing. I . . . I'm not up to this right now."

Penelope went very still. Projecting an outer calmness she didn't feel, she stood up straight, allowing the long skirt to fall over her ass and drift back to her ankles. She smoothed the skirt, adjusted her horn-rimmed glasses, and turned to face Slater with an expression cold enough to frost the Sahara.

"I don't think you know what you just did," she said, her tone as flat as Slater's. "Do you really want to cross me, Raymond?"

She was pleased to see fear bloom in his eyes. The roles they assumed in sex play were reversed outside the sexual arena. Penelope dictated the course of their relationship, because she held all the cards. She had taped their initial encounters without his knowledge, showing him copies the first time he'd tried to break off their relationship. "I am not going to be a casual fling," she'd told him, enjoying the sick look that crossed his face. "You belong to me now, and you'll be mine as long as I want you."

If he didn't play ball, copies of the tapes would go out to the mayor and Slater's wife.

Slater played ball.

And once he accepted the permanence of their relationship, Slater loosened up, embracing it with new enthusiasm. Two wonderful years down the road, Penelope wasn't sure she wanted it to ever end. She'd lately entertained fantasy scenarios wherein Mrs. Slater, a portly hag inexplicably beloved by the community-at-large, met an untimely demise.

"I'm sorry," he said again. He rubbed his eyes and sagged in the chair. "I've had a very bad day." He laughed without humor. "And that's an understatement of epic proportions." His eyes met Penelope's gaze. "Penny . . . do you believe in . . . demons?"

She blinked. "What?"

"There's no way you're going to believe this until you see it for yourself." Now there was real sadness in Slater's expression. "I hate it, Penny, but there's no way to keep you out of this. She's got plans for both of us." His eyes welled with sudden tears. "She's going to make us do the most awful, horrible things, and . . . and . . ." Tears coursed down his cheeks as he began to blubber. ". . . and . . . there's nothing we can do about it . . . oh, Penny . . ."

Penelope slapped him. "Snap out of it this instant, Raymond!"

But the principal just covered his face with his hands and continued to blubber.

Seeing him this way filled Penelope with disgust. She didn't like emotional weakness in anybody, but she especially despised it in men. She expected them to be weak in matters of the flesh. They were just dumb, brute animals, after all, a failing she'd exploited many times with many men. But this sort of thing—this vulnerability—was just vile. For a few fleeting moments, she doubted her devotion to this relationship.

Then she heard his words in her head again and made an association that stirred fresh excitement within her. "My God, Raymond, are you talking about your wife? That's the 'demon,' right? Did she find out about us somehow?"

Slater looked up at her and tried to speak, but his throat was too tight.

Penelope laughed. "She plans to expose us, right? Divorce you and take you for all you've got, right? That cunt." She leaned close to Slater, dropped her voice to a whisper. "Well, we won't let her get away with it, Raymond."

Slater's face was a mask of confusion. "What?"

"Listen to me." She gripped his shoulders and spoke earnestly. "I know what to do about this, love. But you are going to have to be very brave for me, okay? You'll have to be braver than you've ever been. And you'll need to accept in your heart that this is the right thing to do. And of course, you'll need to be able to stand up to questioning."

"What are you talking about, Penelope?"

Penelope rolled her eyes. "Isn't it obvious? Oh, Raymond, I'm talking about killing your wife, of course."

Slater's eyes went wide with horror. "My wife? My God, Penelope!"

Now it was Penelope's turn to be confused. "But I thought—"

Slater shook his head. "My wife's the least of our problems."

Penelope scowled. "I don't see how that's possible."

A strange calm settled over Slater. His tears dried up. He gently removed Penelope's hands from his shoulders and smoothed his rumpled shirt. "You have a student named Myra Lewis in your sixth period Senior English class, correct?"

"Yes. So?"

Slater swallowed with difficulty. "She's our problem. She's the demon, Penny. And she's—"

Penelope's wild laughter surprised him. She threw her head

back and let it peal out. Then she met Slater's gaze and said, "Raymond, you are a funny man. That little girl may be a bit of a hellion, but she's no demon. Jesus, men are so threatened by strong-willed females."

Slater shook his head. "I'm serious. She's a demon. Literally."

Penelope gasped when she heard the office door open. She whirled around and shuffled sideways, instinctively putting a socially acceptable space between herself and the principal. She cursed her foolishness. She'd been so certain the door was locked.

And so it had been—Myra Lewis entered the office, the extra key provided by Slater twinkling between her fingers.

Penelope gaped. "Myra, what—"

"Shut up."

Myra closed the door and locked it. A thin, sly smile dimpled the corners of her mouth. She pocketed the key and dropped into the seat in front of Slater's desk, draping herself over it the way she had earlier in the day.

Penelope looked at Slater. "Why does she have a key?"

Myra chuckled. "Because I wanted it."

Penelope's head swiveled back toward Myra. "That's absurd. The principal doesn't just hand out keys to any student who wants one. You do not belong in here, Ms. Lewis."

Myra sprang out of the chair and clamped a hand around Penelope's throat. Penelope struggled for air. The strength of the girl was astonishing. She tried to pry Myra's hand loose, but to no avail. Myra only squeezed harder.

"Are you going to obey me now? Are you going to shut up?"

Penelope was beginning to feel light-headed, but she managed a nod. Myra loosened her grip, allowing her to suck in a lungful of air. Penelope felt better, but the girl was still holding her by the throat.

"I have something to show you," Myra said. "Something simply amazing, Ms. Simmons."

Slater groaned.

Penelope managed a weak smile. "Okay." Anything to appease this strange, violent girl. "I'd love to—"

Myra's flesh began to ripple and stretch, its smoothness shifting to a rough, scaly texture. Then she grinned. Only it was really a hideous, hellish parody of a grin. Her mouth doubled in size. Tripled. Quadrupled. Her teeth grew and multiplied, became sharp like razors, glistened with saliva. The expansion continued until it seemed the interior of the Myra-thing's mouth encompassed the whole world. There was something at the back of the mouth, something yellow and pulsating, something obscene.

A voice inside Penelope's head said: *Here it comes.*

Then it did.

Penelope fainted.

CHAPTER FIFTEEN

The clock on the digital cable box showed the time as 2:59. Jake felt a rush of anxiety. He needed to be at his mother's house by three thirty. Rockville was a small town. A drive from one end of town to the other would take perhaps fifteen minutes. The Zone was a mere ten-minute drive from Washington Heights. Under normal circumstances, he would be able to hop in his car and get there with plenty of time to spare.

These were not normal circumstances.

He was in bed with Stu's sister. In the guest bedroom in Stu's house. They hadn't made love. Not yet. Still fully clothed, they held each other in the middle of the bed, limbs entwined in the intimate manner of lovers. Jake moaned with every slight shift of her body, enjoying the way her thigh pushed against his erection. Every so often, she cupped the crotch of his jeans and gave him a gentle squeeze.

No. Definitely not normal circumstances.

Kristen breathed softly in his ear. "I don't know why we're fighting this."

Jake, who hadn't been laid once in the four months since breaking up with his latest ex, could think of at least one reason to fight it. This was not the normal course of adult relationships, with the exception of the one-night stand variety, but this didn't feel like something so meaningless. He expected females to maintain a safe emotional distance, a gentle aloofness, at the outset. There should be dates. Dinners and movies.

A natural progression toward that initial sexual encounter. He should not be on the brink of that within hours of meeting someone he liked so much. Not at this point in his life.

Fuck.

So this is how it happens, he thought.

How you know you're getting old.

You turn into a fucking prude.

The cable-box clock now read 3:04.

"I don't want to fight it. I truly don't," he said. He cupped her cheek with a palm, and she smiled broadly, making a noise of pleasure and turning her head into the caress. His heart fluttered. "But fuck, I don't have a choice."

Kristen frowned. "I want this." She put a hand to the back of his neck and drew him to within kissing distance. Her soft lips met his, and the slow kiss that ensued was nearly enough to melt what remained of his resistance. "This is fate, Jake. One of those meant-to-be things."

Yeah. Okay. She had a tendency to make sweeping pronouncements, a willingness to be swept along by sheer emotion. Which wasn't necessarily a bad thing, if tempered by a healthy dose of realism. They had known each other five hours and already she had them cast as the leading roles in some great, epic romance. Jake liked her. An understatement. But he was a more a look-before-you-leap type. He hadn't always been that way, but age and bitter experience had a way of changing things. Sometimes he mourned his loss of youthful optimism more than anything else.

The digital cable box taunted him: 3:07.

Kristen pinched the tab of his zipper between thumb and forefinger, tugged gently at it. "You want this as much as I do."

"Yeah. You're right. But I still have to go."

With much regret, Jake began the process of disengaging himself from Kristen, who sighed heavily. He sat up and looked down at her. "I'm sorry. But I can't think straight right now. I have to get over to my mother's house in about twenty minutes. If I lay here any longer with you, I'd never get over there."

Kristen glanced at the cable box and gasped. "Oh, shit!" Something in her wide-eyed expression made him want to climb atop her. "I'm so sorry! I had no idea it was so late."

Be strong.

He forced a smile. "Time flies when you're . . ." He fumbled for the right words. He'd been about to say "in love," but that was ridiculous at this stage. Wasn't it? Saying those words to someone as intense as Kristen would be a mistake. He coughed and finished lamely: ". . . having fun."

There was a knowing quality in her expression. Of course. She knew precisely what he'd been about to say—and wouldn't be forgetting it anytime soon. Damn.

"Fun. That's one word for it." Her eyes widened again. Jake felt drawn into them. They burned with a kind of rare and magnificent spark, an ineffable quality he'd only glimpsed once or twice in his life.

I am fucking done for, he thought.

He knew then he was completely at her mercy.

He wondered if she knew it yet.

She said, "Hey, I could go with you."

Jake thought about it. He wouldn't mind the company. Going to his mother's house wouldn't be any more pleasant than his last visit. Shit. "No. I'd love to have you along, but I'm afraid your being there would make my mother behave so badly I'd puke."

Kristen's brow furrowed. "Is she really so bad, Jake? You make her sound like Cruella De Vil's illegitimate white-trash sister. Oh. I shouldn't have said that."

"What?"

"I shouldn't have said 'white trash.' I'm sorry."

Jake snorted. "Don't be. The term 'white trash' was invented for families like the McAllisters. Let's put it this way. After my dad died and my mom remarried, she didn't have to change her last name."

"You're kidding. Tell me you're kidding."

"I wish."

"Damn."

"Yep. Hubby number two was my dad's second cousin. Or third. I don't know. It's hard to tell with the McAllisters. It sounds sick, but that's only because it is. Listen, I've really got to be going. I'll swing by with Trey later. Maybe we could all do something together."

She smiled. "Sure. I'd like to meet him."

They kissed good-bye and Jake hurried out of the house. Then he hopped in his car and headed toward the Zone. The old neighborhood was livelier at this time of day, with groups of school-aged kids loitering on corners and playing in pickup baseball and basketball games. It was a bright, sunny day, and the Zone looked as wholesome as any other slice of suburbia. He was glad things had changed for the better here, and he again felt embarrassment that his family's home remained such a blight on the landscape.

He parked at the curb and walked to the front door, taking note of the red Camaro parked in the driveway. Trey's car, he guessed. It looked to be an early '80s model, the kind he'd coveted when he was Trey's age. He again felt the passage of time like a weight pressing against him. To Trey, the Camaro was likely just an affordable junker, maybe even a little embarrassing.

Jolene stood framed in the open front door, watching him as if she'd been expecting him. She'd changed clothes since that morning, losing the tank top and denim cutoffs in favor of low-rider jeans and a cropped purple T-shirt that showed off her flat midriff and accentuated her bust. Jake's stomach curdled as he noted a navel piercing framed by a tattoo of the sun.

He looked her in the eye, nodded, but didn't smile. "Mom."

His mother smirked. "Ain't you the friendly one."

Jake counted slowly to ten, then managed a tight smile and said, "I can play nice if you can. Look, I'm here to see Trey. To help. So let's be civil."

Jolene's smirk gave way to a cold glare. "For Trey's sake, I'll be sweeter than sugar, but just between you and me, you can shove your superior attitude right up your tight ass. Treat me with respect in my house, boy."

She turned and stalked away from him, the screen door flapping shut behind her. Jake felt some of his old anger coming back. His mind treated him to an array of images from his past, beatings and other cruel punishments. Blood roared in his ears. He wanted to scream.

He counted to ten again and entered the house.

Jolene was pouring herself a glass of Wild Turkey, diluting it with a minimal splash of Coke from an almost empty two-liter bottle. She nodded at an empty glass on the table. "Want some firewater, son?"

Jake clenched his fists. His fingernails pierced his flesh. Jolene had introduced Jake to the wonderful world of alcohol on the occasion of his tenth birthday. Things were different on Planet McAllister. Here ten-year-olds were considered old enough to indulge in adult vices. Jake was given a carton of Kools and a six-pack of Bud when he reached that age. Five years later it was Mikey's turn. Poor Mikey never had a chance at a real life. He was a good kid. Kindhearted. Maybe too sensitive. The poor bastard dived headfirst into the world's biggest bottle of whiskey and never resurfaced.

Jake made himself relax. "Thanks, but no." He looked around the dirty kitchen. "Where's Trey?"

Jolene knocked back her drink and slammed the empty glass down. "Trey! Get out here, boy, your brother's here!"

Trey ambled into the kitchen a moment later, his hands shoved into the pockets of his jeans and his gaze cast downward. Trey was a handsome golden boy with dark blue eyes and tousled, longish blond hair that made him look like a displaced California surfer dude.

But something was very wrong here.

Trey displayed none of the abundant confidence described by both his mother and Stu Walker. He seemed fidgety, uncomfortable in his own skin.

Jake was dismayed to see that his mother's concerns were justified. He'd been so certain her worries about Trey were unfounded. He seemed dazed or drugged, and Jake immediately wondered whether the new girlfriend had gotten him hooked on something. Couldn't be meth, the preferred poison of white trash youth. The kid didn't have that jittery, tweaker thing going on, thank God. But maybe it was heroin. Did they have that out here in the sticks? He had no clue, and so he tried to rein in that line of thinking. Jumping to conclusions was a bad idea. He needed to get Trey out of here, take him somewhere where he'd feel able to talk more freely.

"Hey man, why don't we go get a pizza or something. My treat. We've got some major catching up to do."

Trey shrugged, but didn't lift his gaze from the floor. "Sure. Whatever."

"Boy, can't you at least look your brother in the eye?" Jake cringed. His mother's voice was like nails on a chalkboard when she was this hammered. "He came a long ways just to see you, boy, takin' time out of his busy schedule. You owe him some respect."

The rebuke seemed to have some effect. Trey lifted his head, forced his mouth to form an expression that vaguely resembled a smile, and finally looked Jake in the eye. The effort clearly required a great force of will. "Sorry, Jake. I'm just—"

Then the kid's eyes widened and his face contorted with terror.

Jake frowned.

What the—

Something crashed against the sliding glass door behind him, making the door rattle in its frame. Jolene was shrieking as Jake spun around and gaped at the site of a blood-soaked naked fat man pressed against the glass. The sheer strangeness of what he was seeing kept Jake from processing the horrific tableau for a long, elastic moment. Time seemed to slow down, to grind down to an almost complete stop. Then things clicked back into place, the mental gears started meshing smoothly again, and he realized the man at the door was his stepfather.

Jolene dashed to the door, flung it open, and drove the heel of a palm into the center of Hal's chest, causing the man to stumble backward several steps before landing on his back in the tall grass beyond the patio.

"What the fuck are you doing out here, you goddamn son of a bitch!" Jolene's voice achieved a level of shrillness that surpassed even the worst screaming fits Jake remembered from his childhood. "Get off your motherfuckin' ass and get back in the goddamn shed before I cut your nuts off!"

Jake followed his mother into the backyard. Maintaining a cautious distance from her, he moved in a slow semicircle to his left. His stomach twisted when he was able to get a better view of Hal. Jolene kicked at him, driving a foot into his flabby belly again and again. Hal managed to shift his weight and flop onto his side. He cast an anguished gaze up at Jake, and Jake was astonished to find himself feeling actual pity for his stepfather. A series of revelations snapped into place in rapid succession. Primary among them was the brutally evident fact that his mother was insane. Most of the man's fingers were gone. He saw knobs of ugly, cauterized scar tissue just below the knuckles. His genitals were a bloody mess. One of his ears was gone. His whole body was covered with scabbed-over wounds, places where he'd been sliced with a knife or other sharp instrument.

Jake felt dizzy, sick with fear and revulsion, but he couldn't allow himself to be overcome. He wanted to run screaming in the opposite direction, anywhere away from there, but he made himself cling to an unfortunate reality—he was the only person here remotely capable of handling this thing the right way.

He moved closer to Jolene, who was still kicking her husband. Jake stepped over Hal's much-abused body, seized his mother from behind by the elbows, and twisted his head toward the house. "Trey! Call 911!"

Trey stood in the open doorway, his eyes wide and his jaw hanging slack.

Jolene flailed against him, trying to twist out of his tight grip. "Let go of me, you fuckin' asshole! He had it comin'! Let me go or I'll fuckin' kill you!"

"Trey, your mom needs help." Jake glanced at Hal. "And so does your dad. Call 911 now!"

Trey blinked. He nodded and retreated into the kitchen.

Within moments, Jake dimly heard his brother's voice as he talked to the 911 operator.

Jolene threw her head back and released a wail that chilled Jake's blood.

On the ground, Hal cried.

Jake held his breath and prayed for the ground to remain solid beneath his feet for just a little while longer.

CHAPTER SIXTEEN

Jordan was asleep on the sofa in her living room. Overwhelmed by exhaustion and anguish, she'd collapsed there moments after ejecting Bridget from her apartment. Her body twitched and her throat produced a series of mumbled words and moans. Noise from the apartment next door pushed through the wall of sleep, sounds of distress that complemented an already disturbing dream. The shrieks that came from Todd Monroe in the moments before his death changed the tenor of the dream. What had previously been just a disturbing bit of eroticism became a horror show, and Jordan's moans of pleasure became frightened whimpers.

Jordan awoke with a scream. She sat up, gasping for breath, her heart racing, her mind awash in pornographic images. She put a hand to her chest, willing her heart to return to a calmer pace. Despite its awful ending, the dream had been powerfully erotic, and she felt a lingering arousal. Which wouldn't be so bad, except that Bridget Flanagan had played a starring role in the dream.

Jordan experienced a flare of self-disgust. But the erotic images were so vivid, so compelling, that the arousal refused to go away. Even now she could almost feel Bridget's tongue on her clit. She toyed with the idea of masturbating, of indulging in a fantasy about Bridget. But the tide of self-loathing that rose up at this thought stifled the urge.

She sniffed. "I hate you sometimes, Jordan Harper."

She was on the brink of a crying jag, the kind of pity party she had no tolerance for in others. What a dark day in her life this was. A brittle facade of strength had been smashed to bits. There was no way to put a positive spin on it. Her life was a mess. The rough road ahead of her, which she'd contemplated with such conviction before finding Bridget in her apartment, now seemed daunting.

Tears rolled down her cheeks and she made no effort to wipe them away. Her distress made her oblivious to the new sounds emanating from Todd's apartment. At first. Then she began to perceive something. A blunt, flat sound, like some sort of heavy object striking something repeatedly. *Thunk. Thunk. Thunk.*

Thunk. Thunk. Thunk.

Thunk. Thunk. THUNK.

God, it simply wouldn't end.

Jordan frowned.

She'd looked after Todd's cat, a brown tabby named Willow, once while he was away for a week over the Christmas holiday season. She spent hours at a time there, watching his DVDs and poking through his stuff. She felt some guilt over the snooping, but told herself it was harmless. It made her feel a bit naughty, and she sometimes liked doing things she wasn't supposed to do. She discovered no deep, dark secrets. Todd had no secret cache of naked kid pictures, no drug stash, no telltale hint of secret lunacy, or no bomb-making materials, or Far Right pamphlets. About the worst you could say about Todd was that he was terminally geeky. The guy had a massive comics collection, and what Jordan imagined must be the world's largest collection of *Buffy the Vampire Slayer* memorabilia.

Jordan figured she knew Todd as well as you could know a person without actually being friends with them. And there was one thing of which she was absolutely certain—Todd was not the handyman type. The idea that he was over there hammering away at something struck her as unlikely.

The sound came again.

THUNK.

And again, louder.

THUNK!

Another dim sound from next door deepened her frown.

It was laughter. And it had a certain quality that made her uneasy. Then the sound came again, rising in pitch as the hammering continued.

Her stomach clenched.

It was female laughter.

For some reason she thought of Bridget. But that was ridiculous. And paranoid. The laughing girl could be anybody. But it troubled her nonetheless. Todd hadn't had a girlfriend the entire time she'd known him. She rarely saw him in the company of females at all. But maybe his luck had changed. She hoped so. He'd always seemed so lonely. Hell, at least maybe somebody's life had taken a turn for the better.

She thought of the sad state of her own life and darkness encroached. Fuck. She didn't want to think about other people being happy. Not now. The sounds from Todd's apartment taunted her, reminded her of a buoyancy of spirit she'd felt so often, even as recently as yesterday. She went to her bathroom and found a package of earplugs. Then she returned to the sofa and lay down for another nap.

This time her sleep was free of dreams, erotic or otherwise, and she slept for hours. When she awoke again, the day had progressed well into the afternoon. She pulled the foam earplugs from her ears and the first thing she heard was loud, thumping music from Todd's apartment. This, too, was very unlike Todd. He was a considerate neighbor. On the rare occasions when the sound from his stereo bled into her apartment, the volume was too low to be a real nuisance. But this time the music was going full blast. She slammed a fist against her living room wall in protest. She sighed. The music was too loud. She'd have to go knock on his door if this continued much longer.

Her sense of unease returned. She put her ear to the wall and listened to the music. Weird. This wasn't Todd's sort of thing at all. He liked alt-pop stuff. Modest Mouse and Death Cab For

Cutie. This stuff was club music, some kind of bland techno crap. Well, maybe he was going out of his way to please his female guest.

She smiled.

I hope you get laid, buddy.

God knows you deserve it for putting up with that crappy music.

Jordan put Todd's mystery girlfriend out of her mind and got to her feet. She stretched and decided she would fill at least some of the remaining daylight hours by giving the apartment a thorough cleaning. She put on a Tori Amos CD to block the noxious club music. But it wasn't very effective. The mellow Tori songs just couldn't compete with the ultrapercussive bonehead beats coming from Todd's apartment.

"Goddammit!"

She paused in the midst of polishing the coffee table and stared at the wall separating her apartment from Todd's. The dance music was so loud it could have been coming from her own stereo. Tori's ethereal voice was lost in the musical maelstrom. She tossed aside the cleaning rag, set down the can of Pledge, and got to her feet.

Enough of this.

She strode quickly to her front door, intent on marching over to Todd's place to put an end to this crap. But she heard something from outside and paused at the door. She listened and recognized the sound as a clatter of footsteps coming up the staircase. Someone in heels. Jordan's and Todd's apartments were the only ones accessible via the second-story landing on this side of the building, so one of them was about to have a guest. Jordan looked through the peephole of her door and watched Angela Brooks move into view. Jordan's eyes widened. Why was one of Bridget's bitch friends coming to see her now?

Jordan felt sick.

When would Bridget quit playing her stupid little games?

Then Jordan frowned again.

Angela swept past the door to her apartment and disappeared from view. Seconds later she heard the brass knocker rapping against the door to Todd's apartment. Then she heard the creak of the door opening, followed by the excited squeals of two very vapid females exchanging greetings. Now Jordan knew the identity of Todd's female guest. Her initial instinct—the one she'd dismissed as paranoia—had been right all along.

Bridget fucking Flanagan.

That voice—so falsely sweet and lilting—was impossible to mistake. The revelation also explained the horrid music pounding out of Todd's stereo.

It all came together for Jordan in a heartbeat. Bridget had created quite the ruckus upon getting the boot from Jordan, a disturbance which naturally brought Todd running. Jordan could too easily picture what happened next. In her mind, she saw Todd reeling at the sight of a gorgeous naked female outside his apartment. A hot blonde prettier even than the admittedly very fine Buffy Summers. In three-dimensional flesh and blood. He wouldn't have been able to think properly, the poor bastard, and Bridget would have played him with the finesse of a master symphony musician manipulating her instrument. The bitch was likely assuaging her bruised ego by fucking with the guy's head to an extreme degree.

The door to Todd's apartment slammed shut.

Jordan stood there by the door for a long time. She didn't like the idea of her sweet, geeky neighbor being used by those heartless girls. On the other hand, she didn't much relish the idea of confronting Bridget again.

An inner voice taunted her: *You fucking coward.*

Jordan's expression hardened. "No. I'm not."

She looked at her door. Saw her hand gripping the knob, then turning it. Her conscience told her a visit to Todd's place to set him straight on some things was the absolute right thing to do. But then she thought of the smirk on Bridget's face this morning when the comforter fell away from her breasts. And she thought some about the way Bridget's body had looked stretched out in the morning sunlight.

She closed her eyes against a fresh welling of tears. "Shit."

She sighed.

Wiped away her tears.

And went back to her bathroom to find some sleeping pills.

CHAPTER SEVENTEEN

After school let out, Kelsey hopped in his ancient Oldsmobile and headed for the Rockville Public Library, where he checked out an armful of books, most of them musty, old volumes, everything he could find on demonology and related occult subjects. Old Mrs. Cheever, the head librarian since roughly the dawn of time, clucked over his disturbing taste in literature.

Her always stern expression became even more severe than usual. "Such *filth*." Her eyes narrowed and her nose wrinkled. She looked like she'd caught a whiff of something dead and rotting. "Why on earth are you reading this trash, young man?"

Kelsey was caught off guard by her nosiness and fumbled for something to say. "Uh . . . I . . . dunno."

Mrs. Cheever harrumphed. "What, exactly, is the allure of something like this?"

She held up a copy of a richly illustrated text entitled *Succubi: An Illustrated Journey Through the World of Sexual Demons and Possession*. The cover depicted a woman drawn in an exaggerated manner similar to the covers of old fantasy novels. Her feminine attributes were emphasized to a ridiculous degree, with wide, flaring hips, a narrow waist, and breasts like melons. She stood against a lurid landscape meant to represent some hideous layer of hell, with little demons and imps dancing in the background. Clad in a ragged animal skin loincloth and matching top, she stirred something primal within Kelsey.

He felt his face go hot with embarrassment. "I . . . don't know."

The librarian made that clucking sound in her throat again. "I suppose this kind of thing must appeal to boys your age. It's shameful. God forbid you should enrich your minds with real literature."

Kelsey seethed with rage. This wasn't school. This was the *public* library. He didn't need to be lectured by this snooty old bitch. His reading material was none of her damn business.

"Tell you what. I'll borrow my sister's Jane Austen books. That's real literature, right?"

The librarian's wary smile poorly masked a deep-rooted suspicion. This was a woman who clearly did not like young people. At all. "Well . . . yes. But—"

Kelsey grinned. "Good. I'll enrich my ass with brilliant prose. And by that I mean I'll wipe my shit-encrusted bumhole with the pages. And I'll be thinking of you the whole time, Mrs. Cheever."

The librarian shoved the stack of books across the counter. "These are due back in two weeks. Enjoy your drivel, you worthless delinquent."

"Right. Have an excellent day."

Kelsey scooped up the books and got the hell out of there.

Mrs. Cheever summoned young Bethany Haines to the front desk and retreated to her office for a break. She settled into the plush leather chair behind her desk, put the phone to her ear, and made a call.

The beloved voice of a certain delightful young woman answered on the second ring: "Who the fuck is this?"

Mrs. Cheever shivered with pleasure at the sound of the voice. "This is your humble servant, Ellen Cheever of the Rockville Public Library. I believe I have information of interest to you."

Kelsey parked his Olds in the driveway, behind his sister's tan Volvo. It was four o'clock. His parents, still at work, wouldn't

be home until after five. He entered the house through the
front door, moved rapidly through the foyer, and rushed up
the stairs to the second floor. The memory of the unpleasant
exchange with Mrs. Cheever was still fresh in his mind, and
he didn't want his sister subjecting him to a similar interrogation about his choice of reading material.

And she would, given the opportunity.

If anything, she was even more of a literature snob than
Mrs. Cheever.

Upstairs, he walked softly past the closed door to her room.
Low moans and a squeak of bedsprings emanated from the
other side of the door. Kelsey frowned and edged closer to
the door. The muffled sounds of passion continued. He first
thought she might be watching Internet porn, but then he
heard a hoarse voice call out her name.

The voice then beseeched God.

Then called out her name again.

And so on.

Definitely not the Internet.

The voice was so faint he wasn't able to figure out which of
Melissa's many male acquaintances was putting it to her in
there. What he did know absolutely for certain was she would
kick his ass if she caught him playing aural voyeur. His sister
was nearly six feet tall and was a former member of the
Rockville High girls' basketball team. And anyway, listening to
his sister fuck some guy made him feel kind of like a sleaze, so
he continued down the hallway and closed himself up in his
room.

He dropped the stack of books on his bed, kicked his shoes
off, and settled down in front of his television, folding his legs
beneath him Indian style. He switched on his X-Box and put
in the latest version of *Halo*. Ten minutes into the game his
cell phone rang. He pushed the pause button and flipped
open the phone. "Yeah?"

"Dude!"

It was Will.

"Hey, man. I got some real interesting books from the library. Maybe you could——"

"You are not going to believe what I just heard." There was a frantic edge to Will's voice, an almost jittery tone utterly unlike him. "It's just fucking insane."

"Okay. What's happening?"

"Trey's mom was arrested. My brother's girlfriend just called him. Trisha. She lives just down the street from Trey. She saw all the cops show up and everything."

Kelsey was flabbergasted. "Holy shit." He felt like he'd been whacked over the head with something heavy. "Why'd they nab that crazy slut?"

Will laughed. The manic undertone was still there. "Trisha says a bunch of the neighbors wandered out to the scene when the cops showed up. You know how those rednecks are. She doesn't know all the facts, but she did see Trey's dad get carted out on a stretcher and put in an ambulance. She even got a look at the sorry motherfucker before they took off. And this is the really fucked-up part. She said all his fingers were gone. Now, maybe my memory's off, but I'm pretty sure the last time I saw that asshole he had all his fat fucking fingers."

Kelsey whistled. "Goddamn."

He didn't know what else to say, so he said it again. "I mean, goddamn."

Will snorted. "Yeah. It's freaky as shit. Jolene was taken away in handcuffs. Nobody knows exactly what happened, but it's pretty clear she did something pretty fucked-up to Hal."

Kelsey couldn't help the smile that came to his face. "Well . . ."

Will was on the same wavelength. "Right. The motherfucker deserved it. No question. Still, you can't sweep something like this under the rug. Jolene's not getting out of jail anytime soon."

Kelsey had a disquieting thought. "Shit. What's gonna happen to Trey?"

The manic edge seeped out of Will's voice and was replaced

by a quiet but obvious unease. "I don't know. I think he's being questioned by the police right now. You know that older brother of his? He's there with him."

"Jake? I thought he was in Minnesota."

"Yeah, well, he's here now. And unless Trey gets charged with something, I guess he'll have temporary custody."

Kelsey nodded. It made sense. "Do we know where Jake's staying?"

"No. But we fucking need to find out, man."

They agreed to make some calls and get back to each other. Kelsey searched his memory, trying to recall whether Trey had ever mentioned names of Jake's old friends. No specific names came to mind, but the one thing he kept coming back to was a general awareness that Jake was a big drinker. So, say Jake gets into town feeling a little thirsty—where would he go?

Well.

If you weren't into the whole redneck karaoke douche bag scene, there was only one real alternative.

The Good Times Bar & Grill.

Kelsey leaped to his feet, grabbed his shit, and hurried out of the room. He was halfway down the hallway when he heard his sister call his name. He halted. The door to her bedroom stood open. Frowning, he turned and peered into the room. Melissa was alone in the room. There was no sign of her mystery lover, but this barely registered. The shock he felt now exceeded what he'd felt when he heard Will's astonishing news.

She was on her back in her bed, head and shoulders propped on a pile of colorful, plush pillows, and she didn't have a stitch of clothing on. Her long, curly blonde hair cascaded over her shoulders and covered the tops of her large breasts. She extended a hand to her brother and beckoned to him with a hooked finger. "Come, Kelsey. Come in and shut the door behind you. I have some things I want to show you."

He'd seen his sister naked before, of course, but they'd been little kids then.

Innocents.

Melissa wasn't a little kid anymore. Not even close. She was a full-grown woman.

A *beautiful* full-grown woman.

Kelsey's jaw dropped. "Um . . ."

She laughed. "You're so cute when you're flustered, little brother. I've always liked that about you." She giggled. "Among other . . . things. You're looking good these days. Fit. You've finally lost the last of that baby fat." She looked him up and down in a frank, disconcerting way. "Mmm . . ."

Kelsey's face reddened. "Um . . ."

Melissa swung her legs over the side of the bed, planted her feet on the floor, and stood up, posing for maximum effect. "See anything you like?" She giggled again and the motion of her body made her breasts bounce. "Of course you do. Let's stop playing games. Time to admit the truth. You want me, and I want you."

Kelsey was shaking his head before he even realized he was doing it. He felt light-headed, like he might pass out at any moment. This was crazy. It couldn't be happening. "No. You're wrong."

She smirked and took a step toward him. "I've never been so right. Now come over here and fuck me."

Kelsey moved back a step as the initial shock passed. "This is insane. You're my sister. What's wrong with you?"

The smirk deepened as she continued to advance on him. "I'm horny. And so are you." She laughed. "You naughty little boy."

Every bit of Kelsey's essence rebelled against this. It was wrong on a very basic level. It was obscene. Christ. He loved his sister. Adored her, even. But that love had always been a pure thing, absolutely untainted by the ugliness of incestuous desires. He wanted to scream. To cry. When his sister drew to within a few feet of him, he backed out of the doorway, psyching himself to run out of the house.

There was just one problem with that.

A large man was blocking the way to the staircase.

Not just a large man, but a very tall, very muscular man with a black hood over his head. Except for the hood, the man was nude. His cock stood erect and glistening, pointing at Kelsey. Kelsey yelped. His mind was close to cracking. The world had gone nuts. He felt as if he'd fallen through a crack in reality, or as if one of his most hellish, psychotic dreams had materialized into reality.

Melissa put a hand on his shoulder. "Relax, Kel. There's nothing to be afraid of. You'll see that soon. You don't know how lucky you are." Her hand massaged his shoulder. "This is the best day of your life."

The hooded man took a step toward him.

The surge of terror Kelsey experienced broke his paralysis. Before he could think about what he was doing, he rushed forward and swung a foot toward the man's exposed genitals. The man didn't have time to react. His pained shriek was astonishing. He wobbled and stumbled backward. Kelsey pressed his advantage, kicking the man again. The hooded behemoth tumbled down the stairs.

Melissa screamed.

Kelsey rushed down the staircase, leaped over the man's still body as he reached the floor, pulled open the door, and staggered outside. He wobbled but managed to stay upright as he made his way to the Olds. Then the keys slipped from his hands and he knelt to pick them up. As his shaking hand closed around them, he heard footsteps pounding down the driveway. He got to his feet and saw his still-nude sister streaking toward him, a hand clutching a large kitchen knife raised high above her head, her face contorted in an awful expression of pure hatred and rage.

Through some miracle, Kelsey's fingers found the correct key right away and he unlocked the Oldsmobile. He slipped in and pulled the door shut, slamming the lock down just as Melissa arrived at the driver's-side window. She pounded on the window and screamed at him. Kelsey started the engine, tore out of the driveway, and raced away from his home at a reckless speed. A few blocks away, his hands started shaking again, this time so badly that he was swerving all over the road.

A glance at the rearview mirror revealed no sign of his sister.

He pulled over and waited for the shaking to subside. And as he waited, an image floated into his head: the sneering, sadistic face of Myra Lewis. Despite a lack of evidence, he felt certain Trey's girlfriend was responsible for whatever had taken over his sister. It was a gut feeling, an emotional reaction, but he was convinced.

She's a demon.

Fucking hell.

Somehow, Myra had sensed he might be a threat—a threat she needed to eliminate. Kelsey groaned. This was more than he could handle alone. How could he hope to fight something so powerful? People needed to know there was an evil loose in Rockville, something insidious, something that was slowly taking over, but he couldn't imagine anyone believing something so crazy.

Jake McAllister. Maybe.

And Will, of course.

Kelsey froze and stared through the windshield at the empty road ahead.

Fuck.

He had to get to his friend before *they* did.

His hands steady now, he restarted the Oldsmobile, pulled onto the road, and sped out of Washington Heights.

CHAPTER EIGHTEEN

"Shit!"

Will slammed the phone down in its cradle.

He'd never find out where Trey's brother was staying at this rate. How the hell long could his mother and that other woman gab? At least Kelsey's parents had been cool enough to get Kelsey a cell phone. They *cared* about their son. His own parents, well-heeled tightwads, refused to even invest a tiny, tiny little bit of money in a second line. It was ridiculous. His dad was a lawyer. He made twice the combined income of Kelsey's parents. But the old man wanted to teach him the "value of a dollar."

"Shit! Shit! Shit!"

Will's heart slammed in his rib cage. He knew he needed to calm down. Getting all pissed off was no good. It wouldn't help Trey, and it damn sure wouldn't do anything to loosen the parental purse strings. He stared at the phone, wondering how many seconds had passed since the last time he'd checked the line.

A minute?

Maybe a little more.

"Fuck!"

He did what he always did when he was frustrated. He turned to the poster of Jessica Alba pinned to the wall above his bed. Jessica, clad in a skintight black leather outfit, regarded him with an expression that was both stern and knowing. He had a recurring fantasy in which she slipped into his room in the middle of the night and handcuffed him to his bed. Believing he possessed vital information she required for some unknown reason, she interrogated him with a wonderful ruthlessness, strutting about his room on thigh-high black vinyl boots with stiletto heels, resplendent in all that black leather.

He pictured it again and felt a little better.

Until he heard footsteps thumping down the hallway toward his room. He grimaced. These were not happy footsteps. These were not even mildly perturbed footsteps. These were the footsteps of doom, as confirmed by the loud knock on his door a moment later.

His mother's voice cracked at him like a gun blast: "William Henry Mackeson, open this door this instant!"

Will gulped. Anytime his mother used his full name, he knew he was in for it. He slid off the bed and got shakily to his feet. He drew in a calming breath, crossed the room to open the door, and cringed at the expression on his mother's face. "Uh . . . what's the problem, Mom?"

Alexis Mackeson was livid. Her face was red and her eyes bulged in an almost cartoonish way. She wore a pretty floral-print dress with a scooped neck that displayed impressive cleavage. His mother had a nice figure and she liked to show it off. She flirted with damn near every man she met, and Will suspected she was doing a lot more than just flirting with many of them. With the hours his father kept, she had plenty of free time for infidelity. Once upon a time, Will had loved his mother with a kind of starry-eyed devotion. But that was before he learned some unpleasant truths, including the bitter realization that his mother and father only played at being a loving, happy couple. It was a facade they presented for the world. Alexis looked good on Blake Mackeson's arm at social functions, and Alexis enjoyed Blake's money.

Will dreamed of the day he'd be free of their "let's pretend" world.

She shoved her son backward, stalked into his room, and

threw the door shut behind her. "You little snot. I will not tol-
erate rudeness. You damn near *deafened* me when you slammed
that phone down." She gave Will a hard shake. "Goddammit,
boy, I taught you better manners than that."

Will sniffled. "I'm sorry."

At seventeen, Will knew he was too old to allow this kind
of treatment. He wanted to cry, but crying was for pussies.

The phone rang.

Will took an unconscious step toward it, but Alexis stopped
him. "Oh no, you don't. You let that phone ring, child. I have
to teach you a lesson in manners. Make you see why it's wrong
to be such a miserable little snot."

The phone continued to ring.

Desperation contorted Will's face. "Mom, that might be
Kelsey. I have to talk to him. Trey's in trouble. We have to—"

Will was caught off guard by what happened next. She
landed a hard backhand blow across his face that knocked
him to the floor. Will rolled over and stared up at her, his eyes
wide, his jaw aching. He was stunned. His mother had never
been the world's best, but this was the first time she'd ever
struck him. She'd never even spanked him for misbehaving as
a child. The terror he felt now was something new and awful.
For the first time, he believed he truly understood how Trey
felt when his parents got liquored up and turned violent.

He looked into his mother's eyes and saw nothing but hatred. This was new, too. She didn't love him, of course, but
the pure malevolence in her eyes was horrible. That look
penetrated places within him he thought were dead, and he
felt his heart break.

The phone stopped ringing.

Her nostrils flared. "Get up so I can hit you again."

"But—"

She kicked him, the point of her shoe sending a flash of
pain down a shin. "Get up!"

Will experienced an epiphany then. He knew something
was really wrong with his mother, something beyond her
control. Mental illness, perhaps, a chemical imbalance that

could be corrected with the right medications. He held fast to that notion, telling himself that he couldn't hold this against her, that she wasn't as evil, as bad, as she seemed now. He just had to get through this somehow and find a way to get her help.

He looked at her again, his eyes wide and pleading. "I'm sorry, Mom. I know I was wrong. I'll never do it again. I—"

The phone rang again.

Something about the second call, coming so soon on the heels of the first, communicated urgency. Intuition told him it was Kelsey trying to reach him. He had news about Trey, or he'd located Trey's brother. Or it was about something else, something equally important, and Kelsey needed to talk to him about it right now.

"I've got to answer that, Mom. It's probably Kelsey. We're trying to help Trey."

His mom snorted. "Oh, I'm sure it is your little friend. Such a stupid name for a boy, Kelsey. A queer kid's name. I'm not surprised the little faggot's up to no good."

"What?"

The phone fell silent again.

"Don't play innocent with me, child." Something in her tone now disturbed him more than the violence. She sounded like a person who reveled in cruelty. To Will, it was as if he was seeing her as she really was for the first time. Another layer had been peeled away, a mask beneath a mask. "You boys are dabbling in things that are none of your business. You know Melissa Hargrove, don't you? Kelsey's sister? I was talking to her before your rude interruption. Melissa had a very interesting conversation with Mrs. Cheever from the library." She chewed her lower lip and studied her son in a way that sent a shiver through him. "What do you know about demons, boy?"

Will gaped at her. "What?"

His mother sneered. "Idiot. Can't you say anything other than 'what'? Jesus, the average parrot has a larger vocabulary than you."

Tears began to course down Will's face. He couldn't help it. He didn't know what was wrong with his mom. He was so stunned by her hatefulness that it took many moments for the implications of her words to sink in. Then it hit him. And now his mom seemed more threatening than ever. He sat up, planted his hands on the floor, and began to scoot away from her.

She giggled like a teenager. "What's the matter, William? Afraid of your sweet, loving mother?" Her voice became more stern. "I told you to get up, and you best obey me." Her eyes gleamed with feral intent. "Get up so I can kill you."

Will's back met the side of his bed.

His mother took a step toward him.

Will whimpered.

His mother's sneer became an ugly smile. "You have no idea how much I'm going to enjoy murdering you, William. You have no idea how much it will mean for me. Lamia richly rewards willing sacrifices."

The door to the room flew open. Will felt a surge of joy at the sight of his father regarding them with horror. Blake Mackeson was still in his work clothes—khaki slacks, a starched white shirt, and a maroon necktie loosened around his collar. He looked weary, the way he always did after a day at the office.

"What the hell is going on here, Alexis?"

Alexis smiled sweetly at her husband. "The most wonderful thing, darling. I'm going to kill our pathetic son."

Blake's expression changed, became strangely neutral. "Huh. Why?"

"Because he's been messing where he shouldn't be messing. Now be a dear and bring me your gun. I'd like to put a bullet through his head right now."

Blake's entire demeanor changed. He sighed. Will sensed surrender in that sound. And sadness. Maybe even regret. But Will knew he would do as ordered. He could see it in the man's posture and in his eyes—he was his wife's slave.

"Now, Blake!" Alexis snapped. "Don't make me say it again."

"Okay."

His dad left the room. Will slumped against the bed and stared at his mother's ankles. He should be doing something, maybe attempting a desperate dash to freedom, but he felt too numb to act. Too much had happened. The world he'd known had changed forever.

His mother continued to taunt him. "What's it like, William? How does it feel to know that all that remains of your life is a precious handful of seconds?" She laughed. "What do you think it's going to feel like when I shoot you?"

Will imagined high-velocity lead punching through his forehead. Tears welled in his eyes again.

His mom giggled. "If it makes you feel any better, you were going to die tomorrow anyway. I'll just be putting you out of your misery early. Why, you could almost call this a mercy killing."

"You were already planning to kill me? Why?"

"Not me, sweet child o' mine. Lamia. You would have suffered much more horribly at the Harvest."

"The what?"

"The Harvest of Souls. Tomorrow afternoon a special assembly will be held at your school. And Lamia will feast. All your friends will die."

Will didn't know what to say to that, so he said nothing.

His mother had an almost rapturous look on her face. She looked like one of those true believers at a Holy Roller tent revival meeting. Any moment now she'd start clapping her hands and singing a rollicking song of praise. Her eyes were shining and her cheeks were flushed. She swayed a little on her feet, licked her lips, and caressed her hips. There was something more than just a little sexual underneath the faux-religious fervor. It was disturbing, but no more so than anything else that had happened in the last several minutes.

Will heard footsteps entering the room. That would be his dad, returning as ordered with the gun. He closed his eyes and tried to make his mind blank. He knew there would be no last-minute rescue. No chance of escape.

Just make it fast, he prayed.

He heard a loud, metallic sound, the clack of a gun being cocked.

Then he heard a gasp from his mother.

Astounded, Will opened his eyes and saw a miracle. Kelsey Hargrove stood just inside the doorway to the room. His arms were extended in front of him, aiming a .38 revolver at Alexis Mackeson's head.

Kelsey glanced at his friend. "Dude, I'm beginning to detect a weird fucking trend."

Will's mom snarled like a rabid beast.

She turned toward Kelsey, her body tensing for a leap.

Kelsey gulped. His hands trembled. The barrel of the gun wavered a bit. "Don't do it, Mrs. Mackeson."

Alexis grinned. "How nice. This is more than I could have hoped for. Before I kill William, I get to make him watch his friend die."

She moved with astonishing speed, propelling herself at Kelsey like a shell fired from a cannon.

The sound the gun made was very loud in the small room.

Will screamed.

CHAPTER NINETEEN

The world seemed different now to Jake. It had taken on a peculiar, surreal tint. Paranoia colored every thought. He perceived dark schemes and conspiracies behind every word, and a threat in every glance. It was similar in some respects to the way he'd often felt during his brief cocaine period.

He steered his Camry into Stu Walker's driveway and parked it by rote, like a preprogrammed robot. Even that thought fueled his paranoia. How much control, really, did he have over his own body and its actions? Sometimes very little, it seemed. Yet he had no choice but to keep moving forward.

He entered Stu's house through the front door and darkness enveloped him. It was as if the world had blinked out, as if he'd suddenly ceased to exist. There was something so comforting—so tempting—about that notion. Then his eyes adjusted to the twilight gloom penetrating the living room windows that overlooked the front yard. His gaze went immediately to the sofa Kristen had been sleeping on when he first glimpsed her.

She wasn't there.

He groped to the left and found a light switch. Light flooded the foyer and the living room. He locked the front door and went into the kitchen. At a loss as to what to do next, he simply settled into a chair at the kitchen table and closed his eyes. He emptied his mind and focused on the quiet hum of the refrigerator, the low thrum becoming something else as he eased into a state akin to meditation. It was the gentle obliteration of self and feeling, an ascent away from the hurt and confusion his life had become. Maybe if he stayed this focused, he really could float away. His consciousness, his essence, might disperse in the ether, just cease to be.

The sound of heels on linoleum snapped him out of it. He opened his eyes and saw Kristen entering the kitchen through the garage entrance. The sight of her had a curative effect. He came back to himself in an instant, consciousness and awareness slamming home with jarring force.

She showed him a smile, but it became a frown. She wore crisp black slacks and a stylish blazer over a bright white shirt. A business outfit. Her hair was styled and her makeup was impeccable. She hardly resembled the girl he'd met this morning. If anything, she looked far sexier now. He found he couldn't say anything to her, at least not right away. He didn't know how to talk to this new Kristen. Though he was happy to see her, he also felt a stirring of sadness. A woman of this caliber was not meant for the likes of Jake McAllister.

She dropped her purse on the table and took the chair next to him, turning it so they were facing each other. "Sorry, I don't always dress up like this. I was out on a job interview." Her frown deepened as she studied his face. "Jake, what's wrong? Where's Trey? Why aren't you guys out doing male-bonding stuff?"

Jake laughed. It sounded strange coming out of his mouth. He wasn't the least amused, nor was there anything funny in what he had to say. "My mother is in jail. She'll probably be in jail for a long, long time. My brother's at the police station being interrogated. I had to get out of there. I felt helpless. There was nothing I could do. They said they'd call when they're through with him."

Kristen was stunned. "Whoa, whoa, whoa . . . back up a little, Jake. What the hell's going on? *Why* is your mother in jail? *Why* are the police questioning Trey?"

So he told her about the events of that afternoon, taking his time, including every detail he could remember. "So that's why I'm out of sorts. To understate. I don't know what's gonna happen next—Christ, there's so much to consider— but I suppose I'll be at least temporarily responsible for Trey."

Kristen let out a long, low whistle. "My God. How awful. No wonder you're so out of it."

Jake smiled. "Oh, I'm always a little out of it. That's status quo for me. But the reality of what's happened is just starting to sink in. It's too strange. I never anticipated anything like this, of course, but I've always known my mother is capable of great cruelty." His face darkened as images of Hal's mutilated body came back to him. "Someday I'll tell you my personal experiences with Jolene McAllister's idea of the proper way to discipline a child."

Kristen squeezed his hands. "I wish I could make it all better for you."

Jake looked into her eyes and felt those things one feels in the presence of someone special—a tightness in his chest and a fluttery feeling in his stomach. He wanted to kiss her. Not just on the mouth, but on her eyelids, her chin, all along that delicate, lovely jawline. She must have sensed what he was thinking, because she leaned into him for a kiss. Jake shuddered at the contact. He shifted toward her, sliding to the edge of his chair as he encircled her with his arms and drew her close. The kiss deepened, and she came out of her chair, planting a knee on the edge of Jake's chair between his legs. She pushed him against the back of the chair, fell against him, and continued kissing him with a breathtaking hunger.

She broke the contact long enough to say, "I know what you need."

Her eyes blazed with desire matched by Jake's own. But that familiar voice of common decency spoke within him again. He could not fuck Stu's sister. Not yet. And not in this house.

Kristen sighed. "Jesus. I can see those wheels spinning behind your eyes again. Listen up, Jake." She clamped a hand around his jaw and leaned even closer, so close that her mouth brushed his when she spoke. "*Fuck* waiting till we know each other better. *Fuck* every motherfucking thing holding you back." The hand clamped around his jaw moved to the back of his head, where she seized a handful of his hair and pulled his head back. She grinned. "Most of all, *fuck me.*"

Her free hand went to his zipper and started to pull it down. Jake moaned.

He gripped her by the shoulders and, as gently as possible, pushed her back. "We can't."

Kristen groaned in disgust. "Christ, Jake, you're as uptight as my Bible-thumping old granny."

Jake winced. She was right. And he knew what his real problem was—he was afraid of this next step. It wasn't so much that it was happening so soon, but that it was happening at all. Intimacy, in his mind, equated with vulnerability. And being vulnerable terrified him. "I'm sorry, Kristen."

"You're not getting off the hook so easy. There's something you don't know." There was a wicked glint in her eyes, a hint of secret knowledge. "Stu's gone. He won't be back for weeks."

The revelation dampened Jake's libido. "What? He just took off? That doesn't make sense."

Kristen raised an eyebrow. "Oh?"

A furrow in Jake's brow deepened. Stu had struck Jake as the sturdy, dependable type. His sudden absence stirred the paranoia in Jake's mind. Something just wasn't right about this. On the other hand, what reason did he have to suspect something was wrong? "Where did he go?"

"You don't know my baby brother too well. He's very impulsive. One of his exes, Lorelei something or other, came into the bar today. One thing led to another. You know how that is." She grinned. "Anyway, they went away together."

"Just like that? Won't he lose his job?"

Kristen shook her head. "No. Stu's boss, this guy named Russ, is cool about things like that. He and Stu go off camping and hunting all the time. So Stu and Lorelei are gone. They'll be in a mountain cabin Russ owns in the Rockies for a while. Weeks maybe, as I said."

Jake's paranoia eased some. Kristen was right. He didn't

know Stu very well. Still, it gnawed at him that the guy had vanished so suddenly, and without waiting around long enough to let him know in person what was going on.

But now something else was bothering him. "So . . . it's okay if I stay here all that time while he's gone?"

"Oh, yeah." She seized the front of his shirt. "That's not the only thing that's okay."

She got to her feet and pulled him out of his chair. She began pulling him toward the living room. Jake stumbled along after her. Some part of him still wanted to stop this. But Kristen was so beautiful. And she so clearly wanted him. There was nothing at all wrong with this. Not really. Kristen tugged him along until they reached the sofa, where he'd seen her sleeping this morning. She shrugged off her blazer, gripped the front of his shirt again, and fell back onto the sofa, pulling him down on top of her. They kissed and writhed on the sofa for a while, dry-humping like teenagers, then she placed her hands on his chest and pushed him back, all the way to the far end of the sofa. She smiled. She lifted her ass off the sofa and began to wriggle out of her slacks. Once they were down around her ankles, she kicked them away. Then she kicked off her shoes, braced the soles of her bare feet on the sofa, and spread her legs like a flower.

She parted the lips of her labia with a thumb and forefinger. She licked her lips. "Taste me, Jake."

Jake shivered.

He couldn't believe how brazen she was. It excited him. And it frightened him. His heart hammered in his chest. He knelt between Kristen's legs, and she propped an ankle over his shoulder. He leaned toward her and began. She groaned, almost growled like an animal, and writhed against the sofa. Listening to her fueled Jake's excitement, and he began to lose himself in the act, all of his previous inhibitions falling away, sloughing off like a shed skin.

Kristen sat up and gripped his neck. "I want you in me. Hurry."

All Jake could think of now was Kristen and how good being

108 BRYAN SMITH

with her felt. He wanted to get deep inside her and stay there
forever, just disappear, fuck the world and his problems away.
Of all the ways to escape, what could be better? He pulled his
shirt off and cast it aside, then got to his feet and began to
push down his jeans.

The phone rang.

The noise broke the spell. Jake's head turned toward the
kitchen. And he remembered what was going on in the world.
His mother was in jail and his brother was being interrogated
by the police. And what was he doing? He wasn't looking
into his legal obligations. Nor was he doing any of the things
a person in his position should be doing. Nope, he was doing
what he always did—losing himself in yet another form of
intoxication.

Three rings.

Four.

He sighed.

Kristen groaned. "Ignore it."

Stu's recorded voice emanated from the answering machine
in the kitchen: "You've reached the Walker residence. Leave a
message at the beep."

Then the beep, followed by: "Ah . . . if I have the right
number, this message is for Jake McAllister. This is Detective
Myers with the Rockville Police Department. I think you
should get down here as soon as possible."

Myers recited his direct line and hung up.

Jake's shoulders sagged. "Jesus." He put a hand to his forehead. "What the hell could be wrong now?"

Kristen got to her feet and pressed her body against Jake.
She laid her head in the crook of his neck, hooked her hands
over his shoulders, and wrapped a leg around him. "Whatever
it is, you can handle it." She stroked his bare chest. "You're
stronger than you think, I bet."

Jake didn't reply to that.

The soft tips of her fingers slid down his chest, moved over
his deflating cock, and gave it a gentle squeeze. She looked
into his eyes. "I'm not through with this."

Jake made an exasperated sound. "Kristen—"

She shushed him. "Quiet." She relinquished her hold on him. "You have duty to attend to, I know that." She smiled. "But I expect you to finish what you started later tonight."

Again, Jake didn't reply.

The sensation he experienced then was akin to a mental free fall. The world felt shaky beneath his feet. He loved the way this woman's body felt against his, and he loved being in her arms. She just made him feel good. So why did he have this nagging feeling that plunging headfirst into a sexual relationship with her was a dangerous thing?

He grimaced when she tightened her grip on him and dug her nails into his shoulders.

She drew the nails down his back.

His breath grew shallow as Kristen drew blood.

CHAPTER TWENTY

Trey wanted to die. Through everything, he'd managed to hold on to some shred of sanity by believing he could rescue Myra from whatever horrible force was using her body. But he didn't believe that anymore. The girl he'd known as a pretty outcast and fellow high school senior had never really existed. Myra was an illusion. A facade. A disguise. Brilliantly conceived and rendered, but a disguise nonetheless. Coming to grips with this should have brought him a measure of peace, but it had not. With the well-being of his illusory girl-friend no longer a consideration, his thoughts had initially turned to saving himself. But he knew this wasn't possible.

So he wanted to die.

He heard it again.

That mad, sadistic laughter inside his head. *Her* laughter. Wherever she was now—and he'd lost track of her earlier in the day—part of her remained with him. Inside him. She was able to reach into his mind regardless of physical proximity. She was privy to his every thought, his every emotion. It was maddening. And terrifying. It made him want to claw out of his own skin.

The cops thought there was something wrong with him. He could see it in their eyes. And it was evident in the way they flinched every time he reacted to Myra's mental taunts. That one guy, the detective who dressed like a businessman, had put a halt to the interrogation when Trey had slipped and yelled at

Myra to get out of his head. And his court-appointed attorney had said something about an "evaluation."

Trey knew what that meant. And the prospect of it frightened him almost as much as Myra. They thought he was a head case. So they were gonna lock him up in some padded room, somewhere deep in the bowels of a horror movie madhouse, where he'd spend the rest of his days doped up on tranquilizers, and even that would provide no relief—Myra's voice would always speak inside his head.

Trey stared at the scratched surface of the interrogation room table. He heard voices in the hallway. One of them was the detective. Myers. His voice was too dim for Trey to distinguish much, but he heard enough to get the gist—Jake was coming back. He still wasn't sure why his brother had left in the first place. Trey didn't know the guy very well, but he sensed there was something broken inside him. Not in the usual McAllister way. He was a smart dude. And accomplished. He'd done something with his life. But that sense of something wrong inside him was strong. He didn't seem able to cope with the harsher side of life. It made Trey sad. If he didn't get sent to the loony bin, Jake would be expected to take care of him.

Which meant Jake would have to deal with Myra.

And Trey knew his brother would be as powerless against her as anyone else.

Maybe more so.

I can't let it happen, he thought.

I have to die.

The laughter filled his head again.

And this time Myra spoke: *Oh, Trey, such a grandiose sense of importance you have. You were never important, little boy. You were a means to an end. You've served your purpose. You want to die? Okay.*

Trey frowned.

Maybe Myra was just fucking with him some more, but he didn't think so. She got off on making him think his torment would be eternal. She reveled in his pain and humiliation.

He'd been forced to endure agonizing physical punishments. If the police ever got a look at the welts covering his body, they'd assume the marks were inflicted by Jolene. And he'd been made to do such vile things. Though he hadn't willfully killed anyone, his body had been used as a killing instrument. Even now, if she wanted to, she could pull his strings from afar, make him do something to himself.

Or to someone else.

But now she was through with him?

He flashed back to his suicidal thoughts of a few moments ago, and now he found he didn't want to die just yet. He had to warn people, let them know what was going on in Rockville. But who would believe his crazy story? The police? Like hell. Jake? Probably not. Kelsey and Will would believe him. But they were kids, too. No adult would ever believe any of them. Still, he would have to try. And soon. If Myra meant to have him killed, he would be killed. There was no way around it. So fuck it, he'd spill his guts to Myers when the detective returned. Caution be damned. Let them toss him in that padded cell and throw away the key. At least he would have tried something. And maybe—just maybe—Myers would be smart enough to take a longer look at some of the odd things that had been going on in his town.

He heard a scuff of boots on the room's tiled floor. He looked up in time to see the guard posted at the door moving toward him. The uniformed female officer was pulling her service pistol out of its holster.

Trey gasped. "No."

The officer was tall and slender. Her long, blonde hair was pinned back. Trey was sure she was one of the women he'd seen in the clearing that first night. The gun looked large and imposing, bigger than life, like a cannon wielded by an angry goddess. It was aimed at the narrow space between his eyes.

The woman thumbed back the hammer and grinned. "Now you die."

The voice was Myra's. It sounded strange emanating from the

blonde officer. Her mouth just hung open while the words came forth: "It's going to look like you attacked this woman. You're unstable. You're ill. She'll kill you in self-defense." Myra's laugh came out of the woman's open mouth. "Are you ready for the bullet? Your brains will look lovely painted all over that drab wall."

Again, the laughter.

"Nobody will ever believe that." Trey glanced pointedly at the video camera mounted high on the wall in a corner of the room. "It'll all be on tape."

Myra's vessel looked at the camera. "Oops." Then she looked at Trey again. "No matter. This acolyte is expendable. Her sacrifice will be rewarded in the next world. Say good-bye, Trey."

Trey screamed.

The door to the interrogation room flew open and two uniformed cops ran in. The blonde officer whirled around as they were drawing their weapons. One of them, a muscular black man, had just pulled his 9mm clear of its holster when a hard, concussive noise filled the room. The black man's life ended as a bullet penetrated his brain. He hopped backward and spasmed before falling to the floor, blood jetting from the opening at the back of his head. Another bullet knocked down the other officer, and the blonde woman swung back around, again aiming the gun at Trey's head.

Trey felt paralyzed. There'd been times in his life, especially after seeing a particularly thrilling action movie, when he'd visualized himself in a situation like this. He always saw himself acting decisively, heroically, making some kind of bold move. He'd never imagined this. He felt impotent. He was a coward. Myra, whatever she really was, had been right about that.

So Trey just stood there, waiting for the bullet that would end his life.

The woman advanced on him, keeping the gun aimed at that place between his eyes. She backed Trey all the way to the wall. He whimpered and began to slide to the floor.

Other people entered the room. He heard raised voices. Screaming. Someone out in the hallway was crying hysterically. There was a shouted command. He recognized Myers's voice. He was telling the blonde woman to put down the gun. Telling her he would shoot her. As if that mattered. Trey almost laughed. There was no way Myers could know this woman was one of Myra's acolytes. No way he could know no threat would sway her from this task.

The barrel of the gun pressed against his lips.

He heard Myra's voice again: "Suck it."

Trey was as helpless as ever. He opened his mouth and drew in the barrel of the gun. He licked the cold steel, and the blonde woman moved the barrel in and out of his mouth, mimicking the motion of a thrusting cock.

He heard Myers say, "Jesus fuck . . ."

Someone else said, "Aw, shit, man. Fucking shoot her!"

This was the voice of his brother. Trey felt an instant of mortification at the thought of Jake seeing him like this. But then he laughed around the barrel of the gun. He was about to die, but Myra would lose this follower. And maybe the strangeness of the blonde woman's behavior would merit investigation of possibilities the cops might otherwise have ignored.

Trey saw Myers move into view over the blonde woman's shoulder. The man was big and beefy. He had a helmet of thick black hair and a bushy black mustache. His brown eyes looked hard and determined. He placed the barrel of a 9mm pistol against the blonde woman's temple. "Let's stop this right now, sugar." The cop's accent was old-time Southern-fried hard-ass. "You don't wanna hurt this boy. And I don't wanna shoot ya. But I sure as shit will put a hole through your fuckin' head in about one more second if you don't step off."

The woman's head snapped toward him, and she flashed him a feral grin. "Okay."

She eased the pistol from Trey's mouth.

A look of uncertainty crossed Myers's face. The detective knew something unnatural was happening here. Trey could see it in the man's eyes. He wanted to cry. He thought there was at least a ghost of a chance this man might believe his story now.

Then a forced grin replaced the uncertain look. "That's a good girl. Put the gun in my hand."

Keeping the barrel of his own gun on her temple, Myers extended a hand.

Her smile then was saccharine sweet. "Yes, sir."

A strangled cry emerged from Trey's throat. He wanted to scream at Myers not to trust her, but he couldn't get his vocal cords to work. He wasn't paralyzed with fear, not this time, but Myra was again pulling his strings. He seethed with frustration.

The woman's gun grazed Myers's fingertips.

Then, before the detective could react, her hand moved with superhuman speed and jammed the barrel of the gun against the detective's stomach. She squeezed the trigger twice, and the detective staggered backward. Blood blossomed across the front of his starched white shirt as he tumbled dead to the floor. His gun flew out of his hand, struck the wall close to Trey, and spun across the floor. The other officers that had entered the room behind Myers were shooting at the female cop and she was returning fire. As Trey stared up at her, chunks of blood-red meat flew from her back as her tan uniform blouse turned a dark shade of crimson.

Yet she remained on her feet, firing until her gun clicked empty.

Someone yelled at her to drop the gun.

Trey was flabbergasted.

Didn't these people get it yet?

This bitch was not about to surrender.

She ejected the 9mm's spent clip and calmly reached to her belt for a fresh clip. She slammed the clip home, racked a bullet into the chamber, and aimed again. The stupid Rockville cops finally decided to start shooting again, but they continued directing their fire at her torso.

Fuck it, Trey thought.

He pushed away from the wall and scrabbled across the floor. Two more of Rockville's finest fell down dead before he managed to get to his feet with Myers's gun in hand. Imitating the two-handed firing stance of the cops, he aimed the barrel at the side of the woman's head and pulled the trigger. The bullet punched a hole through her head just above her ear, and a red spray like water shooting out of a hose erupted from the other side of her head. The force of the shot threw her sideways, but, to Trey's astonishment, she still managed to remain upright. Goddamn, it was like trying to kill a zombie in a video game. And if he'd learned nothing else of value from playing video games, there was at least this—*nothing succeeds like overkill.*

So Trey moved in and fired another bullet through the center of her face.

She fell back against the wall.

Trey fired again.

And again.

Until the gun was again empty and the blonde woman's head was a pulped ruin.

Somehow, her body was still upright, but it jerked like a malfunctioning mechanical doll. Then, all at once, the life went out of her, and she dropped like a lead weight to the floor.

Trey's heart was hammering.

Someone said, "Fucking *finally.*"

Trey derived little real satisfaction from stilling this agent of Myra's wrath. He knew all too well she could make him turn the gun on himself if she wanted. But he didn't feel her presence in his head now. She'd retreated, at least for the time being.

He felt sick.

This was all a game to her.

All these dead cops.

A grand distraction.

He flinched when his brother laid a hand on his shoulder. "She's going to kill us." He turned to look into Jake's shocked face. "She's going to kill us all."

Jake's expression was strained. "It's gonna be okay."

He didn't sound like he meant it. Not one little bit.

Shuddery laughter trickled out of Trey's mouth. "No. No, Jake, it's not."

Another suit-and-tie-clad detective escorted them out of the room. Trey kept his eyes closed until he was in the hallway.

He didn't want to see any more blood.

Not now.

Not ever.

CHAPTER TWENTY-ONE

Jordan awoke with a start when she felt something cold graze the back of her hand. She jerked the hand away from the side of the bed, over which it'd been dangling while she slept. Her heart thudding, she sat and searched frantically about the room for the intruder.

But she was alone.

She sighed. "Shit."

The obvious occurred to her—she'd been dreaming again. An unwelcome touch in her dream had seemed real. It was a sensible explanation, and just thinking it had the immediate effect of calming her.

Until she heard the sound of something skittering across the floor behind her. She gasped and spun about on the bed, again scanning the other side of the room. She saw nothing. There was a temptation to chalk up the sound to a mind befuddled by too many tranquilizers, but a strong voice rose within her.

That was NOT your imagination!

Jordan trembled as she remained rooted to the center of the bed. There was something in the room with her. Some animal. Maybe a snake. Her trembling became more pronounced as images of venom-spitting snakes entered her head. She had long feared snakes.

How would a snake have gotten into her room?

She didn't know. Nor did she care. All she knew was that it was here, probably coiled up beneath her bed right now. She visualized moving off the bed—and in her mind saw the snake dart out from under the bed to sink its dripping fangs into her bare ankle.

Jordan whimpered.

She remembered the cold sensation of something grazing the back of her hand. Now she was almost certain she hadn't dreamed it, that the snake had been inspecting her, looking for a suitably juicy morsel of flesh to clamp its jaw around. On some level, Jordan realized what she imagined wasn't typical snake behavior, but, as was so often the case, fear overwhelmed logic.

The snake was here.

She believed it wholeheartedly.

And she was trapped on this bed, as helpless as an abandoned baby in a stroller. She sensed movement to her left. A rustling. With as much caution as she could muster, she inched closer to the edge of the mattress and looked at the floor at the side of the bed. Something pushed against a dangling bedsheet, stretching the fabric and pulling the sheet away from the bed.

This did not look like the head of a snake distending the fabric. Whatever it was, it was too large, too lumpish. An idea came to her, something that made her feel foolish. This was no snake. But maybe it was a cat. How a cat would have gotten into her apartment she had no clue, but she found herself eager to embrace the idea. It was possible that a cat had slipped through the front door when she'd ejected Bridget from her apartment. She'd been so upset she might not have noticed. The cat could have been hiding under her bed all day, frightened out of its wits by its new surroundings. The cold sensation she'd experienced a few moments ago had probably been the cat's nose sniffing at her hand, trying to determine whether she was a trustworthy biped.

Jordan smiled, feeling a sudden warmth toward the cat. "Here, kitty, kitty . . ."

The thing from underneath the bed slipped free of the sheet, revealing itself to Jordan for the first time. It was not a cat. Jordan didn't know what it was. It looked reptilian, with scaly green skin, a gargoylelike head, and a wide, froggy mouth brimming with rows of sharp, glistening teeth. A forked tongue emerged between two of the teeth and slithered toward her face. She felt it on her chin and knew then what she'd really felt moments before.

She screamed.

Instinct propelled her backward off the bed. Her ass struck the floor hard and a bolt of pain arced up her spine and jabbed into her head. The creature's head popped into view a moment later. Its mouth widened and the rows of teeth seemed to lengthen. A steady hiss emerged from the mouth, and the forked tongue flicked in and out. A pair of three-fingered hands appeared, gripping the edge of the bed as the thing began to stand. The sight of its body, with its long, multijointed limbs and elastic, segmented torso, sent a ripple of repulsion through Jordan.

It was hideous.

And it was coming for her, an awful hunger evident in its dark, pulsing eyes. Jordan screamed and lurched to her feet, galvanized by adrenaline. She felt fully alive for the first time all day, all five senses engaged as the sluggishness she had felt since that morning gave way to a single, clear purpose—escape. Through the bedroom doorway and down the hallway she dashed, her mind intent only on getting to her front door. She had a good head start on the creature, but she heard its pursuit with a heart-jolting clarity, the razor-sharp nails of its three-fingered hands scraping along the corridor walls behind her.

She sprinted through the living room and reached the front door. Her hand closed around the knob. Alarming thoughts flashed through her mind in a fraction of a second. She didn't have her keys, therefore she couldn't use her car. Her feet were bare. She didn't have a clue what she would do once she was on the other side of this door. But she had no time to contemplate the implications of any of that, so she yanked the door open, stepped outside and pulled it shut behind her. Would a thing like that know how to work a doorknob? She didn't know. Jesus Christ, she didn't even know what in the goddamn hell that fucking abomination was. It had managed to get into her apartment somehow, so she had to believe it could work its way out. And that meant she had to keep moving.

Get down those stairs.

Maybe run down the street to the QuikMart, get one of those stoner clerks to call 911.

And she would have done just that had the staircase been unobstructed. She got to the first step, glanced down, and loosed a shrill cry. There were more *things* there. Awful, grotesque creatures that looked like mutations, like things that couldn't exist outside of nightmares. Long, slithering snakelike things and smaller variations of the lizard-monster she'd locked in her apartment. Some of them looked malformed, like genetics experiments gone horribly awry, with misshapen heads and eyes protruding from stalks, elongated, twisted jaws with long teeth that curled over bloated lips. When they saw her, they became agitated, bouncing and chittering, some of them communicating excitedly in a language she didn't recognize.

She backed away from the monstrous horde, turned and ran to the other end of the landing. She banged on the door to Todd's apartment, screaming for help and eying the approach of the strange creatures with mounting panic.

Then the door opened and she was greeted by a sight so startling it made her forget her terror for a moment. She'd forgotten all about Bridget and how she'd sleazed her way into Todd's place, but it all came back to her now. Bridget shrieked with delight.

"Hey, girl!" She clamped a hand around one of Jordan's arms. "Come on in and join the party." She giggled. "We're, uh, just having Todd for dinner now."

Jordan smelled cooking meat. It made her mouth water, and her stomach rumbled. She hadn't eaten all day. Another woman inside the apartment laughed. Jordan then remembered seeing Angela Brooks that afternoon. Then she saw Bridget's friend appear behind her. She grinned and draped an arm around Bridget's shoulders. Both women were completely nude. They were dripping wet, as if they'd recently showered. Jordan wondered whether they'd showered together. The thought brought forth a strange pang of jealousy. Then she felt something, a slim tendril, curling around her ankle and she snapped back to reality. She kicked loose of the tendril, rushed into the apartment, and threw the door shut.

She sagged against the door, breathing hard. "There's monsters out there."

Bridget and Angela exchanged a glance, then looked at Jordan. Bridget arched an eyebrow. "Monsters? Really?"

Jordan heaved another heavy sigh. "Yes, monsters. Look, I know you don't believe me, but it's the goddamn truth. There was one in my apartment, a big, skinny, slimy lizard-monster. And now there's a bunch of them out on the landing. I'm not lying. I'm not hallucinating. I swear to fucking God."

Bridget shrugged off Angela's arm and brushed past Jordan. Jordan was pretty sure the brief physical contact was intentional, but she chose not to dwell on that for the moment. She wanted to scream when Bridget opened the door. "Don't!"

Bridget peered around the edge of the door. She was silent for a while; then she giggled. "Aw, aren't they cute?"

Jordan's eyes went wide with disbelief. "Cute!?"

Bridget knelt and picked up one of the creatures. Cradling it in her arms, she came back into the apartment, kicking the door shut behind her. The thing in her arms looked like a mottled beach ball with tiny arms and legs. It had a face like a Halloween pumpkin come to life. Thick strands of saliva hung from the corners of its mouth. The moisture plopped on the floor, sizzling like bacon grease on a hot stove.

Bridget stroked the top of its head. She grinned at Jordan's horror-struck expression. "Oh, he's just a little guy."

Jordan spluttered unintelligibly, then said, "What the fuck is that thing?"

"This?" There was a note of mock innocence in Bridget's voice as she glanced again at the vile thing nestled in her arms. "Oh, it's just one of Lamia's minions."

Jordan didn't know what to say to that. She didn't know this

Lamia person. And she didn't know what to make of Bridget's nonchalance in the face of something so horrible. She seemed unafraid of the awful creatures. Indeed, she appeared to feel real affection for them. Maybe she really *was* hallucinating. She'd never taken LSD, but maybe someone at Mondo Video, some hateful asshole, had dosed her coffee. That had to be it. Nothing else could account for what she was seeing, because none of it could be real.

Bridget opened her arms and let the beach ball on legs drop to the floor. It bounced and rolled for a moment before regaining its footing. Then it leered up at Jordan and began to waddle toward her. Jordan screamed and backed away. Bridget and Angela laughed hysterically, like two drunken bimbos clowning it up for a *Girls Gone Wild* camera crew.

Jordan shrieked at them. "What the hell's wrong with you!? What is this!?"

The women advanced on her, circling around her as the little creature backed her up against Todd's overflowing entertainment center. For the first time, Jordan noticed the living room. There was a dried, dark brownish substance all over everything. It looked like it might be blood. Her head snapped toward the kitchen, which was visible beyond a partition separating it from the living room.

We're uh, just, having Todd for dinner now.

Jordan's stomach lurched at the memory of Bridget's words.

Panic gripped her. She was trapped in this apartment with a couple of murdering cannibal women. Murdering cannibal women with a host of creepy-crawly things as pets. Her immediate future was clear—painful death.

Angela Brooks gripped her by a wrist and twisted her arm behind her back. She seized a handful of Jordan's hair with her other hand and jerked her head back. Bridget put a hand on Jordan's hip, stroking it with surprising gentleness.

"Oh, sweet, sweet Jordan." She laughed. "I'm going to make all your dreams come true." The hand moved up under Jordan's shirt, caressed her flat stomach. "But you look hungry, so maybe you should have a bite to eat first."

Angela began to push her toward the kitchen.

The beach ball thing waddled ahead of them.

Jordan sobbed, begged them to let her go.

"Oh, I don't think so, Jordan, dear." Bridget picked up a plate, forked a chunk of brown meat, and held it in front of Jordan's face. "Have a bite of Todd."

Jordan's knees buckled, but Angela, stronger than she appeared, kept her upright.

Bridget squeezed her mouth open and pushed the warm meat inside.

Jordan spit it out.

Bridget smiled. She forked another chunk of meat. "That's okay. There's more where that came from. A lot more. And we've got all night, baby."

Jordan thought about that.

And she made a promise to herself.

She would wait.

Do whatever these monsters—human and inhuman—demanded of her. Suffer any degradation.

And hope for an opportunity.

CHAPTER TWENTY-TWO

Raymond Slater dressed for bed with the numb precision of an automaton. At no point was he conscious of the process. His fingers moved of their own accord, following patterns established over decades, drawing on his silk pajamas, pushing buttons through buttonholes, squeezing a small twist of toothpaste onto a brush that needed replacing. He spit out toothpaste foam in the bathroom sink, blotted his face with a paper towel, and stepped back to appraise his reflection. But the image in his mirror triggered something in the recesses of his mind, a dangerous spark of awareness.

He muttered a curse: "Shit."

He flicked off the bathroom light and returned to the tastefully, and expensively, appointed bedroom he shared with his wife of twenty years, Patricia Louise Winston Slater. He flipped back the plush Laura Ashley comforter and crawled beneath freshly laundered sheets that smelled vaguely of pine needles. His wife, clad in a blue silk nightgown, set down the latest issue of *Vanity Fair* and shifted her considerable bulk, rocking the canopied bed as she turned to face her husband.

Raymond sighed. His wife always knew when something was bothering him. She was excellent at reading his moods, almost to a scary degree, but luckily, wasn't so good at detecting hints of infidelity. He dreaded what was coming—one of those intensely earnest, supposedly heart-to-heart talks, the intent of which was to purge him of stress and set everything right in the world again. It never worked. Oh, he allowed Patricia to think the talks did him some good. He played that game, that age-old conjugal dance of deceit, and he played it well. Normally, he considered it a small price to pay, a necessary hoop to jump through so she wouldn't suspect his real obsessions.

Patricia Slater made a clucking sound. "Something's bothering you, dear."

A statement. Not a question. Words that would brook no denial. He sighed again, an indicator of reluctance, of difficulty finding the right way to phrase how he really felt. It was a stalling tactic. Jesus, what could he say to her? He suppressed an inappropriate burst of laughter, twisting the smile that twitched at the corners of his mouth to look like a grimace of pain (this wasn't difficult).

He imagined telling her the truth: *Well, dear, today was a very interesting day. A truly singular day, in fact. I've never quite experienced the likes of it before. You see, a girl, one of my students, is a demon. Yes, a demon. I mean that in the most literal sense. A spirit. An incarnation of evil. A fucking DEMON. And, well, she's forcing me to participate in something horrendous tomorrow. I suspect I'll be dead soon. No, there's absolutely nothing I can do about it. And how was your day, dear?*

What he actually said was, "I suppose."

"Hmm." She touched his arm. Raymond only barely managed not to flinch. His grimace deepened as he watched her face form an expression of sympathy, which looked ghastly behind her mask of facial creme. "Is it that dreadful business at the police station? That boy, what was his name?"

"Trey McAllister."

Patricia's fingers stroked his forearm, her manicured nails lightly grazing his skin and sending an uncomfortable tingling down the length of his arm. "Yes, Trey, that's it. He's a student of yours, correct?"

Raymond answered with a grunt. He was trying not to acknowledge the steadily increasing intimacy of his wife's touch. It was just possible she was feeling horny. She didn't attempt to seduce him all that often, probably because she was having at least one extramarital affair of her own. He hoped like hell it wouldn't happen now. He groaned when her hand left his arm and dipped under the comforter. Her fingers fiddled with the snap of his pajama bottoms before Raymond gave up and tossed the comforter back. Best just to get it done so he could get to sleep. Patricia giggled. She lifted the hem of her nightgown and straddled her husband. She gripped his limp penis with her left hand and slapped him several times with her right hand. He grew hard in her hand. This was the way they always did it now. It was the only way Raymond could perform with her. She mounted him and rode him until he spurted inside her. In the moment before orgasm, Raymond saw Myra's face in his mind. The memory of the way she'd looked straddling his lap that afternoon was the thing that pushed him over the finish line.

Then, spent, he recalled the way Myra had looked moments later.

He whimpered.

Patricia's face crinkled with concern. The layer of facial cream made her look like some sort of demon herself, like a bloated gargoyle. "Oh, honey. It's awful, I know. I hoped I could take your mind off it for a while, but I can see how heavily it's weighing on you."

Raymond thought: *Not as heavily as you, I can tell you that.*

He wanted her to dismount, but he didn't say so. This "intimacy" was bad enough—really, it was just shy of vomit inducing—but offending her was the last thing he wanted. The many people who loved Patricia would never believe the level of cruelty she was capable of in private, but her wrath was a truly awful thing to incur. Raymond put up with it because her worst moments were very rare. Enduring them was preferable to going through a very expensive and messy divorce.

He coughed. "Yes. It is. Very much so." Best just to go along with this load of steaming horseshit. "I've had a rough time of it. I know I can't protect my kids the way I'd like to."

When Raymond wanted to subtly showcase his sensitivity, he referred to the students at Rockville High as "my kids." Patricia fell for it every damn time, and this time was no exception. She made a noise of empathy, and Raymond decided to lay it on a little thicker. "Trey McAllister has a special place in my heart, you know. I've long suspected abuse by his parents."

Patricia shook her head. "It's awful. Simply awful. There ought to be a minimum IQ requirement for becoming a parent in this country. Those McAllisters are trashy people. I well remember all the trouble you had with Trey's older brothers."

Raymond frowned. "You do? But . . . that was so long ago."

"Mmm, yes, it was." Patricia's eyes were closed, and there was a dreamy quality to her voice. She tightened her vaginal muscles around Raymond's shrinking cock and her large, drooping breasts undulated beneath the fabric of her nightgown. She rolled her massive hips and her torso began to sway. Her eyes came open—they were glazed. "I have a good memory, Raymond. An excellent memory, in fact. Photographic, you might say. Jake and Michael McAllister caused you tremendous aggravation back in the day. You would tell me about their escapades over dinner. That was back when you still loved me and would willingly share your troubles with me."

The motion of his wife's body felt nice. This was odd. He was enjoying physical contact with Patricia for the first time in . . . well, in a very long time. He grew hard inside her, and her rocking rhythm increased a little. Now this was beyond odd. An encore performance with Patricia? That hadn't happened in many years. He smiled. And this time some of the day's stress really did begin to dissipate. He felt very mellow, very relaxed, and pleasantly aroused.

He moaned.

He closed his eyes and focused only on the physical sensations.

Then his eyes snapped open. "Wait. Wait. What did you mean by that?"

Patricia smiled. "Mean by what, dear?"

"You know exactly what I mean. You referred to my love in the past tense." It was true that Raymond didn't love Patricia. He hadn't for a very long time. But having this reality verbalized by Patricia made him angry and defensive. "That's just ridiculous. It's . . . cruel."

Patricia laughed. "Is it?"

Raymond's face contorted with rage. "It fucking well is. How dare you—"

"Oh, shut up."

Patricia bit her lower lip and began to buck like a bronco, rattling the bed and abusing her husband's spine. It hurt. The hell of it, though, was that he was more turned on than ever. Patricia clamped a hand around his throat and applied considerable pressure. She was choking him, but it only served to intensify his pleasure. She spewed verbal abuse at him. He built quickly toward orgasm, and when she eased the pressure on his throat he went off like a rocket.

Raymond laid there panting for several moments.

"Oh . . . oh . . . Jesus . . ."

Then he met his wife's steady gaze, saw her smirk. "What was that all about?"

"It's a reminder." Patricia's eyes went flat. Her voice was icy when she said, "And a going-away present."

Raymond felt a flicker of alarm. This was so unlike Patricia. Even when she was treating him like an idiot stepchild, she never sounded like this. Never this cold. "Patricia, what's wrong? Have I done something? Please tell me." A welling of tears surprised him. "I promise I'll fix whatever's wrong."

"We're past that, Raymond. I wanted you to remember that I know what makes you tick. I had to remind you that your wife is still the best fuck you've ever had—or ever will have." Her lips twisted into a sneer. "Tell me, Raymond, be honest, has that little slut English teacher you've been screwing ever made you come that hard?"

Raymond's eyes widened. He spluttered. "Wh-wh . . . what?"

Patricia laughed again. "That's right. I know all about it.

And I have pictures. Graciously provided to me by a concerned, albeit anonymous, friend."

Raymond felt a pain in his chest. Panic ripped through him like a virulent virus. His world was falling apart. Suddenly. Without warning. And he felt powerless to halt its disintegration. "Patricia, you've got to listen to me."

Patricia's eyes widened in mock surprise. "Me? Listen to you?"

She threw her head back and laughed heartily.

Raymond strove to keep his voice calm. He had to make her see reason. Only by keeping a level head might he see his way through this storm. "I've been blackmailed. It's been horrible. A nightmare. I've had no choice."

Patricia glared at him. "And I don't care. I'm through with you, Raymond. I'm getting a divorce. I'm getting this house and all your fucking money. And then I'm getting the hell out of this podunk town you've trapped me in all these years. There's nothing you can do about it. You'll agree to whatever I want." She grinned. "Unless you want everyone you know to see the pictures."

The thought of it made Raymond pray for a heart attack. He imagined his daughter, a college freshman, seeing those pictures and wanted to scream.

Raymond's chest hitched.

He sniffled and his vision blurred.

"Awww." Patricia mocked him again. "Poor little baby. Is my soon-to-be ex-husband about to cry?"

Raymond wiped moisture from his eyes. He met his wife's fiery, horribly satisfied gaze and felt a long-dormant piece of himself flare briefly to life and then die. It all hit him at once. The tragedy of his broken life. He'd had it all. A wife, a beautiful child, money, and a rewarding career. Not anymore. Piece by piece, bit by bitter bit, he'd dismantled his slice of the American Dream through his own arrogance and stupidity. Looking into Patricia's eyes, he knew it was all over.

He sniffed again. "I'm sorry. I really am." The sentiment was sincere. Now that the big secret, the thing he'd worked so hard to conceal, was a secret no more, he was seized by a need to come clean on everything before it was too late. Tragedy could still be averted. The desire frightened him because he knew the risk involved was probably life threatening, but he plunged ahead anyway. "There's something I have to tell you. Your first instinct will be to scoff, but I beg you, Patricia, I *beseech* you, please listen with an open mind. So many innocent lives are at stake. We have to warn people. A student at Rockville High is a . . ." He hesitated. Here it was, the big moment. But now he felt ridiculous. She would never believe this. He sighed. "She's a demon."

Patricia laughed again louder than ever. "You grandiose, delusional fool!" Hilarity rendered her voice shrill. "You ridiculous man. Egads, how lucky I'll be to be shed of you!" She rolled her eyes. "A *demon!*"

Raymond's shame and self-pity intensified. He felt small. Impotent. Then he heard something incongruous, barely audible through his wife's laughter. A creak. And another. A sound like someone moving with deliberate stealth. When Raymond saw what was looming over Patricia's shoulder, he opened his mouth to scream.

It was too late.

Patricia's laugh became a squeal as her head was jerked roughly back. A long, curved blade was then pressed against her throat. The gloved hand holding the blade's handle gave it a savage jerk and Patricia's throat opened like a zipper. Blood geysered from the massive wound, splashing Raymond's face and getting inside his mouth and nose. He felt another pain in his chest, this time so intense he thought he really might have a heart attack. Then the big blade, similar to a machete, returned and ripped at Patricia's neck again.

The strength of her attacker was phenomenal, almost inhuman.

Her head came free of her body.

Penelope Simmons jumped onto the bed and kicked the lifeless body aside. Clad entirely in black and wearing a dark wig and sunglasses, she looked like something out of a piece of spy fiction, a sexy paid assassin. She stood over Raymond, the top of her head nearly grazing the bed's canopy; then she grinned at her lover.

"I heard you, Raymond. You big tattletale, you." Her blue eyes burned with excitement. "You've been naughty. You better hope you-know-who doesn't cut your tongue out. That would be a shame. I'm rather fond of your tongue." She gave Patricia's severed head a hard shake, pumping it like an especially enthusiastic cheerleader waving a pom-pom. "Aren't you glad this stupid cow is dead? We're free at last, Raymond, free at last. Praise Lamia."

Raymond just blubbered, incapable now of speech or screams.

Penelope cackled. "Catch, baby."

She tossed Patricia's head to Raymond.

This time he did manage to scream.

And he screamed for a while, straining his vocal cords.

Until Penelope made him shut up.

CHAPTER TWENTY-THREE

The beer was good. Better than good, like liquid nirvana. Kelsey and Will stood in the kitchen, calming their nerves with some of Blake Mackeson's German beer. Save for a single flickering candle on the counter, the room was dark. All the lights were off. The intent was to convey the impression of an empty house. After what had transpired over the last several hours, they imagined themselves surrounded by enemies, lurking assassins just waiting for the right opportunity to pounce.

Kelsey polished off his third Warsteiner and set it on the counter. "That beer is the shit, man. I don't know if I can ever drink Bud again."

Will nodded. He didn't bother with a verbal reply. He'd barely said anything since knocking his mother unconscious. The violence disturbed him. Though his mom had meant to kill them both, he felt guilt. She was his mother. She wasn't much of a mother, true, but there was still an emotional attachment. He could no more excise the part of himself that still cared for her than he could cut off his own hand. Hell, cutting off his own hand might be easier.

He flashed on an image: . . . *that gash in her forehead, the shocking flow of blood, staining the carpet red* . . .

Will's mom had tackled Kelsey after his shot went astray. She'd pinned him to the floor and wrapped her hands around his throat. She would have killed him had Will not intervened. Now, bound with duct tape and gagged with a sock, she was stuffed in the closet in Will's bedroom. Blake Mackeson was bound to the leather chair in his office, where he'd been since Kelsey knocked him unconscious with a fireplace poker. According to Kelsey, Will's dad had been in the process of loading his gun. Kelsey, who had quietly entered the house moments after Mr. Mackeson's arrival, had eavesdropped on enough of the conversation in Will's bedroom to know it didn't bode well for Will.

Will recalled the sight of the ruined radio on his nightstand, which had been struck by the misdirected bullet. "Kelsey . . ."

Kelsey popped the top off another Warsteiner. "Yeah?"

Will swallowed a lump in his throat. This wouldn't be easy to say. "I think we should call 911."

Kelsey gaped at him. "Are you kidding? Why, for fuck's sake?"

Will swallowed some Warsteiner. He didn't like beer as much as Kelsey or Trey, but liquid courage seemed absolutely necessary right now. "Because I hit her with a fucking baseball bat, man. She could have a concussion. Hell, maybe even brain damage. She could be dying right now."

Kelsey shook his head, made an exasperated sound. "I don't think so. You didn't hit her that hard. That wasn't any Babe Ruth swing, bro. And we got the bleeding to stop, right? She's fine. And I hate to say it, man, but her health is the least of our concerns right now."

Will glared at his friend. "Easy for you to say. She's not your mother."

Kelsey held the gaze for a long, uncomfortable moment, then sighed. "All right. Fair enough. But you know something, Will? I'm the guy who was attacked by his own sister. I may have killed a man to make it out of my own house alive. You're not the only one who's had a rough time today."

Will's anger evaporated. His shoulders sagged. "I'm sorry."

Kelsey shrugged. "It's okay. Look, we need to be thinking about our next step, figure out a plan of action before this special assembly you say your mom told you about."

"I think she was serious about that. You should have seen

her when she was talking about it." Will shuddered at the memory of his mom's rapt, almost aroused expression. "My God, Kelsey. They're really gonna do it. Kill hundreds of teenagers. Our friends."

"Oh, I believe you. I'd believe damn near anything at this point. But we're gonna stop them. Somehow."

"Right." Will swallowed. "Somehow."

Somehow.

The word sounded empty to his ears. Hollow and unconvincing.

Kelsey scratched his chin and looked thoughtful. "Look. We can't stay here all night. Whatever's going on, your parents are involved. Myra's people knew enough to get after us in the first place, so I kinda have to believe somebody will come here sooner or later to check shit out. It'd be a good idea to be gone by then."

Will made a vague sound of assent. He knew Kelsey was right, but he was still having a hard time getting his head around the notion that they had unwittingly uncovered a vast occult conspiracy. It seemed too fantastic, too much like the plot of one of Jake McAllister's lurid novels, to believe. Yet, the proof was all around him. And it was intimidating. How could two high school kids hope to combat forces so powerful?

Will looked Kelsey in the eye. "We are fucked, you know that? We are fucking fucked."

Kelsey chuckled. "I believe that's what Mr. Brennaman would call a 'defeatist attitude.' Hey, we're the good guys. We *can't* lose. It's like we're in a horror movie, right? And in horror movies good always triumphs over evil some kinda way or other." His expression turned uncertain. "Right?"

"No."

Kelsey frowned. "Anyway, that's sort of beside the point. What we've—"

"*The Blair Witch Project*?"

"Huh? What about the fucking *Blair Witch Project*?"

"Evil triumphed, dude."

"Okay, but—"

"*Night of the Living Dead.*"

"That's zombies, man. This is not a living-dead situation."

"But that black dude, the hero, that redneck fuck shot him in the head in the end."

"Again, that's—"

Will had turned pale by now. His hands shook slightly. "*Halloween.* Michael Myers gets shot six fucking times with a .357 Magnum and falls off a balcony. Motherfucker gets up and walks away. The End, fade to black."

Kelsey put a hand to his left temple. He was starting to get a headache. "Right, but—"

"And Jason Voorhees, you can't kill that guy at all. Not permanently. He always comes back. Evil always comes—"

"STOP!"

Will blinked. "Okay."

Kelsey picked up his beer again. "Sorry."

"No, I'm sorry. I think I may be on the verge of a nervous breakdown."

"You and me both, man. Listen, I've got no idea how to solve this clusterfuck we're in, but I may know something. I've detected a pattern."

Will cocked an eyebrow. "Yeah?"

"Yep. It's the women."

"What do you mean?"

"Think about it." Kelsey swigged beer. He started to pace, moving from one end of the kitchen to the other and back again. The beer bottle moved in his hands, punctuating his thoughts. "Imagine a chain. Myra's the lead link, she's the focal point. She's made our boy Trey her slave. Mrs. Cheever is another link in the chain, a conduit of information. What do they both have in common? You guessed it, they're women. Then there's my sister, Melissa. She tried to kill me. Again, she's a woman. To state the fucking obvious. That guy in the hood, I'm not sure what the deal with him is, but he looked like a subordinate. It's the *women.* They're the leaders of this thing, this whatever-it-is, this black magic coven, this satanic club for girls, what-the-fuck-ever. Need more evidence? Look at your mother. After Mrs. Cheever blabbed to her, she set out to kill you. And it's real obvious your dad is just another slave. Maybe if you dig around in his office, you'll find a black hood."

Kelsey ceased pacing. He stood in the middle of the kitchen, facing Will. He needed a moment to catch his breath. Then he said, "So . . . what do you think?"

Will swallowed some beer. "I don't know. This is all so . . . weird."

"And that, ladies and gentlemen, is the understatement of the motherfuckin' century."

Will eyed the half-empty bottle of Warsteiner in his hand. He considered taking another sip, but he set it down without drinking. He was calmer now, thanks in part to the alcohol, but he wanted to keep a clear head.

He looked at Kelsey. "You should slow down on the beer. If more men in black hoods show up, or more demon women, whatever, you don't want to be fucked up."

Kelsey glanced at the almost empty bottled in his hand. "Good point."

He dumped out the rest in the kitchen sink. "Wish I'd thought of that a beer or two back. I'm feeling a little light-headed. Got any soda?"

Will opened the refrigerator, took out two cans of Dr Pepper, and passed one to Kelsey. He popped the tab on his and took a swig. He chugged down half the can.

"Do you think it's all the women in Rockville?" Will asked. "That would mean thousands of them. Shit, they can't *all* be involved. Can they? Every mother? Every sister? Every adult female? Every little girl?"

Kelsey shook his head. "No. Of course not. I don't think so. I mean, that doesn't sound . . . feasible. But let's say there's a large number involved. The fact that both your mother and my sister just happen to be involved in this points to a large-scale operation. I don't believe in coincidence. Still, I'm guessing Myra's followers have to be, at most, in the hundreds, not thousands. And consider this—she's actively disliked by a large percentage of the chicks at Rockville High."

Will found himself nodding along as Kelsey spoke. "Cindy Wells."

Kelsey jabbed a finger at Will. "Yes! Cindy has never been hostile to Myra. But Myra popped her in the jaw. Why? Who the fuck knows? You know what?" He snapped his fingers. "I bet Slater's got a fucking black hood in his office! *That's* why he didn't suspend the cunt!"

Will groaned. "Great. What if Slater's just the tip of the iceberg? I bet other people with authority are involved. Cops, businessmen. Hell, maybe even the mayor."

Kelsey's eyes widened. "Aw, fuck. You were right, man. We are fucking fucked. Maybe we should just phone in a bomb threat to the school tomorrow afternoon and get out of town."

Will didn't say anything for a while. He didn't believe something as simple as a phoned-in bomb threat would do the trick, especially if Slater and other Rockville High administrators were in on the whole mass murder plot thing. He was trying to recall something, a word, some strange name his mother had used before Kelsey showed up. He'd been so frightened at the time it had scarcely registered. Now, for some reason, remembering it seemed vitally important.

Then it came to him: "Lamia."

"Say what?"

"Something my mom said before you showed up: 'Lamia richly rewards willing sacrifices.'" The memory of the exact phrasing made him shiver. "Jesus, that's creepy. Who, or what, the fuck is Lamia?"

Kelsey resumed pacing, but at a more thoughtful pace this time. "My God, maybe that's it."

"The hell are you talking about?"

Kelsey stopped in the middle of the kitchen again. "Say the names, Will. Repeat them, run them together. Lamia, Lamia, Mia, Mia, Myra, Myra . . ."

Will shook his head. "No. They don't really sound alike. That's a big stretch."

"Is it?" Kelsey crushed the empty Dr Pepper can in his hand and retrieved a fresh one from the refrigerator. He popped the tab and chugged. "We're dealing with a cult, right? Every cult needs a figurehead, a leader. Evidence indicates Myra is that leader. Maybe she's a for-real demon, maybe she's not. Maybe the demon acts through her. The name 'Lamia' rings a vague bell. Let's get on your dad's computer and do a Google search, see what we can come up with."

The idea galvanized Will. He finished off his soda and moved toward the archway that led to his dad's office.

Kelsey started to follow his friend, but came to a dead stop in the center of the kitchen. Something stirred within him, raising the hairs on the back of his neck. He sensed a presence behind him, something trying to move without making a sound.

Kelsey saw Will step through the archway.

The presence behind him shuffled closer, not so furtive now.

Kelsey tugged Blake Mackeson's .38 from his waistband. He heard Will shriek, then reappear through the archway, backpedaling and stumbling as something closed in on him. Kelsey's breath caught in his throat. He had a terrible knowledge that he would have to kill again if he wanted to live beyond the next few moments. He gripped the revolver in both hands, whirled around, and pulled the trigger. The big, concussive boom rocked him again, but this time his aim was true. A big, machete-wielding man stood prepared to cleave his head in two. The bullet slammed a hole through the middle of the black hood that obscured the man's identity. The would-be assailant flew backward and crashed into another hooded man. This second man knocked the body of his comrade aside and charged Kelsey. Kelsey stood stock-still, adjusted his aim, and fired again, just as this new attacker tried to decapitate him with a strange double-bladed axe.

Something struck his back.

Will, stumbling into him.

Kelsey spun about, saw that this next attacker was too close, and jabbed the barrel of the gun into the man's stomach. He yanked the trigger twice and watched the man skip backward.

He'd fired the gun four times. Two bullets left. Strike that. Five times. He'd forgotten the shot in Will's room. One goddamn bullet left. He hoped like hell there weren't many more of these hood-wearing motherfuckers skulking about.

Will stared at him, wide-eyed and shaking. "Oh, fuck. Oh, fuck, fuck, FUCK!"

"Calm down. We've got to leave."

Will trilled nervous, high-pitched laughter. "Oh, hell yeah. Let's get moving."

Kelsey shook his head. "Not yet. Follow me."

He led the way through the archway this time, leading with the pistol. They rushed down the short hallway and entered Blake Mackeson's office. Kelsey's stomach flipped at the sight of Will's father, who was still duct-taped to the leather chair. His throat had been slit. The gaping wound looked like a second mouth. Kelsey wrenched his gaze away from the hideous tableau and rushed over to the still-open gun cabinet. He shoved shells into his pockets. Then he opened the .38's cylinder, filled the chambers, and snapped it shut.

He looked at Will.

Will's gaze was riveted to his dead father. He was sobbing.

Kelsey gripped him by the shoulder and stepped in front of him, blocking his view of the dead man. "We're going, Will. This sucks. I know. But we're fucking going."

He tightened his grip on Will's shoulder and turned him around, steering him toward the archway. Another hooded figure surged through the opening.

"Goddammit!"

Kelsey shoved Will aside, took aim, and fired.

And missed.

The bullet punched through the throat of yet another hooded man, but Kelsey didn't see that. He was too consumed with his imminent death. The man he'd missed was fast. And strong. He seized Kelsey's wrist with one hand, twisting the gun away as he swung his other hand around. A big hunting knife sliced through the air on a precise, direct arc toward Kelsey's temple.

But the man's aim faltered.

The air exploded out of him and he bent over at the waist. It took Kelsey a moment to realize that Will had propelled himself headfirst into the man's midsection. Will was on the floor, dazed by the impact. Kelsey touched the .38's barrel to the top of the gasping man's head and pulled the trigger. Blood and brains blew out the back of the man's head as he toppled backward.

Kelsey extended a hand to Will and helped him to his feet. "Move!"

They got out of the office in a hurry and made it through the kitchen without encountering any more of the hooded assassins, then left the slaughterhouse that had been Will's home. As Kelsey fumbled with the keys to his Oldsmobile, the sound of sirens rose in the distance.

"Shit!"

He managed to locate the right key and get the door open. Then he reached across the seat and unlocked the passenger-side door. Will slid into the passenger seat and yanked the door shut. Kelsey got the engine running just as the first flashing lights appeared at the far end of the street. Leaving his headlights off, he put the car in gear and backed out onto the street.

A quick glance in the rearview mirror put the closing cruisers at three blocks away.

He shifted gears again, stomped on the gas pedal, and slipped away under the cover of darkness.

For a while, the only sounds were the hiss of tires on asphalt and the receding sirens.

Kelsey finally exhaled. "Fuck. We got away. I don't believe it."

Then it came—the hitch in Will's breath.

He cradled his face in his hands and sobbed for a long time.

Kelsey kept his mouth shut. No words of comfort could possibly be adequate. He kept his eyes on the road and allowed his friend the opportunity to vent his grief.

CHAPTER TWENTY-FOUR

They watched television. The late news played like a series of reports from the front lines of some new war. It was crazy. All this shocking news coming out of the formerly sleepy community of Rockville, Tennessee. In addition to the police station massacre—a story that had even made the national news—sketchy reports were coming in of yet another mass killing in Rockville, this one in an affluent neighborhood called Oakdale. One channel showed a live scene from a helicopter—police cars and ambulances with flashing lights jammed the street in front of an opulent home.

Trey groaned. "Jesus."

Jake glanced sideways at him. "What's wrong?"

Trey's face twisted with worry. "I know that house. One of my best friends lives there. Will Mackeson. Fuck."

Jake watched the footage of sheet-covered bodies on stretchers being loaded into ambulances with increasing dread. The names of the dead hadn't been released yet, but things didn't look good for Trey's friend. One of the reporters said, "According to a police source, there is no one alive in the residence." The reporter's permed blonde hair shifted minutely in a stiff evening breeze. "Very grim news, indeed, for a town that's already endured so much tragedy this evening."

The brothers flinched when the phone rang. Again. It had been ringing all night, and Jake was tired of answering calls from scoop-hungry reporters. What part of "No comment" didn't these piranhas understand? This time, he stayed where he was. The ringing continued until the answering machine picked up, and yet another reporter left a message and a string of phone numbers.

Jake pushed a button and the television screen went black. He set the remote on an end table and turned to face Trey, whose limp posture made him resemble a rag doll at the other end of the sofa. Trey's eyes were red and his eyelids hovered at half-mast.

"Why don't you go on to bed? You can take Stu's room. Come on." He got to his feet. "I'll show you where everything is. We'll crash and start dealing with all this shit tomorrow."

Trey's posture changed in an instant. He sat up straight and scooted to the edge of the sofa. He stared up at Jake, his eyes wide with a mixture of fear and excitement. "Not yet, okay? I have to tell you some things. You won't believe any of it, but please listen. There's this girl—"

Then some kind of seizure rippled through him, distending his jaw and making his eyes and veins bulge and his body shake. The fit lasted just a moment. All at once, Trey's limbs stopped jerking and awareness returned to his eyes. As he looked at Jake, his eyes were brimming with tears. "She's back!" He gave his head several emphatic shakes and wailed like a baby.

Then he screamed.

Jake was scared shitless. What had he just seen? Trey was too coherent for that to have been an actual seizure. Probably it was just a delayed reaction to all the day's trauma. But was Jake really prepared to care for someone as obviously disturbed as his half brother? He wanted to do it. It felt right to do it. But maybe this was a job for professionals. Maybe the kid should be under observation somewhere for a few days, until his mental condition stabilized. It didn't sound unreasonable, but just thinking it made Jake feel guilty. He had a duty, a solemn obligation, here. He was all the kid had left.

"Trey . . . are you okay?"

Trey sniffled. "Yeah. I'm sorry. I think I'll be all right."

"You sure? You mentioned a girl. Who—"

"Nothing." Trey stood and tried on a smile that looked false. "You shouldn't listen to me right now. You're right. I am tired. I need to sleep."

Jake eyed him suspiciously, but said, "Fine, we'll let it go for now. But tomorrow I want you to tell me about Myra. Okay?"

Trey flinched at the mention of her name. He shrugged. "Okay." His gaze went to the floor, and for a moment his demeanor reminded Jake of the way he'd been at Jolene's house this afternoon. "I guess."

Jake wondered whether he should change his mind about waiting till tomorrow. It was easy to put difficult things off. Too easy. He had a lot of personal experience in that regard. It was one thing to make bad choices in his own life. It used to be, he wasn't hurting anybody but himself if he decided to take a drink. That wasn't the case anymore. Whether he liked it or not, he had responsibilities and he was determined to live up to them. Still, he couldn't see any harm in letting the poor bastard have some rest before being made to deal with the hard stuff.

"Look at me, Trey."

Trey shoved his hands into his pockets and shifted his weight from one foot to the other. Then, as if it took tremendous focus, he raised his head, very slowly, and looked Jake in the eye.

Jake nodded. "Good. You and I are going to talk about some serious things tomorrow, and that includes your girlfriend. Got it?"

Trey shrugged. "Sure."

"Great. Let's go get you settled."

Jake returned to the living room a few minutes later. He was relieved to have his brother out of the way for the rest of the evening. He needed some time to decompress, to finally step down from crisis mode. A beer would hit the spot right about now. He considered going into the kitchen to fetch one, but, instead, he settled into a recliner, aimed the remote at the television, and watched some more of the news.

Two black-and-white photos, probably yearbook pictures, filled the screen. At the bottom of the screen, the words, ARMED AND DANGEROUS. A reporter was speaking: "The suspects are Kelsey Hargrove, age seventeen, and William Mackeson, also age seventeen. Police are advising citizens not to approach the boys, but to call police immediately if they are sighted."

"Fuck." Jake was very glad that Trey wasn't awake to see this. "The world has gone insane."

The latest revelation turned his thoughts again to alcohol. Alcohol was good in these situations. It eliminated problems by blotting them from consciousness. The effect was temporary, of course, but that rarely swayed him. He imagined the taste of cold beer filling his mouth, and the shivery sensation of anticipated pleasure almost sent him to the kitchen to fetch a bottle.

But he stayed where he was. He stared some more at the television. The sensational coverage brought to mind previous tragedies, the mass killings at Columbine and Virginia Tech, and he was struck by how surreal it was to have a personal connection to one of these televised real-life dramas. And he thought some more about his responsibilities to Trey. For the first time since arriving in Rockville, he allowed himself to think about the year of sobriety he'd flushed down the drain. He thought of AA meetings. He remembered reciting the Serenity Prayer while holding hands in a circle. And he recalled the new sense of confidence and peace that had come into his life during that year.

Gone, now.

The most important accomplishment of his adult life and he'd trashed it, surrendering himself to the darkness again with hardly a struggle.

Two days had elapsed.

Two drops in a very large bucket.

Nothing, really.

He could reverse the damage. He could get back on track.

He was sober, *right now,* and he could stay that way if he so chose. If he had the strength.

He heard a door slam somewhere in the house, then a jangle of keys, and he turned toward the kitchen.

"I'm home!"

Jake smiled.

Kristen.

Just knowing she was here made him feel better. He looked forward to holding her again. To kissing her. To, yes, making love with her. He felt a twinge of guilt, but this time it had little power. There was nothing wrong with the way she made him feel. Nothing wrong at all with how much he desired her. Not really. They'd known each other only a very short time, true, but the intense, instant chemistry between them rendered that meaningless. And Kristen was right. There was nothing wrong in giving yourself over to passion. And losing yourself in a new romance was certainly a better way to escape reality than booze.

He called out to her: "I'm in the living room!"

She came into the room through the archway behind him. The faint whiff of perfume that preceded her intensified his desire for her. She leaned over the recliner, kissed his cheek, and said, "I missed you."

Jake smiled. "I missed you, too."

Kristen's mouth went to his ear. Her warm breath felt good on his skin. "I have a present for you."

Jake turned to look at her, his smile growing wider. "Yeah?"

There was a hint of mischief in her smile. She placed a beer can in his hand, popping the tab for him. "I made it just for you." She laughed.

Jake's smile stayed frozen in place a moment, then it slowly faded. He eyed the can with the wariness of a soldier preparing to pull the pin on a grenade for the first time. He opened his mouth, intending to tell her he didn't feel like drinking tonight, that he was too tired. A lame excuse, yes. A way of biding time. Jake recognized this as slippery-slope thinking, a strong indication that his newfound conviction wasn't really a conviction at all—it was just a fleeting, insubstantial fancy, an illusion of strength. It was ludicrous, really. His whole life served as a vivid illustration of how little mental toughness he possessed.

He closed his mouth without saying anything.

Kristen slid into the recliner with him, slipping an arm around his neck and curling her legs up on his lap. There was another open can of beer in her left hand. She took a swig from it, seemed to savor the beer a moment, then swallowed it with a sound of pleasure. She smiled. "What do you say we get drunk and screw all night?"

Jake managed a strained chuckle. "To paraphrase Jimmy Buffet, that great American poet."

Kristen giggled and swallowed some more beer. "Let's waste away again in Rockville!"

Jake looked into her dark eyes and immediately felt again that erotic hunger that had been there before. He ran a hand through her raven black hair. "You are so beautiful, Kristen."

She rolled her eyes. "Gee, haven't heard that one before."

His fingertips glided along her delicate jawline. "You're like something out of a dream. Like something that can't be real. An angel come to life."

Her expression grew more solemn. She drew in a deep breath and let it out slowly. "Wow." She spoke in an awed whisper, and there was a glimmer of moisture in her eyes. "That's the most beautiful thing anyone's ever said to me." Her face darkened a little. "Please tell me that's not a rehearsed speech you give every girl."

"No. It's just for you."

"Jake . . ."

"Yes?"

She shook her head. "Nothing."

She kissed him. Jake wouldn't have thought it possible, but this clinch was more intense, more passionate, than every previous kiss they'd shared. The pleasure seemed to touch every nerve ending in his body. He knew he could lose himself in this girl. Completely. Forever.

Kristen broke the kiss off and knocked back another swallow of beer. She disengaged herself from Jake and got to her feet. She stood before him and finished off her beer. "Drink." The word was a command, not a request. "Drink, then ravage me."

She laughed.

Jake looked at the beer can he was holding. He had almost forgotten about it. He looked again at Kristen, who was unbuttoning her blouse. She tugged the blouse open, and his heart raced a little at the sight of the smooth, flat expanse of her belly. Then his gaze went to her full breasts, displayed to devastating effect in a pretty, frilly black bra. She shot a pointed glance at his still-full beer, then pooched out her lower lip and pouted. "Don't you want me, Jake?"

Jake swallowed thickly. "Yes."

The beer can came to his mouth. He turned it up, and his throat bobbed several times as he swallowed the can's entire contents.

Kristen's pout became a smile. "Good boy." She crooked a finger at him. "Now, get over here."

Jake put the empty can down and shakily got to his feet.

Kristen pulled him into an embrace. She bit his lower lip and drew it into her mouth for a moment. "Mmm." She dipped a hand into his jeans, gripped his growing erection. She made a sound like a growl low in her throat. "I've waited long enough." Her upper lip curled in a way that made Jake shiver. "And now I'm gonna eat you alive."

Outside, a crow was perched on a windowsill.

It studied Kristen's unsubtle seduction of Jake through a blind slat bent crooked.

After a time, it flapped its wings, rose away from the house, and flew into the night.

CHAPTER TWENTY-FIVE

"I want to kill her."

Zack Bishop, Rockville High's starting quarterback and prom king, set down the issue of *Maxim* he'd been reading and looked at his girlfriend. "You shouldn't talk that way, Cin. People might think you're serious, then you'd be in even more trouble."

Cindy Wells stood in front of the mirror above Zack's desk, regarding with disgust the imperfect image reflected there. The bandage affixed to her nose marred an otherwise flawless countenance. She had a beautiful face. A model's face, as so many had told her, with high cheekbones, big blue eyes, a graceful jawline, and imminently kissable lips. Until this morning, her nose had been perfect. Narrow and graceful. Now it was a bent, broken thing, a boxer's nose.

The rest of her still looked wonderful. Her clothes, a sleeveless, lime green top and a sleek miniskirt, showed off her svelte body to stunning effect. She had a long, slender neck (which her mother variously described as "swanlike" or "like Audrey Hepburn"), long, shapely legs, and a perfectly contoured figure. All topped off by a flowing mane of lustrous blonde hair. She'd been the school's reigning beauty.

But not anymore.

Now I'm a beast, she thought.

Until now, Cindy had never considered herself shallow.

She was self-aware enough to know she was exceptionally beautiful, but she'd accepted this as a simple fact of her existence, an asset, certainly, but not a thing that elevated her above other people. She took more pride in her intelligence and academic achievements. Her GPA was a rock-solid 4.0. She was gifted in math and science. She also had a passion for literature, and she'd displayed talent as a writer of fiction. She had long been torn between, on the one hand, accepting a scholarship at a school renowned for its science programs and, on the other hand, attending a school known for producing accomplished artists and writers.

None of these things mattered at the moment.

She applied the tip of a finger to her damaged nose and winced. Her upper lip curled, further marring the image of beauty. Anger flared inside her again. And the real thing, not just teenage petulance. Raw, burning fury. She imagined her hands wrapped around Myra Lewis's scrawny neck and she clenched her fists. She could almost feel that fragile flesh collapsing beneath the force of her righteous wrath. This frightened her, mostly because giving herself over to anger was such a new and strange thing for her, but she was close to embracing it.

She glanced at the stacks of *Maxim* magazines next to Zack's bed. She'd always regarded the beautiful, busty women on the covers with a mixture of pity and disgust. Women who displayed their bodies for profit, whether they were Parisian supermodels or porno "actresses," were little better than whores. Or so Cindy had always believed.

Beauty is power, she thought.

The truth of it struck her hard. Her looks *had* made her special. They *had* made her better than all the other girls. And they had granted her some degree of power over nearly everyone she had ever encountered. Extra-special emphasis on the past tense, however, because fucking Myra Lewis had ruined much of that power with one blow.

She turned away from the mirror. "I mean it." She stalked

over to the bed and stood glaring down at Zack. "I want to kill the bitch."

Zack frowned. "You're scaring me a little, Cin." He sat up, clasped hands with Cindy, and drew her near. He sighed. "This isn't easy to say, but . . . look, I know you told me you didn't provoke Myra in any way, and I want to believe you, but it just doesn't make any sense. I can't believe you'd get a suspension for no good reason."

Cindy fumed. It took all her willpower not to strike Zack. "What are you accusing me of, Zack? Are you saying I'm a liar?"

Zack flinched. "No. I'm just . . . well, not exactly."

"What!?"

Zack swallowed a lump in his throat. Cindy thought she saw fear in his eyes. A part of her, she was stunned to discover, enjoyed seeing it. It made her feel powerful again. It was particularly gratifying that the man in question was Rockville High's king stud. She wondered how he'd react to a backhand across the face. The thought stunned her—but only for a moment.

And Zack sensed the hostility. He let go of her hands and scooted backward on the bed, putting some distance between them. "Jesus, Cin, relax. Obviously I'm not calling you a liar." He shrugged, and looked at her with a helpless expression. "Maybe . . . I'm sorry, I know I'm not saying this right. But maybe you offended her in some way you don't know about. Some offhanded comment she took to heart, maybe."

Cindy sneered. "Are you fucking serious? You dick. You're calling me thoughtless."

"No, I'm not." Zack seemed to become a little more sure of himself. "And I'm really about done talking about this. You're in some weird kind of denial, Cin. I think you did say something to that girl, maybe something really out of character for you, something mean. And maybe you feel so guilty about it you can't acknowledge the truth. Christ, Cindy, girls like you don't get suspended without a really good reason. And now this crazy talk about wanting to kill Myra. It scares me." His voice had grown solemn. "I think we shouldn't see each other for a few days. Just until you've had some time to really think and deal with all this."

Cindy gaped at him, unable to believe what she'd just heard. Sudden tears welled in her eyes. "Zack, no . . ."

He looked away from her. "I'm sorry, Cindy. But it has to be this way. Please leave. Now."

Cindy's anger surged back to the surface, burning through her tears and setting her hand in motion before she knew what she was doing. Her palm smacked hard across Zack's jaw, snapping his head to the side and leaving him dazed long enough for her to continue the assault. She picked up the magazine he'd discarded, rolled it up tight, and battered him about the head with it until he at last managed to snatch it away from her and seize her by the wrists.

"What's wrong with you!?" he screamed.

Cindy struggled in his grip. She ached to strike him again. Slapping him had felt good, but it hadn't been enough. Swatting him around with the magazine had felt even better, but even that had fallen short of completely satisfying. The terror and confusion in his bugged-out eyes sent a pleasurable shudder through her. This new urge to do violence was intoxicating.

No . . . that wasn't quite the real truth of it.

Hell, she thought, *it turned me on.*

Her nipples had stiffened. And she was wet *down there*.

She recognized this reaction as wrong and probably crazy, but she didn't care.

She *loved* it.

She thrashed against Zack and eventually managed to wrest one hand free. Her thumb and middle finger went to his eyes and began to press. Zack yelped and leaped away from her. He picked up one of his athletic trophies and brandished it like a club. "You stay away from me, you crazy bitch!"

Cindy got off the bed, clasped her hands behind her back, and began to move toward him, rolling her hips and arching her back so that her breasts jutted. "Come on, Za-cky baby. You're not afraid of little ol' me?" She laughed. "Are you?"

Zack's expression was grim. "Don't take another step. I'll bash your brains in, I swear to God."

Cindy shook her head in mock disappointment. "Look at you. A big, strong boy like you waving that trophy thingy at me. Don't you bench-press two or three times my weight, Zack? What could I do to you?"

Zack took a step backward. His back met the wall. "You're a fucking psycho. What an actress you are, Cindy. I can't be-lieve I never saw how completely fucking nuts you are." His voice grew hoarse with emotion. "I loved you. Please . . . don't make me hurt you. Please stay back."

Cindy eyed the trophy. She smiled. "I don't think you could do it. You're too much of a good guy to really hit a girl with that thing. Oh, you'd want to, if I really came at you, but you wouldn't. You'd hesitate." Her smile broadened. "Yes, you'd hesitate, and I'd be digging your eyes out before you could do anything."

Zack was shaking now. His grip on the trophy was slip-ping. He looked defeated, like a beaten, broken thing. Big, bad Zack. King stud.

King pussy, more like.

Cindy giggled at the thought.

Zack scooted sideways down the wall, getting into position to bolt toward the door. But his gaze never wavered from Cindy. "Stay away from me."

Cindy licked her lips. "You really are pitiful. But you don't need to run, baby. I'm leaving. I'm gonna go find a more chal-lenging foe. Myra Lewis. And I'm really gonna do it, Zack. I'm gonna kill the cunt."

Zack's horrified expression almost made her laugh again. She shrugged. "C'est la vie, baby. I'm leaving now." Her eyes twinkled with mischief. "Who knows? Maybe we'll meet again. Soon."

Then she left his room and descended the stairs to the first floor. Zack's mother, a pleasant-looking woman with short, permed hair, greeted her with a smile in the foyer. "Leaving so soon, dear?"

Cindy's own smile was just as pleasant.

So Lizzie Bishop was likely shocked when her favorite son's golden goddess of a girlfriend slugged her hard in the stomach. The blow expelled the air from her lungs and made her double over. Cindy pounded a fist against the crown of the woman's skull, sending her to her knees. She lingered over the woman a moment, contemplating ways to inflict further damage.

Then the logical part of her mind reasserted itself for a moment. The fragile thing that had masqueraded as her conscience was gone forever, utterly destroyed. But her self-preservation instinct remained intact. She shouldn't have assaulted Zack's mother. Not because there was anything wrong with what she'd done (Cindy was quickly reassessing all her previously held notions of right and wrong), but because the woman might call the police to report the attack.

Cindy heard footsteps behind her.

Then a horrified screech.

"Oh my God! What have you done?"

Zack brushed by her and knelt next to his stricken mother. The woman was sobbing. She was curled up in a ball on the floor, hugging herself and shaking.

"Mom? Mom, are you okay?"

Cindy cast her gaze about the foyer. She spied something that might be useful, then glanced down at mother and son.

Zack glared up at her. "You crazy bitch! You were wrong, Cindy. I will fight back. You've gone too far."

He started to rise.

Cindy drove the toe of a high-heeled shoe into his stomach, sending him back to the floor. Then she swept past Zack and his mother, grabbed the pruning shears Lizzie Bishop had set aside upon returning from her garden, and pounced on Zack. She buried the blades in his throat and felt a more intense ripple of the same pleasure she'd experienced in Zack's room moments ago.

She punched the blades into his body again and again, dozens of times.

On and on, ripping his body to shreds long after he had died.

Then she turned her attention to Lizzie Bishop, who hadn't moved.

The woman was smiling through her tears.

"My sacrifice." She palmed some tears away and kept smiling. "I'm so happy."

Cindy gaped at the woman. What she had done felt right. It was insane, she recognized that, but it felt right. Nothing had ever felt so right. Her entire life as she'd known it—along with all her extravagant plans for the future—was over. Something new, something breathtakingly, unexpectedly better had come along.

It was incredible, a startling revelation, an epiphany. Nothing should surprise her now.

But this—well, frankly the woman's attitude was shocking.

Cindy had just butchered her son before her eyes.

And she was . . . happy?

It didn't make sense.

"What the hell's the matter with you, you fucking old hag?"

Lizzie Bishop's smile still radiated unabashed joy. "I should've known all along. You're special. You're one of her chosen ones."

Cindy shook her head. "Chosen ones? Who are you talking about?"

Lizzie seemed surprised. "Why, Lamia, of course."

"I don't know who the fuck that is."

"You will, dear."

"You know something? Don't call me 'dear,' okay? I've always hated that."

Cindy disengaged herself from Zack's ruined body. She straddled Lizzie and flexed the blades. She leered at the woman. "Are you ready for this?"

She wanted to see terror steal into the woman's eyes, but

there was no fear there. Lizzie was still smiling. "I've never been so ready. Not for anything."

Cindy frowned. "Stop that shit. You're freaking me out."

She went to work with the blades one more time.

Then she stood up and surveyed the carnage. The formerly immaculate foyer was awash in crimson. The lifeless bodies at her feet possessed a grisly beauty. She felt a strange kind of pride. She had snuffed them. The work of her own hands had splashed all this blood around.

She felt powerful again.

More than that—she'd never felt so good in her life.

And she shivered with delight at the knowledge that there was still one more thing that could make her feel even better—Myra Lewis dead at her feet.

The cunt's face reappeared in her mind.

Cindy grinned.

"Here I come, bitch, ready or not."

She opened the front door and stepped outside.

Then froze.

Myra Lewis was sitting on a white wicker chair on the porch, one leg curled beneath her as she nonchalantly smoked a clove cigarette. She looked at Cindy and smiled. "Hello, darling." She glanced at the bloody shears and expelled a cloud of pungent smoke. "I see you've been busy."

Cindy snarled and raised the shears high over her head. A delirious sensation of purest ecstasy swirled inside her. Her fondest wish was about to come true. And the stupid bitch was just sitting there, waiting for it. As if she didn't have a care in the world.

I'll fix that, Cindy thought. And pounced.

Or, rather, she *tried* to pounce.

She couldn't move. Something had reached inside her and paralyzed her. She saw the flicker of amusement in Myra's eyes and knew at once the bitch had done it. The sense of power she'd so reveled in moments ago was gone. Terror now welled inside her. She wanted to cry. Because whatever else Myra Lewis might be, one thing was clear—she wasn't human.

Myra flicked the cigarette away. She unfolded the leg tucked beneath her and scooted to the edge of the chair. "You don't need to be afraid, Cindy." Her voice was low and earnest. And a strange thing happened—Cindy believed her. "I had a hunch about you. I thought I could provoke some interesting things." She smiled and shot a glance at the open door behind Cindy. "Turns out I was right. I want you to join me, Cindy. I want you to help me kill them all. Will you do that?"

Cindy felt some of the paralysis slip away. Her legs remained frozen, but her upper body was under her own control again. The shears slipped from her hands and landed with a clatter on the porch.

"Yes." She sniffled. "I think I want that more than anything."

Myra smiled again. "Good. A change is coming, Cindy. A storm. Soon Rockville will be a ghost town. You're going to kill a lot of people for me."

Hot tears spilled down Cindy's cheeks. "Thank you. Oh, thank you . . ."

"But now I need you to do something else for me first." Myra's eyes gleamed, and there was a new intensity in her voice. "A symbol of your subservience and devotion to me."

Cindy's legs prickled with a pins-and-needles sensation. Her body was fully under her control again. "What do you want me to do?"

A corner of Myra's mouth twitched. "I want you to come to me on your hands and knees. And then I want you to kiss my feet."

Only moments earlier the prospect of such a thing would have made Cindy sick. But now there was only pleasure and the desire to prove herself worthy to Myra. Before she could even consciously decide to obey, she felt her bare knees touch the cold concrete surface of the porch. Then she leaned forward and placed the palms of her hands on the concrete.

"Come to me," Myra said.

"Yes, Lamia."

Cindy almost frowned.

CHAPTER TWENTY-SIX

Jordan burped.

She put a hand over her stomach and groaned. "I don't think I can eat any more Todd."

Bridget put down the length of fried intestine she'd been nibbling on. "Yeah, I've kinda had my fill of him, too."

Angela belched.

All three of the women seated around Todd's kitchen table laughed. Jordan glanced down at the beach ball–shaped monster that had nuzzled against her ankles throughout the meal. It looked up at her with its leering pumpkinlike eyes. She dropped a Todd morsel and the creature snatched it out of the air with its tongue.

Bridget grinned. "I think you've made a friend."

"I think you're right," Jordan said.

Bridget reached across the table to stroke the back of Jordan's hand. "It's nice to see you getting into the spirit of things. The idea of cannibalism makes most people kind of, well . . . uptight."

Angela giggled.

"Now that you've explained about Lamia, I feel a lot better about things," Jordan said. "I can see why you thought I wouldn't fit in with you guys, but you were wrong."

"Hmm. Do you really think so?" Bridget bent one of Jordan's fingers backward, just enough to hurt. "I still don't think you're fit for anything other than slave duty." She smiled. "Tell me, why do you think I'm wrong?"

Bridget pushed Jordan's finger backward some more. Jordan gritted her teeth, but she didn't cry out. Nor did she attempt to yank her hand away. She'd already learned the price of resisting Bridget's various tortures. Her hair was still a bit damp from the multiple toilet-bowl dunkings, and her back was raw from the belt-lashing she'd endured prior to that. Oh, they had been very cruel. But Jordan wouldn't have expected anything less from such sadists. Yet, she had survived this much. It couldn't get much worse. Or so she hoped.

Her smile wavered a bit, but she managed to reinforce it. "The way I see it, Lamia is all about female empowerment. She's the ultimate feminist. Knowing what you know about me, you should see how perfectly her objectives mesh with my ideals."

Angela snickered. "You don't understand anything at all."

Jordan tried to sound hurt. "Oh?"

Bridget nodded. "She's right, Jordan. Yes, women assume the leadership roles within Lamia's ring of power. Lamia sees that as the natural order of things. But the *really* important thing for all of us is the glorification of Lamia. She's a deity, you know. A goddess. A divine being. All-powerful. And in the end, even the women of Rockville must fall at her feet and praise her."

Jordan frowned. "Look, I believe you. Given what I've seen, that's a no-brainer."

Angela brayed more of that idiot laughter Jordan so hated. "Like Todd. He's a *real* no-brainer now. We ate 'em up, yum yum." She made a lip-smacking sound. "Mmm, brains . . ."

Jordan rolled her eyes, but otherwise ignored the interruption. "Okay, Lamia's a goddess. Granted. We've established that. What I don't understand, though, is the need for this . . . what did you call it?"

Bridget said, "The Harvest of Souls."

"Yeah, that."

Something subtle but significant changed in Bridget's expression. And when she spoke next her tone was more serious than before. "It's simple. Lamia derives energy, power, from souls. Yes, by the way, the soul is a real thing. Every human, every dog, every cat, every insect, every microorganism possesses one. Obviously, the soul-energy in, say, your average locust is negligible. But Lamia doesn't bother absorbing the souls of the lower creatures. It would be a waste of her time. She has other uses for animals. Human beings, however, are loaded with soul-energy. Lamia can subsist on a handful of souls for years at a time. However, every hundred years or so a harvest must occur. What it does for her is hard to explain in human terms. You could compare it to recharging a car's battery, I guess. But for Lamia one recharge will take her through another century."

During this speech, Bridget had relinquished her grip on Jordan's finger. Jordan folded her hands in her lap. "I guess I can buy that." She glanced again at the beach ball creature. "I guess at this point I can buy anything." She met Bridget's gaze again. "But I don't understand why a truly divine being would need a recharging."

Angela made a disgusted sound and sneered. "Why are we bothering explaining this shit to this bitch? We should just kill her skinny ass." The sneer became a smile. "I'm still hungry. I bet her eyeballs would be tasty fried up in a skillet."

Bridget smiled "There's more interesting things to do with Jordan than kill her." She picked at the remaining morsels on her plate for another moment before setting her fork down again. She looked at Jordan. "I don't think any of us ever truly understand divine beings, not even chosen ones like me."

"Chosen ones?"

"Those personally selected by Lamia to carry out the Harvest."

Jordan felt a chill go through her. "You mean . . ."

Bridget nodded. There was a very intent look in her eyes. A deeply disturbing *eagerness*. "Yes. Chosen ones do the actual killing. There's a very complicated energy-transference process. Well, you'll see how it works at the Harvest."

"And that happens when?"

"Very soon. At Rockville High School."

"Why there?"

Bridget rolled her eyes. "Isn't it obvious? It's true that Lamia derives substantial energy from any human soul she takes, but the souls of the very young contain the most raw energy. A teenager's soul is the equivalent of spiritual crack or Ecstasy." She shrugged. "I don't know which analogy is more accurate, but that's my basic understanding of it."

"So why can't I join the club? Why are you a chosen one?"

Bridget sighed. "You can't join the club because you're not from here. Lamia chose this place as the site of the next Harvest long ago. And since then all women born in Rockville have been by birth members of her inner circle, whether they know it or not." She giggled. "And in fact, they very often *don't* know it, not awakening to their true nature until late in adolescence. I was an early bloomer. I began to sense my connection with the goddess even before I entered puberty. Anyway, that's why no amount of pleading on your part can get you into the club. It doesn't matter that you're trying to get on our good side to find a way out of this. Even if I believed you were a true convert, it wouldn't matter. Lamia wouldn't have you."

Jordan's brow furrowed. "Doesn't this goddess ever bend her own rules? If I could somehow prove myself to her, maybe she'd make an exception for me."

Bridget shrugged. "Doubt it. But who knows, stranger things have happened. Anyway, you'll get a chance to ask her yourself. You'll be meeting her soon."

Jordan didn't say anything. The revelation was unexpected and shocking. Before, the goddess had existed to her only as a concept, an intellectual puzzle to figure out. She hadn't considered, even for a moment, the possibility of an actual encounter with the flesh-and-blood manifestation of this supposed deity. Thinking about it made her heart race and her breath grow shallow. If she couldn't make these two bimbos believe she was sincere, she didn't stand a chance of convincing Lamia.

She cast her gaze about the kitchen surreptitiously, moving her eyes without moving her head as she searched for weapons. There was a large—and bloody—carving knife on a chopping block on the counter. Angela had used it to chop lengths of intestine. Jordan recalled the image of the glistening viscera, a long, wet rope of it coiled on the chopping block, and felt her stomach rumble.

Angela's eyes narrowed. "Why is she staring at that knife?"

Bridget raised an eyebrow. "Yeah, Jordan. Why *are* you staring at that knife?" She laughed. "Tell you what, we'll make a contest of it."

Jordan's heart skipped a beat and she felt a tightness in her chest. "What are you talking about?"

"I know you have a low opinion of my intelligence, Jordy-poo," Bridget said, "but you should know better by now. You know I'm not the ditzy bimbo I pretend to be. You're so transparent." She giggled again. "You're easier to read than a best-selling novel. What I'm saying is, you'll never make it in Hollywood."

Angela laughed. "She's no Meryl Streep."

"Marisa Tomei is Meryl Streep compared to this hag-in-training."

Angela snorted. "That one-fluke wonder. Hell, that's nothing. You ever see Paris Hilton in *House of Wax*? That's some Juilliard School of the Arts shit compared to Jordan."

Jordan felt something cold and hard settle within her. "You know what, fuck both of you."

Bridget gave her a mock pout. "Oh, you'd love to fuck me. We're already aware of that."

Jordan wanted to lash back at Bridget, but the pure truth of the matter was she was right. She bit her lip and said nothing.

Bridget grinned. "Now about that contest."

Jordan eyed her warily. "Yeah?"

Bridget leaned across the table and leered at her. "It's really more of a race. Here's the deal. We'll have Angela here count to three. On three, you and I make a dash for the knife. Get there first, you get to live. Get there last, you get to hurt. Sound fair?"

"No."

"Why not?"

Jordan glanced at Angela. "Because I'm outnumbered. Even if I got there first, this cunt would come after me."

Bridget shrugged. "Yeah, maybe. But it's the only chance you've got. Ready to start the countdown?"

Jordan's heart was racing. She looked at the knife. She looked at Bridget, felt her mouth go dry at the look of almost feral anticipation she saw there. "No. Please. It doesn't have to be this way." She felt moisture well in her eyes. "Look, I'm sorry. I don't want to die."

Bridget leaned even closer. Her eyes sparkled prettily beneath the ceiling light. "You weren't listening like you should. I said, 'Get there last, you get to hurt.' I didn't say a thing about dying. When I get my hands on that big-ass knife, I'll have Angela hold you still while I cut on you for a while. But I'm not gonna kill you."

Jordan swallowed thickly. "Why not?"

"It's like I told you. You have a meeting with Lamia in your future. And you'll need to be alive for that." Her smile then radiated sheer madness. Seeing it made Jordan want to curl up in a ball in a dark corner somewhere. "At least for a little while."

Jordan was shaking. Her breath hitched. A sob worked its way out of her throat, followed quickly by a moan of despair. A part of her felt shamed by this display. She should show some courage, or at least stoicism, in the face of this awful development. Anything to dampen the sadistic glee they were deriving from this.

But she simply couldn't help it. She didn't want to die. Not like this. With no one who loved her around to help ease the transition into eternal darkness. With no goddamn dignity at all. "Please . . . please . . . I don't want to die. . ."

Bridget and Angela laughed in unison.

Jordan dabbed tears from her eyes. "Can't either of you see how insane this is? Don't either of you have a shred of human decency left? Why would you want to participate in this . . . this . . . *evil*?"

Bridget smiled. "Aside from being born into it, you mean?" She shrugged. "Frankly, I get off on it."

"Ditto like a motherfucker," Angela said.

Jordan groaned. "God . . ."

Bridget's tongue darted out, slowly traced the length of her lower lip. "Mmm. To be honest, I just love the way being all evil and shit makes me feel. All hot and bothered, you know?"

A visible ripple of pleasure went through Angela. "Fuck, I'm getting all horny just thinking about it. I sure hope we get to kill somebody else tonight."

Bridget said, "I think you can count on it. And speaking of counting, you should start."

Jordan sat up straighter in her chair. "Wait!"

Bridget shook her head. "No more waiting."

Angela said, "One . . ."

Bridget pushed her chair away from the table and scooted to its edge. "This is gonna be so much fun. You ready to start hurting again, Jordy-poo?"

"Two . . ."

Jordan looked at the knife.

Any moment now, Angela would utter the final number.

Jordan leaped out of her chair, seized the knife, and whirled around to face her tormentors.

She smiled at their identical thunderstruck expressions.

Angela smacked the table with her palm and glared at Jordan accusingly. "No fair!"

Relishing the feel of the word in her mouth, Jordan said, "Three."

CHAPTER TWENTY-SEVEN

The first thing Stu Walker was aware of upon regaining consciousness was the strange medicinal taste in his mouth. He couldn't identify it, but a powerful chemical smell clogged his nostrils, too.

Chloroform?

At first blush, the very thought of it was crazy. It made him think of scenes from movies. Guy walking down a street, some black-clad guys pop a white cloth over his mouth, and the poor bastard gets shoved into the back of a black limo. Maybe he's a superspy, maybe James Bond himself, and he'll wind up outwitting his abductors. Or maybe he's just some guy in over his head, a gambler in debt up to his eyeballs. Guy like that, you'll never see him again. He'll end up chained to a cinder block at the bottom of a lake or buried beneath the goalpost at a football stadium. Anyone could conjure up a thousand similar scenarios with ease. Because it was so cliche. Any casual observer of popular culture had seen countless variations on it.

So it was ridiculous, really.

But.

Maybe it wasn't.

Maybe chloroform or some other chemical agent had been used to knock him out. The smell and the sore-throat tickle at the back of his throat made it hard to deny. But there was a bigger question to consider. Who would do this? He thought about it and hit a brick wall. He didn't have any real enemies, certainly no one who hated him enough to do something like this. The whole situation just didn't make any sense. Well, whatever was going on, he had been out like a light for hours. He knew that by the darkness visible through the bedroom window.

He was in the master bedroom of the spacious lakeside cabin Lorelei's parents owned. The room was dark, the only light courtesy of a single candle on the nightstand to his right. Its light revealed little of the room. He could see the nightstand, the bed's gleaming brass headboard, and the window. The darkness was deeper at the other end of the room. He could just make out the shadowy outline of the bedroom's open door. He sensed movement in the hallway beyond, motion defined by changing shades of darkness. He wondered who was out there, what kind of predator might have invaded the remote cabin, and that made him think of Lorelei.

My God, what have they done to her?

He pictured her as he'd last seen her, nude save for her stylish stiletto-heel boots, sprawled invitingly across the plush white rug spread in front of the fireplace. The image was the last thing he remembered. He marveled at the stealth of the intruder (or had there been more than one of the bastards?). He couldn't recall any sense of danger. And he usually noticed such things. That ability to suss out danger—and to know when a tense situation was tilting toward violence—had served him well as a barkeep. Not many barroom brawls went down on his watch. But he couldn't remember anything like that. There'd been no creak of the hardwood floor, no shadow falling over him, no warm breath tickling the hairs at the back of his neck.

There'd only been Lorelei.

Then the smell.

Followed by the long, dreamless void of unconsciousness.

His breath caught in his throat as he heard a click of heels on the hardwood floor. Something was moving through the deep darkness at the other end of the room, gaining definition as it approached, taking on a familiar form.

A smile trembled around the corners of Stu's mouth; then he let out a gasp of relief. "Lorelei. You're alive."

He tried to rise as she approached the bed, but the ropes binding him to the headboard held him in place. He'd been so weak—and so groggy—that he'd been unaware they were there. He turned his wrists a bit, testing the bonds. There was no give to them at all. Someone had done an expert job of securing him to the bed.

Lorelei stood over him now. "Hello, Stu."

"I'm so glad to see you." Stu coughed. He felt lousy. Nauseated. The medicinal taste made him feel sick, like he was on the verge of coming down with the flu. He craved a cold beer to flush the taste away. "I was so afraid they'd done something horrible to you."

Lorelei laughed. "It's yourself you should be worried about."

Stu frowned. "What? Why? They must have left, right? Otherwise you wouldn't be in here. I don't know why they didn't finish us off, but I'm so grateful they weren't killers. But they might come back. You never know. You need to find a knife, a sharp one, and cut these ropes off me."

Lorelei didn't answer.

Stu looked at her with a mixture of awe, love, and sudden fear. She was as beautiful as she'd been all those years ago. Her perfect, trim body was as toned as it had been in their high school days. It was as if the last decade had melted away. They were back together, as they'd been destined to be all along. How empty his heart had been during all those wasted years. He'd never stopped wanting her, and, like a miracle, she was his again. But maybe not. Because she was behaving very strangely. And it made no sense that ruthless home invaders would leave her alive and unbound. A quick study of her nude, and very lovely, body revealed no marks or damage of any kind.

"Lorelei . . . what's going on here?"

She smiled. "I'm doing my duty. This is my sacrifice. My way of honoring the goddess. I do love you, Stu. But I love Lamia more."

Stu coughed again. "I . . . I don't know what you're talking about."

Lorelei's smile broadened. "Of course you don't, baby. And you don't need to. And I'm sorry, but the worse it is for you, the greater my eventual reward will be."

Stu's head was swimming. He felt like he was in a dream. He knew now Lorelei meant to harm him. Probably kill him. And as bad as that was—he definitely didn't want to die—the inability to understand what was going on here was even worse. He wanted to know *why* this was happening. Maybe she had lost her mind at some point during their years apart. That must be it. It was the only thing that could explain the nonsense talk about "sacrifice" and "honoring the goddess." And as he considered the likelihood of Lorelei's madness, the terror that had taken root within grew exponentially. His heart slammed in his chest and his eyes filled with tears. He had so much left he wanted to do in life.

It couldn't end like this. So soon and unexpectedly.

It wasn't fair.

Lorelei knelt and lifted a black plastic garbage bag off the floor. She flashed a smile disturbing in its gleefulness and dumped the bag's contents on the bed next to him. Stu lifted his head and saw a funnel affixed to a length of vacuum hose, a roll of duct tape, a knife, and a bottle of extra-strength Drano.

He let out a whimper and showed Lorelei a beseeching look. "No . . . nonono . . . you can't."

Lorelei laughed. "Oh, but I can."

Tears spilled in hot streams down Stu's face. "No. Jesus . . . no . . ."

Lorelei's eyes turned hard. "It's Lamia you should be praying to, Stu."

She picked up the length of vacuum hose and shoved it through his wide-open mouth, killing a burgeoning sob. Stu's eyes went wide and he tried to push the hose out of his mouth with his tongue. But Lorelei climbed atop him and planted a knee on his chest, then used her leverage to shove the hose deeper down his throat. He gagged and coughed, and the rapid slamming of his heart sounded like thunder in his ears. Through it all, Lorelei laughed.

She wrapped several layers of duct tape around his head to better secure the hose.

Then she used the knife to cut him.

The cutting went on for a seeming eternity. Lorelei licked his wounds and painted her body with his blood.

The pain was immense. Staggering. All of existence was pain, it seemed. And yet, it afforded him a small measure of peace, because he knew it couldn't get any worse than this.

But he was wrong.

Lorelei picked up the Drano and slowly twisted the cap off the bottle, savoring the agony and helplessness in his expression.

She smiled. "Bottoms up, baby."

She picked up the funnel and began to pour.

And for Stu, things got a lot worse for a little while.

Then he was gone.

CHAPTER TWENTY-EIGHT

There was something strange about the rat in the corner of Jolene McAllister's jail cell. Her cell was one of eight at the Rockville police station, and tonight she was the township's lone prisoner. She'd been grateful for the solitude in the beginning. She wanted to be away from people, away from the reality of the royal mess she'd made of her life. Here in this cell, removed from the detectives and their endless questions, she'd experienced a strange kind of peace. She could close her eyes and pretend she was in her own bed in her own home. The cot in her cell was a good deal less comfortable than her own bed, so it took a bit of imagination.

But she managed.

And she even succeeded in slipping into a blissful, dreamless sleep for a time. Until she heard the chittering of the rodent. The sound drew her back to grim reality. She heard the rodent scuttling across the floor of the cell, and the fleeting sense of peace she'd known deserted her. She was in *jail*. She was *alone*. And there was nothing at all she could do about it. She was going to spend the rest of her life behind bars. Never again would she see Trey, her best-loved son. The long-dreamed-of pilgrimage to Memphis, the city where she was born, would never occur. Her days of determining the course of her own life had come to an abrupt, irrevocable halt. The stark prospect sent her tumbling into depression, and she began to imagine ways she might kill herself.

Then her gaze went to the corner and she saw the rat for the first time.

Shit.

That's no motherfucking rat.

Jolene's mind whirled and her vision went blurry for a moment. The thing in the corner was an impossibility. So this could only be a dream. Except that the uncomfortably thin mattress upon which she lay felt exceedingly real. She could feel every ache in her old and creaky joints.

Her vision cleared and she risked a peek at the corner again.

Still there.

Fuck.

There were a lot of things wrong here. Scratch that. A lot of things *weird* here. And not just the central mind-fuck threatening to explode what remained of her sanity. For one thing, she shouldn't have been able to see the thing in the corner at all. The corridor lights were off, rendering her cell and the others as dark as the inside of a coffin. Yet she could see the thing. Its eyes glowed like tiny specks of yellow neon, and the dim light allowed her to see the hazy outline of its little body.

Jolene whimpered. "Go away! You're not real!"

The creature waddled closer and now she could no longer deny the reality of what she was seeing. Nor could she pretend her mind was playing tricks on her. The thing was definitely not a rat. And the sounds emanating from its tiny mouth weren't rodent sounds. The thing on the floor was her husband, somehow reduced to rat size. He was trying to talk to her, but he was too small for his words to be intelligible from this distance. Jolene would have to get down on the floor, put her ear down close to his shrunken body, to hear what he wanted to tell her—but she had no intention of doing that.

Her mind again rebelled against the idea that Tiny Hal was real. Jolene was a junior high dropout, but she wasn't completely stupid. She thought she had a pretty firm handle on what things were possible in the real world. What she was seeing now just wasn't possible.

And yet . . .

The thing that could not be continued to stumble toward her cot. As it drew closer, Jolene was able to make out finer details, including evidence of her own handiwork, the ragged stumps where she'd cut off his fingers and cauterized the open wounds with an acetylene torch. And she could see the terror in his eyes. He was gesturing wildly and opening his mouth wide to scream at her.

Jolene closed her eyes. "This is a dream. A nightmare. I'm going to wake up now."

Just because this felt real didn't mean it was. She'd had dreams like that before. Some far worse than this. Real doozies, like the recurring one in which a masked serial killer chased her endlessly through a dark forest. The killer would inevitably close the gap between them, getting close enough to reach out to her with a gloved hand—and then she'd wake up with a gasp, drenched in sweat, her heart pounding. The serial killer dream always seemed so real—the danger, the rough forest floor beneath her bare feet—and so it seemed safe to dismiss this episode as mental silliness, a case of her mind weaving her tragedy into a kind of dark farce. Very vivid and compelling, but a farce nonetheless.

Jolene began to drift toward unconsciousness. She spoke again, a groggy but defiant jab at the darkness: "People don't shrink. I'm not crazy."

A sound close to her ear snapped her awake.

She glanced down and saw her diminutive husband attempting to climb up one of the cot's metal legs. Jolene's eyes went wide and she let out a yelp. Hal cringed. Her shrill shriek seemed to overwhelm his little ears, probably sounding to him like feedback from a wall of amplifiers at a rock concert.

Jolene acted without thinking.

She snatched Hal off the cot leg, sat up, and swung her legs over the edge of the cot. Hal struggled in her grip and almost got loose, but Jolene tightened her fingers around him. Maybe a bit more tightly than was necessary. Hal's face turned red.

He struggled to draw in breath. Jolene eased the pressure slightly. Hal immediately began trying to speak to her again, but she still couldn't make out what he was saying.

"Oh, just shut up!"

She'd intentionally pitched her voice at a high level, smirking as it achieved the desired effect. Hal's fat face crinkled, and he surely would have cupped his mutilated hands over his ears had he been able to work them free of Jolene's grasp.

Jolene smiled.

"Well, shit, I guess this is real." She gave Hal a slight squeeze, delighting at the way the small amount of pressure made his eyes bug out. "Have to say I like you better this way, you fat sack of fucking ugly-ass shit. You're easier to handle at pocket size. Although you were pretty damn manageable out in that shed. That was a good time. You know what, though? This has some real nice possibilities." She nodded. "Yeah. I think I like this even better."

Hal tried to speak again.

Jolene made a tsk-tsk noise and pinched the sides of his head with the thumb and forefinger of her other hand. "Didn't I tell you to shut up? I think you might want to obey me, you fucking cocksucker. Unless you want your fat little head squished, I mean."

Hal's mouth slammed shut.

Jolene examined the visible parts of his little body with interest, marveling at the minuscule eyes, nose, and mouth. She turned him slightly to see where she'd sliced off one of his ears. She laughed. "Jesus jacked-up Christ on a cracker, this is a fuckin' trip." She cast a glance up at the invisible ceiling in the darkness before returning her gaze to little Hal. "I reckon somebody upstairs must like me. I couldn't have asked for a better present." She shook her head. "Though I gotta say the way your eyes are glowin' like that is a mite creepy." She shuddered before smiling again. "You listen to me, shit stain. I'm gonna put you up to my ear, and you're gonna tell me how this happened? Got it?"

Hal nodded.

Before she could do that a sound came from outside the cell. It was a metallic sound. A lock turning. Then the corridor lights came on and she heard footsteps clicking down the concrete floor. And voices. A flash of panic sizzled through Jolene. The very strange thing that had happened to her husband still freaked her out, but she did not want to give him up. The opportunity to torture him again, in new and previously unimagined ways, was a dream come true. It was a gift. A beautiful gift from someone, some god the nature of which she couldn't fathom. And she would not be robbed of it. She considered ducking under the covers again and pretending to be asleep.

But there was no time.

It was a short corridor. Her visitors would be at her cell in seconds. So she leaned back against the cold wall adjacent to the cot, turned on her side, and pushed the hand holding Hal under her pillow.

The footsteps came to a stop outside her cell.

Then Myra Lewis was staring in at her with a strange, knowing smile, her thin lips stretched so thin they looked as if they might snap like rubber bands. With her was a plain-clothes police detective and the officer on duty. The detective said something to the officer, who inserted a key into the cell's lock, turned it, and threw the door open.

Myra muttered something Jolene couldn't hear.

The detective nodded and the cops departed.

Myra strutted into the cell. She looked as she always did, like an insolent, sneering, rebellious teenager. She was wearing a studded leather jacket, a midriff-exposing black Misfits T-shirt, and tight leather pants. The sight of her filled Jolene with revulsion. The girl looked every bit the corrupting tramp she'd described to her skeptical older son. The little cunt was the realization of her worst nightmares, a harlot who would be the ruination of her perfect, angelic Trey, who had been the one and only good thing in her life for so many years.

Jolene shook with hatred. "What the fuck are *you* doing here?"

"I've come to fetch you."

Of all the things Jolene might have expected to hear, this hadn't been among them. "Fetch me? What am I, a fucking dog? You gonna throw me a stick? Make me do some fuckin' tricks? The fuck are you talking about, whore?"

Myra chuckled. "Let me ask you a question or two, Jolene." She came several steps closer to Jolene, with the ease that comes from supreme confidence. Jolene gulped. She wished she could slip through the wall behind her back, just step through it like a ghost. The need to be away from Myra was sudden and intense.

There was something . . . wrong . . . something *very* wrong with her baby's girlfriend, something she sensed on a primal level. It was palpable, rolling off her like Louisiana swamp stink. Her eyes watered and she began to feel nauseated. How had she never sensed this wrongness before?

Myra was standing over her now.

She smiled again. "Do you like my present?"

"What?"

Myra rolled her eyes. "Oh, don't play dumb. Wait. You are dumb. Still, brains aren't everything." She looked Jolene over, appraising her in a slow, frank way that made the fine hairs at the back of her neck tingle. "Hmm, not a bad little body for an aging piece of white trash. It's much as I remember it."

Jolene's confusion deepened. "Remember? What the fuck kind of sick-ass game are you playing here? Why'd those cop bastards let you in here?"

Myra reached into a jacket pocket, brought out a pack of cloves and a Zippo. She sparked up and blew smoke at Jolene. "I own them. Like I own practically everyone else in this town. Now let me ask you another question—do you remember the time you got down and dirty with Moira Flanagan?"

Jolene gaped at the girl. Her heart seemed to stop for a long moment. Her mouth opened, moved as if to form words, but no sounds emerged.

How could the bitch know about that?

Fuck, it was impossible.

Nobody knew about that.

Myra exhaled another stream of pungent smoke. "I remember, Jolene. Because I was there."

Jolene scowled. "Bullshit. You couldn't have been no more than a baby."

Myra smiled. "I remember how surprised you were when I showed up at your door alone that day." She licked her lips and her eyes shone with a mischievous gleam. "And I remember how easy it was to seduce you. Later you told me how much it turned you on to fuck your son's girlfriend."

Jolene's mouth continued to work, but she still couldn't speak.

Myra flicked the half-smoked clove away. "But enough of Memory Lane. Let's get back to the matter at hand." She giggled. "In your hand, that is."

Jolene at last was able to push a few halting words through her numb lips. "You . . . you're not her. Moira's dead. You . . . look nothing like her."

Myra's face contorted with sudden anger and her voice boomed out in the cell: "ENOUGH!"

Jolene cringed and whimpered. That voice. Holy Mother of God. No human voice could ever be that loud. What was she really dealing with here? She couldn't begin to guess. She recognized then how helpless she was. Terror burned in her guts like acid. "Please . . ."

Myra's features smoothed out. An almost serene smile touched the corners of her mouth. "You don't need to be afraid. Now about your husband . . ."

Jolene sniffed. "My . . . husband?"

"You know, the abusive asshole clutched in your grubby little fist."

Jolene felt Hal squirm in her loosened grip and clenched her fingers tighter around him. "That was . . . you?"

Myra nodded. "Yes. I did that. It's my goodwill gesture to you. It's not the kind of thing I can do too often. Too much of an energy drain this close to the Harvest. But I think it was worth it in this case."

Jolene shuddered. "What do you want from me?"

"Now we're getting somewhere." Myra sat down next to Jolene, draping an arm over her shoulders. "As you've seen, I've got a lot of power. I can do amazing things to people. I can make most of them do whatever I want them to do. Some people, though . . . well, let's just say I sometimes find it useful to find alternate ways of manipulating them. Let me ask you another question."

"Okay."

Myra started stroking Jolene's hair. "Would you say your son Jake is an ungrateful little piece of shit?"

"Yes. Yes, I certainly would." Jolene nodded.

"Good. I can see you and I are on the same page now."

Jolene closed her eyes and savored the feel of Myra's fingers gliding through her hair. All of her previous anger and fear dissipated. She'd badly misjudged this girl. Something about her touch made all the bad feelings go away. She shivered when Myra's fingertips brushed the back of her neck. A little erotic tingle went through her. It felt nice. More than that, it felt . . . familiar.

Myra leaned close and whispered into her ear. "I'm getting you out of here, Jolene. In more ways than one, I'll be your liberator. But I'll be expecting a favor in return. There'll come a time when I'll ask you to help me hurt Jake."

Myra's other hand settled on Jolene's knee.

The girl's breath was nice and warm on her earlobe. "Will you help me with that, Jolene?"

"Yes. I'll do anything you ask," Jolene sighed.

Myra smiled. "Of course you will."

She gave Jolene's knee a squeeze, then got to her feet.

She held out a hand and Jolene let the girl pull her off the cot.

Then, arm in arm, they walked out of the jail.

CHAPTER TWENTY-NINE

Bridget's gaze was riveted to the knife in Jordan's hand. "You cheated."

Jordan sneered. "Think I give a shit?"

Bridget smiled. "Guess not. The concept of fair play's for chumps anyway. Should have done it myself."

Jordan glanced back and forth between Angela and Bridget. Though possession of the knife gave her a theoretic advantage over them, her elation didn't last long. The other women possessed amazing, unnatural strength. She wasn't at all certain she could win against either of them, unarmed or not.

Against the two of them working in tandem . . .

She shivered.

"Look, she's getting scared," Angela said with a chuckle.

Bridget locked eyes with Jordan. Jordan's throat felt thick and her heart fluttered. "I see that. She'll pee herself any second now."

Jordan's expression hardened. "Shut up." She brandished the knife in a general way. "Keep your fucking mouths shut. You think I won't use this? Okay, maybe I am scared, but I'll do whatever I have to do to get out of this."

Bridget covered her mouth. She looked as if she were attempting to suppress hysterical laughter. But Jordan knew the truth—the bitch was just mocking her again. Bridget's hand came away from her mouth and she laughed heartily. "You're so cute, Jordan. You with that knife, so big in your scrawny little hand. You're a child playing at grown-up games." She licked her lips. "So it's time to start treating you like a child. You've been extra naughty. So I'll be bending you over my knee for a spanking in a minute."

Angela leered. "Oooh, now you're just turning her on."

Bridget giggled.

"Go. To. Hell," Jordan seethed.

The mirth vanished from Bridget's face at once. Her expression now was cold and unforgiving. "I'm tired of indulging your pathetic rebellion." She glanced at Angela. "Get the bitch." She looked at Jordan. "Now."

Jordan gasped and took an unconscious step backward. She waved the knife again. "Stay back!"

Angela rose from her chair, stretching to her full height, which was just an inch or so shy of six feet. She cut a very impressive figure, with long, lean legs, a flat, concave stomach, and toned and gleaming muscles. She was the sort of woman people had in mind when they used the term "Amazonian." She stood still for a moment, smiling softly and holding Jordan's gaze, intimidating the smaller woman with her physicality. Then she began to approach Jordan, slowly, with a slight sway to her hips.

Jordan was unable to suppress a whimper. The hand holding the knife shook visibly. She was sure it would tumble to the floor any moment. "Stop." Her voice was a hoarse, desperate whisper. "Stay right there."

Angela just kept coming.

"I'm about to take that knife away from you, little girl." There was something hungry in her expression. Something eager. "And I'm gonna put it in a real uncomfortable place."

Jordan's body was close to betraying her. Her knees were shaking and the world around her had become soft-focus. The floor felt slippery beneath her, almost insubstantial, as if it could swallow her like quicksand. She felt unspeakably weak, like a failing wisp of a thing, barely alive.

Angela said, "Why don't you save us both some trouble?

You know you won't be able to do anything to me. Don't embarrass yourself. Hell, you're almost down for the count already." She was within a few feet of Jordan now. She held out her hand. "Just hand it over."

Jordan's grip tightened on the knife. She bit her lip hard, and some of her strength and focus came back. Just enough, as it turned out. Animal instinct drove what happened next—she slashed at the extended hand, and the sharp blade cut a deep trail across Angela's open palm. Angela shrieked as blood gushed out of the wound.

Bridget said, "Shit."

Jordan pressed her new advantage, moving in to slash at Angela again. The blade opened a deep cut just below the woman's collarbone. She stumbled backward, blood pouring over her breasts. Her eyes were wide with pain and fear. A part of Jordan thrilled at the sight of it, a savage, primal piece of her psyche she had never been in touch with before. It scared her, but she also knew she needed to embrace it to have any hope of getting out of this place alive.

Angela was holding her hands up for protection.

A torrent of words spilled through her trembling lips, panic-driven cries for mercy.

Jordan loved it.

Reveled in it.

The big, bad bitch was *begging*.

Jordan slashed her with the knife again, a strike that went deep into the meaty part of a forearm. She had to dig the blade out. Angela screamed some more and staggered backward. Then there was a loud squeal, the source of which wasn't immediately apparent to Jordan. Then Angela tumbled over something and landed hard on the linoleum. The squeal came again, and Jordan saw that Angela had tripped over the beach ball creature. The thing that had been described to her as one of Lamia's "minions" opened its wide mouth and displayed rows of sharp, jagged teeth.

Then it took a chunk out of Angela's left calf.

Angela spasmed on the floor, kicking her leg in a desperate

attempt to dislodge the creature, which again chomped down on her leg.

Bridget shot up out of her chair. "Stop!"

Angela tried to rise, but Jordan kicked her in the stomach. Driven again by that savage, unforgiving part of her psyche, she dropped to her knees next to the fallen woman, raised the knife high above her head, and slammed it down. The blade punched through Angela's chest wall, impaling her heart and stopping it cold.

Jordan watched the life fade from her vanquished foe's eyes.

A shudder of revulsion made her stomach lurch. The knife slipped from her hand. She pitched forward, her open palms slapping against the floor. Then it came, an awful tide of bile that filled the back of her throat before exploding out of her wide-open mouth. Fluid mixed with partially digested pieces of Todd splattered against the linoleum. The sight of the vile remains of her neighbor made her stomach heave again, and her entire body spasmed as she sprayed more vomit on the floor.

She became aware of a presence close to her. Bridget. The knowledge should have frightened her. She had to defend herself. She knew it, but for the moment she was incapable of doing anything about it. She was shaking harder than ever, her body beyond her control. That sick weakness returned, engulfing her. Sweat bloomed on her brow and a chill swept through her. She ached all over. She was so miserable she didn't give a damn what happened to her.

She even prayed for her own death.

She turned her head a little to the right, glimpsed Angela's lifeless, sliced-up body, and experienced another ripple of nausea, but this time it was a less violent dry heave. There was nothing left to throw up. Her eyes filled with tears again. She'd only meant to defend herself. What the hell had possessed her?

Bridget knelt next to her and placed a hand on her back.

Jordan's breath caught in her throat.

Bridget stroked her, a soothing, sensual touch.

"That . . . feels nice," Jordan said.

"Mmm." Bridget's hand moved up between her shoulder blades. "Let me guess. Something came over you. You didn't feel like yourself. But it felt *good*."

Jordan shuddered again. She sat up slowly and allowed the other woman to embrace her. "How . . . how did you know?"

Bridget smiled. "You felt the touch of the goddess. She was inside you."

"But . . . how? You said—"

Bridget shushed her with a finger across her lips. "Never mind all that. I was wrong. Wrong about everything." She smiled ruefully and shook her head. "This will sound nuts to you, but hear me out. I think there's some things about yourself, about your origin, that you know nothing about. You've been lied to about your early life, I imagine."

"But—"

"Relax." Bridget touched her face, stroked her cheek. "Think about it. What's your earliest memory? How much of your childhood do you really remember?"

Jordan scowled, shook her head in disbelief. "What the hell are you saying? I had a perfectly normal childhood." But now she was thinking about it. A strange feeling came over her. Her scowl became a frown. It was odd, but she never thought much about her preadolescent years. She tried to cast her mind back to that time, but all that came to her were murky, dreamlike images. It was like a kind of mental block. "Well, this is . . . listen, just because I can't remember anything . . ."

Bridget's smile was full of sympathy. "It's okay. You don't need to be afraid. I can help you with this. Guide you. I can show you the truth."

Jordan shrugged out of the embrace. "Why are you suddenly being so nice to me?"

Bridget's smile didn't waver. "There's been one wild motherfucker of a paradigm shift, that's all." Her expression became more contemplative, but she seemed no less serene. "I hated you until a few moments ago. Not for any good reason. That's just the kind of bitch I am. I'm as close to the goddess

as any mortal can be. I think I have a special relationship with
her. But the reality is that I'm just a mortal. I can't know
every facet of her grand design. I can only perceive or understand portions of it. You were a part I didn't understand." She
hesitated, and a flicker of unease was apparent in her eyes.
"Until now . . . I guess."

Jordan's expression was a study in confusion. "Oh, give me
a fucking break, Bridget. I've had enough of this insanity. I'm
not a part of anything to do with your fucking goddess."

"But you are." Bridget reached out to her, clasped hands
with her. "Here's what I do know. You are Lamia's daughter.
Sired by a human man. She told us you were out there. That
one day you would return and become aware of your true nature, and that you would join us in the glory of the Harvest.
You should embrace this gift, Jordan. Allow yourself to know
the joy that is your birthright. You're a half-breed, darling. Part
divine, part human."

Jordan snorted. "Bullshit."

Bridget squeezed her hand. "It's okay if you don't believe.
Trust me, this is hard for me, too. I guess I sort of hoped I
might turn out to be the one." Her expression turned strangely
shy, very unlike the Bridget she knew. Her laughter was more
than a bit nervous. "I fantasized about it, envisioned this great
cosmic awakening. And it even would have made sense. Once
upon a time Lamia masqueraded as my older sister, Moira.
Alas, it was not to be."

Jordan couldn't stop shaking her head. "No, no, no. This is
ridiculous. Deities don't procreate with humans."

Bridget brushed long strands of golden blonde hair from
her face. "You're proof to the contrary."

"Look, even if Lamia had a daughter, how could you know
I'm the one?" Jordan laughed without humor. "I was trying to
stay alive, so you'll have to offer more proof than . . . what I did
to Angela."

Bridget's expression changed again, her sky blue eyes projecting total confidence now. "When you were attacking her,
you . . . well, you . . . *changed.*"

"What do you mean?"

"Your face . . . it changed. Morphed." Bridget's tone was a mixture of fear and awe. "Your face became her face. You and the goddess are inextricably, uniquely linked. Like I said, she told us about you. Not about your human identity, but about your existence. And she said your true nature would be revealed to us one day, in this very way." A shiver rippled through her. "And there's more. So much more. Wondrous things, Jordan."

Jordan's heart was beating fast. "What are you talking about?"

Bridget shook her head. "Some things are not for me to reveal. You'll know more when you meet your mother." She smiled. "Your *real* mother."

Jordan frowned. "Fuck this. I don't believe any of it. It's crazy. And if that goddess of yours is really my mother, and if she's so fucking omnipotent, why did she let you and your bitch friend torment me so?"

Bridget's eyes betrayed a deepening fear. She shivered. "I think I know. I . . ."

Jordan clamped a hand around Bridget's jaw, forced the girl to look her in the eye. She saw terror in her expression. The real thing. Pure and vibrant. The kind even the best actress could never fake. And despite her doubts, Jordan became aware of a new strength thrumming within her. She moved her hand to Bridget's throat, felt the life pulsing there, felt how easy it would be to snuff it.

"Tell me." Her voice was hard. "Now."

Bridget's jaw quivered as she struggled to speak. "I . . . I suspect she wanted this to happen. She . . . must have wanted us to goad you to a breaking point, to where you'd feel compelled to defend yourself, to . . . kill."

Jordan rose to her feet. No trace of her former weakness remained. She felt strong. Powerful. Invincible. Like some kind of fucking superwoman. It was amazing. And though it made her mind reel, she now knew Bridget was telling the truth. She felt it down to her DNA. Glaring down at her former adversary, she felt a resurgence of what she'd felt just before Angela's death.

Bridget cowered at her feet. "Please . . ."

"WHY, Bridget?" Jordan was screaming now. "WHY WOULD SHE WANT THAT!?"

Bridget sobbed. "I don't . . . know. Part of a process, a . . . transformation . . . maybe. I don't really know. There's nothing more I can tell you. Please believe me."

"YOU'RE LYING!"

Bridget's face was streaked with tears. "No . . . I swear . . ."

"I ought to kill you."

Bridget bowed her head. "If . . . if that's what you want." Her body quaked with the force of her fear. "I submit to you as I would your mother."

Jordan thought about it. She wouldn't even need the knife. She could snap Bridget's neck as easily as she'd snap a twig. Or punch through her chest wall and rip out her still-beating heart. The knowledge was exhilarating—and terrifying. She felt a strange and unnatural energy pulsing within her, something dormant come to full, screaming life, and she felt a strong urge to revel in it. Yet, a part of her was repulsed by it. This was the voice of her conscience, she supposed.

Yes.

Her mother was a goddess, which meant she had some aspect of the deity within her. But she was of the human world, as well. Her humanity had shaped her, not that secret touch of the divine. She had a soul. A *conscience*.

Her body relaxed. She let out a deep breath. "I'm not going to kill you."

Bridget looked up at her. "You're not?"

Jordan shook her head. "And I'm not killing anyone else, either. You can tell my mother that when you see her. Neither is she. I'm going to find a way to stop this massacre she has planned."

Bridget gaped at her. "But that's impossible."

Jordan smiled. "You're wrong. This time, you're really wrong."

Jordan found the clothes that had been forcibly removed from her hours earlier. She put them on and left the apartment without another word. Lamia's minions tensed at the sight of her as she emerged onto the landing. They sensed the change within her, felt the power flowing through her, and they parted as she walked down the stairs, allowing her passage as she brushed past them.

Jordan stood in the parking lot and stared up at the clear night sky.

Her smile was a cold, almost dead thing, her voice quiet but hard. "I'm coming for you, Mother. And there's nothing you can do about it."

A dark cloud passed over the silver moon.

And somewhere far away, a scream resonated in the night.

CHAPTER THIRTY

Jake awoke feeling sick. The glare of the sun through the open mini-blind slats didn't help things. Nor did the blare of AC/DC's "Highway To Hell" coming from the living room stereo. The CD apparently had been left on repeat play mode all night, and though the speakers were in another room, the sound was loud enough to make the hangover ache behind his eyes throb mercilessly. With a groan, he rolled onto his back and covered his eyes with a forearm. He stretched out his legs, kicking a crumpled beer can over the edge of the bed. The vague bad feeling that was always there after a night of hard drinking arrived on cue, and he couldn't help thinking there was something seriously wrong, something he couldn't remember.

There'd been a lot of sex. He remembered that much. The kind of sweaty, alcohol-fueled sex that goes on seemingly forever. And there'd been a great deal of drinking.

Kristen, it turned out, was no casual drinker. She matched him drink for drink throughout the night, eventually revealing that this kind of binging was a regular thing for her. He thought it odd she hadn't mentioned this when he'd told her of his struggles with alcoholism, but she shrugged it off when he pushed her about it. She didn't see the omission as a big deal. But Jake wasn't so sure. At times, she seemed to play on his weakness for booze, manipulating his emotions by plying him with drink and offering up the endless temptations of her body.

In the harsh light of this new day, she didn't seem quite so wonderful anymore. He felt anger—both at himself and at Kristen—as he reflected on the events of the previous day. So much of it seemed unreal now, like a half-remembered dream. Their instant, mutual obsession made him wince with embarrassment. It was probably unhealthy.

Jake sighed.

There was just one conclusion to draw—he would have to break off this thing with Kristen before it went any deeper, before they could do any more damage to each other's psyches. And though he recognized this as true, the reality of it hit him hard. He would do what he had to do, but you don't go through something that intense with a person and not feel pain at the prospect of its demise.

The AC/DC CD was abruptly shut off by someone in the living room.

A short moment later he heard his name: "Jake?"

For the first time, Jake realized Kristen wasn't in bed with him. He drew his forearm away from his eyes and saw her standing in the open doorway. She was wearing one of his shirts like a dress, her face looked slightly puffy, and her hair was rumpled, but she looked as beautiful as ever. He felt another pang of regret as he looked at her, a pang so strong it took him a moment to look beyond her beauty and see the distress on her face.

He sat up fast. "What's wrong?"

For some reason, his first thought was that something bad had happened with Trey. But that was ridiculous. His brother had spent the night right here, safely sacked out in the guest bedroom. There was nothing to worry about. He was just being paranoid. But he couldn't help that. Not after all that had happened. He felt dizzy for a moment, as the rest of yesterday's madness came rushing back. His mother in jail, Trey suddenly in his custody. The police station murders. Thinking of the traumas his brother had endured made his own troubles seem trivial. And now he dreaded the next words out of Kristen's mouth, fearing what fresh hell they might bring.

She looked away. He could tell there was something she didn't want to say. Not good. Not fucking good at all. Jake's paranoia approached redline status. His breath caught in his throat. He wanted to scream at her to spit it out already. But then she walked over to the bed, sat down, and clasped his hands.

She cleared her throat and took a deep breath. She hesitated one last awful moment, then finally made herself say it: "Your mother is out of jail."

Jake gasped. "What?" He shook his head. "How the hell did she make bail?"

Kristen's strained smile was awful. There was no humor in it. "She didn't. All charges against her were dropped."

"You're kidding."

"No."

Jake didn't say anything else for a while. The revelation was so far out of the realm of reason that he just couldn't believe it. It was yet another in a seemingly endless succession of psychological wallops. He'd chalked up yesterday's extreme weirdness to the stars being aligned in a once-in-a-billion-years superbad-mojo configuration that dumped a decade's worth of grief on him in one day. Which was ludicrous, but he couldn't think of a rational explaination for the endless shit parade his life had become.

Kristen slowly exhaled a deeply held breath. "That's not all."

Jake eyed her warily and steeled himself for another blow. "I don't think I can take any more drama, Kristen."

Kristen sighed. "I'm sorry. I wish I didn't have to say it. But . . . Trey's gone."

Jake had a sick feeling, a queasy sense of tumbling helplessly down a steep, bottomless hill. He had a shameful, brief impulse to pack up his stuff, get in his car, and put several hundred miles between himself and Rockville. He dismissed the idea right away. An irresponsible act like that was a relic of his past, a self-destructive option no longer open to him. He had to take care of Trey. It was his duty. Nothing else mattered as much.

His grip tightened around Kristen's hands. "Do you have any idea where he went? Was he gone when you woke up?"

Kristen nodded. "I went into the kitchen to make us some breakfast. I turned on the news and heard the story about your mother. There was a note attached to the refrigerator. Jake, he—" She hesitated.

"Just say it."

"Jake . . . he's gone back to your mother. He says you should leave him alone, that everything yesterday was just a big mistake."

Jake's eyes went wide with disbelief. "A 'big mistake'? What the fuck is wrong with him?"

Kristen winced. "Jake, don't bark at me. None of this is my fault."

Bullshit.

She had gotten him loaded. Fucked him. Distracted him. If he had been sober—if he had been paying attention—this wouldn't have happened. Trey would still be safe.

Again, there was that urge to scream at her.

She seemed to sense the building rage within him. Her jaw quivered and she appeared to be on the verge of crying.

He counted to ten, forced himself to calm down a little.

He wasn't being fair. He could not lay the blame for anything solely at her feet—or at all. This was another of the things he was supposed to have left behind. Blaming others for things that were his own damn fault. He'd allowed himself to be distracted. And, ultimately, it'd been *his* choice to drink last night.

His expression softened. "I'm sorry, Kristen. You're right."

He swung his legs over the edge of the bed, found his jeans, and began to pull them on. He got to his feet, hopping until the jeans were up around his waist. He scooped a shirt off the floor, pulled it over his head, and sat down again to put on his shoes and socks.

"You're not going over there," Kristen said.

It was a statement, but it sounded like a question—with a note of pleading in it. "I damn well am going over there. He's my brother. That woman, my worthless fucking mother, is a psychopath. A sadist."

He stood up and snatched his keys off the nightstand. He looked down at Kristen, who was still on the bed, her legs curled beneath her and a worried look on her face. "No way am I letting him stay with her. I'll drag him out of there if I have to."

Kristen had a worried look in her eyes. Jake thought he knew what was coming, but let her say it anyway. "I guess I understand why you want to do this. Hell, I'd probably want to do the same in your shoes. But you're not looking at this rationally. He's there of his own free will. You might get in trouble, real legal trouble, for something like this."

Jake nodded. She was right. He knew he was rushing headlong into probable disaster. But knowing this on an intellectual level changed nothing. "I've gotta go, Kristen."

"I'm going with you."

"Kristen—"

She bounced off the bed, found her own jeans, and stepped into them. "Don't even start, Jake. I'm part of your life now. I want to be there for you."

Jake watched her for several moments without speaking. He was surprised by her resoluteness. They would be entering hostile territory today. No one was saying it, but there was a remote possibility of violence. Yet she seemed utterly unafraid. Also, that "part of your life" stuff bothered him. The sensible thing to do would be to disabuse her of such notions right now.

She smiled.

And Jake sighed, knowing he didn't have the heart to go there yet. "Okay. Let's get going."

They left the house and drove across town to the Zone, Jake exceeding the speed limit by at least fifteen miles an hour the whole way. Several times he nearly had an accident, Kristen gasping sharply each time.

She shuddered as Jake turned the Camry down a narrow road leading into the Zone and slowed down. "I think I just saw my life flash before my eyes."

Jake smirked. "You were never in danger. You were merely witnessing an expert display of high-speed precision driving. Richard Petty, eat your heart out."

Kristen rolled her eyes. "Right. Precision driving. I confused that with suicidal recklessness. My mistake."

Jake turned the Camry down another narrow road and drove all the way to the end. A sudden attack of shame assailed him as they neared his childhood home. Again, he was struck by the difference between the ramshackle dump at the end of the lane and the much-better-kept lawns and houses of his mother's neighbors. He winced at the sight of the rusted-out old Camaro up on blocks in Jolene McAllister's front yard. The lawn still hadn't been mown. Shards of broken brown glass reflected the early morning sunlight. The place embodied all the worst assumptions of snooty urbanites about white trash slobs living out in the boonies.

Jake parked at the curb. "Well, here we are. Home sweet hell."

Kristen kept her expression neutral as she scanned the trash-strewn yard. "This is . . ."

Jake laughed without humor. "Don't spare my feelings, Kristen. This is a dump. A redneck wasteland. And this is where I come from."

She touched his arm. "I'm sorry."

"Yeah. So am I. Fuck it. Let's go."

They got out of the car and began to stroll across the yard to the front door. Jake kicked a Miller Lite bottle out of his way. It skittered across the lawn and exploded against a stack of mud-encrusted old bricks. "Ninety-nine bottles of beer on the ground, ninety-nine bottles of beer . . ."

Kristen surprised him by picking the tune up: ". . . pick one up, throw it in the trash, ninety-eight bottles of cheap-ass beer on the ground."

Jake surprised himself with a laugh that felt real.

Kristen put a hand on his shoulder as they stepped up onto the porch. "You shouldn't feel so bad about this, Jake. You got out of here. You made something out of yourself."

Jake didn't reply.

He jabbed the doorbell and stepped back.

He heard voices inside the house. Jolene and Trey. Then he heard the lock turn. Jolene pulled the door open and stood behind the still-closed screen door. She wore her usual uniform—low-slung, tight denim cutoffs and a skimpy pink tank top. The grin on her face was new, though. Jake couldn't remember ever seeing his mother look so smug.

She chuckled. "Well, look at this. It's my backstabbing son come to say howdy." She turned to Kristen. "And he's brought his new whore with him." She looked Kristen up and down, licking her lips in a lewd way that made Jake's stomach churn. She caught Jake's sickened expression and her grin broadened. "Aren't you going to congratulate me for beating that bum rap, baby?"

"I'm not your fucking baby," Jake said. "And you ought to be in goddamn jail. Where's my brother?"

Before Jolene could say anything else, a shadowy figure came up behind her. When Trey came into view, Jake was astonished at the difference in him. No trace remained of his former sheepishness. He glared at Jake, his eyes wide and his nostrils flaring. The teenager threw the screen door open and strode outside. He bore down on Jake like a heavyweight champion springing out of his corner at the sound of a bell, making Jake flinch and take a step back.

Trey stopped a few inches shy of Jake, standing chin-to-chin with his older brother. "You're not welcome here, motherfucker. You set my mother up. You tortured my dad and blamed it on her. The police know all about it. They're gonna drag your worthless ass into jail soon." He sneered. "That's if I don't kill you first."

Jake was flabbergasted. He tried to say something, anything, for several moments before giving up. He needed to marshal his thoughts, to regroup. Of all the things he might have expected to hear from Trey—well, this wasn't even on the list.

The best he could manage, finally, was a weak, "What?"

"You heard me." Trey jabbed his chest with a strong forefinger. "Get the hell off our property." He pitched his voice higher and leaned closer to Jake. "NOW!"

Jake blinked. He looked to Kristen for help, but she looked just as flabbergasted. She even looked a little afraid. "Have you lost your fucking mind, Trey? This is bullshit and you know it." He pointed a finger at Jolene. "She's crazy. You know that, too. I don't know what the hell's gone wrong here, or what's happened to sway you to her side, but some part of you must know this isn't right."

Trey's answer came in the form of a fist to the throat that sent Jake tumbling backward. Kristen screamed. The lawn's tall grass cushioned his landing somewhat, but he landed hard nonetheless, the back of his head thumping against the ground. He winced and turned his head to the left, saw a shard of broken green glass inches from his face. He didn't seem to be cut, so he'd lucked out in that regard, but he hurt like hell all over. He gagged and his vision misted. Then he looked up and saw his brother standing over him. Trey's fists were clenched.

"Get up." His voice was flat and hard, betraying only one emotion—pure hatred. "Let's finish this right now."

Kristen knelt over Jake, putting her body between the brothers. She glared up at Trey. "Don't touch him! We're leaving." She put a hand on Jake's face and gazed down at him. "Are you okay?"

Jake drew in a deep breath. His throat still hurt, but at least he was able to breathe again. He gripped Kristen's hand and drew himself to his feet. He looked Trey in the eye. "I don't know what's wrong here, brother, but I'm gonna find out."

Trey scowled. "There's nothing to find out."

"I doubt that."

Jake spun away from his broken family and strode rapidly back across the lawn to his Camry. The world spun and he wobbled some, but he managed to stay upright. Kristen caught up with him, taking him by the hand again as they reached the car. By then he was shaking all over. She pulled him into an embrace and he allowed her to hold him as he fought to get control of himself.

"It's okay," she whispered into his ear. "We'll figure this out. I promise."

Jake nodded.

He looked over her shoulder and saw Jolene standing on the sidewalk with her arm draped around Trey's waist. With her other hand, she waved to Jake. "Bye, baby. Tell that whore of yours to come see my other baby if she ever wants a taste of a real man."

Jake felt another surge of nausea.

Kristen whispered in his ear: "Don't say anything else. This is not the time. You'll only make it worse. Let's get out of here and figure out what to do next."

Unable to bear the sight of his mother's leering face another moment, Jake decided to follow Kristen's advice. He eased out of her embrace and got back inside the Camry. Moments later they were out of the Zone and speeding back toward Washington Heights.

CHAPTER THIRTY-ONE

The name of the place was GUN CITY USA. It was a sort of firearm superstore. A Walmart for hunters and aspiring mass killers. The store offered rifles, shotguns, and sidearms of every make and caliber imaginable. Some of the rifles looked like the kind of thing a motivated sociopath might easily convert into a fully automated killing machine.

Raymond Slater was appalled.

These were the things that had haunted his pre-Lamia nightmares. Every time a story broke about some new school shooting a chill went up his spine. He lived with an ever-present dread that something similar might occur at Rockville High one day. On his worst days, a Columbine-style massacre at his school seemed inevitable, which he realized wasn't entirely rational, and so he'd sought the help of a therapist, who'd dispensed antidepressants and antianxiety meds by the fistful. The pills helped some, but the affair with Penelope had been the real cure for his stress. But now even that was lost to him, though she didn't know that yet.

Because the time had come for Raymond Slater to make a stand.

Following a long night of degradation and humiliation, Penelope had left him to his own devices this morning. That bitch. So smug. So certain he was again a thoroughly cowed man. He knew his place in Lamia's scheme and would perform as required. It was a given. They thought he was a spineless, weak-willed man incapable of rebellion. The threat of torture and death would certainly be enough to keep a cretin like him in line. And if by some remote chance he should develop the testicular fortitude to oppose them, well . . .

Josefina.

Sweet little Jo . . .

Something tugged at his heart at the thought of his daughter's name. His only child. She was all he had left. And they had threatened her. She would die in the slowest and most agonizing manner possible if he attempted to stop today's planned mass murder at Rockville High. This was according to Penelope, who said she was relaying the message on behalf of Lamia. And though Jo was at a college hundreds of miles to the north, Raymond knew this was no empty threat. So he had been forced to weigh the possible loss of his beautiful daughter against the potential loss of hundreds of young lives.

The decision to rebel was the hardest he'd ever been forced to make.

He felt hollow inside.

Desolate.

But he knew this—a man forced to sacrifice so much must do his damnedest to get the job done.

He sucked in a deep breath, exhaled slowly, and turned away from a display of various trinkets emblazoned with NRA-approved slogans. The morbidly obese man in red suspenders behind the register at the checkout counter eyed him with obvious suspicion. Raymond forced his mouth to form something that may have resembled a smile. And he stood there. Still not moving. The big man still watching him, slowly moving a green toothpick from one corner of his mouth to the other. The store was nearly empty this time of day. Raymond had actually been counting on that. But now he was wishing he had come at a busier time. Now he wanted nothing more than to blend in with a crowd. To be anonymous. What if this man was in cahoots with Lamia?

Was he paranoid?

Maybe.

But that didn't mean it wasn't true.

Raymond approached the counter and coughed. "I would like to purchase a firearm."

The man behind the register smirked around his toothpick. "Didn't figure you were here for milk and cookies," the man said in a slow redneck drawl. He removed the toothpick and noisily sucked moisture from the corners of his mouth. "Whatcha lookin' for?"

"Excuse me?"

The man made a sound that might have been a laugh or a grunt of contempt. "What I mean is, do you need something for protection or . . ." He hesitated, smirked. "Or something to hunt with?"

Raymond cleared his throat and stepped closer to the counter. "Hunting."

"No shit."

Raymond leaned over the counter, dropped his voice an octave. "I would like to buy a handgun and some type of shotgun, something with serious stopping power. The best you've got. Price is not an issue."

"Mister, have you ever fired a gun in your life? Because, no offense, but—"

Raymond's face reddened as he bristled at the man's questions. "Is this not a place of business? Do you regularly interrogate potential customers? Because if you don't want my money, I'm sure—"

"Now hold on, don't get yourself all riled up." The big man grinned. "I don't mind takin' your money. Was just curious, is all. Let me show you some stuff."

The big man showed him an array of handguns and shotguns. He spent a lot of time extolling the relative virtues of each piece. Most of the finer points went over Raymond's head. There was something else he'd been thinking about and while he listened to the man talk he tried to work up the nerve to broach the subject.

To his relief, the man went there for him. "'Course, you know there's a waiting period. Federal law."

Raymond struggled to keep his face blank as he said, "I've, uh, heard . . ."

The man grinned, showing him a lot of yellow, uneven teeth. "This here's the South, son. Federal laws are made to be broken, you know that. We can negotiate. I get the feeling you're wanting these here hunting weapons sooner rather than later. Am I right?"

Raymond swallowed hard. "Yes."

"Thought so." The clerk grinned again. "I'll have to sell you something that ain't from official stock. And you'll have to pay cash. A lot of it. That a problem?"

This was a point Raymond had anticipated. He'd fattened his wallet with a thick wad of hundred-dollar bills prior to coming here. "Not at all."

"Good." The man put his fingers in his mouth and whistled loudly. "Roscoe! Cover the register while I talk to this man in back."

A big, bearded behemoth of a man emerged from an aisle and approached the register. He looked like a younger version of the the clerk. Father and son, Raymond had no doubt. "Got it, Pa."

The older man fished a fresh toothpick from his shirt pocket and wedged it in his mouth. "Good boy." He looked at Raymond. "Now let's do some business."

Raymond followed him to the rear of the store, where they stepped through a door, through a room stacked with boxes, and then through another door.

Raymond's jaw dropped. Then he closed his mouth and let out a low whistle. "My God . . ."

The clerk chuckled.

Raymond squinted as he moved deeper into the room. "Jesus . . . is that a . . . a bazooka?"

The man clapped a hand on his shoulder. "That, son, is a shoulder-mounted AT-7 antitank weapon."

"I'll take it."

Some of the gun seller's good humor evaporated. "Ain't

for sale. I may skirt the law a lot of ways, but selling heavy ar-
tillery's a good way to wind up in the slam for a long stretch
of years. Besides, you could be with Al Qaeda or some other
batch of assholes. Nah, that sucker's just for show. But looky
here, I got some good stuff . . ."

Thirty minutes later Raymond Slater exited GUN CITY
USA thousands of dollars poorer and in possession of the
first firearms he'd ever owned, a Glock 9mm and a Mossberg
pump-action shotgun. He'd also purchased several boxes of
ammunition for both weapons. After stowing his booty in the
trunk of the Lexus, he sat behind the wheel of the car for several minutes as he considered what to do next.

He was exhausted. It was possible he wasn't thinking
straight. The night before he'd watched his mistress decapitate his wife while his dick was still inside her. It was the sort
of thing that would unhinge any man. By all rights, he should
be a gibbering, useless mess, but here he was, a man on a mis-
sion. A man with murder on his mind.

So now he asked himself: *Can I really do this?*

But he'd been around the block with that one countless
times and knew the answer.

I have to.

I have no choice.

If not me, then who?

Never in his life had Raymond Slater felt so alone. It wasn't
fair. This burden was more than any one human being should
have to shoulder.

And yet . . .

I have no choice.

"Fuck!" He pounded the steering wheel with his fist several times, each blow punctuated with another curse: "Fuck!
Fuck! Fuck!"

Then his fist missed the wheel and glanced off the horn pad,
producing a single loud squawk. He winced and looked at the
storefront. The big man—the older one—was behind the register again. At the sound of the horn he turned away from

another customer and stared straight at Raymond. Raymond's heart skipped a beat. If the man had any doubts about the wisdom of doing business with him, those doubts had likely edged closer to certainty. Raymond didn't think the man would call the cops. That would mean at least as much trouble for him as it would for Raymond. Still, putting some distance between himself and the man's suspicious eyes was probably a supremely excellent idea.

He started the Lexus and reached for the gearshift.

A knock at the driver's-side window startled him.

Raymond let out a little squeak and reached for his chest. "Jesus!"

His heart slamming, he turned and saw Cindy Wells staring down at him through the closed window. She smiled and waved. The smile looked grotesque beneath her bandaged nose. Dark sunglasses obscured her eyes. The shades hid a dark shiner inflicted by the thing pretending to be a teenage girl named Myra Lewis. The thought sent a chill through Raymond. He believed in coincidence, but he did not believe in capital-C Coincidence. This was just too much. The idea that Cindy was now allied with Lamia struck him with sudden force and unassailable certainty. Rockville High's expelled golden girl wouldn't just happen to be outside a gun shop at the exact moment he was leaving the place.

She was following him.

Keeping tabs on him.

Raymond's throat tightened. For a few tense moments, he saw all his grand plans going down in flames. He desperately wanted to bolt. His hand hovered near the gearshift as he debated a quick, rubber-burning departure.

Cindy was still smiling, but the expression was beginning to falter at the edges. She made a rolling motion with her hand and said something that was unintelligible through the window.

A thought struck him. His hand came away from the gearshift. He was suddenly sure he should talk with her, if only long enough to allay any suspicions he might be planning something that could piss off Lamia. He pressed a button and the window lowered a few inches.

Cindy's smile brightened again. "Hello, Mr. Slater."

Raymond cleared his throat. "Hello, Cindy. What—" He stopped, realizing he'd been about to ask why she wasn't in school. Stupid. He knew the answer to that. Instead, he settled for the next obvious question. "What are you doing here?"

Still smiling, she said, "Following you."

Raymond gulped. His gaze flicked to the gearshift. "I, uh . . ."

Cindy's expression turned solemn. "Don't." A note of pleading entered her voice. "Listen to me, okay? I need to talk to you about Myra Lewis. I know you'll think I'm crazy, but I think she's planning to hurt a lot of people. We need to do something to stop her."

For a moment, Raymond felt something that might have been hope. More than anything, he didn't want to do this alone. He touched the button again and the window lowered another few inches. He leaned toward Cindy and dropped his voice to a whisper. "I have a plan. It's not much, but it's better than—"

He let out a startled shriek as Cindy stuck her head through the newly widened opening and wriggled in to her waist. Her right hand went for the key ring dangling from the ignition, but he batted it away. She laughed and reached for the keys again. Raymond knew he had to do something drastic or risk losing his chance at salvation. He backhanded her with a tight, hard blow, knocking the sunglasses off her face. Cindy howled in agony and started screaming about her nose. Raymond unclipped his seat belt, twisted in his seat, and braced his palms against the top of her head. The fleeting thought that her soft, conditioned hair felt nice against his fingers whistled through his mind like a bottle rocket; then he gave her a mighty shove and she fell back through the opening. She staggered backward, wobbling on high heels for a moment, then fell hard on her ass. He saw that she was dressed in a tiny halter and a tight black miniskirt. They made her look like a cheap hooker. Nothing at all like the effervescent, brainy head cheerleader he'd known for four years. Seeing her lying there on parched asphalt with her long, shapely legs splayed open triggered a spark of crazy lust.

He gave his head a hard shake and put the Lexus in gear.

Cindy began the laborious process of getting to her feet.

Slater backed up the Lexus and executed a quick three-point turn. Then he stomped the gas pedal down and the car shot to the edge of the parking lot.

He hit the brakes and let out a scream of frustration. An 18-wheeler was blocking his way, slowing down as it neared the intersection. Raymond glanced at the rearview mirror. Cindy still wasn't upright. The older gun-shop clerk was at her side, offering his assistance. A knife appeared in her hand. The blade flashed in the morning sunlight before she stuck it in the man's throat. Raymond whimpered and whipped his head back toward the street. The 18-wheeler was rolling slowly through the three-way stop. He heaved a sigh of relief and let his foot off the brake, allowing the Lexus to roll closer to the edge of the street.

Then Cindy was there again, screaming and launching herself through the halfway-open driver side window. Raymond might have cursed his stupid failure to close the window had he been capable of coherent thought in that moment. Instead he matched Cindy's scream with an impressive one of his own as he dodged the bloody blade in her hand. Then he looked in front of him and saw that the street was clear again. He hit the gas and the Lexus surged into the street, straight toward the brick wall of a building on the opposite side. He spun the wheel hard to the left and the car swerved back to the street.

There was a massive thump and Cindy loosed a scream of sheer agony. Raymond realized two things in the next moment.

One, the lower half of the psychotic cheerleader's body had struck a telephone pole with extraordinary force.

And two, the Lexus was still speeding down the street.

He pulled his leaden foot off the accelerator and hit the brake. Then he twisted the steering wheel and ducked down an alley, dragging Cindy Wells's now very limp body along with him. He slammed the gearshift to the park position and sat there struggling not to hyperventilate for several moments. After he had calmed down some, he forced himself to look at Cindy. She was very still and at first he was sure she was dead. Then he looked at her throat and saw the slow throb of a weak pulse.

He thought about taking her to a hospital, but dismissed the idea as ridiculous. Doing that would doom everything and Cindy would probably die anyway.

Frustration made Raymond pound the steering wheel again. "Fuck!"

His breath hitched and a sob worked its way out of his throat. A series of progressively more wrenching sobs followed. This lasted until it hit him that he was living down to Lamia's worst assumptions about him. He wiped the tears from his eyes and looked at the rearview mirror. There was no one behind him. A glance through the windshield confirmed that the opposite end of the alley was also deserted. But it wouldn't be for long.

He got out of the car. The sight of Cindy's badly mangled legs made him gag. They were twisted and broken, though he saw no compound fractures, no shards of bone sticking through punctured flesh. In that regard only she'd been lucky. Not that it mattered. Cindy's limited future remained very bleak. Raymond choked down bile and forced himself to act quickly. He extracted the girl from the shattered window and dragged her to the rear of the Lexus. She whimpered softly, but did not regain consciousness. Raymond opened the trunk, hoisted her up, and dropped her inside. He hesitated a moment, his hand poised on the trunk lid, ready to slam it

CHAPTER THIRTY-TWO

Trey McAllister sat at the chintzy little kitchen table in his mother's house and stared at his fists, feeling sick as he remembered how his brother had fallen beneath the force of his punches. A sickness surpassed only by the guilt he felt at the memory of the shock and betrayal he'd seen in Jake's eyes.

He told himself it had been necessary. That he'd done it only to protect his brother. Once again he reviewed the morning and laughed bitterly. He recalled the lies he'd spewed to drive Jake away and laughed again, and this time he felt a sting of tears. It had been the performance of a lifetime. Real Oscar-caliber work. If by some miracle he managed to make it to tomorrow alive, he would have to give some serious thought to pursuing an acting career.

The thought of surviving triggered yet another round of that numb laughter.

That wasn't going to happen.

He was a walking dead man and there wasn't a damned thing he could do about it. Which was kind of okay. He'd been through a lot. Had seen a lot of awful things. Had been made to do things so gruesome and deranged that the thought of living with the memories horrified him nearly as much as the acts themselves.

So, yeah, dying—preferably sooner rather than later—would probably be for the best.

He thought of the hopelessness of his predicament some more and laughed one last time.

"What's so funny, child?"

Trey's breath caught in his throat at the sound of her voice. He clenched his fists tighter as he struggled not to scream.

The voice turned colder. "I asked you a question. I expect an answer."

Trey consciously reminded himself to breathe. He exhaled slowly and unclenched his fists with great deliberation. Then he turned to look at Myra. And he did the only thing possible. He told the truth. He couldn't lie to her. There would be no point even if he could. "I was just thinking about everything. About my brother. About how much I hate you. And about how fucked up this all is." The depth of his despair came through in his voice. He made no attempt to hide it. "And I was thinking about how there's not a fucking thing I can do about it."

Myra was nude save for a tiny black thong. He looked at her slim, pale body and tried to feel even a ghost of the overpowering lust he'd felt for her just days ago. But there was nothing. It made sense. The compact little body he'd once found so enticing was only a facade.

She smirked. "You're right about that. But you're wrong about the other thing. I could make you feel lust for me again if I really wanted."

Trey felt a chill. She was still inside his head. Still knew his every thought. It was a violation. A mental rape of sorts. And just one more thing he could do nothing about. "I know. But it wouldn't be any more real than the girl I'm looking at."

Myra ran a hand slowly down one side of her sleek body. "Oh? I could alter my appearance, you know. Change my shape, make it more pleasing."

Trey shook his head. "That's not what I mean and you know it."

"I suppose I do, at that."

She stared at him for several long, exceedingly uncomfortable moments, her dark, glittering eyes boring into his skull like lasers, making him squirm. Then she turned away from him and opened a cutlery drawer. Trey heard a clank of steel as she sorted through the contents. He sucked in a breath when she turned toward him again. The gleaming carving knife looked impossibly big in her little hand. She approached the table with a slow roll of her hips and set the knife down before him.

"What—"

"I'm giving you a chance to take yourself out of the equation, but I'm leaving it all up to you, darling." She grinned at his thunderstruck expression. "You can live for a while or die right now. If you choose the latter, you can do the job with that easily enough. It'll hurt, of course, horribly, but that won't last long. Well, not *too* long."

Trey looked at the knife and thought about it.

And thought about another possibility or two.

Myra snorted. "Yeah, right. Try and I'll pop a vessel in your brain before you even get the fucking thing off the table. Now put that idiot thought away before I take this choice away from you. You'll want to think about this very carefully, Trey. It's the last time you'll ever have any say in what happens to you."

Trey stared at the knife another long moment, then pushed it away with a sigh. "I . . . can't."

"Because you're a coward."

Another sigh, then, very quietly: "Yes."

Her laughter was smug and very satisfied.

Trey hated himself more than ever in that moment.

"What's going on in here?"

Trey turned his head away from Myra's hateful face and cringed at the sight of his mother sauntering into the kitchen. She wore only a grimy white T-shirt and a pair of lacy pink panties. She winked at Trey and patted Myra on the ass on her way to the refrigerator. She took a can of Old Milwaukee from the fridge and popped the tab.

She took a long swallow from the can, made a sound of almost sexual satisfaction. "Got-damn. Tell you what, ain't nothin' hits the spot like a beer after getting laid."

Trey struggled not to throw up.

Myra had elected to stay inside and out of sight during the confrontation with Jake. She was not yet ready to reveal herself to the older McAllister boy for some reason. After Jake and his girl left, Trey and Jolene came back inside. Myra had been very pleased with the way the whole thing had played out. And she had chosen to show her pleasure by dragging Jolene into one of the tiny home's two bedrooms. Trey had retreated to the kitchen at the sound of the first orgasmic squeals.

And now here they were again. Utterly shameless. Making no attempt to disguise what they had been doing. Quite the opposite, in fact.

Jolene finished off the beer and tossed the crumpled can into the overflowing sink. Then she sidled up next to Myra and slipped an arm around the girl's waist. Keeping her eyes on Trey, Myra smiled and leaned into the embrace. Jolene slipped a thumb beneath the band of Myra's thong and gave it a snap. "Mmm . . . your girl's primo stuff, boy. Knows her way around a woman's body better than any *man* I ever knew, that's for goddamn sure. If I'd known that, I never would've given you so much fuckin' grief about her."

"She's not my girl."

Jolene ran a finger along the delicate line of Myra's jaw and made a purring sound. "You mean I can have this fine piece all to myself?"

"Be my guest."

Jolene made that purring sound again and said, "Oh, I think I will."

Trey stared at his hands and tried to make his mind a blank while they noisily made out for several minutes. But the effort was doomed. There was too much to think about. Too many awful things had happened. And there was the prospect of a near future awash in blood and violence to consider. So his mind wandered. He thought about Lamia. He understood in a general way her need to harvest souls and replenish her energy for another long stretch of years. And to some degree he understood some of the machinations necessary to put all the right pieces in place and arrange a successful harvest. He was less sure about why she did so many other things that seemed unnecessary. All the random murder and mind games. And she had some kind of fixation on Jake. Some kind of connection she refused to clarify. Trey didn't have much left that mattered to him, but his brother did matter. He wished he could talk to him, convince him to head out of town, to run like a mad bastard, and keep running until he was hundreds or thousands of miles away.

He felt like crying now.

Because he knew it wasn't possible. He knew that Jake was just as doomed as he was.

"You're right about that."

Trey flinched. He looked up and saw that Jolene had left the kitchen. Myra had moved closer to him while his mind was elsewhere. She stared down at him, her dark eyes cold as ever but also amused. "You can't warn him. And he won't escape. He was always meant to be here at harvest time."

"Why?"

She shook her head ruefully. "You know better, darling. I don't like to reveal all my secrets at once. Why ease your mind when it's so much more fun to watch you writhe in torment?"

"You're evil."

"Well, fucking *duh*, Trey." She laughed and her modest breasts jiggled in a way he would have found thrilling only a short time ago. "As for the rest of it . . . the seeming lack of a method to my madness . . . let's just say that most of it is fun and games."

Trey shuddered. "Murder. Torture. Fucked-up head games. Those are fun and games?"

She shrugged. "I'm old beyond your ability to comprehend, little worm." She smiled and stroked his cheek with the back of a soft hand. "I get bored. Even a goddess, an immortal, can get bored. Maybe even especially a goddess. So many years, Trey. Endless. The centuries. Millennia. I have to amuse myself somehow."

"You're not a goddess."

BRYAN SMITH

She lifted her chin, tilted her head. "Excuse me?"

"You heard me. This goddess bullshit . . . it's just your way of fooling your followers into believing you're more important than you are." There was contempt in his tone now. He knew he was pushing it, that he risked invoking her wrath in a big way, but he was powerless to keep this inside. It wouldn't matter anyway—she would just look inside his head and know what he was thinking. "No, the truth is you're just some kind of fucking demon. Satan kicked you out of hell or something."

Her hand moved from his cheek to his neck, encircled it.

She applied pressure.

His eyes bugged out and he couldn't breathe.

Then she released him and smiled again. "No. That would be too easy. I want you around to see everyone and everything you care about go down in flames."

Trey touched his tender throat and smiled weakly. "Okay. But I'm right. I know I am."

She shrugged. "It doesn't matter. And Satan? Please. Just an idea. And I was a player long before it was even conceived. And goddess or not, I *am* immortal. Perpetual. I'll survive the end of the world. Doesn't that make you feel small?"

Trey didn't have an answer for that.

Myra smiled. "Not that it matters. I'm almost done with you anyway. With both of you."

"What does that mean?"

She touched a hand to his forehead. He felt her invading his mind again.

She said, "Forget."

There was a fuzzy moment. Trey shook his head and looked up at her. "What . . ."

He frowned.

Something had happened, but he couldn't remember what it was. It was probably just another symptom of his exhaustion.

"I'm back!" Jolene threw an arm around Myra and laid a loud, wet smack on her cheek. "Did you miss me?"

Myra smiled. "Of course."

Jolene had returned with a largish Tupperware container. Trey frowned at the dark shape visible through its opaque side.

It was . . . moving.

Jolene caught his puzzled look and cackled. "Oh! That's right. You don't know about your daddy yet. Check this shit out, boy."

She disengaged herself from Myra and peeled back the container's purple top. Trey peeked inside and let out a gasp. "Holy . . ."

His head swam.

He thought he might faint.

"That . . . it's not . . . it can't . . ."

Jolene loosed another burst of mad laughter. "That's what I thought, baby, but I was fuckin' wrong. Myra did it for me. A special gift." She beamed at Myra. The girl's eyes shone with amusement. "And I fetched him now 'cause I figured out what I want to do with him." She giggled. "You're gonna love this shit. It's perfect."

She hurried across the kitchen and popped the open container in the microwave. A series of beeps followed as she set the timer, followed by the hum of the machine working. Several seconds later there was a loud *PLOP!* And something wet splashed against the microwave's little window.

There was a good deal of feminine laughter then.

Trey shoved himself away from the kitchen table, put his head between his knees, and heaved.

This elicited more laughter.

And then he did faint.

CHAPTER THIRTY-THREE

The first thing Jordan thought as she began to wake up was that she was hungover. Her mouth was dry. She felt thick-headed, engulfed in a mental fuzz obscuring memories of the night before. An ache throbbed somewhere behind her eyes. Her stomach fluttered. A taste of bile at the back of her throat hinted at a big meal her digestive system wanted no part of, probably something fried and drowned in grease.

Must have really tied one on.

She'd probably gone out to the Grill again. Their whole menu was chock-full of things the food nazis would scream about. Loaded with fat and deep fried to hell and back. She had to stop eating there. Had to change her habits while she was still young and thin. And . . .

Wait.

She still wasn't fully awake. But she was close enough now to find certain things curious, verging on alarming. She became aware of various aches throughout her body. Then she felt the hardness beneath her. She wasn't in a bed. She stretched and groaned. Her foot kicked something hard that skittered away. Maybe she'd crashed for the night on the floor for some reason. Too drunk to make it the bed or sofa, maybe. She rolled onto her back and groaned again. A frown twitched at the corners of her mouth.

Something about the hardness beneath her felt . . . wrong.

It was too . . . lumpy.

And now she felt something else. A sweet, mellow warmth on her face. It felt nice. Familiar. She knew what it felt like, but it wasn't something she should feel crashed out on the floor of her apartment. And yet the warmth on her face felt like sunshine. Couldn't be. Like many people her age, she liked to have a few drinks, maybe even get pretty tipsy, but she'd never been the type to get completely hammered and pass out outdoors.

Then she felt something wet and rough on her face.

She flinched away from it.

What the hell?

She felt it again. What could that possibly be?

Then it hit her.

Something's licking me!

Her eyes snapped open.

The big dog's lolling tongue lapped at her face again.

Jordan screamed.

She sat up and scooted away from the golden retriever. It sat on its haunches and grinned at her in its simple doggy way. The dog had company. A loose circle of animals surrounded her, all of them staring at her. A German shepherd sniffed at her feet. A squirrel sat on its hind legs and chittered at her. A big gray tomcat approached her from the right and nuzzled her hand. And there were more of them. Cats and dogs. A rabbit. A skunk. A row of gleaming blackbirds peered down at her from a telephone wire. Jordan scanned their faces and tried to tell herself this was just coincidence, all these creatures gathered around her like this. Christ, it was like being surrounded by Lamia's minions again.

Jordan's eyes went wide.

Fuck.

It all came back then, all the madness of the night before. The tortures she'd been forced to endure. The depravity. The cannibalism. She'd *eaten* bits of her next-door neighbor. Her stomach fluttered again and she thought she would be sick. But then she remembered how it had all changed, how the tables had turned. How powerful she'd felt while killing

Angela. That unnatural energy thrumming within her as she
ripped the bigger girl apart with the knife. And then there was
the matter of Bridget's crazy claims about her true nature.
About her true mother.

Lamia.

She shook her head as the memories unspooled like a
forgotten reel from a long-lost film. "No. No way.
Nonononononono. A lie. A big fucking lie. All of it."

But it wasn't.

In her heart, she knew it was all true.

And now she remembered the rest of it. How she'd left
Todd's apartment in search of her mother, with no destination in mind. On foot. Hunting by instinct. She had walked
the streets of Rockville for hours, that unnatural energy
awake and alive within her the whole time, steering her re-
lentlessly toward Lamia. She'd felt the connection between
them, a sort of spiritual tether that was as real and palpable to
her as any physical object. A connection so intense she
couldn't understand how she'd gone her whole life without
being aware of it. She walked for miles and miles, the minions accompanying her the whole way, reverted as they were
now to an animal form so as not to unduly alarm the clueless
citizenry. Her winding path took her out of the upwardly
mobile part of town surrounding the Rockville Community
College campus to the farthest outskirts of the community
until she'd arrived here.

The Zone.

And she remembered how the power had swelled within
her as she'd entered the streets of the sprawling old neighborhood. Her flesh tingled. Her whole body felt like a live wire.
But it wasn't a wild energy. She sensed she could focus and
control it. Direct it. Shoot bolts of electricity from her fingertips if she wanted. It sounded particularly fanciful, but
she'd really believed she could do it. And even now she believed it.

But something had stopped her.

Some . . . presence.

She shivered as she recalled how it had invaded her mind. She'd felt it initially as a darkness stealing into her mind. A malign tendril slithering into her psyche. This was followed by an overwhelming sensation of cold. Freezing cold in the near-summer heat. And within moments that incredible power had deserted her, and the connection she'd felt with Lamia began to wane. But she soldiered on, continuing for a time in what she felt was the right direction.

Until an implacable voice spoke in her mind: *STOP.*

She obeyed immediately and without question. Whatever this presence was, it was many times more powerful than she. Defiance was not an option.

The voice spoke one more time: *IT IS NOT YET TIME. NOW YOU WILL SLEEP.*

The minions took over then, guiding her to the backyard of an uninhabited house, where she had spent the night. Jordan looked beyond the circle of animals and surveyed her surroundings. She saw the back of a small, one-story house. Some of its windows were boarded over. The barren backyard would need to be reseeded should the next owner wish to have a proper lawn. A sagging chain-link fence surrounded the rear of the property. The gate through which she and the minions had entered stood open. Another German shepherd crouched near it like a guard. No. Not *like* a guard. It actually *was* a guard. Jordan felt certain it would have ripped to shreds any intruder during the night. She wondered about this. Lamia didn't want to see her, not yet, but she wanted her to be safe.

I came here to stop her.
Maybe to kill her.
So why not just kill me?

Maybe the answer was as simple as maternal love. Maybe Lamia did care for her in some twisted way. She supposed it was possible the creature did not relish the prospect of a confrontation with its daughter, one in which it might be forced to harm or possibly kill her. Jordan wasn't at all certain this was true. It didn't feel quite right. Whatever the truth was,

218   BRYAN SMITH

she was left now with the matter of what to do next. And where to go.

She looked at the big golden retriever. Its grin widened and its tongue slopped out the side of its mouth. She sensed a genuine joy from the creature at her attention. A strong intuition told her this was the animal form of the beach ball creature from last night. She sighed at the thought. This whole situation was miles beyond fucked up. She couldn't imagine a possible future beyond this day. Couldn't imagine how she might slip back into her old life, the one devoid of strange creatures and grounded in everyday reality, a world that now seemed as distant and unreachable as the gates of heaven. But there was an odd comfort in knowing that this creature felt this simple, stupid love for her. That she was being looked after, guarded and kept safe.

She held out a hand and the dog came to her eagerly, smiling broadly as she patted its head and scratched its neck. "You're a good boy. Christ, what am I saying, you're not . . . look, could you do me a favor and stay in dog mode full-time? No offense or anything, but I really like you better this way."

The creature's only answer was to lick the back of her hand.

"Good enough."

Time to get rolling.

Jordan still didn't know what her next move should be, but she did know she couldn't stay here all day. So she got to her feet and brushed herself off. She started toward the open gate and her new entourage followed her. The German shepherd guarding the gate greeted her with a friendly bark. She paused a moment to scratch the animal behind its ears, then continued through the gate.

A moment later she was standing in the middle of a narrow residential street. She saw a few cars parked in driveways and at the side of the street, but other than the distant buzz of a lawn mower there was little evidence of human activity. Of course. The kids were in school and the adults were at work. The emptiness creeped her out a bit. Knowing the reason for it didn't help at all. After the shrieking madness of the night before, she craved the company of normal human beings. Stranger or friend, it didn't matter. She'd be happy to en-counter absolutely anyone unconnected with Lamia and her sick schemes.

She caught a flicker of movement in one of the parked cars. The Oldsmobile was parked a house down on the other side of the street. She moved a few steps toward it and was able to make out a human shape behind the wheel. It was hard to tell more about it because of the glare of the sun on the windshield. She couldn't swear to it, but she was almost certain there'd been no one there a moment ago. This was a little strange, she supposed, but she wasn't too worried. Noth-ing too bad could happen in broad daylight. Besides, she was tired and not up for another long walk back across town. Maybe she could hitch a ride. As she continued slowly toward the car, another shape popped up in the backseat and leaned through the gap between the seats. She still couldn't make out much, but the person in the backseat seemed to be speaking in an animated fashion, gesticulating wildly for a moment be-fore pointing a finger straight at Jordan.

Jordan began to feel a little afraid. She stopped moving to-ward the car. The golden retriever and one of the German shepherds sensed her fear and moved into position in front of her. Jordan's heart hammered as her head filled with lurid vi-sions of abduction and rape. How stupid she'd been to think nothing like that could happen in daylight. It happened all the time. Newspapers and A&E true crime shows were filled with such stories. She was suddenly very happy to have the minions arrayed around her. Then she remembered how she'd dealt with Angela and the sound of her own laughter startled her. She felt the power stirring within her again and knew she had nothing to fear from mundane human predators.

The Oldsmobile's engine started and the black car rolled slowly toward her.

Jordan stood stock-still with her hands splayed before her, feeling that strange, potentially deadly energy crackle in her fingertips.

"Bring it on," she whispered.

By now she almost hoped these guys really were would-be rapists. She was kind of curious to see what exactly she could do with this power.

The car rolled to a stop next to her. The driver side window slid down and she saw two skinny teenage boys staring at her with wide, frightened eyes. The boy in the backseat pointed a gun at her. The dogs snarled and leaned toward the car, readying to leap through the open window. Jordan touched the backs of their necks to calm them.

She looked at the boy with the gun and said, "Put that away, child. I don't want to have to hurt you."

The boy gulped. His hands started to shake, but he kept the gun aimed at her. "No. You're one of *them,* aren't you?"

The word "them" was invested with such contempt that Jordan knew at once what he meant. "I'm not one of Lamia's followers, if that's what you're asking me."

The driver frowned as he scanned the faces of the agitated animals. "We saw them follow you. All those animals. Like they were escorting you. You must be one of them."

Jordan sighed. "Who the fuck are you guys?"

The boy in back laughed, but there was no real mirth in the sound. "We're dangerous outlaws."

"Right. Look, can you guys give me a ride?" She forced a smile. "I promise you have nothing to fear from me. I'm not one of them. I want to stop them."

The teenagers conferred in whispers for a few moments. Then the driver cleared his throat and said, "We'll give you a ride, but those animals are staying behind."

Jordan considered this for a long moment before nodding. Then she went to a knee and whispered in the golden retriever's ear. "I'm going away for a while. I'll be okay. And I have a feeling you can find me again if I need you. Am I right?"

The dog answered with a single, emphatic bark.

"Good boy."

Jordan stood and got in the car.

CHAPTER THIRTY-FOUR

The first several minutes of the ride back from the Zone were very tense. Jake didn't talk and Kristen allowed him some mental distance. He was grateful for both her company and her sensitivity. A lot of women he'd known would have pressed him to talk about what had happened right away. Her first overture was nonverbal. A hand on his leg. A gentle, re-assuring squeeze. Jake let out a huge breath and felt some of the tension drain out of him.

He spoke in a soft monotone: "I guess there's nothing more I can do."

"That's not what you were saying back there." She hooked a thumb over her shoulder. "You didn't sound like a guy about to give up."

Jake's laughter was bitter. "You don't know me as well as you think you do. I give up on shit all the time."

Kristen shook her head. "I don't think so. You've got an inner strength most guys lack."

"You're wrong about that. But I don't want to argue about it. The situation is what it fucking is. For some reason I don't understand, the local law's sided with my mom. The reality is there's not a damn thing I can do about that. I think it's time to say fuck it, pack my bags, and head home."

Kristen took her hand from his leg and folded her arms beneath her breasts. The atmosphere in the car changed. "You could really do that, couldn't you?" Her voice sounded tight, strained, each word thick with a barely contained fury. "You could just walk out on me like I was some kind of one-night stand. A casual fuck-buddy you hooked up with for your triumphant return home. You know what, Jake? Fuck you."

Jake didn't say anything at first. His first instinct was to confirm her worst fears. He and Kristen couldn't be good together over the long term. It didn't take a genius to see that their mutually self-destructive ways were a recipe for disaster. The smart thing here would be to make a relatively clean break. Just say nothing and allow this new rift to grow of its own accord. Hardly more than an hour ago he'd been certain that getting away from her was the smart thing to do. And now she'd provided him with the perfect opening. He only had to let it happen.

And yet . . .

Admit it.

Okay. He didn't want to be alone. Too much had happened. Too much had changed. Too much fucking drama in too short a time. Alone he'd be more vulnerable than ever. Perhaps he'd even be a danger to himself. It wasn't until this thought struck him that he was able to face the real truth lurking beneath his fears. The self-destructive part of him—the part he'd worked so hard to suppress in the past—didn't want to break it off with Kristen. That part of him wanted her more than ever. It was selfish and stupid, but Jake recognized it as fact. And in the aftermath of the morning's disasters, it was too easy to allow that part of his psyche to rule the other.

At least for a while.

He took one of her hands in his and squeezed it. "I'm sorry, Kristen. That's not what I meant. I couldn't leave without you. Hell, maybe you could even leave with me."

Oops.

Where the hell did that come from?

The words had just popped out of him. He felt more like a thoughtless idiot than ever. He wanted to retract the impulsive offer, but knew he couldn't. That was the thing about words. Once they were out there, you couldn't take them back. And of course he knew what she would say. There was a strange sense of the course of his life proceeding along a predetermined path. He knew now what was next on that path and there was no longer anything he could do about it.

So he just waited for her to say it.

And she did.

"Okay."

Jake nodded. "Yeah. Okay."

She leaned over to kiss him on the cheek. "You won't be sorry." Her breath was soft against his ear, and he began to feel a stir of arousal. "We'll be great together. I promise."

Jake swallowed a lump in his throat and shifted in his seat. "Yeah. I think so, too."

He didn't believe it. Not really. But maybe if he said it and thought it enough times, it would come true.

Kristen's cell phone buzzed in her purse. She sighed and nipped lightly at his earlobe. "Let me see who this is."

She retrieved her purse from the floor, fished out her slim little phone, and looked at the number on the screen. "It's my uncle. What the hell does he want?"

She flipped open the phone and said, "What's up?"

There was a long moment of silence as she listened, but there was a dramatic change in her demeanor at once. Jake looked at her and frowned. Her eyes were bright with sudden tears. Her mouth hung open and her jaw quivered. She slapped her free hand over her mouth in shock. Jake dimly heard the caller's voice, but couldn't make out what was being said. It was obvious, though, that it was something very, very bad. His stomach clenched as he waited to hear the bad news, whatever it was.

Her voice quavered as she said, "Yes, I heard you. Yes, I understand. I know, I know. I'm sorry. I love you, too."

She snapped the cell phone shut.

And then she screamed.

She smashed the cell phone against the dashboard. The broken phone slipped from her hand and she bashed the dashboard with her fists. She screamed again, a sound that shifted to an anguished wail. Then she was crying and hugging herself, rocking on the edge of the seat. She shook her head and plaintively said the word "no" over and over.

They were out of the Zone now. Jake spied a convenience store and pulled into its parking lot. Kristen gave no sign of realizing they'd stopped. She buried her face in her hands, tucked her head between her legs, and wailed. Jake watched her and said nothing. He was afraid to ask her what was wrong. He tried to think of what might be horrendous enough to affect her this way. He still didn't know her very well at all. It could be anything. Thinking this, he again felt a stab of doubt. He had to be out of his mind to get in so deep with her so soon. But the doubt gave way to guilt as he heard her sobs.

Stop being an asshole, he thought.

He laid a gentle hand between her shoulder blades and for a moment the strength of her sobs only increased. Her whole body quivered. Then she came to him and he took her in his arms, stroking her hair and whispering reassuring nonsense into her ear as she cried against his neck. After maybe ten minutes of this, she eased out of the embrace and looked at him through red-rimmed eyes.

She wiped moisture from her flushed cheeks and sniffed. "Stu's dead."

The news hit him like a hard blow to the gut. His chest felt tight. He couldn't breathe for a few seconds. He thought about Stu's kindness in offering him a place to stay. Christ. Stu dead. It made no sense. And then it hit him that he'd scarcely known Stu any better than he knew Kristen. It was a shock, yes, but the anguish he felt was more intense than it should have been. Part of it was the guy's giving, generous personality. He'd just been an all-around good guy. You didn't have to know the man in and out to see that. The world became a darker place every time someone like that died. And Kristen had known and loved him over the course of a lifetime.

He at last found his voice and somehow managed to keep it steady. "I'm so sorry, Kristen. What happened?"

Her face crumpled at the question and fresh tears streamed down her face. She swiped at them furiously and said, "Some piece of fucking shit *murdered* him. My poor brother. Oh, Jake . . ."

Then the sobs came again and again he held her.

In a while she was able to tell what she knew of the story. Someone had invaded the mountain cabin during the night. Stu had been tortured and murdered. Lorelei was missing and presumed dead or abducted. A massive search was underway for two suspects fingered by an anonymous caller. The same tipster had alerted authorities to the crime. Police were urging the caller to come forward again, but so far it hadn't happened.

Jake comforted her there in the car for a long time.

He never noticed the black Oldsmobile parked next to the Dumpster at the side of the convenience store.

It was there the whole time.

And when Jake drove away from the convenience store to take Kristen home, it followed them.

CHAPTER THIRTY-FIVE

Raymond Slater did the only thing he could think of after stuffing Cindy's mangled body in the trunk of his Lexus.

He went home.

The journey back through the familiar streets was hellish. He kept to a few careful miles over the posted speed limit the whole way, but he spent every moment convinced some bored Rockville cop would pull him over to fill his ticket quota. One big problem was the shattered passenger-side window. There was a spray of glittering safety glass on the leather seat and floorboard. Some of it was tinged crimson with Cindy's blood. A fragile wedge of glass remained at the bottom of the window frame. Raymond had been sure some busybody cop would see that as a red flag and use it as an excuse to stick his nose in his business. So he stopped at a little strip mall for a quick clean-up job. He knocked the remaining glass out of the frame. Then he used a rolled-up newspaper to sweep the safety glass to the floor and under the seat. The biggest bloodstain was on the floorboard. He unfolded the newspaper and placed it over the stain. He surveyed his work and judged it passable. Not perfect by any means, but good enough not to arouse any immediate suspicion.

So he got back in the car and resumed the journey home. The next half mile passed without incident and he began to relax. In another few minutes he would be home and safe. He would be able to decompress and take some time to consider his next move.

Then he heard it.

A noise in the trunk.

He might have missed it had the radio been on, it was so soft. But he'd turned off the radio after leaving the alley, finding the sound of music grating under these circumstances. When he heard the noise, he wished he'd left the radio on. His ears perked up and he listened intently while his heart raced. A few moments of silence allowed him the brief illusion that he'd been hearing things.

Then he heard it again.

And there could be no mistake.

The bitch is alive!

The whimper coming from the trunk was low and weak, but it was clearly the sound of a person in unbearable agony. Raymond gripped the steering wheel tighter and let out a whimper of his own.

"Fuck me running."

Then there was the sound of something shifting in the trunk, followed by a louder whimper.

"Jesus Christ!" Raymond punched the steering wheel. "Die already!"

Raymond replayed the words in his head. He had never felt lower in his life. He felt like a monster. A badly injured young girl was trapped in the trunk of his car. It wasn't her fault she'd fallen under the spell of Lamia. She was just a child. This was the truth. And yet it didn't matter. He couldn't change what had happened. He couldn't take her to a hospital. So he was left with a grim reality—if she didn't die on her own soon, he would have to speed the inevitable along.

By the time he arrived at last at his large estate in the wealthiest part of town, he was a trembling, mewling wreck. He pulled up to one of the garage doors, fumbled with the automatic opener clipped to the visor above him for a moment, then watched through a veil of tears as the maroon door rolled up on its tracks. He pulled the Lexus into the open space, fumbled with the opener again, and rested his forehead against the steering wheel for several minutes in the gloom of the garage. His sobs only masked the intermittent cries still emanating from the trunk.

His hands at last came away from the steering wheel. He curled them into fists, dug the nails deep into his flesh, instinctively knowing he needed the pain to cut through the whirlwind of emotions engulfing him. He desperately needed something real and immediate to center him. He bore down harder. His hands shook. Then he let out a big breath and opened them, saw blood leaking out of the deep grooves. And there was pain, yes, enough to make him grit his teeth, but he felt focused again. In this case, instinct had served him well. Maybe that was the key. He shouldn't overthink any of this. It would be hard. He was an educator. Thinking things out and reaching logical conclusions was the backbone of his life. He nonetheless knew he would have to reach beyond that now. Silence that coldly analytical side of himself and trust his gut.

He sat back in the seat and thought of nothing for a time. Blanked his mind as thoroughly as possible given the circumstances. He saw a workbench with tools on it through the windshield. To the left a door led to a small anteroom. His eyes saw these things but his mind was elsewhere. Simply *gone* for a time. His eyes glazed and his breathing evened out. His heart was no longer racing. He remained in the trancelike state for more than ten minutes. Then something—maybe his newfound friend Instinct—told him it was time to wake up and start dealing with the mess.

He almost smiled. A small twinge of that aching desperation returned.

Such a fine euphemism. So delicate. So thoroughly removed from the truth of the situation.

The "mess" moaned again.

Raymond popped open the trunk and got out of the car. There was no conscious decision involved with this. Instinct was guiding him. Instinct would enable him to do what needed doing without having to think about it. And that was good. Better than good. It was like a gift from the gods. Because what needed doing was so overwhelmingly awful. It was vile and despicable, an act normally committed only by the most depraved. What could be worse than the cold-blooded murder of a helpless human being?

Shit.

He was thinking again and that would only get him in trouble. It would slow him down, and the sooner this terrible thing was done, the better. So much was at stake. Cindy was just one girl. The fates of hundreds more young people hung in the balance.

The first thing to do was shed some light on the situation. It was full daylight outside, but the garage-door windows were small and dusty. He didn't want to see Cindy's twisted and broken limbs again, but there was nothing for it. He would need to see clearly to get this done fast and with some degree of mercy. So he found the light switch and flipped it. The overhead fluorescent lights flickered and came on, bathing the interior of the garage in a harsh glare. Patricia's sleek black Jaguar gleamed in the space next to his Lexus. Patricia, whose body was moldering in the hole Penelope had forced him to dig out back during the night. He felt another sharp pang of loss, but pushed the emotion away, into a remote corner of his psyche. One day he might let it out again. And on that day he would allow himself to experience the full spectrum of pain, regret, and loss.

If, of course, he lived long enough.

He moved to the rear of the Lexus and lifted open the trunk lid.

Cindy's face was pressed against the trunk floor. She flinched at the sudden light and lifted her head to look at him. Her face was red and shiny with sweat. Her legs looked as if they had been worked over by a couple of especially sadistic mafia enforcers. No, that was a movie thing. Mere fancy. Allowing instinct to guide him was all well and good, but he would not

turn away from truth. Her legs were broken bones sheathed in
trembling flesh. And this had happened because he'd been
careless with the window. Because he'd driven her at high
speed straight into a fucking telephone pole.

She lifted a shaking hand toward him. Her class ring glittered as the light struck it.

"Please . . ." she said. "Please . . . help me . . . it . . . hurts. . ."

Raymond sighed.

I can do this.

Cindy moaned some more and sobbed softly.

Raymond again gave himself a mental prod. This needed
doing. And now, not later. In theory, it could be done easily
enough. He could find something from the workbench to
finish her off. It was filled with a number of things that
could accomplish the grim task efficiently enough. But he
didn't move. He stood there and stared at the girl. Memories from the last few years taunted him. Cindy had been a
star at Rockville, existing at a rarefied level of popularity
known only to a tiny elite. Girls like her didn't come along
every year. Maybe once or twice a decade a student with
that special combination of beauty, brains, and personality
graced the halls of Rockville High. She'd really been something special. What he had to do was a crime in more ways
than one.

She was looking at him again. For the first time, he saw
more than pain in her eyes. They were clear and focused. She
was analyzing him. Looking for an angle. "You can't kill me."

Raymond blinked. "I . . ."

She shifted again and a fresh jolt of agony made her cry
out. Then her eyes were on him again, hard and unflinching.
"She'll know. She's inside me, and she'll fucking know. And
she'll come get you. Make you fucking pay."

Raymond swallowed hard and stared at her. The fierce
conviction evident in her eyes made him waver for a moment. Maybe Cindy was right. Maybe Lamia would come for
him if he killed the broken golden girl. But instinct told him
otherwise. Lamia wouldn't have put her on his tail in the first

SOULTAKER

231

place if she was really all knowing and all seeing. A theory had been formulating quietly in his subconsciousness and now it surged to the surface.

Lamia was powerful. Extremely. Of that he had no doubt at all. She was something very old. Something not human. A force of nature beyond the ability of men to comprehend. But she was not the goddess she claimed to be. She was instead a magnificent manipulator. She displayed her admittedly impressive abilities only when it suited her. When it benefited her. She terrorized people into following her, bullied them into believing she controlled everyone and everything. Well, maybe she could control one person at a time. Maybe two or three. Four or five. Maybe more. But nothing close to everyone in town. Yet he understood why her followers believed she could. Until today he had believed it, too.

Cindy squinted at him. "Whatever you're thinking is wrong."

Raymond wiped sweat from his brow. "I'm sorry, Cindy, but I don't think so."

Cindy sneered. "You're dead. Fucking dead. You'll see. Lamia will fix me and I'll dance on your fucking grave."

Raymond opened his mouth to respond, but the words never made it out.

The door to the anteroom flew open and banged against the wall. Raymond's eyes went wide as Penelope strutted down the stairs and into the garage. She wore a tight, see-through white blouse and a beige miniskirt that revealed almost everything. It was not normal workday attire, but as Penelope had informed him before leaving for work this morning all the normal rules had been suspended. She could do whatever she wanted and no one would lift a finger to stop her. She was drunk on what she saw as her elevated new station in life. Lamia had fooled her as effectively as she'd fooled anyone.

She saw Raymond and scowled. "*There* you are! Where the fuck have you been, Raymond? Why didn't you show up for work this morning? I told you—"

Then she was standing next to him and looking down at the trunk. "My God . . ." She looked at him. "What have you done?"

Raymond's emotions were complex in that moment, a mixture of guilt, terror at being caught, and self-directed anger at allowing the situation to slip out of his control.

"Penelope . . ." The plaintive, strained tone returned to Cindy's voice. "Please help me. He kidnapped me. I think he was going to rape me."

Penelope chortled. "Oh, please. Raymond likes a bit of slap and tickle, but he doesn't have the cojones for hard-core stuff." She looked at Raymond again. "What really happened?"

Raymond felt deflated. He'd been caught. Found out. It was all over. There was even a kind of relief in knowing he wouldn't have to make like some kind of tweed-wearing Rambo. "It was an accident. She came after me."

"An accident, huh?"

"Yeah."

Penelope smirked. "I can see that, I guess. And you brought her here, not knowing what else to do. Figured you'd finish her off in private and . . . then what?"

"I don't know."

"Of course not." She slapped him. "That's for being such a fucking pussy. You expect me to believe you would've offed this chick while she was still awake and talking to you?"

Raymond was silent. He didn't have an answer for that.

Cindy let out another little cry of pain. "Penelope . . . please . . ."

"Shut up."

Penelope spun on her heel and stalked toward the workbench. There was a clank of metal as she sifted through the various implements there. When she returned, a long iron spike was gripped in her right fist. It was a rusty thing, something Raymond had found in the yard years ago after construction was finished on the house.

It had a very sharp tip.

Cindy saw it and whimpered.

Penelope sat on the lip of the trunk and leered at Raymond. "She's no use to Lamia like this, so I'll do what you weren't man enough to do." She reached inside the trunk and ripped the flimsy and shredded halter away from Cindy's body, exposing the girl's tanned torso. She directed another leer at Raymond. "Look at her. Still a hot young thing from the waist up, Raymond. Sure you don't want to have a bit of fun with her before I do this?"

Raymond's face twisted in disgust. He took an unconscious step away from her. "You sick bitch. You can't be serious."

Penelope's eyes gleamed with amusement. "Oh, but I am. Think about it. You can't tell me you never fantasized about getting nasty with Miss Hot Stuff here. This is your big chance, Raymond. You'll never get another."

Raymond had indeed fantasized about Cindy Wells. Her and many other young girls throughout his career at Rockville. The memory shamed him now. His voice was tight as he said, "No. And don't ask me again, you psychotic bitch."

Penelope's leering smile faded. "Very well." She looked at Cindy and a hint of mirth again twitched at the corners of her mouth. "Time to say good night."

Cindy moaned. There was terror mingled with the agony in her cries now. "No . . . please . . . please . . . please . . ."

Penelope raised the spike over her head and slammed it down. Raymond saw the tip of the spike punch through Cindy's quivering stomach and cringed at the sound of the girl's scream. It was astonishingly loud in the closed garage, seeming to shred his ears. Nearly as awful was the sound of the spike thunking against the trunk floor after passing through the girl's body. Penelope yanked the spike out and slammed it down again. Another puncture. Another fountain of blood. Raymond forced his eyes away from the girl's ravaged body, but what he saw now was perhaps more disturbing. Penelope slammed the spike down over and over. A dozen times. More. At some point Cindy stopped screaming and Raymond knew she was finally dead. But Penelope just kept slamming the spike down. And she was laughing, her mouth open in a broad, almost manic grin. She glanced at Raymond once with delight radiant in her eyes. She bobbed her head, as if in time to a jaunty tune only she could hear. Her formerly white blouse was splattered with crimson.

And in the midst of Penelope's murderous frenzy Raymond rediscovered his resolve.

Penelope was distracted. She was obscenely absorbed in the act of mutilation.

Raymond quietly opened the Lexus's rear door. He removed the Glock from its box and loaded it the way the gun-shop clerk had showed him. He moved to the rear of the car again and aimed the gun at the back of Penelope's head. She continued thrusting the bloody spike into the dead girl's very still body.

He waited until she was done.

She dropped the spike in the trunk and looked at him. She didn't flinch at the sight of the gun.

She smiled.

And licked flecks of blood from her lips.

She took a step toward him, swinging her luscious hips seductively. "A gun, Raymond? Really? Put that thing away before I—"

Raymond's voice was cold as he said, "Not this time."

Then he shot her in the face.

CHAPTER THIRTY-SIX

Bridget Flanagan returned to her own apartment around the time Jordan was waking up in the backyard of an empty house in the Zone. She'd been at loose ends in the wake of Jordan's departure, not sure whether she should stay there and await Jordan's return or go looking for Lamia. An attempt at establishing a telepathic connection with her went unanswered, as did multiple calls to her cell phone. It was frustrating, but it happened on occasion. Lamia was very busy preparing for the Harvest and sometimes was not able to respond.

She tried not to worry. Lamia was strong. And she was wise. So she fell a little short in the omnipotence department once in a while. So what? No one could hurt her. No one could stop her. The success of the Harvest was not in doubt.

Yet she was certain the goddess would want to know all about what had happened. Jordan's brief transformation to the serpent form, for instance. And how she had awakened to her true nature in the aftermath of Angela's death. These things the goddess would consider vitally important. What most concerned Bridget, however, was the threats the bitch had made against Lamia.

Whoops.

The reflexive contempt she felt for Jordan was still there. She would have to work at suppressing it. Her personal feelings regarding the girl were no longer important. Jordan was Lamia's daughter. She was to be respected, honored, and worshiped. Lamia would expect nothing less. And in her total devotion to the goddess, Bridget would accept nothing less from herself. For so long she'd been Lamia's special one. Her favorite. Now Jordan would usurp her place. Knowing this hurt her deeply. But she found some consolation in reminding herself that she remained a member of Lamia's Sacred Circle, that exclusive group of upper-echelon acolytes. The ones who would also reap the fruits of the Harvest. She and the other women of the Circle would become immortal and serve the goddess throughout eternity. Bridget entered a state of near ecstatic bliss every time she thought of it. How glorious! To live forever at Lamia's side!

Bridget forced her head out of the clouds. She was tired, having slept only in brief fits throughout the night. Like all other Circle members, she was stronger and more resilient than a normal person, but her energy reserves weren't bottomless. She needed to rest and recharge. So when Jordan failed to show by morning, Bridget returned home. She remained worried about the threats Jordan had made, but not enough to feel any real urgency. Jordan just needed time to adjust. And even if she did somehow track down Lamia, she wouldn't be able to hurt her. She was strong, but not that strong. And, hell, for all Bridget knew, Lamia was already aware of her daughter's awakening.

Bridget parked her car, got out, and slung the strap of her purse over her shoulder. The walk across the parking lot seemed an endless slog in her exhausted state, but she finally made it to the building and trudged up the stairs to her third-floor apartment.

She entered the apartment and threw the door shut behind her. The tiny studio apartment wasn't as nice as Jordan's place. There was a lot less room and the building was much older. The threadbare furniture was all secondhand. The carpet had stains no amount of shampooing or vacuuming could excise. All in all, it was a pretty shabby place to live. But Bridget didn't care. It was just a place to sleep. It was temporary. Greater things awaited her. Soon, perhaps as early as tomorrow, she would leave all this behind. Besides, most of Bridget's discretionary income went to things like clothes, makeup, and salon visits. Looking good mattered more than living in the lap of luxury. Looking good enabled a girl to reach for bigger things. Bridget reflected on that last thought and frowned. The philosophy was an echo from a person who no longer existed. The pre-Lamia Bridget. Bridget 2.0 no longer gave a shit about using her looks to snare a man with a fat wallet. All men were beneath her. She was a woman, after all. And not just a woman, but a follower of the goddess.

One of the chosen ones.

She giggled. "And this chosen one is fucking *beat*."

She dropped her purse on the cluttered coffee table. Then she kicked off her shoes, stripped off her skirt and blouse, and collapsed on the couch. She reached for the thin blanket folded over the top of the couch, shook it open, and tucked it over her shoulders. She was asleep within moments. She slept deeply and when she awoke she knew hours had passed. She lay there in a state of semiconsciousness for several moments before becoming aware that something wasn't quite right. She tried to dismiss the feeling, but it persisted. As she neared full consciousness, she realized another person was in the room. A cold finger of fear tickled the length of her spine.

Someone had broken in while she was asleep.

A burglar, maybe. Or a rapist.

She wondered whether she should play possum. Just keep her eyes closed and pretend she was still asleep. She saw one immediate problem with that. She was a snorer. Every chick she'd ever bedded complained about it, as had her occasional male partners. The intruder had been here while she was sleeping and would know it, too. She didn't doubt her ability to physically overpower any man. She was of the Circle. Snapping his neck would be child's play.

But . . . what if he has a gun?

Fear gave way to terror. She wasn't yet immortal. A burgeoning scream welled inside her. The thought of surrendering the eternal reward promised her by the goddess was more than she could bear.

A voice she recognized said, "Open your eyes."

Bridget relaxed at once. She blew out a breath and stretched her long, lean body. Then she opened her eyes and saw Myra Lewis—Lamia—staring down at her with her usual blank expression. She smiled and tossed the blanket aside. "Please tell me you're here to have your way with me," Bridget said.

Lamia said nothing, but something in her eyes hardened.

Bridget rolled off the couch and went to her knees before the goddess. She bowed her head and closed her eyes again. "Have I offended you in some way, Dark Mother?"

"Stand up."

Bridget stood and looked the goddess in the eye. She tried not to tremble. As much as she loved Lamia, it was hard to peer directly into that endless darkness. She half suspected anyone attempting to hold that gaze for too long a time would go insane. "Whatever I've done, I'm sorry. You know my loyalty to you is total. I would never—"

"Shut up."

Bridget flinched. "I have things to tell you. Jordan Harper—"

The backhand blow sent Bridget flying over the couch. She landed in an awkward heap on the floor and a shock of pain ripped through her body. She cried out and rolled onto her back. Tears obscured her vision for a moment. When she could see again, Lamia was standing over her. The goddess planted the hard sole of a black Doc Marten boot on her bare chest and exerted enough pressure to render breathing difficult. Bridget opened her mouth to beg for mercy, then remembered what had triggered the attack. She closed her mouth and waited for Lamia to speak.

There was a brief pause. Perhaps a minute elapsed. Long

enough for Bridget to feel her ribs grinding beneath the pressure of the combat boot.

Then Lamia said, "I already know of my daughter's awakening. I am not here to talk about that."

The goddess removed her foot and Bridget sucked in a deep, wheezing breath. Then she frowned as she watched Lamia strip off her leather jacket and toss it aside. The cropped Misfits shirt came off next. The black bra after that. Bridget stared at Lamia's milk white breasts and their jutting pink nipples and felt a stirring of lust. Lamia leaned against the back of the couch and removed the thick-soled Doc Martens. Finally, she peeled off the tight leather pants and was entirely nude. A thick sheen of sweat covered her entire body. A thick drop fell from her nose. She looked paler than usual. Almost feverish. Bridget glanced at the jumble of clothes on the floor and saw they were sopping wet.

"What's wrong with you? You look . . . sick. I thought . . ."

Lamia wiped a fresh swelling of sweat from her brow and flicked fat droplets from the ends of her fingers. "You thought what?"

Bridget frowned. "I . . . don't know. I guess I thought you couldn't get sick."

"I can't."

"Then . . ."

Lamia smiled. "You wouldn't understand and there isn't time to explain. You have been a faithful servant. I have made many promises to you. I must now break them all."

Bridget's heart lurched.

"Wh . . . what?"

"Do you remember Moira, dear?"

The mention of her sister confounded Bridget. Moira had been dead for many years. Bridget rarely thought of her. "I . . . what about her?"

"I killed her. Used her body for a time. It wasn't suitable as a permanent home, but it sufficed long enough. And now the time has come to shed this skin, sweet Bridget. The Harvest must happen today. I am not strong enough in this used-up shell. I require a new host." She straddled Bridget and pinned her wrists behind her head with strong hands. "Your body is perfect and should serve me well for the next hundred years."

Bridget's head spun. The Harvest was today? Lamia had told the members of the Sacred Circle they would know the exact day and hour of the Harvest weeks ahead of time. But apparently this was just one lie among many. There was no time for Bridget to grieve the loss of all she'd been promised, or to appreciate the depth of Lamia's betrayal. She was about to die. She now knew no eternal reward awaited her. No bliss of any kind. Just darkness.

She opened her mouth to scream.

But Lamia forced Myra Lewis's mouth open wider.

Far wider.

Something long and scaly slithered out, moving too fast to perceive in detail. Then it was inside Bridget. Bridget twitched and convulsed, the back of her head banging against the dirty carpet for several moments as the now-dead body of Myra collapsed to the floor and went still. In a while, Bridget, too, was still.

Bridget Flanagan, her essence, expired.

Her body let out an abrupt gasp and sat up.

Lamia had a new home.

CHAPTER THIRTY-SEVEN

The house felt like the inside of a long-sealed tomb. Some ancient pharaoh's crypt, maybe. A dead place, devoid of even the hint of life. It was just an illusion, but that's how it felt. Kristen was somewhere nearby. She was in one of the bedrooms. Jake could just make out her voice from the living room. She was talking to yet another relative, but mostly listening, only on occasion responding with a few clipped words. She sounded subdued. Numb. Much the way he'd felt in the immediate aftermath of his own family drama yesterday.

Thinking about that caused him to reflect again on his confrontation with Trey. His jaw still stung from the blows he'd absorbed. The memory of the hate in his brother's eyes caused a different kind of hurt, one he knew would last far longer than any physical pain.

The air conditioner kicked on and Jake welcomed its uneven hum. It made the thick, oppressive silence a touch more bearable. The old window unit sent a blast of cool air his way that felt good on his face. It soothed him inwardly, too, allowing him to banish the bad thoughts for a time. It didn't matter that the relief was only temporary. He needed a mental respite, however brief. And he needed to gather strength for the hard times ahead. Because more hard times were coming. It was the one thing of which he was absolutely certain.

He sat slouched on the sofa, at a loss as to what else to do. Kristen had family duties she would need to deal with, of course, and he'd help her with these if he was able. But for now—and at least for a few minutes more—he was on his own. He relished the relative solitude and wished it could last longer. Wished again he could be somewhere far from this cursed town.

He shifted on the sofa and one of his feet kicked a leg of the coffee table. A crumpled Budweiser can toppled over. The coffee table's surface was littered with empty cans and bottles. An ashtray was filled with Kristen's cigarette butts. Looking at all the dead soldiers awakened the old thirst again, and in a few moments he craved a drink with a burning intensity that easily matched anything he remembered from his worst pre-AA days. The urge to get up and go to the kitchen to fetch a beer from the fridge was almost too powerful to resist. He thought again of the way Kristen had plied him with drinks as part of perhaps the most unsubtle seduction in the history of sex. There was still a bit of regret attached to this memory. It didn't say much good about him that his resolve had crumbled so easily. But now the hangover haze had lifted and other, more pleasant memories were coming back to him. A flashing image of Kristen, nude and bent over the edge of the sofa as he thrust into her from behind, made his breathing quicken. They'd gone at it with heedless abandon, in several positions, here on the sofa, on the living room floor, up against the wall, on the hallway floor, on the bed, in the fucking shower . . .

Christ.

It was all coming back to him in a wild, X-rated rush, like a series of scenes from the hottest porn movie ever. An erection pushed against the crotch of his jeans as memory shifted seamlessly to fantasy. He imagined Kristen on top of him again, straddling him on the sofa, writhing against him while thrusting her tongue into his mouth. His hands kneading her soft breasts, thumbs massaging swollen nipples . . .

He shook his head to dispel the images before he could get lost in them. These were not appropriate thoughts. Not with Stu dead and Kristen crying softly in a room down the hallway. The craving for a drink returned to fill the void. No. Fuck that. Maybe he'd have that drink later. Maybe he'd have a few of them. But now was certainly not the time.

Then he thought of something productive he could do to occupy himself until Kristen needed him again. He got up and went into the kitchen, where he looked under the sink and found a box of plastic garbage bags. He shook one open and returned to the living room. He and Kristen had made quite the mess over the course of their wild evening. Cleaning up prior to the inevitable appearance of other Walker family members was the least he could do. The bag soon grew heavy with the weight of empty bottles and cans. A few of the bottles still contained an ounce or two of flat beer. These he poured out in the kitchen sink before dropping them in the bag. This all took maybe ten minutes. The last thing was dumping the contents of the overflowing ashtray into the bag. This done, he began to tie the bag with the intent of taking it out to one of the big garbage cans outside. A sudden sound startled him before he could finish.

"What the . . ."

The sound came again and this time he recognized it as the rapping of the brass knocker against the front door. He twisted together the loops of plastic threaded through his fingers and set down the bag. Then he went to the door and peered through the peephole. A young girl he didn't recognize stood on the front porch. She appeared to be alone. She was slender, with hair the same dark shade as Kristen's, but cut in a pixie style. His hand moved to the doorknob, but he didn't open the door immediately. Though he was sure he'd never seen her before, there was something familiar about her. Something in the set of her features. Frustration gnawed at him. His mind was struggling to make some kind of connection, but it was eluding him.

The girl let out a frustrated puff of breath and reached for the door knocker again.

Yet another strident rap on the door, this one close enough— and loud enough—to rattle his fillings.

"Jake!" Kristen cried from her bedroom sanctuary. "Will you get that, please?"

"Sorry! I've got it!"

It hit him that this was probably some member of the Walker clan. Which probably also accounted for that nagging sense of familiarity.

He turned the doorknob and pulled open the door.

The girl's lower lip pushed out in a display of youthful petulance. "It's about fucking time."

"Sorry. I was just—"

He stopped talking because two teenagers with guns were suddenly filling the open doorway. The boys must have been crouching out of view while the girl knocked. Their guns were aimed away from Jake, but that gave him little comfort. The crazy thing was he wasn't afraid. Not yet anyway. He was too angry to be afraid. This was ridiculous. How many more insane things could happen in one fucking day?

He glowered at the juvenile home invaders. "Do me a favor, assholes, and save it for another day. I've got enough shit on my table for now."

One of the boys piped up. "We're not here to rob you. We just need to talk to you. You're Jake McAllister, right?"

"Yeah. What do you want with me?"

His hand tightened on the doorknob. He weighed the advisability of simply throwing the door shut in their faces. Shutting and locking the door would take hardly more than a second. And even if they were here for some nefarious purpose, he doubted they'd shoot their way in. This was the middle of the day in a nice neighborhood. Gunfire would bring the cops running in minutes. So, yeah, a quick door slam seemed the wisest course of action.

"What's going on here?"

Kristen's voice, behind him.

Jake groaned. "It's nothing. Stay back, okay?"

"Stay back?" He could hear her getting closer, curiosity apparently overriding the urgency in his voice. "Is it Uncle Don? I'm expecting—"

She pushed his hand off the doorknob and opened the door wider. She gasped. "Oh my God." She flashed Jake a terror-stricken expression. "Jake, is it . . . *them?*"

"Them?"

She put a hand to her chest and stumbled back a step. "It's them. The bastards who killed my brother. Oh my God."

One of the teenagers said, "Dude, what is she talking about?"

Jake glowered at him. "Her brother was murdered last night. Tortured and murdered. And now here you are waving guns around. Connect the fucking dots."

Both boys looked aghast at the implication. The taller of the two said, "Oh. Shit. Look, I'm sorry. I know this looks bad, but you've got to believe me when I say it just can't be helped. We did not torture and murder anybody last night."

"Or ever," said the other one.

"Right. Or ever," the tall one continued. "We sure as shit shot a bunch of motherfuckers yesterday, though. But that's only because they were trying really fucking hard to kill us."

"Which we sort of took issue with."

The tall one nodded. "Right. We've been through a lot, Mr. McAllister. And it's not over. A lot of people are in danger. It is extremely important that we talk to you."

Jake was aware of Kristen trembling next to him. He grabbed one of her hands and held on tight. "I sympathize, guys. I really do. But we've got major problems of our own to deal with, and this sounds like a matter for the police anyway."

The shorter kid gave his head an emphatic shake. "Uh-uh. Fuck the police."

Something stirred in the back of Jake's mind. He peered more closely at the boys. There was something familiar about them, too. Then he had it. He couldn't breathe for a moment. He'd seen their faces on the late news last night. They were Trey's friends. That surely had something to do with why they'd come to see him. But Jake wanted no part of them. They were wanted for several murders. Maybe they were telling the truth and maybe not. It didn't matter. They were fugitives and he wanted them gone, pronto. Let them sort their shit out elsewhere. It wasn't his problem.

"Look, guys—"

"Oh my God."

Jake glanced at Kristen. She seemed a little less on the verge of falling to pieces. She was staring intently at the girl on the porch. "Kristen? What's wrong?"

She shook her head, her features set in wonderment. "She looks so much like you. Can't you see it?"

Jake looked at the girl. It wasn't something he would have noticed on his own, but a closer study of the girl's face did reveal some similarity. They had the same strong cheekbones and full lips. He and the girl also had the same shade of dark brown hair. And the eyes . . .

Fuck.

The similarity was too strong. He didn't know the girl and had never seen her before. But given the hyperpromiscuity of the McAllister clan, that meant nothing. Factor in an absurdly high level of infidelity and the strong possibility of a familial connection became a probability. She was almost certainly the product of some sordid one-night stand or back-door rendezvous involving a McAllister male and some poor woman. But he couldn't dwell on it or allow himself to get sidetracked.

He put himself between Kristen and the fugitives and began to close the door. "Sorry, but I can't help you. Now get off this property before I call the cops."

The boys traded a single quick glance, then surged through the narrowing space between doorjamb and door. Jake cursed and pushed back against them. His feet slid on the hardwood floor. He was older and stronger than either of them, but it was two against one and a losing battle. He threw all the strength of his upper body into the effort, but his feet continued to slide backward. Then the girl who looked so much like him joined them and the battle was lost. Jake let go of the door and staggered backward as the three intruders came stumbling into the house. The girl threw the door shut and turned the lock.

Jake struggled to catch his breath. He looked at Kristen.

"Go . . . out the . . . back. Run to the nearest . . . neighbor. Call the cops."

But Kristen just stood there. Her eyes pleaded with him. *Rescue me,* they said. *Please make this go away.* He'd been angry before, but now he was shaking with barely checked fury. He burned with the need to beat the shit out of these little snots for putting her through this so soon after the trauma of losing her brother.

The taller boy recognized the promise of violence in his eyes and held up his hands. "Whoa, whoa. Hold on. Just listen to me for one goddamn minute, okay? If you still want us to leave after I've had my say, we'll get out of here and figure something else out." The boy had been panting, too. He paused to catch his breath before continuing. "That fair enough?"

Jake held his breath and counted to ten. He unclenched his fists. "No. I'd rather take those popguns and shove 'em up your fucking asses. But I just want you gone, so I'll take you at your word. Have your say and get the fuck out."

The tall one tucked his gun in the waistband of his pants. He looked Jake in the eye and said, "This has to do with your brother, our friend Trey, and his demon girlfriend."

The other boy said, "He means that, by the way. Literally."

"Excuse me?"

The tall one said, "Trey's girlfriend is a demon. A for-real demon. She feeds on the souls of young people, and later this afternoon she'll pig out on the students of Rockville High."

"The Harvest of Souls." The girl stepped closer. The eyes that so resembled his own shone with a startling intensity. "I only learned about it last night. They're telling the truth. I wouldn't have believed it myself, but last night some things happened. Incredible, horrible things. And now I know. Demons are real. I'm half demon myself, you see."

Jake blinked slowly before his eyes went wide.

He felt as if he'd been slapped.

He surprised himself with a laugh. "Is this a joke?"

The girl and the boys exchanged glances. They fidgeted a

little. Jake tried to find some meaning in the silent communications passing between them. Some instinct told him they were far too earnest to be lying. They knew their story would sound absurd to other ears, but they believed what they were saying. Maybe they were on drugs. No. Jake knew drugs, was very familiar with the effects of all major narcotics and hallucinogens. Dope wasn't the culprit here. A simple solution occurred to him and it made him groan inwardly. These were just kids, after all. And perhaps very gullible or suggestible ones.

"If this isn't some kind of stupid prank or joke—"

"It isn't!" the girl snapped.

Jake held up a hand to head off any further outbursts. "Chill a sec, okay? I take it you're all aware of what I do for a living?"

The girl blew out a breath. Her features conveyed disdain. "What? Are you supposed to be somebody important? I never fucking heard of you before today."

One of the boys said, "You write horror novels. I've read them. I liked the first one."

His friend said, "I have them, but haven't read them."

Jake smiled. "Okay then." He directed his next comments at the girl. She was the most volatile of the three and he figured he should establish a more intimate rapport with her. "And no, I'm not important. I'm nobody. You haven't heard of me? Guess what? Hardly anyone has. My books are supermarket paperbacks. They're on the racks for a few weeks and then gone forever. I'm not complaining, mind you. I like what I do. But in my chosen genre there are some stock cliches, things that have been done a million times. One of the most hackneyed is the plot involving a writer, often a horror writer, who returns to the small town of his youth only to wind up battling a real supernatural evil. So . . . think about it. What you're telling me is I'm living the cliche." Another of those unexpected laughs came. It was followed by another. He choked back yet another.

He wouldn't let the laughter take him again. For Kristen's

sake, it was time to wrap up this farce. He coughed and sat up straighter. "I'm sorry." He strove for a more sober tone and almost made it. "Really I am." He heaved another big breath and this time successfully killed off the last of the hysteria that had been bubbling inside him. He looked the scowling girl in the eye and said, "Trust me on this, okay? Whatever you think is going on . . . there's a logical explanation for it. You've maybe let your imaginations run wild and—"

The girl said, "It's all true and I can prove it. Right now."

Jake stared at her with his mouth hanging open for a long moment, his mind still stuck on his interrupted sentence. Then he did another slow blink and shook his head. "Come again?"

The girl's scowl vanished. A small, almost imperceptible smile crimped the edges of her mouth. "I told you. I'm half demon. I can do things. I'll show you. Then you'll believe."

Jake stared at her a moment before saying, "Uh-huh. Okay." He looked at Kristen, who was staring at the girl with a rapt expression, hanging on her every word. There was no evidence of the anger he'd expected to see there. He looked at the girl again and smiled. Okay. Whatever. As long as Kristen wasn't freaking out, he could play this game, too. See it through to its logical—and quite likely anticlimactic—conclusion. "Fine. You're a demon and you can prove it. What are we really talking about here? Magic tricks?"

The girl's inscrutable smile remained in place as she shook her head. "A kind of magic, yes. But *real* magic. There won't be any trickery involved."

Jake grinned. "Cool. Awesome." He rubbed his hands together and clapped them once. He shot a wink Kristen's way. "Hit me with the smoke-and-mirrors routine, girl."

"The name's Jordan." A corner of her mouth twitched, a near smirk. "And I'm about to wipe that smug grin off your face. I told you. No trickery. No smoke and mirrors. Just real-deal magic."

Jake shrugged. "Okay, okay. Show us your stuff, Jordan. I'm expecting some serious razzle-dazzle here."

Jordan moved to the center of the room. The rest of them backed away from her, instinctively giving her space to do her thing. Space for what, Jake couldn't imagine. Jordan closed her eyes and bowed her head. She held her hands in front of her, splayed fingers pointed at the floor. The pose made her look as if she were praying. She moved her lips and sounds emerged, but nothing intelligible. Jake scanned the faces of the others. The attention of all was focused solely on Jordan. They were absolutely spellbound. It was absurd. Nothing was happening. Why—

And then he felt it.

A sudden shift in the atmosphere. The fine hairs at the back of his neck stood on end. His heart began to speed up and he felt a strange kind of crackling in his fillings. A strange warmth suffused the air, displacing the air-conditioned chill in the space of maybe a second. He glanced at the others again, saw they were all feeling the same things. Kristen's hands were clenched in tight fists at her sides. Her knuckles were a stark white. Her cheeks looked gaunt, the flesh stretched taut. It was then that Jake began to experience true terror. A terror of the unknown. He had written of this feeling in his books, but he knew now he'd gotten it all wrong. He had never fully conveyed how it could strip a man of his defenses and lay him bare. He was in the presence of something unnatural and dangerous. Something *supernatural*. Accepting the truth of this in his gut made him feel exquisitely vulnerable. Like he knew nothing and understood nothing. He hadn't felt anything remotely like this since those childhood nights of crouching in a dark closet while his drunken parents screamed and threw things at each other. And even that had been a mere shadow of what he was feeling now.

The hell of it was she hadn't even done much yet.

There'd been no genuine supernatural pyrotechnics of the sort he wrote about in his books. The kind of things he always pictured as rendered in cheesy CGI.

As if sensing his thoughts, Jordan lifted her head and her eyes snapped open.

They were red. Not just the pupil and the iris. Each eye . . . the whole fucking orb was *red*.

And they were glowing, projecting a sinister light that lit up her whole face. Sinister because there was a strange darkness swirling in the midst of that fiery, unnatural light, a shifting, half-formed presence that suggested capering shadows and phantoms. It was like a glimpse of hell. She smiled and Jake sensed the same darkness in the expression. He was starting to think maybe the boys had gotten it all wrong. *This* girl was the real threat, not Trey's punk girlfriend. He glanced at them and saw awestruck expressions he figured must mirror his own.

Then Jordan lifted her hands and aimed her outstretched fingers at him.

Jake gulped.

Maybe the time had come to make a run for it.

Before he could act a field of unnatural energy enveloped him. He wanted to scream, but couldn't open his mouth. Every inch of his flesh tingled in a way that was almost pleasant. Waves of blue-white electricity rolled over his body. Then she lifted her hands higher and he began to float.

Even as it was happening he thought, *This is not possible*.

The top of his head touching the ceiling seemed to suggest otherwise, though. He looked down at the others staring up at him and felt for a flashing moment like a man in the midst of a particularly weird dream. It was tempting to believe that. The problem with it was he'd never felt so alive and real than he felt in this moment.

And in the very next moment the unnatural energy suffusing the room's atmosphere simply turned off, as if someone had thrown a switch.

Jake gasped and dropped.

Kristen screamed.

His rear end hit the floor. Hard. A jagged spike of pain shot up his spine as he rolled over. Then Kristen was at his side, her fluttering hand on his back as she alternately cursed Jordan and begged him to tell her he was all right. In a moment he realized he was okay, except for the lingering pain caused by his awkward landing. Nothing was broken. He was intact. Well, his body was. His mind felt as if it might fly into a million pieces any second now. He got up muttering assurances to Kristen.

He looked at Jordan. She looked normal again.

Then he looked at each of the boys. Both looked stunned. Jake shook his head.

He settled into the recliner again and was silent for a long moment.

Then he said, "Well, fuck me."

Jordan bit down on a smile. "Told you."

"That you did. I'm sorry I didn't believe you. Sorry I made fun of you."

She looked sheepish now. Almost shy. She looked at the floor. "It's okay."

Jake grunted. "No. It's a long fucking way from okay." He slapped his knees and stood again. He put an arm around Kristen, felt the live-wire thrum of her body. "We're taking this party to the kitchen. I need a drink like never before. And then I want to hear your story in detail. Every fucking bit of it. Including why you think I can do anything about your problem. Got it?"

He waited a beat.

Nods and half-mumbled words of assent followed.

Jake led them into the kitchen.

CHAPTER THIRTY-EIGHT

After wasting perhaps fifteen minutes debating how he should dispose of the bodies stinking up his garage, Raymond Slater realized the only sensible course of action was to do nothing. There was no reason to spend hours digging more big holes in his backyard. No point in carting both bodies out to some remote backwoods spot for dumping. It would only make him feel grubby, like the kind of banal serial killers he'd seen on A&E true crime shows. Besides, he would almost certainly be dead himself by the end of the day. He wouldn't be around to sweat police inquiries.

He slammed shut the trunk of his Lexus, sealing off forever the sight of Cindy's horribly mutilated body. He covered Penelope's corpse with a tarp and shoved it under the Lexus.

Good enough.

Someone would discover the bodies in the coming days. And not just the bodies here in the garage. The authorities would find the mound of freshly turned earth in his backyard. They would dig up Patricia. He would be branded a psychotic murderer by the media. His daughter would spend the rest of her life hating him and cursing his name. But that would be fine. At least she would be alive. He no longer really believed hitmen would be dispatched to her university the instant he deviated from Lamia's instructions for the day.

Two reasons.

For one thing, this was the day of the Harvest. The day

when he was to call for a special assembly of all students at two P.M.

Except that he had gone against her will.

He wouldn't be there to call that special assembly. Hours had passed. It was early afternoon now. He suspected Lamia would have a fallback plan in place. Someone else in the school's administrative staff would summon the students to the auditorium at two.

But *he* hadn't done it, by God.

That was something, at least.

The other thing was the deal clincher. The thing that mattered to him more than anything else. Josefina. She was out of it now. She would be okay regardless of what happened in Rockville this afternoon. He knew this because he'd talked to her only moments earlier. Seated behind the wheel of Patricia's Jaguar, he stared at the cell phone in his right hand and resisted the urge to hit redial. He badly wanted to hear his only child's voice one more time, even though it would mean again interrupting the impromptu adventure she'd set out on this morning. Turned out she wasn't even at the school, having blown off the day's classes to head up to Niagara Falls with her boyfriend. They wouldn't return until the next day. And by then it would all be over. She was *safe*. That knowledge alone was enough to make the decision for him. He flipped the cell phone shut and dropped it in the cup holder. Josefina Slater had talked to her father for the last time.

Let her have one last good day, he thought. *I owe her that much. One more carefree day of youth in the company of a cute boy. This will be my gift to you, Jo. My very last gift.*

If he called her again, his voice might crack.

She would sense something was wrong.

So, no. It wasn't an option.

As he drove to the school, Raymond gripped the Jag's steering wheel and cried quietly for a few moments. It was over fast. He wouldn't allow himself the fleeting comfort of an emotional surrender. Time was running out. The hour of truth was almost at hand. He wiped the tears from his eyes and stared

through the windshield. Soon he was parked at the far edge of
the staff parking lot at Rockville High School. The school day
was still in full swing, so the lot was mostly full. The auditorium was over on the other side of the main building. The lot
on that side was packed tight with student-owned vehicles. His
immediate problem was figuring out how to get from here to
there without having to walk all the way around the school in
full view of anyone who might be looking through any of the
many classroom windows. The sight of the school's principal
crossing the school grounds would not alarm the vast majority
of potential witnesses. Most would not even be aware of his
absence today. But there was a strong chance that at least a few
of those prying eyes would belong to members of Lamia's insidious cult. He couldn't risk being intercepted before he had a
chance to take his shot (literally) at putting an end to Lamia's
evil scheme.

So he was stuck.

He thumped the steering wheel. "Damn it all. What do I
do? Christ, what do I do?"

He sat there stewing in frustration a while longer, intensely
aware of the seconds and minutes ticking by, time rushing
forward in a relentless tide toward the appointed hour. The
forceful knock on the window made him gasp and jump in his
seat. Flashing memories of this morning's disastrous encounter
with Cindy Wells zipped through his head. His head snapped
to the left and he saw the face of Carter Brown, a member of
the school's security staff, peering down at him. Brown's expression was neutral, but Raymond nonetheless glimpsed a
flicker of suspicion in his eyes.

Raymond's heart raced.

He felt paralyzed, temporarily incapable of logical thought
or action. It was very much the way he'd felt when Penelope
had come bursting into his garage. The security guard's eyes
narrowed and his features fell into a jowly frown. Instinct
guided Raymond's hand to the power-window button. He
pressed the switch and the window whirred down.

Brown tugged at his broad black belt, raised his sagging gray uniform jeans. "Afternoon, Mr. Slater. Any kind of problem here? Saw you banging on that steering wheel and got a mite worried."

Raymond forced a smile. It was difficult and he was sure the expression was just a grotesque parody of mirth. "No problem. I, uh . . . just realized I left something I need at home. My, uh . . ."

He trailed off because he realized Brown was looking past him now, at the long white box on the passenger seat.

The box containing the Mossberg pump-action shotgun.

The box clearly labeled MOSSBERG, adorned with a picture of a Mossberg pump-action shotgun.

Hell.

Brown's eyes flicked from the box back to Raymond's face. They locked gazes for a moment that seemed to last years. Then Brown reached for the radio clipped to his belt. Raymond's stomach did a slow, agonizing roll as he realized there was only one way out of this. He reached into his coat, pulled out the Glock, and aimed it at Brown's large belly.

Brown's thumb froze on the radio's talk button.

"Listen to me carefully, Brown."

Brown's jowls trembled as he swallowed a lump in his throat. His face reddened. A sudden sheen of sweat glistened at his brow. He managed a single terse nod. "Okay."

"Put the radio back on your belt."

Brown did as ordered. More sweat rolled off him. His face flushed a deeper shade of scarlet. The poor man had to be scared out of his wits. In all his years on the job—and he'd been at Rockville longer than Raymond—he'd probably never had a gun aimed at him. He looked like he was about to have a heart attack. Raymond couldn't have the man collapsing out here in the open. And he couldn't allow himself to feel sympathy for him. He was just a man doing his job. But it didn't matter. He was in the way.

"Open the door behind me. Get in the back."

Brown's lower lip trembled. "You're not going to . . . kill me . . . are you?"

Raymond forced another of those fake smiles, hoping this one would be more convincing than the last. "Of course not. I just need to talk to you. I need your help, Brown. I'm not here to commit a crime. I'm here to stop one."

Brown still didn't look convinced, but he was too frightened to do anything other than what he'd been told. Raymond tracked him with the barrel of the Glock as he reached for the door behind Raymond, opened it, and slung his considerable weight inside. The Jaguar bounced slightly as his butt hit the seat.

Raymond twisted in his seat and aimed the gun through the gap between the front seats. "Close that door."

Brown stared at the gun. The door stayed open. He looked at Raymond. "You can't stop her."

Raymond sighed.

Until now he'd harbored a small shred of hope. Hope that he could convince Brown of the threat facing Rockville's students. That he could talk the man into helping him put a stop to it. But she'd gotten to him first, and probably long ago. It was a smart move on her part. Probably every member of the security staff had been corrupted. It would make things harder than he'd already expected.

"I'm sorry, Brown."

He leaned through the gap between the seats and plunged the Glock's barrel deep into the man's big belly. Terror spurred Brown into action. A meaty fist arced toward Raymond's head, made contact with his jaw at the same instant his finger squeezed the trigger. The blow sent him crashing against the dashboard. His head wobbled and the gun slipped from his fingers, landing on the Mossberg box. Everything went gray for a few moments. Panic gripped him when everything snapped back into focus.

He groped for the fallen Glock.

He had to stop Brown before he could raise the alarm.

But Brown wasn't going anywhere. He was dead, his body slumped forward on the backseat. Blood leaked from the hole in his gut. Raymond glanced around, expecting to see other members of the security staff bearing down on the Jag. But there was no one in sight. He hoped Brown's soft belly had muffled the sound of the blast. Maybe it had. His ears were ringing, but that could be attributed to having his bell rung by Carter Brown as the man's last mortal act.

A renewed sense of urgency got him moving again.

He could hear the seconds ticking away in his head again, loud and resonant like the ticking of an old grandfather clock.

He reached between the seats and shoved Brown's corpse aside, then crawled into the back and pulled the door shut. He didn't spare the body a glance as he returned to the front seat. Three people had died today at his hands, either directly or, in the case of Cindy Wells, indirectly.

He chose to think of these deaths as necessary sacrifices.

God's way of steeling him for the greater violence to come.

He started the Jaguar, put the car in gear, and headed toward the other side of the school.

It was 12:30.

CHAPTER THIRTY-NINE

It was 12:45.

Or maybe 12:49.

The Camry's digital dashboard clock made it difficult to tell. One of the little LED filaments had given up the ghost some time ago. Five could be nine nine. Eight could be six. Numbers like three or four weren't a problem. It was easy to connect the digital dots, so to speak. But with the problem numbers the only thing you could do was wait another minute to see which way the little glowing bars would rearrange themselves. The necessary time passed while the others piled into the Camry.

Jake watched the clock as he put the car in gear and backed out of Stu Walker's driveway.

The clock moved forward a minute.

12:50.

Damn.

Jake changed gears again and hit the gas. The Camry sped down the narrow residential street. But this was not a time for caution. The situation was urgent. This he'd realized after only a few additional minutes of conversation with the kids back in Stu's kitchen.

They were with him now, bunched together in the back.

Jordan, Kelsey, and Will.

Kristen sat next to him, riding shotgun. He almost laughed at that. He wished she did have a shotgun nestled in her lap.

Their only weapons were handguns. The Glocks the boys were carrying and Stu's .38. Kristen had retrieved it from a closet shelf in Stu's bedroom. It looked like a cannon clutched in Kristen's smallish hands. Looking at her, he wished again she'd stayed behind, but she'd been adamant about accompanying him, and there'd been no time to argue.

He slowed down at a three-way stop. A quick scan in either direction revealed no oncoming traffic, so he executed a quick right turn without coming to a full stop.

He straightened the car out and looked at the clock again. 12:51.

That sense of urgency intensified. Time seemed to be moving faster. He imagined the hands of a clock moving in a fast-forward circle, minutes falling away like seconds. No. Faster. Like tiny fractions of a second. The thought roused the paranoiac within him. He'd seen things that challenged his concepts of reality. He thought again of Lamia and what these kids swore she could do. Things he no longer had any reason to doubt. And if she could do those things, was it possible that she could speed up time, or at least somehow alter the way they perceived the passage of time?

No.

He was willing to believe a lot. She was a demon. Okay. She had powers. The ability to bend people to her will by reaching into their minds. She was strong. Powerful. Almost inconceivably ancient. But even a demon would not have the power to alter the rules of time and space. He had to calm down and concentrate on the reality of the situation. Focus on what he knew and what he could do. A surrender to irrational panic would only serve to further Lamia's goals.

He made another hairpin turn and checked the rearview mirror. The kids looked as if they were nearly as afraid of his daredevil driving as they were of the demon. Their faces were ashen, their eyes wide. Jordan sat between the boys. Her hands clutched the edge of the seat between her legs. She was holding on for dear life. And she looked not at all like a person capable of levitating a human being merely by concentrating.

"Kelsey!"

The taller of the two boys flinched at the sound of his name. He looked at Jake's reflected eyes. "Yeah?"

"Tell me again about your idea."

"I'm not sure it'll work. It was just something I read in a book on ancient mythology. Could be just a lot of ancient bullshit."

They were out of Washington Heights now and headed down a wider avenue. Traffic heading into town was thicker than he would have imagined for this time of day and so he was forced to slow down. He resisted the almost overpowering temptation to weave recklessly through the tiny gaps in traffic. With his luck, they'd sideswipe an SUV or Hummer and crash, go down in an inglorious blaze. Or worse, a cop would try to pull them over. He shuddered at the possibility. There were so many ways an encounter with the police could lead to unmitigated disaster. He had two armed fugitives in his car. He could be arrested as an accomplice or accessory. Or the cop might turn out to be loyal to Lamia. Guns would be drawn. There would be shooting. Death. Maybe even his own.

Shit.

He glanced at the rearview mirror again. "That might be true, Kelsey. But we're gonna have to roll the dice here. We're damn near out of time and options. So tell us again what the book said."

Kelsey shifted in his seat and shot an uncertain glance at Will. "The book says you can't kill a demon. They're immortal. There's nothing we can do about that." He paused as he glanced at Will again. The other boy nodded and Kelsey continued: "The only way to get rid of the bitch is a banishment spell. It would expel her from the mortal realm. Maybe send her to hell or some other dimension, fuck, I don't know. The book wasn't real clear on that part."

Will said, "Somewhere *else* anyway."

Jake waited for a Mazda to ease past him and did a quick lane change; then his eyes went back to the mirror. "Sounds good. I don't care where she goes, so long as she's gone from here."

Kelsey cleared his throat. "Um . . . there is a bit of a catch."

Jake tensed. He'd figured there would be a catch. He'd hoped he was wrong about that. Hell. He was always right about things on the negative side of the scale. "Spill it."

Kelsey's jaw tightened. He didn't want to say it, but forced the words out anyway: "It would require a . . . blood sacrifice."

Kristen's head snapped toward Jake. He looked at her and was startled by the change in her. She'd said nothing since leaving the house, had just sat there staring straight ahead, looking numb and zoned out. But now she looked alert and anxious. She still didn't say anything, but her eyes conveyed a warning of some kind. A silent rebuke. But why? It was strange but he couldn't worry about it right now.

He glanced over his shoulder at Kelsey. "A blood sacrifice? Would that be like a voodoo thing, with an animal?"

Kelsey grimaced. "No. It has to be a human sacrifice."

Jake laughed and shook his head. "Well, of fucking course it does. We wouldn't get off that easy. Any other insane requirements for this barbaric ancient ritual? I understand those long-ago jackasses were big on sacrificing virgins. Usually young female virgins." He laughed again as he made another lane change, sliding in behind an old but immaculate Lincoln Continental with a single, incongruous sticker on its bumper: LET YOUR FREAK FLAG FLY! "Because I don't know about the rest of you, but I think we're gonna have a problem locating one of those within an hour."

"Book didn't say anything about virgins or the sex of the victim, just that it has to be human."

"Great. Chalk up one for our side, I guess." Jake drummed his fingers on the steering wheel. He was feeling more anxious by the moment. There was so much they didn't know. So many things they were probably overlooking. The drumming rhythm intensified as he tried to kick his mind into gear. Then he thought of something. "Say . . . where is that book now?"

"Um . . ."

"Spit it out."

"Well . . ." Kelsey sighed. "It's back there." He jerked a thumb over his shoulder. "In the Oldsmobile. We left in such a hurry . . ."

Jake groaned. "Right. Of course." He'd insisted on leaving the Olds behind. The police were looking for it, after all. See? Here was one of those overlooked things. A potentially fatal miscalculation. "And I suppose the book has info we need to do this thing up right?"

Kelsey shifted in his seat again. "The book lays out the whole ritual for performing a banishment spell. How to perform the sacrifice. With a knife, by the way. There are chants the person performing the sacrifice has to, uh, chant."

"The chants are in the book?"

"Yeah."

Jake ceased drumming the steering wheel and wrapped his fingers tight around the hard plastic. "We need that fucking book."

Jordan leaned forward, poked her head between the seats. "We don't have time to go back. We do that, the Harvest will begin without us. We'll be too late."

Jake glanced at the clock.

Almost 1:00.

Kelsey had risked sending a text message to one of his friends, a fellow student at Rockville High he was sure he could trust. The friend verified that a special assembly had been called for two P.M. If Will's mother had told him the truth—and there was no reason to doubt she had—this would be when Lamia would initiate her Harvest of Souls. Jordan was right. Going back for the book at this point was out of the question.

Now Kelsey leaned forward and Jordan retreated. "She's right. But there's a Barnes & Noble on the way, at a strip mall right off the street. It's a long shot, but they might have another copy there."

Kristen said, "We are not performing any goddamned blood sacrifice."

Jake ignored the comment. He knew she was on edge. Brittle. She might fall apart any moment. Getting into an argument with her would be counterproductive. To understate.

He looked at Kelsey. "Right. We make a pit stop at Barnes & Noble. Think. Is there anything else we need before we get to the school?"

"Just a knife."

"I've got an old switchblade in the glove box. Will that do?"

"I guess it'll have to."

"Did you hear what I fucking said?" Kristen's eyes flashed as she leaned toward Jake. Her nostrils flared. There was a harsher, more emphatic edge in her voice now. A tone indicating no tolerance for disagreement. "We're not doing this. Are you stupid? Who are you thinking of sacrificing anyway?"

Jake looked at her. He hesitated. He knew what he needed to say would only incense her further. But there was just no way around it. He'd intuited the only solution the moment Kelsey told him the victim only needed to be human. And it sucked. It really did. He didn't particularly want to die. He made his expression as sober as he could and said, "It has to be me."

"What!?"

Kristen's scream reverberated in the car.

Jake cringed and looked away from her. "It's the only way."

"Bullshit it is!" Kristen leaned closer and grabbed a handful of his shirt. "You're all I've got left. I won't let you do this."

Jake peeled her hand away and smoothed his shirt. "What do you propose we do, then? Just let all those kids die?"

"Fuck them."

Jake gaped at her. "Kristen—"

"I mean it. They're nothing to me." She glanced at the kids in the back. "Them, too. I don't care what happens to them. We should just drop them off and skip town. You said you'd take me back to Minnesota with you, remember?"

Jake put a hand to his temple. Her ranting was making his

head hurt. He'd known his impulsive offer to take her with him when he left might come back to haunt him, but he hadn't expected it to happen so soon. "We can't do that. Think about what you're saying, Kristen. One of those kids you don't give a shit about is Trey. I understand that you're upset. This on the heels of what happened to your brother has to be almost too much to bear. But—"

"ALMOST!?"

Her voice rose to screech level now, felt like a knife going through his skull.

She went on: "And as for *your* precious brother, he didn't seem too interested in your help this morning. He hit you, remember? So, yeah, fuck him, too."

Jordan made a sound of disgust. "Could you please shut the fuck up? And by the way, I don't care what happens to you either, bitch."

Jake's stomach began to knot up. He could feel the situation spinning out of control, and didn't have the first clue what to do about it.

Kristen twisted in her seat and aimed Stu's .38 at Jordan's midsection. "Talk to me like that again and I'll shoot you. You do not want to fuck with me."

Jordan sneered. "Right. I'm half demon, remember? What could your bullets do to me?"

"I don't know, bitch. Maybe I should pumps six rounds straight into your face and find out."

Jake's hands were shaking on the steering wheel. He'd sensed before that Kristen harbored a fearsome temper. That it could be so . . . overwhelming, though, came as a revelation. He recalled what she'd said about her boyfriend kicking her out for unspecified transgressions and knew he should have headed off any sort of relationship with her in that moment.

Hindsight, as always, was a motherfucker.

He braced a hand on Kristen's shoulder and shoved her back into her seat. She gasped in surprise and glared at him.

Jordan laughed. "Oooh. Boyfriend lays the smack down."

Kristen screamed again and lunged toward the gap between the seats.

Jake shoved her back again and said, "STOP!" He glanced at the rearview mirror, sought Jordan's eyes and found them. "That goes for both of you. Knock it the fuck off."

There was a lull in the battle then. Kristen sat panting in the front seat. That and the thrum of traffic around them were the only sounds for more than a minute.

Then Jake relaxed his grip on the steering wheel and exhaled a long breath. "I've made up my mind, Kristen. This has to be done. There's no one else. I'm sure as hell not asking one of these kids to take my place. I told you before to stay home, but you didn't listen. If you want, I can drop you off at the bookstore. You could call a taxi to take you home."

Kristen looked at him. She was outwardly calmer now, her expression smooth and unreadable. But a glint in her eyes hinted a still-raging storm within. "No. You're stuck with me."

"Even if it means watching me die?"

Kristen didn't say anything, just stared at him.

Kelsey said, "Hey, there's that mall."

Jake saw the strip mall coming up on the right. The Barnes & Noble looked to be the main attraction here, dominating the center of the retail space. He flicked on the blinker, switched lanes, and slowed down as they neared the parking lot. The lot was crowded, so he pulled to a stop outside the store's entrance and fished his wallet out of his back pocket. He extracted a fifty-dollar bill and passed it back to Kelsey.

"That should cover it. Get on in there and find that book or something similar. I'll cruise the lot and circle back."

Kristen said, "You're forgetting something."

Jake braced himself for another argument, but made himself look at her anyway. "Yeah?"

Kristen's expression remained placid, her tone even. "The police are looking for him. He shouldn't be showing his face in public."

Jake cursed himself for overlooking something so obvious. "Oh. Right."

Kristen twisted in her seat again and extended a hand toward Kelsey. "Give me the money. I'll go get the book."

Jordan snorted. "Yeah, right. And pretend not to find it."

She snatched the fifty from Kelsey's fingertips and climbed over him. She pushed against the back of the seat with an unnecessary level of force, jostling Kristen as she reached for the door handle. Then the door was open and she was standing outside.

She leaned down and peered through the open window. "What's the name of that book?"

Kelsey told her.

She shot a distinctly unfriendly smile at Kristen and said, "I'll be right back."

Then she turned away from them and headed into the store.

Kristen seethed. "I could strangle her. I swear."

Jake didn't reply.

He put the Camry in gear again and drove away from the curb.

CHAPTER FORTY

The auditorium was abuzz with excitement as the students of Rockville High began to file in. Some hurried to claim the premium seats up front, while the usual mix of stoners and burnouts went immediately to the seats at the very back. The reason for the special assembly still had not been announced, but rumors were flying about a special performance by a local rock band that had just been signed to a major record label. The rumor was spread by Lamia's small contingent of student followers, who would die alongside their classmates today. These students believed their sacrifices would be rewarded in the afterlife. Of all the many lies Lamia had told them, this had been the most compelling. She had convinced them they would rule as kings and queens in a vague ethereal kingdom.

Lamia found it amusing.

They were in for quite the surprise on the other side of the veil.

Eternal misery instead of eternal bliss.

It gave her great pleasure to think of the eons of pain awaiting them. However, she did feel a grudging appreciation for how effectively they had spread the rumor. Although they were not actually here, the band rumored to play was real enough. Their fliers were up all over town. And most of the students now seemed convinced the closed curtain at the front of the stage would soon part to reveal musical instruments and stacks of amplifiers. This was good. It kept the stu-

dents interested and happy and diverted speculation about
other reasons for the special assembly. And it eliminated the
need to spend too many minutes waiting for stragglers. The
auditorium was filling quickly.

Most of Lamia's adult acolytes had gathered for the event, as
well. Some of them were positioned at the various entrances to
the auditorium, forming a sort of rear guard that would inter-
cept any students attempting to flee once the Harvest was underway. The others were with her in the backstage area. They
talked quietly among each other, but anticipation was evident
in their eager expressions. Here was another thing from which
she derived significant pleasure. How willing these simple fools
were to sacrifice their offspring. She wandered among them
with an enigmatic smile on her face, nodding when some
greeted her by speaking the name of her new host. Here was
the mayor with a glass of brandy in his hand, conversing in low
tones with the chief of police. And over here was Mrs.
Cheever, the elderly librarian. A young Novice was on his
hands and knees before her, licking the soles of the librarian's
shoes. The gullibility of humans never failed to amuse Lamia.
There was no real difference between Novices, Adepts, and
Priestesses. These titles implying a complex level of hierarchy
were all just things she'd made up over time and carried no real
weight with her. Humans were all equally loathsome in her
eyes. And, of course, none of them knew they would all die
after she'd finished with the students, a sort of after-dinner
snack. There were no real "chosen ones," either. The ones
she'd favored had served a single, simple purpose—to keep the
rest in line when she wasn't around. She looked forward to de-
vouring them all. The soul-energy harbored by adults was not
fresh and strong, but she would take it anyway. Lamia always
felt greedy at harvest time. Today she would gorge herself.

She stopped at a table and poured herself a glass of vodka-
spiked punch. She tossed the drink back and poured another.
A pleasant warmth began to suffuse her. Of all the sensory
pleasures available to her in the human form, the effects of alcohol ranked a close second behind sex. This made her think

of Jake McAllister, her favorite human in recent memory. And also her best object lesson. Her relationship with him during her time as Moira had been intense. Lots of booze. Lots of sex. Lots of reckless behavior in general. He was the closest she'd ever come to losing control. And that time was the closest she'd come to losing sight of her real purpose, which was simply to perpetuate her existence throughout the ages. She had felt something for him. Something almost like human love. And it had frightened her. She'd had to fight to reclaim her true nature. She eventually succeeded, of course, but by then an incredible, impossible thing had happened—Jake had impregnated her. In all the many thousands of years of her existence, it had never happened before. She'd thought it *couldn't* happen, but there'd been no denying the nature of her condition.

Drastic measures had been called for.

An accident was staged. Moira "died."

And Michael McAllister died for real.

Lamia retired to the shadows for a time and eventually gave birth to a baby girl. Half human. Half demon. And, as far as Lamia knew, an absolute one of a kind. There were many other demons. None of them had ever procreated, as far as she knew. The mystery of how and why it had happened had troubled her. Was it a sign of decay? A signal from the gods that her natural cycle was at long last near an end? She knew demons could not die. But the arrival of her child was unusual enough to spur many wild musings. For a brief time, she considered killing the baby, but could not bring herself to do it. She instead recruited an ostensibly normal family to raise the girl, whom they christened Jordan.

And now a reunion was in the offing. Jordan and her father were on their way to the auditorium, were perhaps outside the building even now.

Lamia couldn't deny it.

She was looking forward to seeing them again.

A young woman approached her at the refreshments table.

"Hello, Bridget. Where's Angela? I thought she'd be with you."

Lamia spooned more punch into her glass and looked at the woman, a plumpish brunette named Megan. "Why did you think that?"

Megan smirked. "You're lovers, aren't you? Least that's what I've heard on the grapevine."

"We broke up," Lamia said. "I don't know where she is."

Megan assumed an expression of pity. A not-so-subtle mocking quality was just beneath the surface. "Oh, that's too bad." Then her expression brightened and she flashed a phony smile that dripped venom. "I'm sure you'll find some other dyke to lick your rancid twat soon enough."

Lamia's smile never faltered. "You don't like me much, do you?"

"How did you guess?"

Lamia sipped punched and stared at the woman over the rim of her glass. The temptation to snap the woman's neck was strong, but she'd hoped to hide in her new host a little longer. She lowered the glass and smacked her lips. "Go away, Megan."

Megan laughed. "Why? Did I hurt your feelings? And what have you done to yourself? Those clothes look like you dug them out of a time capsule. And what's with the Bon Jovi circa 1989 hair? Somebody not tell me about a costume party after the Harvest?"

She had wondered when someone would comment on her new look. It was something she had cooked up solely for Jake McAllister's benefit. Bridget's familial resemblance to Moira was strong to begin with, but she'd realized there were some things she could do to emphasize it. Some quality time in front of a mirror with a can of Aquanet went a long way toward painting the proper picture. The rest of it was a matter of selecting the proper clothes and applying the right makeup. She wore a denim jacket over a frilly blouse and a tight black miniskirt. The whole outfit screamed '80s groupie slut, an impression completed by a dramatic application of eye shadow and a thick layer of mascara that emphasized her cheekbones.

Jake would look at her and think immediately of Moira.

Exactly as he remembered her.

She couldn't wait to see his shocked expression.

"Are you even hearing me?"

Lamia blinked. She'd been vaguely aware that Megan was still speaking, but she'd tuned the woman out. "Excuse me?"

Megan rolled her eyes. "Idiot. I would say all that hair spray has scrambled your brains, but you didn't have a lot going on upstairs to begin with, did you?"

Something cold and filled with an ageless hatred flexed inside Lamia. It was an instinct she was helpless to quell once it asserted itself. An imperative delivered straight from the primal center of her psyche. She finished the last of her punch and set the glass on the table.

Then she gripped Megan's wrist and snapped it.

Megan's high-pitched scream silenced all backstage chatter and temporarily quietened the collective rumble of voices from the auditorium. Lamia kept a grip on Megan's broken wrist with one hand and slapped the other over the woman's gaping mouth. She twisted the mangled wrist and Megan dropped helplessly to her knees. Lamia forced the trembling woman to meet her gaze. There was an immediate spark of recognition in the woman's eyes. She began to whimper.

A man nearby said, "Oh my God. It's her."

A breathless female whisper: "Lamia."

Then there was silence again. Lamia surveyed the faces of those present. Some averted their eyes. Others dropped to their knees and bowed their heads. The chief of police put a hand down his pants to stroke a sudden erection. A few minutes passed and the roar of the crowd began to build again. The building was alive with anticipation. The students would have their show soon. It wouldn't be what they were expecting, but it would be memorable. Too bad for them they wouldn't be around to remember it.

Lamia smiled. "I believe this cunt's husband is present. Correct?"

A tall, slender man in a cheap blue suit stepped forward. "Um . . . that would be me."

"Elliot, correct?"

The man licked his lips. He was nervous. Scared shitless. For good reason. He wiped his mouth with the back of a hand and nodded. "That's right."

"I'm about to kill your wife, Elliot. You have anything to say about that?"

The man's eyes danced nervously in his sockets. He was sweating. He looked at his trembling wife and a shadow seemed to pass over his face. He shuddered. "Nothing." He coughed and straightened his tie. His composure returned and he even managed a small, shaky smile. "Nothing at all, really. Other than wishing it'd happened a long time ago."

Lamia's smile broadened as she forced Megan to look her in the eye again. "Hear that, Megan? You're about to die. On your knees at my feet. And no one in the world gives a damn. Not even your pedophile husband. Oh, yes. It's true. He's a baby raper. Carry that pleasant thought to hell with you."

Megan whimpered again.

Tears spilled from her eyes in a hot rush.

There was a collective gasp from the others in the room as Lamia pushed her fingers through Megan's pliant flesh and began to peel her face off. That was only the beginning. Megan remained alive for several more minutes as Lamia plucked her eyes from their sockets and pulled out her tongue. She only finished off the woman as she began to go into shock. Lamia then tossed the corpse aside and grinned at the thunderstruck expressions of her acolytes.

"So much for the warm-up act. It's time for the main event. I've waited long enough. A hundred years, to be exact."

Lamia left the backstage area, passed through a small hallway and began to walk across the mostly bare stage. She reveled in the growing roar of the crowd as she strode toward the narrow gap between the drawn curtains. The curtains began to part and the crowd noise reached a crescendo. There was applause punctuated by whoops and whistles. Students stamped their feet on the floor. It really did feel like the buildup to a rock-and-roll show. But the excitement gave way to a growing confusion as the lack of drums and guitars became obvious.

Lamia approached a podium at the front of the stage and waited for the murmurs of discontent to abate. Then she leaned toward a microphone and said, "I realize most of you were expecting something else. Something fun." She giggled. "But there will be no more fun for any of you."

A few members of the audience shouted insults. Most of these emanated from the burnout contingent in the back rows.

Lamia raised her hands and signaled for silence. She didn't get it, but the noise tapered off enough to again address the students. "Please direct your attention to the doors at the back of the auditorium and those to the left and right of the stage."

The students twisted in their seats and craned their necks. Lamia grinned at the sea of confused faces as men wearing hoods linked door handles with heavy chains and secured them with big iron padlocks. The tone of the murmurs began to change. Lamia felt a sudden arousal as she detected the first inklings of fear. It was delicious. Intoxicating. And it was only an appetizer. She felt stronger now than she had in a long time. Very soon she would be stronger than she'd ever been. This would be the most bountiful Harvest since medieval times.

Her laughter boomed over the auditorium's speaker system.

"It's all over, children. No more studying for exams. No more trying to dodge that bully in the hallway. No more fretting about not living up to your parents' expectations. These earthly concerns are beyond you now. I know you'll all be grateful to be relieved of these burdens."

Someone screamed, "Fuck you, slut!"

There was a bit of nervous laughter, but it was a token thing. The eyes of most were glued to her, and the expressions of those staring at her were nearly identical.

They were afraid.

So delightfully afraid.

A group of football jocks got up and strode purposefully toward one of the chained entrances. The boy in the lead pointed a finger at one of the hooded men and said, "Get out of my way, motherfucker!"

The hooded man did not flinch.

Lamia said, "The time has come. This is the Harvest of Souls. Time to die, boys and girls!"

The hooded guard produced a handgun and shot the lead jock between the eyes.

Shocked silence. Maybe a full second of it.

Then came the screams.

Lamia smiled and spread her arms wide as she walked to the edge of the stage.

Students surged out of their seats. The auditorium erupted in pandemonium. The kids fought and crawled over each other in a blind rush to get to the exits.

More screams.

More gunfire.

Energy flowed from the ends of Lamia's outstretched fingertips. The air crackled and a dazzling light filled the auditorium. Sizzling strands of blue-white electricity arced out of her fingers to form a glowing, pulsing web on the ceiling.

Lamia threw back her head, exulting in the glory of it all.

The Harvest had begun.

CHAPTER FORTY-ONE

It was starting already.

Raymond could feel it in his bones and at the back of his mouth like the sting of a poison. Even here, hunched down in the floor of Patricia's Jaguar, the atmospheric shift was palpable. The air felt charged the way it did before a storm. There was that same pregnant stillness in the last moments before that first furious clap of thunder. And yet a glance through the Jaguar's windows revealed only a clear blue sky.

Raymond crawled out of the floor and stared at the back of the school.

The rear entrance—which opened to a hallway directly adjacent to the backstage area of the auditorium—stood open. Ten minutes ago there'd been two men there, standing guard, admitting a steady stream of local luminaries, as well as a handful of people he didn't recognize. The mayor was here. So were the chief of police and a couple of city commissioners. A number of heavy hitters in the local business community were also present. Many of them wore formal attire, as if they were arriving for the opening night of an opera or play. They parked their cars in the lot of the nearby public library and walked across a short expanse of green lawn, looking almost regal in the brilliant sunlight. You would never guess these respectable-looking people had gathered to revel in the deaths of so many of Rockville's young.

Raymond had wedged the Jag into a narrow space at the end

of a row in the student parking lot. He'd had to run the driver side tires up over the curb to fit the Jag in the space. More than an hour had passed since he'd had to shoot Carter Brown. The Jag's interior was thick with the sickly sweet stench of recent death. He yearned to be out of the car and away from the corpse, but he hadn't dared to make a move with the guards around. But now they were gone, presumably to grab a ringside seat for the slaughter.

The slaughter . . .

The full weight of the situation fell upon him again and his breath caught in his throat. It was happening. People were dying in that building *right now*. Kids. Hundreds of them.

He was terrified.

Yet he knew he couldn't wait another second.

He sucked in a big breath and expelled it fast.

"Go," he told himself.

He reached for the driver side door handle, pulled it, and kicked the door open wide. He stepped out and stood erect. He checked the Glock. Safety off. The pockets of his black trench coat were heavy with the weight of spare clips and shotgun shells. He reached back into the car to retrieve the Mossberg. Then, with the Mossberg pointed at the ground in one hand and the Glock in the other, he began to move toward the rear entrance.

He was halfway there when one of the guards stepped back through the door and noticed him. The man gaped at him for a moment, obviously not believing what he was seeing. Raymond thought of how he must look—like a heavily armed outlaw approaching the OK Corral at high noon—and a grim smile curved the corners of his mouth.

He increased his stride and cut the remaining distance in half.

The guard snapped out of it and reached for his weapon, but by then it was too late. Raymond squeezed the Glock's trigger. The gun boomed and a bright patch of red bloomed at the center of the man's gray uniform shirt. He fell dead to the ground with his weapon still in its holster. Raymond was close enough to the open door now to hear the screams, high and keening, aural testimony to intense agony and horrible death.

Raymond started running.

In another moment he was past the dead guard and through the open entrance. He was in a hallway now, with rows of gray metal lockers to either side of him. There was an open door on the left, some ten yards ahead. It also stood open, like an invitation to hell. Come on in, it seemed to say. We've been waiting for you. Raymond shivered and started toward the door. The screams were louder now. It was the most awful sound he'd ever heard, like something from the worst nightmares of a madman come to life. And there was another sound, something like the whine of a large generator working at peak capacity.

He stepped through the door and went up a short set of stairs to another door. This one was closed. He tucked the Mossberg under his arm and turned the knob. He threw open the door and waited a beat. No one came to investigate. There were no shots. But the terrible screams were louder still. That, more than anything else, got him moving again. He went through the open door and moved down a short hallway past a dressing room.

Then he came into the larger backstage area and saw them. All those local bigwigs with their spouses and/or lovers. They stood with their backs to him, watching the show from the wings.

Raymond hesitated.

He knew he had to kill as many of them as possible. At least any of them who got in his way. But for a moment he couldn't bring himself to start shooting at their backs. It was something basic hardwired within him. Every boy raised on old Westerns knew it was cowardly to shoot unarmed people, especially in the back.

One of those backs stiffened abruptly.

A man in a tuxedo turned toward him.

It was Sheldon Prather, the chief of police.

He opened his mouth to say something, perhaps raise the alarm.

Raymond shot him in the face.

A hole appeared between the man's eyes and a larger hole erupted at the back of his head. Blood and tissue from the exit wound splashed the front of Mrs. Cheever's evening gown as the dead man's body staggered backward a step before toppling to the floor. They all turned to face him then, and their expressions were a mixture of shock and hatred. And then outrage. He saw it in their eyes. He was here to spoil it. To stop the sacred Harvest. Raymond spared another second to study the faces of men and women he'd thought he'd known so well. Friends and neighbors. Colleagues. Formerly God-fearing members of several local churches.

Secretly monsters, all of them.

Raymond set his jaw and advanced on them.

Fuck them all.

He squeezed the Glock's trigger again and again. The gun bucked in his hand, a wild thing working at his will as he kept his aim steady enough to mow them down. They fled to the stage and he started after them, firing at their backs, no longer caring a damn about whether it made him a coward. They fell, one by one, holes appearing in their torsos and heads. He felt like an avenging angel come to earth to invoke the wrath of God.

He paused a moment to eject the Glock's spent clip and slap another one home.

He raised the gun to resume the righteous slaughter.

Then he felt it.

The cold steel barrel against the back of his head.

No.

He was so close. It couldn't end this way. The screams of the children taunted him. He was their only hope. He would not surrender. Not now. Not ever. Instinct caused him to spin and lash out at the son of a bitch who'd gotten the drop on him. He struck the man's arm in the millisecond before the gun went off. Raymond staggered backward, a burst of bright pain setting his torso afire. The Mossberg flew out of his left hand and went spinning across the shiny floor.

But the Glock was still in his right hand.

He raised it and managed to squeeze off one round in the same instant another bullet punched through his stomach and sent him to the floor.

The pain was extraordinary. It unmanned him. He cried out for his mother and knew he was finished. But he managed to raise his head and saw the guard on his knees, with a hand held over a bloody hole in his own belly. Raymond raised the Glock one last time and shot the man in the throat, finishing him.

The gun slipped from his numb fingers and thunked on the floor.

He knew there was no way he could lift it again.

I've failed, he thought.

They'll all die. All the children.

And it's all my fault.

This was his last conscious thought before slipping beyond the veil.

The harrowing screams from the auditorium continued unabated.

CHAPTER FORTY-TWO

It was after 2:00.

It was already happening.

The fucking Harvest.

Jake cranked the Camry's steering wheel as he blew through the four-way stop where Marlowe intersected with Spillane Boulevard. A blue Hyundai slammed on its brakes in the middle of the intersection as the Camry missed sideswiping its left fender by inches. The Hyundai's driver shook a fist at him and honked his horn. Jake was too busy getting the Camry turned in the right direction to give a shit about the other guy's righteous indignation. The Camry's passengers let out startled cries and swayed from one side of the vehicle to the other. Jake felt their pain, but they'd wasted too much time already. Traffic laws and the potential for collateral damage en route to Rockville High were the least of their concerns.

Damn the torpedoes and full speed ahead.

He looked at the clock again.

2:04.

Fuck.

He whipped the steering wheel back the other way and now they were roaring along at seventy-five miles an hour down Spillane, where the posted speed limit was forty.

Rockville High loomed up ahead, now only a quarter mile away.

They should already have been there. Should already have

made their big play. It could all have been over by now. All
things considered, they would have been better off turning
back to retrieve the book from Kelsey's Oldsmobile. Jordan
wound up spending too much time inside the Barnes & Noble.
The store didn't have a copy of the same book. Other books
on ancient mythology alluded to the banishment ritual, but did
not contain the necessary chants. They took a detour to the
west side of Rockville to check out a used bookstore Will
knew about. By then all bets were off. They all scrambled out
of the Camry and rushed into Rhino Used Books, no longer
caring whether anyone recognized the boys. And again they
spent too much time in the store. The shelves in the nonfic-
tion sections were all double stacked. Some were triple stacked,
with old musty paperbacks tucked into every available nook
and crevice. Still others were packed tight inside boxes on the
floor. They'd had to pull out the stacks and sort through the
titles individually. They did this with a callous disregard that
upset the clerk on duty, who yelled at them about tossing
books on the floor. He threatened to call the cops at one point.
Kristen ushered him into a back room at gunpoint, secured
him somehow, and returned to flip the Open sign on the
front door over to Closed.

Then, at last, Jordan turned up the right book. It was even
the same edition. A price of one dollar had been scrawled in
faded pencil on the first inside page. At Jake's direction, Jordan dropped the fifty-dollar bill he'd given her earlier on the
desk as payment and they got out of there.

Jake prayed the delay wouldn't prove too costly.

Prayed that not too many kids had died already.

He tapped the Camry's brakes as they neared the school,
twisted the wheel hard again, then gunned across the main
parking lot toward the far side of the school. He pulled to a
screeching stop between two rows of cars. An instant later the
Camry's doors popped open and its occupants again scrambled out. They didn't bother to shut the doors, knowing they
might have to beat a hasty retreat.

They all saw the same thing in the same moment.

Will said, "Holy shit."

Jake felt a sickness swell inside his belly. Bile touched the back of his throat. If he'd harbored any lingering traces of denial or doubt, the sight of the dead guard vanquished them forever. He fought back the tide of nausea and placed himself in front of the others.

He looked at Kelsey. "We're going in. No time to fuck around, get the lay of the land, any of that shit. You got that book ready?"

Kelsey raised a hand, his fingers bookmarking the proper page. It was a strange juxtaposition. Mythology book in one hand. Glock in the other. He looked like a deranged scholar. "Got it."

Jake nodded. He looked at each of them in turn, sparing none of them more than a second. Not even Kristen. She seemed to have cast her reservations aside and was as swept up in the moment as any of them. She looked him in the eye and nodded.

Jake heaved a breath. "Right. Let's go."

He turned away from them and led a grim march toward the school.

Kelsey moved closer to Will as they neared the school's rear entrance. There was something fucked up happening in there. The screams alone told him that. But there was more to it. The atmosphere surrounding the school was alive with some kind of unnatural energy. It made his flesh tingle and his nads shrivel. It was similar to the way he'd felt during Jordan's levitation trick, only intensified a thousandfold. A sudden and very intense desire not to venture inside the school gripped him.

Who the hell did he think he was anyway?

John fucking Wayne riding to the rescue?

Who was he kidding?

He searched Will's pale face and saw at once his friend was

thinking similar thoughts. He could also tell Will knew the same unfortunate truth. Their fear didn't matter. Their friends were in there. *Trey* was in there. And his only hope of salvation was this banishment spell, which, by God, better not turn out to be a bunch of made-up ancient hokum.

It was their only shot.

We're doomed, he thought. *Oh fuck. We're doomed.*

He nudged Will with an elbow. "You ready for this, man?"

Will swallowed and nodded. "I . . . think so."

"Well, that makes one of us."

And then there was no time left for idle conversation. They'd arrived at the entrance and the screams ripped at their ears. Kelsey worked hard to control the sudden tremors rippling through his body as they passed through the entrance and stood in the hallway, but it was impossible. His mind flashed on the movie *Saving Private Ryan.* Those soldiers in the landing boats, most of them hardly more than kids themselves. Crossing themselves and saying final prayers in those last moments before storming the beach at Normandy. For the first time, he thought he truly understood how it must have felt to have been in one of those boats.

A door on the left stood open maybe ten yards ahead.

The screams grew louder still as they approached it.

They were a few strides away when a door to their right flew open and Alexis Mackeson came at them in a rush, a scream tearing out of her mouth as she veered toward her son. Will froze in his tracks and gaped at her. There was a large bruise on her forehead. And matted blood in her hair. She was wild-eyed. A savage. She was nothing at all like the very proper society lady Kelsey had known.

There was a knife in her hand.

A big one.

Kelsey's mind reeled.

What the hell?

The last they'd seen of her she'd been tied up and stuffed inside a closet. How had she gotten here? Who had released her?

She had lain in wait for him.

Had somehow known he would come here.

In the time it took for these thoughts to flit through his head, she brought the knife around in a savage arc and ripped a gash in Will's throat. Blood leaped from the wound as Will staggered backward and banged into a row of lockers.

"NOOOOOO!"

Then the booming report of a gun overrode his cry of grief. Kristen stood ramrod straight in a classic shooter's stance and pumped several rounds into Alexis. The woman's body jerked as each slug tore through it, then toppled to the floor.

Will was on the ground now.

On his back.

His eyes staring up at the ceiling tiles.

Kelsey dropped to his knees, the book slipping from his fingers.

He scooted across the floor.

Stared down at his friend's eyes.

His dead, sightless eyes.

In the next moment a scream of his own joined the chorus of agony issuing from the auditorium.

He could feel it all slipping away, his control of the situation pouring like sand through his fingers.

No.

Not like that.

Like blood from a mortal wound. A deep gash in the neck, say. And no matter how desperately you wished to stop the hemorrhaging, you just couldn't do it. Jake stared at the dead boy on the floor and for a moment was stunned insensible. He just stood there. He didn't know what to do next. Didn't have the first *inkling*. He'd known he was heading into a life-or-death situation. Knowing that on an intellectual level was all well and good. But it did nothing to prepare you for that first moment of sudden, shocking violence. He doubted anything could prepare a person for this. He looked at Kelsey's tear-streaked face and wished he could ease the boy's pain somehow.

But there was one thing he could try to do.

The only thing left.

He reached for the fallen book.

As he knelt he became aware of a new sound rising above the screams from the auditorium. It was an ominous sound he associated with the impending storm. He was down on one knee when he heard Kristen shout his name. The alarm in her voice diverted him from the task of retrieving the book. He looked up and saw several pieces of notebook paper come swirling down the length of the corridor, buffeted by a powerful, rushing . . .

WIND.

Now hold on a second.

This didn't make sense.

A wind originating from *inside* the school?

How—

And then it hit him. It was like being struck by hurricane winds. The force of it knocked him off his feet and sent him sliding several feet down the hallway. He rolled onto his stomach and saw the mythology book go flying past him, the slim volume's pages flapping in the gale, looking for a moment like a wounded bird struggling to stay aloft. For a nanosecond, he saw it framed in the light visible through the open back doors. Then it was gone.

Someone screamed.

He didn't know who.

Could even have been himself.

A burst of adrenaline slammed into him and he surged to his feet to stagger after the book. The wind continued to buffet him, slamming him against the lockers more than once, but he managed to stay upright through a monumental effort of physical will. Then he was through the doors and back in the parking lot. The strange wind followed him out of the building, blew past him, and lifted the book off the asphalt. He dove for the book and a fingertip brushed its spine for a moment before it flew high into the sky and disappeared forever.

He screamed and pounded the pavement with his fist. He was so lost in feelings of impotent rage that he hardly noticed the wind had ceased blowing.

Then Kristen was kneeling next to him, a trembling hand on his back. "Jake? Baby, get up. We've got to get out of here."

Jake found a fresh reserve of strength and pushed himself to his knees. He stared at the open rear entrance, saw only the dead security guard. He looked at Kristen. "Jordan. Kelsey. Where are they?"

She hesitated a moment; then her shoulders sagged. "Still in the school."

Jake got to his feet and started walking back toward the school.

Kristen hurried after him, grabbed him by an elbow, stopped him. She spun him toward her. "Did you hear me? We have to go. Now."

Jake shook his head. "I'm not leaving them in there."

Kristen made a sound of frustration. "You don't even know them! Don't you get it yet? This is bigger than us! There's nothing we can do to stop it. The fucking army couldn't stop this. We have to leave before we're dead, too."

Jake looked at her and felt a bone-deep weariness. The day had started off with a monster hangover and he was still feeling some of its effects. He was in nowhere near peak physical condition to begin with. Factor in an ass-kicking at the hands of his jock brother, an afternoon spent speeding around town like some kind of berserk meth-head, and what you wound up with was an exhaustion so enervating all he wanted was to find a comfortable bed and sleep twenty-four hours straight. And yet he knew he couldn't just run away. Not this time. Maybe he couldn't save the Rockville High class of 2009, but he could at least try to save two people. And it didn't matter that they were strangers. They were human beings. The girl was maybe even related to him somehow. He wouldn't be able to live with himself if he didn't make the effort.

"I have to try."

Kristen made a face. "Fuck."

Jake started toward the school again. "You can leave without me. I understand."

She followed him. "Right. You know I can't do that."

"Just so you know. I wish you would go. But there's no time to waste trying to convince you."

They stepped through the rear entrance again. Pages of notebook paper—the contents of someone's discarded folder—littered the floor. Kelsey was where they'd left him, still knelt over the corpse of his best friend.

Jake approached him, put a hand on his shoulder. "Kelsey . . . where's Jordan?"

Kelsey sniffled and looked at him through eyes shiny with tears. "I don't know," he said in a numb monotone. "She was gone when the wind stopped."

Jake grimaced. "Fuck."

Of course.

It fit right in with everything else that had happened today. Nothing could go down the clean and easy way. If he'd found them, he would've heeded Kristen's advice. She was right. They couldn't win. They'd been stupid to ever believe they could. But with Jordan missing, he felt obligated to look for her.

"You didn't see where she went at all?"

"I just told you, I looked up and she was gone."

Jake sighed and looked at the open door to the auditorium. His stomach churned and he felt faint. It was the only place she could have gone. He would have to go in there.

He took a step toward the door.

Kristen grabbed him by the arm again, more forcefully this time. "No. I mean it. You're not going in there. If I have to, I'll shoot you in the fucking foot and drag your stupid ass out to the car."

Jake looked at the door again.

Then he looked at Kristen, saw the fierce determination on her face. She would really do it, he knew. Shoot him to save him from himself. He could feel his resolve diminishing. It was so tempting to just admit defeat and slink away.

Then something happened that frightened him more than anything else that had happened.

The screams stopped.

There was a long moment of frozen silence. None of them moved. None of them said a word. Jake felt a deep coldness pierce the center of his being.

They all knew what that silence meant.

They were all dead.

All the kids.

Jesus fucking Christ.

Jake's breath caught in his throat and tears stung his eyes. He would have collapsed to the floor had Kristen not been holding on to his arm. The enormity of the loss hit him like a blow to the gut from a heavyweight champ. His knees sagged and Kristen drew him close, wrapped her arms around him.

A sound broke the silence.

Jake's heart started hammering again.

Footsteps.

Coming from somewhere on the other side of that open doorway.

Someone on high heels.

Then the person came through the doorway and he thought his heart might stop altogether. His mouth opened. He forced the word out. "Moira."

The demon smiled. "Hello, Jake. I've missed you."

Kelsey got shakily to his feet and moved backward a step. "Something's not right. That's not her. Not Myra. But . . ."

Kristen's grip on his arm tightened. "Jake? Who is this? Do you know this person?"

Jake didn't reply. He was temporarily incapable of speech. A mind-bending sense of surreality gripped him. This thing was their enemy. Lamia. And at the same time it was Moira Flanagan. The hair. The clothes. The eyes. The mouth. That same knowing smirk, so playful and full of sexual promise.

And yet . . . there were little differences, slight subtleties in the shape of her face. A moment after he sensed this, he saw through the disguise. Moira Flanagan was still dead. This was her baby sister, the girl he'd met at the Grill his first day back in town. Bridget. He couldn't fathom why she would have gone to such lengths to look like her dead sister.

Lamia moved a step closer. "It's true. This is Bridget's body. But I am Moira, Jake. And I am Lamia. I am the woman who was the center of your world for a few precious years. The one you made love to in the back of your car down by the dock. The one you read your first stories to. You've never loved anyone like you loved me."

Jake shook his head. "No. Moira's dead. She went for a ride with my brother Michael. There was an accident. They both died."

Lamia smiled again. "Moira's body died, yes. But the essence you loved lived on, just as it has lived on through the ages." She held out her hands, looked at them, then looked at Jake again. "This is just a shell. I can inhabit any female body. You like this one, yes? I can take another if it's not suitable."

The sense of surreality intensified. Too many horrific revelations in too short a time span. The dead love of his life had never really died. Had never been truly human. He thought of all those drunken, wasted years he'd spent mourning a monster and would have laughed if not for the tragic circumstances.

He found his voice at last and said, "You killed them all, didn't you?" He nodded at the open door behind her. "All those kids. They're all dead."

Her smile remained placid. "I fed, yes. It's irrational to hate me for it, Jake. It's simply my nature."

"And now you're going to kill me?" He glanced first at Kristen, then at Kelsey. "And them."

She moved another step closer, raised her hands, splayed her fingers. "Them, yes. Not you."

Jake moved backward a step, dragging Kristen with him. He

felt her tremble and drew her close, wrapped an arm around her. "Why not me?"

She laughed. "Because I enjoy you. I want you around. The others are nothing to me. I'll feed on them as I fed on the children. Then I'll feed you some of their essence. I can do that. I wasn't strong enough ten years ago, but now I am. You'll become stronger, too. And you'll live a long, long time. Hundreds of years, if I wish."

Jake's throat constricted but he managed to push out the words: "I'd rather die."

Lamia shrugged. "I don't believe that. But it hardly matters. The choice is mine, not yours. You are mine. You will do as I say."

He shook his head. "Fuck that and fuck you."

The time to run had come. No more talking. There was nothing more they could do here other than die. He spun around and Kristen turned with him. Then Jake's heart sank as he realized they wouldn't get to make a break for it. The way out was blocked out by at least a dozen big dogs and an array of other animals. The dogs bared their teeth and growled at them. Huge droplets of saliva drooled from the mouths of each. Jake sensed these weren't normal animals. The strangely glowing eyes told him that. And there was the way they'd sneaked up on them without making a sound to consider. An immense frustration tore at Jake. There was nothing to do now. No way to run. No way to fight. They could tangle with these creatures or Lamia, and either way they'd be equally fucked.

Then he looked at the .38 Kristen still held and thought maybe there was one last option, after all. He didn't like it, but it beat the hell out of a surrender to the monster. He looked her in the eye and saw the same grudging acceptance. He pressed his lips to hers and felt equal measures of regret and longing in the way they yielded to his.

"Stop that."

Lamia's voice was harsher now. Angry.

Jake heard the click of her heels on the floor tiles as she

strode rapidly toward him. Jake wrapped one arm around Kristen in an awkward embrace as his other hand went for the .38. He had to do this fast without thinking about it. Had to get off two quick shots. One straight between Kristen's eyes, then swallow a bullet himself.

BOOM!

Jake jumped at the sound, recognizing it immediately for what it was. He let go of Kristen and turned back toward Lamia, gaping at the sight of the massive and bloody exit wound just below her sternum. Then he looked beyond the demon and saw Jordan Harper. The girl pumped another round into the shotgun's chamber and took aim again.

Instinct pushed Jordan through the open door as Kristen took aim and fired at the knife-wielding bitch who'd murdered Will Mackeson. Though she'd found temporary solace in the company of others, she knew she was the only one who stood a chance against Lamia. She had to act while the others were otherwise occupied, before they could get themselves killed by trying to face the monster.

Much of her bravado vanished as she entered the backstage area and saw all the elegantly attired bodies on the floor, all of them leaking blood from still-fresh gunshot wounds. The rest of it disappeared as she moved beyond them and got a look at her mother, who was still working her dark magic at the edge of the stage. The body belonged to Bridget, but strong, undeniable intuition told her the girl she'd known no longer inhabited that body. It was her mother. Lamia. She stood at the edge of the stage with her hands raised high over her head. Bolts of electricity arced out of her fingertips to weave a tapestry of light over the ceiling. The students screamed and screamed. The ones that were still alive, that is. Bodies were piled up at the chained doors and in the aisles between seats. The bodies looked ravaged, as if they'd been hollowed out from the inside. The eyes of the dead appeared to have burst, the sockets filled with bloody pulp. Every few seconds a finger of electric light would descend from the ceiling tapestry to strike at yet another of the screaming students huddled between the rows of seats. The light would enter through the mouth, suffusing the flesh of the victim with an incandescent glow. The body would convulse and quickly wither. Jordan watched this and felt her resolve wither just as quickly. The energy emanating from the edge of the stage was as powerful as anything a faulty nuclear reactor might generate. Stronger. She'd only just started learning how to tap and harness her own abilities. They would be no match for what her mother could do. So she watched in numb shock as the massacre went forward unimpeded, feeling paralyzed, unable even to retreat. She knew she ought to get back to the others, warn them it was hopeless, but she remained riveted to the spot until it was nearly over.

When she saw that only a few students remained alive, the shock gave way to a simple, reflexive act of self-preservation. She moved backward and tripped over the body of a man in a long black trench coat. She landed awkwardly, twisting her ankle as she hit the floor. The last of the screams from the auditorium cut off as she lay there. Then she heard footsteps coming toward her across the stage. She had only a few seconds to act and rolled under a table laden with a punch bowl, plastic cups, and various refreshments. Another dead body was nearby. She pulled it close, hiding behind it as she held her breath and waited for Lamia to pass. The sound of her mother's heels entered the backstage area and continued through to the hallway beyond.

Jordan let out a breath and shoved the dead body away. She crawled out of her hiding spot and spied the shotgun's barrel sticking out beneath another table. She retrieved the weapon and hurried after her mother, a wild idea sparking inside her as she examined the gun. She knew how the thing worked. Her only high school boyfriend had been into guns and had shared much of his knowledge with her. In truth, he'd been more into those guns than he'd been into her. Which was fine, because she wasn't into him either, but a girl was supposed to have a boyfriend. When he'd kiss her, she'd close her eyes and pretend he was Laura Miller, her number-one crush at the time. But his stubble made the illusion a fragile one. Well, at least now maybe some good would come of that sham of a relationship.

Her plan was simple. She would sneak up on Lamia and blast her host body full of holes. And she would hope this would weaken the demon sufficiently to successfully engage her another way. It probably wouldn't work, but there was nothing else she could do.

She stepped into the hallway and aimed the gun at Lamia's back, acting quickly before the others could see her and give her away. She squeezed the trigger and the shotgun's stock slammed against her shoulder, but she'd been taught how to absorb the weapon's recoil and was able to keep it steady as she took aim again. Lamia started to turn toward her as the next shell took out the back of her skull and sent bone shards and bits of brain matter flying. The demon's mouth opened and a sound like a thunderclap split the air.

Jordan chambered another round and fired again. The third shell took the demon full in the neck and nearly decapitated her. The head lolled sharply to one side, but the demon remained upright as she turned fully toward Jordan and began to stagger toward her. Jordan retreated down the hallway as she chambered yet another round. The next blast hit Lamia between the breasts. It staggered her for a moment, but she kept coming nonetheless. Any one of the blasts would have knocked a human woman off her feet, but Lamia was able to keep Bridget's mortally wounded body erect and mobile. It was frustrating. And now there was another complication. The minions streamed past Jake and Kristen, past Kelsey, and Lamia herself.

Jordan tensed, expecting an attack. They were Lamia's minions, after all. Instead they surrounded her and formed a barrier between herself and Lamia.

A few of the dogs even growled at Lamia.

Jordan heard Jake say, "Well, damn. Look at that."

Jordan kept a wary eye on Lamia while directing a response at Jake. "I've got this. You guys get out of here."

"Are you sure? Because—"

Jordan screamed and raised the gun again.

Jake frowned.

Now what?

In less than a heartbeat Jordan had gone from relatively calm to terrified, and he had no clue what had happened to cause the change. She raised the shotgun to fire again. The blast hit Lamia's midsection again, but failed to even rock her. Then the demon's host body began to convulse. She ripped at her bloody clothes, shredding them and pulling them free. Her flesh rippled and shifted as something moved beneath. Then her skin began to split in several places as something inside started to push its way out.

Kristen cringed and clung tighter to him. "What the hell's going on?"

Kelsey aimed his Glock at Lamia's blister-covered back and fired until the gun clicked empty. None of the wounds seemed to have any effect, except perhaps to accelerate the change occurring.

Kelsey looked at Jake. "Why won't she fucking fall down?"

The shotgun boomed again. The shell hit Lamia's neck again and now the head hung by a single thick strand of tissue. But now something else surged through the neck stump. Another head. This one green and triangular, with hard, pebbled flesh and rows of sharp, glistening teeth. The rest of Bridget's dead flesh fell away and a reptilian creature the likes of which Jake had never seen stood hissing in the hallway. It had short, stubby arms, somewhat longer legs, and a long, thick tail. And it began to grow as they stared at it in awed, paralyzed terror. The body expanded to perhaps three times its original size in seconds, its head bowing to avoid scraping the ceiling. Its arms grew and long black talons appeared at the tips of its fingers. The minions whimpered and retreated as it reached for Jordan. A flick of its thrashing tail knocked Jake and the others off their feet. The back of Jake's head smashed against the combination lock of a locker and a bright, flashing pain obliterated everything else for a moment. Then he rolled onto his back and lifted his head to get a look at what was going on.

And he felt a small flicker of hope.

Because now Jordan was changing, too, her body morphing, becoming something very similar to the reptilian demon without having to shed her skin. The creatures lunged at each other and clashed in the hallway, slamming each other from wall to wall. The auditorium door was knocked off its hinges. Lockers collapsed like crepe paper beneath the force of the body slams.

Jake realized what was about to happen an instant before it did.

There was no time to get out of the way.

He closed his eyes and hoped it wouldn't hurt too much.

Then the thing that had been Jordan crashed into him and the world went black.

The first thing he felt when he woke up was pain. Pain all over. He wondered for a moment whether he was paralyzed, but then realized he wouldn't feel this all-over pain if he'd been paralyzed. He carefully tested his arms and legs, rolled his neck from one side to the other. It hurt like hell, but nothing seemed to be broken. A miracle. Now he'd just have to hope he hadn't been hit quite hard enough to trigger some kind of internal bleeding.

He drew in a deep breath, braced his palms against the slick floor, and pushed himself up to a sitting position. He held his breath as he surveyed the carnage around him. Kristen sat slumped against a bank of lockers, unconscious but breathing. She looked okay otherwise, with the exception of a bruised face and a bloody nose. Then he saw Kelsey and felt a pang at the center of his chest. The boy was facedown on the floor. His neck had been snapped during the monster melee. He wasn't breathing. Jake considered a CPR attempt, but knew it would be useless. The floor was littered with pieces of Bridget Flanagan's exploded body.

He frowned.

They were gone.

There was no sign of Jordan. No sign of the thing she'd become. No sign of Lamia in Godzilla mode. All the animals were gone, too.

What the fuck happened?

Kristen groaned and her eyes fluttered open. She blinked slowly and in a few moments was able to focus on Jake. "Jake . . . what . . . happened?"

He sighed. "Your guess is as good as mine."

He got to his feet and went to her. He took her outstretched hand and pulled her gingerly to her feet. They walked out of the school and she held tightly to him as they made their way to the Camry. He got her settled into the front passenger seat and said, "I have to go back inside for a minute."

Some of the bleariness drained from her eyes then. "No. Jake . . . please . . ."

"I have to. I won't be long, I promise. You stay here. I just have to check on something."

He turned away from her and left without another word. Back inside the school, he moved quickly past the bodies in the hallway and stepped through the open door leading to the auditorium. In the backstage area, he stopped and stared for a moment at the bullet-riddled bodies of the adults. These were the people Lamia had recruited to assist her in arranging the Harvest. All dead. Good. Fuck them. He moved past them, found his way to the stage, and felt the strength drain from his body as he saw what had happened in the auditorium.

They were all dead. Just as he'd feared. Every last one of them. If Trey's body was out there somewhere, he would never be able to identify it. The withered corpses barely looked human.

He dropped to his knees and just stared at the horror for a long, long time.

Then he heard footsteps behind him.

A moment later, a soft hand on his shoulder.

"Jake . . . let's go."

He looked up at her through eyes wet with tears. "Okay."

He took Kristen's hand and she helped him to his feet. Then they left that slaughterhouse and never returned.

EPILOGUE

Their first stop after leaving Rockville High was his mother's house in the Zone. He kept his mind a blank as he kicked open the front door, not wanting to acknowledge any notion of his brother having remained safe at home. There was no point in hope by then.

They did find Trey at the house.

But there was no miracle.

He was dead.

And so was Jolene.

Their bodies had been torn apart. They found arms, legs, fingers, and genitals in different parts of the house. He found Trey's head floating in the toilet bowl. His mother's head was in the microwave oven. Lengths of intestine were spread out on the table. Some of them had been cooked and gnawed on. There was an eyeball on a toothpick. Just one. Jake didn't care to guess what had happened to the others. He grabbed an un-opened twelve-pack of Old Milwaukee from the fridge; then they got the hell out of there.

They left town.

What else was there to do?

Kristen drove as he drank beer after beer, crumpling the empties and tossing them into the back. After six of them, Jake had her pull over. He threw the door open and heaved his guts out and listened to cars whiz by on the interstate. He sat there with his head hanging out the door for several more minutes, sweat pouring down his face as his body continued to spasm long after his stomach had been emptied of its contents.

Then he pulled himself back inside and shut the door.

"You okay?"

"Yeah . . ." He was still working to get his breathing under control. "I'll be fine. Just go."

Kristen stared at him a moment. Then she shrugged and put the car back in gear.

Jake started in on the rest of the beer.

They drove and drove, with only brief convenience store pit stops. Jake would empty his bladder and buy more beer while Kristen pumped gas. This continued all the way through to the next day, when they stopped in Austin, Texas. By then Jake was running on fumes. He didn't want to sleep, fearing the nightmares that would come. But sleep was coming. There was nothing he could do about it. They found a cheap motel and Jake used his debit card to pay for a week's stay. He slept deeply that night and did not dream.

The next day they explored the town. Jake didn't feel much like sightseeing, but it was better than just sitting in that gray, depressing room all day. Austin was a funky college town, a bastion of liberalism and creativity in the heart of conservative Texas. Under other circumstances, he might have found it a fascinating place. But he was still too numb to care. Too numb to have even begun a proper grieving process.

That night they ventured back out to a bar they'd stopped by earlier in the day. It had a long wooden porch with benches. The front door was open and music spilled out. There was loud talk and laughter. As Jake stepped through the door with Kristen, he knew this was what he needed. To be surrounded by people. To hear their boozy, carefree conversations. To feel their normality. Maybe if he soaked in enough of it, he could forget about the monster he knew was out there somewhere.

The jukebox was playing "Stagger Lee," some version he didn't recognize. A very attractive brunette in tight denim shorts gyrated in front of the jukebox. A table beside her was filled with other extremely attractive women. They were talking and laughing. Their table was littered with empty beer bottles and shot glasses. One of the women, a leggy black chick, spotted his roving eye and winked at him.

Jake smiled and followed Kristen to the bar. There they ordered two pints of Shiner Bock and watched the television bolted to the wall behind the bar. The news was on. Coverage of the mysterious massacre at Rockville High was still nonstop.

Jake felt a deep melancholy settle over him. There were answers he wanted. Questions he could never ask. He sipped his beer and looked at Kristen. "Do you think she did it on purpose?"

Kristen frowned. "Did what?"

He cleared his throat, looked at the television again, and frowned. "At my mom's house. Do you think she did what she did to Mom and Trey knowing I'd be back there to see it at some point?"

Kristen shrugged. "Maybe. Or maybe she just did it for the sheer evil thrill of it. She's a demon, remember." She touched his knee. "Best not to think about it, really."

Jake nodded. "Yeah. I know."

They sat there and drank several more beers. Then they staggered out of the bar and picked up another twelve-pack on the way back to the motel. Back in their room, they sat on the bed, conversing intermittently while they drank beer and watched TV. At some point Kristen took charge of the remote and dialed up a pay-per-view porno movie. As the first sex scene began, she nibbled on his ear and kissed his neck.

Her hand went to his crotch and squeezed.

The erection surprised him, considering how much he'd drank. Considering everything that had happened.

Kristen made a soft sound somewhere between a grunt and a laugh. "Let's do it," she said, her voice a breathy whisper. "What better way to take our minds off things?"

Jake didn't argue.

Maybe she had a point.

Besides, it felt good. And his philosophy had always been that if something feels good, it must be good.

They shed their clothes as they made out and groped at each other. When they were fully nude, Kristen shoved Jake backward. She straddled him as he fell onto his back. He sighed at the silken smoothness of her thighs against his hips, then gasped as his hardness plunged into her. She smiled down at him and rode him with a slow, rocking rhythm.

She licked her lips. "Mmm . . . you like that, baby?"

A weak smile twitched the corners of Jake's mouth and he let his eyes flutter shut for a moment. "Yeah . . ."

"Can I ask you something?"

"Anything."

Then he felt her hands around his throat. Soft, but strong.

The balls of her thumbs pressing.

His eyes snapped open.

She wasn't smiling now. "Did you really think I'd just walk away?"

Jake's heart began to race. "What do you mean?"

"You know."

Jake stared at her hard, unflinching eyes.

He did know.

"What happened to Jordan?"

"Our daughter? I consumed her, of course."

Daughter?

Jake felt a profound ache of the spirit.

He had a daughter. And she was dead.

Like everyone else.

The creature atop him seemed to sense his thoughts and smiled again. "Not all is lost, darling. I know you like this body. I saw it in your eyes when you were kissing the bitch. And now you'll get to enjoy it for a long, long time."

Jake closed his eyes.

Lamia's hands closed another notch tighter around his throat.

The slow, rocking rhythm gave way to a more frenzied one.

The headboard banged against the wall as Jake grabbed Lamia's arms and held on. It went on for a long time. Jake feared she would break him in half before it was over. Then it was over and he was still intact, at least physically. She drew him into her arms and wrapped a leg around his midsection, holding him tight, not letting him move.

She whispered in his ear. "Now I have to punish you. Teach you a lesson. The first of many."

Jake tried to scream.

She didn't let him.

GORD ROLLO

AUTHOR OF *THE JIGSAW MAN*

The small town of Dunnville is no stranger to fear. Evil has stalked its dark streets once before. These days, no one in the town likes to talk about it much. Some folks deny it ever happened….

But four boyhood friends are about to discover the truth, though no one will believe them. Their parents think they've been listening to too many scary stories. But what the boys have released from an icy well is no legend, and it will soon terrify Dunnville to its very core. Unspeakable horror is running free…and the nightmares of the past are about to begin again.

CRIMSON

ISBN 13: 978-0-8439-6195-9

BRIAN
KEENE

They came to the lush, deserted island to compete on a popular reality TV show. Each one hoped to be the last to leave. Now they're just hoping to stay alive. It seems the island isn't deserted after all. Contestants and crew members are disappearing, but they aren't being eliminated by the game. They're being taken by the monstrous half-human creatures that live in the jungle. The men will be slaughtered. The women will be kept alive as captives. Night is falling, the creatures are coming, and rescue is so far away. . . .

CASTAWAYS

ISBN 13: 978-0-8439-6089-1

RICHARD LAYMON

For two families, it was supposed to be a relaxing camping trip in the California mountains. They thought it would be fun to get away from everything for a while. But they're not alone. The woods are also home to two terrifying residents who don't take kindly to strangers—an old hag with unholy powers, and her hulking son, a half-wild brute with uncontrollable, violent urges. The campers still need to get away—but now their lives depend on it!

DARK MOUNTAIN

ISBN 13: 978-0-8439-6138-6

EDWARD LEE

Author of *Brides of the Impaler*

From the bones of the dead…from a long-buried secret …through an ancient ritual…they rise to kill. What was first created to protect has now been perverted and twisted into servants of evil, commanded to exact a bloody, brutal vengeance. The original golem was molded from clay centuries ago to serve and defend the innocent. But today new golems will stalk the night to bring terror and death to the quiet Maryland coast. For one young couple, their dream home will become a slaughterhouse when they discover that nothing can stop the relentless walking horror known as…

THE GOLEM

"The living legend of literary mayhem. Read him if you dare!"
— Richard Laymon, Author of *Beware*

ISBN 13: 978-0-8439-5808-9

To order a book or to request a catalog call:
1-800-481-9191
Our books are also available at your local bookstore, or you can check out our Web site **www.dorchesterpub.com** where you can look up your favorite authors, read excerpts, or glance at our discussion forum to see what people have to say about your favorite books.

RAY GARTON

Author of *Ravenous* and *Live Girls*

Something very strange is happening in the coastal California town of Big Rock. Several residents have died in unexplained, particularly brutal ways, many torn apart in animal attacks. And there's always that eerie howling late at night...

You might think there's a werewolf in town. But you'd be wrong. It's not just one werewolf, but the whole town that's gradually transforming. Bit by bit, as the infection spreads, the werewolves are becoming more and more powerful. In fact, humans may soon be the minority, mere prey for their hungry neighbors. Is it too late for the humans to fight back? Did they ever have a chance from the start?

BESTIAL

"Garton has a flair for taking veteran horror
themes and twisting them to evocative
or entertaining effect."
—*Publishers Weekly*

ISBN 13: 978-0-8439-6185-0

✂

☐ **YES!**

Sign me up for the Leisure Horror Book Club and send my FREE BOOKS! If I choose to stay in the club, I will pay only $8.50* each month, a savings of $7.48!

NAME: _____

ADDRESS: _____

TELEPHONE: _____

EMAIL: _____

☐ I want to pay by credit card.

☐ **VISA**　　☐ **MasterCard.**　　☐ **DISCOVER**

ACCOUNT #: _____

EXPIRATION DATE: _____

SIGNATURE: _____

Mail this page along with $2.00 shipping and handling to:
Leisure Horror Book Club
PO Box 6640
Wayne, PA 19087
Or fax (must include credit card information) to:
610-995-9274
You can also sign up online at **www.dorchesterpub.com**.
*Plus $2.00 for shipping. Offer open to residents of the U.S. and Canada only. Canadian residents please call 1-800-481-9191 for pricing information.
If under 18, a parent or guardian must sign. Terms, prices and conditions subject to change. Subscription subject to acceptance. Dorchester Publishing reserves the right to reject any order or cancel any subscription.

GET FREE BOOKS!

You can have the best fiction delivered to your door for less than what you'd pay in a bookstore or online. Sign up for one of our book clubs today, and we'll send you *FREE* BOOKS* just for trying it out... **with no obligation to buy, ever!**

As a member of the Leisure Horror Book Club, you'll receive books by authors such as **RICHARD LAYMON, JACK KETCHUM, JOHN SKIPP, BRIAN KEENE** and many more.

As a book club member you also receive the following special benefits:
- **30% off all orders!**
- **Exclusive access to special discounts!**
- **Convenient home delivery and 10 days to return any books you don't want to keep.**

Visit **www.dorchesterpub.com** or call **1-800-481-9191**

There is no minimum number of books to buy, and you may cancel membership at any time.
*Please include $2.00 for shipping and handling.